The Bride of Rosecliffe

REXANNE BECNEL

St. Martin's Paperbacks

"I CAN'T LET YOU GO.
YOU NEED TO UNDERSTAND THAT."

"And you need to understand that I cannot be your willing prisoner."

"Then you will be my unwilling prisoner." She stood there between his outstretched legs, looking down into his dark, opaque eyes, which glinted the flickering firelight back at her. When he spoke again, the low timbre of his voice seemed to vibrate through her. "I wonder just how unwilling a prisoner you shall finally prove to be."

Her heart began to pound, like the surf booming against the rocks, like thunder rattling the heavens. Her heart pounded, her body trembled, and she knew she was in grave danger of succumbing to this enemy she wanted to despise. . . .

St. Martin's Paperbacks titles
by Rexanne Becnel

HEART OF THE STORM
THE MAIDEN BRIDE
DANGEROUS TO LOVE
THE BRIDE OF ROSECLIFFE

To Benny
Benjamin James Becnel
1944–1997

Prologue

Ae fond kiss and then we sever!

—Robert Burns

Prologue

London, October A.D. 1133

Randulf Fitz Hugh lay naked on the bed. Beside him Marianne, wife of the aging Earl of Carland, lay just as naked as he. But while she curled into the warmth beneath the heavy marten coverlet, he reveled in the chill air on his sweat-slicked skin. While she slept as evenly as a babe, he stared morosely up at the dark plank ceiling.

He'd used her roughly, though that was not the cause of his foul mood. He'd been angry with the king—furious— and although he should not have, he'd vented his frustrations on her.

Not that she'd minded. Marianne was an insatiable lover. In that, they were well suited. But tonight he'd not been interested in the pleasures of her deliciously wicked body. He had more pressing matters on his mind.

A squat candle sputtered on the three-legged table beside the door. The pale light danced weakly across the bed-chamber.

Damnation! Hadn't he won every battle and overcome every foe that stood between King Henry and absolute power over his enemies? Hadn't he done enough to earn a just reward? But King Henry was a crafty old fox. Today in court Rand's drunken older brother, John, had renewed his fealty to the king, and as his father's heir, had received his official title, Earl of Asdin. Though it had grated, Rand had expected it. Then the king had turned his watchful gaze upon Rand and announced his reward. In front of the entire court he'd granted Rand lands in the name of the King of England, in the wilds of northern Wales.

Rand had been stunned. Northern Wales was as far away from the center of power in London as was possible to go and yet still remain within Britain. Henry had continued. He was to build a castle at the mouth of the River Gyffin, something impregnable. A mighty castle situated midway between Chester and Anglesey. He was to suppress any opposition to British authority in Wales, a task Henry claimed was an honor reserved only for his most powerful and trusted man.

Perhaps it was. But Rand knew also that sending his faithful supporters to the Welsh marches was the king's way of controlling those men whom he deemed too powerful for *his* own comfort. The lands granted him were extensive. He would be veritably a king in his own kingdom.

But Wales was not the kingdom he wished to rule! In effect, the king had banished him from London, the seat of all power.

Rand snorted in disgust. Perhaps he should be mollified that the king had begun to fear his growing wealth and influence. But he was not mollified. It took years to build a castle. He'd be an old man before he could return to London.

"God's bones!" He surged up from the disheveled bed, too frustrated to lie still, and lit another candle.

Marianne's husband was not in town and Rand knew he could linger the night with her if he chose. But he was not interested.

It may be a long while before you have so adept a lover, a voice in his head whispered as he poured water in a shallow basin and bathed himself. *Make use of her while you can.*

But he ignored the voice. There were women in Wales and he'd heard they were freer with their bodies than English women. Again he snorted. If that were true, they must lie in the streets with their skirts thrown up and their legs spread wide. In his experience, the women in Henry's court would sleep with anyone so long as there were coins or jewels to be had for their efforts.

Not that he objected. He'd sated many a noble wife with sex, rewarded them with baubles, and used them for his own political gain. For information and insight. But cast away in the farthest reaches of Wales, he would no longer have access to those sources. He would be seven days' journey from London. It might as well be the ends of the earth.

He slapped the washrag down. The woman behind him shifted in the bed. He knew without looking that she'd awakened.

"I'm not finished with you," she murmured in the warm purr she used so effectively to attract men. "Come here. It's your turn on top."

Rand stared at her with a dispassionate eye. Marianne was a beauty. She'd been his lover for almost a year now, longer than he stayed with most women. Then again, she was better connected than most women. But in the end, her connections hadn't helped him at all.

Could those connections, indeed, have *hurt* his cause with the king?

He blinked at that unsettling thought, but once insinuated into his head, it would not go away. Had her husband used his influence with the king to send Rand to Wales?

But why would he? Carland had his own mistress, the matronly Lady Ferriday, the only woman at court said to be willing to hold the old man to her ample bosom like a child, and rock him while he suckled her. Rand's lips curled at that disgusting image.

Still, something was amiss. Carland might not have undermined him, but someone had. Rand vowed to ferret out the truth.

"I have other matters to attend," he said as he drew on his braies.

She watched in silence for a moment. "Surely that can wait. You needn't leave for Wales until spring."

"There's much to do between now and then," he countered. "Men to hire. Materials to purchase. The king wants a castle. I want it done swiftly."

The mattress ropes creaked as she rose to her knees. The marten coverlet slid down to puddle around her legs. Her waist-length hair half hid, half revealed her lush body. Her breasts were full, her nipples large. The thought of her toothless husband nuzzling at them like a child made Rand suddenly disgusted. He looked away.

"I'll miss you, Rand. Will you miss me?"

Rand shrugged into his shirt. The fact was, he wanted to get away from her, but he wanted the truth more. He chose his words carefully. "I'll miss you as much as you will miss me, and we both know you'll have a new lover within the week."

Her eyes narrowed in quick fury, just as he'd expected. "What does that mean? Have you some other woman ready to take my place? Are you bringing her with you to Wales?"

"Now Marianne, you are married. Why should you concern yourself—"

"Who is she?"

"There is no one."

"So you said when you pursued that DeLisle bitch—" She broke off, but it was too late. He frowned.

"The DeLisle bitch? That was a marriage contract, nothing more." Then all at once it made sense. Stephen DeLisle had initially welcomed Rand's offer to wed the man's only child, a pretty young woman approaching marriageable age. Marianne had been miffed, but once Rand had assured her that she was far more appealing than the younger woman, she'd been appeased. Indeed, she'd told Rand that it would be a strategic match, a political coup. But she'd not been above pointing out the girl's lack of physical endowments. At the time he'd attributed her caustic words to simple female jealousy. But had it gone further?

Two of the king's advisors, Robert Hartley and Emery Ives, had certainly taken their opposition further. The two resented anyone whose power threatened their own, and they recognized that a union between Rand and DeLisle would give Rand control of a huge amount of property. Emery Ives especially knew how to manipulate Henry. A hint here, a word of caution there, and Rand had become one more of the king's casualties—men too powerful for their own good. Yes, Ives had played a part in this, he knew, and Ives was Marianne's cousin.

God, how could he have been so stupid? Marianne had been a conduit straight to Ives. Had she been so jealous that she'd killed Rand's marriage plans? Rand was suddenly sure she had.

"The DeLisle bitch, as you call her, was hardly that. Indeed, she was a sweet young thing, an innocent virgin—or at least she used to be," he added. Though he'd never touched the girl, he wanted Marianne to think he had. He was not fully prepared for her furious reaction.

"You wretch!" She came at him with claws bared, nearly toppling him over. In a moment he wrestled her down, then held her writhing on his lap. She raged at him. "You bedded that skinny bitch—"

"No, I did not. But I see now the lengths you would go to stop me—the lengths you *did* go. 'Twas you who ruined my agreement with DeLisle."

She went limp in his arms, a sure sign of her guilt. But still she protested. "It was not me. The king put pressure on DeLisle—"

"And Emery pressured the king, after you pressured Emery."

She turned in his lap, but instead of trying to escape, she

clutched his shirtfront. "I did not pressure him, Rand. I only complained that I would be unhappy to see you in another woman's bed. Is that so terrible? I am a jealous lover and I want you all to myself. But I am not to blame. 'Twas my cousin's idea to thwart your marriage plans, not mine."

Perhaps she told the truth. Perhaps not. In any event, the result was the same. He was exiled to Wales. While other men increased their political strength, he would be raising stone walls and fending off Welsh madmen.

With a sharp curse he thrust her off his lap. But when he rose to his feet, she clasped her arms around his legs. "Don't leave yet. Not like this," she begged from her position on her knees.

" 'Tis done between us," he said, trying to dislodge her hands.

But she clung even more tenaciously. "One more time, then. One more time, for memory's sake." She rubbed her bountiful breasts back and forth across his thighs and clutched his buttocks with her hands.

Despite his anger, Rand was not immune to her blatant behavior. When she felt his manhood stiffen, she smiled up at him and slowly licked her lips. "One more time," she purred.

Rand started to object. He'd spent too much time with her already; that was his biggest mistake. But he'd not make that same mistake again. Then she loosened his braies and Rand reluctantly tangled his hands in her hair.

Only once, he told himself. Only once. After tonight he'd never let any woman affect his plans again.

Part One

Hear the voice of the Bard!
Who Present, Past, & Future sees
Whose ears have heard
The Holy Word
That walk'd among the ancient trees

—William Blake

One

Carreg Du, Wales
March A.D. 1134

" 'Winter's end is . . . is nigh.' " Josselyn glanced at Newlin, and when he did not respond, she repeated the translation. " 'Winter's end is nigh.' That is correct, is it not?"

The misshapen little man looked up at her. It was clear his thoughts had wandered away from today's lesson. Josselyn's brow creased with worry. During the long weeks of this bitterest of winters he'd often become preoccupied. Was he unwell? Or did the ageless bard sense some disturbing change in the air?

"Winter's end is indeed nigh," he echoed, but in their native Welsh. "And with its end will come an end to these lessons," he added, looking at her with his peculiar mismatched gaze.

Josselyn shrugged. "Perhaps for a while. There will be much to do once spring is truly upon us. But summer will bring me more time."

"Summer may see you wed and tending to your husband."

"And who will that husband be?" she asked in the

French language of the Normans. *"Anyone I know?"* she finished, in the rougher Saxon tongue of the English.

He smiled at her, though only the left side of his mouth turned up. The right side of his face remained in its perpetually down-drawn expression. Indeed, the entire right side of his body was thus: arm shriveled, leg twisted. He walked with a pronounced limp and had only his left arm with which to perform his daily tasks.

But the blessings that God had withheld from his body, He'd made up for by gifting the man with an astonishing mind. Newlin was widely acknowledged as the wisest and most intelligent man in Rhofoniog. From the English border in the east, to the wide sea far west of the wildwood surrounding the village of Carreg Du, he had no match. He spoke four languages fluently, their own *Cymraeg,* both the French and English he'd taught her, and the Latin tongue known primarily to the priests.

He knew the stars, how to cipher, could foretell the weather, and understood the animals as well. He forgot nothing he'd ever heard, and throughout the long dark winters enthralled the people of Carreg Du with his tales of old and predictions of times yet to come.

He had no age and no one was certain whence he'd come. He'd always lived in the *domen* near the meadow, and though no one else would dare seek shelter under those burial stones beside the hill laced with climbing roses, no one argued his right to do so.

The two of them sat now, perched on a rocky outcropping halfway up the slope of that hill. Josselyn stared below them to the rough meadow, not yet showing any signs of spring save the spongy ground, soaked with the winter thaw. Newlin's gaze, however, turned toward the crest of the hill, toward the cliffs. After a moment he began to clamber upward.

"Wait. Where are you going?"

"To the sea."

"The sea? What of my lesson?" she called out as he

scuttled away with his strange sideways gait.

"Winter's end is nigh," he called back in English. "And spring shall give birth to a future we cannot escape," he added, though this time in their mother tongue.

Josselyn knew better than to press him regarding the meaning of that. Newlin revealed what he wanted, when he wanted to. His predictions, when they came, were frighteningly accurate. What this future was that they could not escape, Josselyn did not begin to know. But she scrambled up after him, hoping for an explanation.

They reached the crest of the great stone outcropping together. The wind was bitter across the dark churning sea. Bitter with the cold. Bitter with the damp. Josselyn stood up against it, though, ignoring the icy fingers of wind that tore at her wool kirtle and cloak, and whipped her soot-black hair around her face. This was the pinnacle overlooking the lands of her people. Though not the highest point, it nonetheless was imbued with an essence that defined the wild freedom of northern Wales.

The great stone outcropping was known as Carreg Du, the Black Stone. Many, like herself, had adopted it as part of their name. She was Josselyn ap Carreg Du, just as her father had called himself Howell ap Carreg Du.

Their family had been a part of this land since before recorded time, since before the oldest tales of the early kings, and their struggles to survive. She loved everything about this green fold of wildwood between the mountains and the sea. That's what had driven her out of her uncle's snug house this third Sunday of the Lenten season, the need to be out on their lands. Now she looked down the cliffs to the sea, and marveled as she had so many times before that roses should grow in so inhospitable a place.

She breathed deeply of the salty air, then shivered at the cold. But that was all right. She could bear the cold a little longer. After all, winter's end was nigh. She looked around for Newlin and found him staring off to the east, rocking forward and back as he so often did when his thoughts delved deep. Forward and back. Forward and back.

Her gaze followed his out to sea, to where the sun pierced the heavy clouds and cast diamond glints against the waves. But it was not only the sun glinting off the sea in brilliant flashes of white. There was something else. A sail. A ship. Josselyn squinted, trying to make it out.

"The future we cannot escape," Newlin stated. Each word came out in a frigid puff, immediately dispersed by the north wind.

"Is it a good future, or a bad one?" Josselyn asked, feeling even colder now than before.

The odd little man shrugged his one good shoulder. "Like all futures, 'tis good for some, and not so for others. Still," he added with his familiar twisted grin. "You must agree that *any* future is better than *no* future."

True. But as they made their way back down from the rose cliffs, then parted ways—she for her village, he for his mean abode beneath the *domen*—Josselyn was filled with a nameless foreboding. She'd lived these past nine years with her aunt and uncle. They had no children of their own and they'd been happy to take her in when her parents had died. She'd been safe with them with no need to look to the future.

But change was in the air. She knew it and so did Newlin. And she didn't like it at all.

"They've erected tents on Rosecliffe. And they continue to remove an endless stream of supplies from their ship."

Josselyn listened to Dewey's report as did the rest of the villagers gathered in her uncle's hall. Uncle Clyde sat without moving, pondering his scout's disturbing news in that silent manner he had. As the moments stretched out, Josselyn had to restrain herself from prodding a response from him. She loved her uncle dearly, but he was most certainly not a man given to impulsive action.

"Post a watch on them," he finally ordered. "We need to know numbers of men, amounts of materials." He paused. "Send for the scribe. Madoc ap Lloyd will want to know of this as well."

He ignored the murmurings generated by that remark. The lands of the Lloyd family lay just west of Carreg Du, but the fact that they were neighbors did not mean the two families were friendly. The Lloyds were as greedy as the English king, albeit on a different scale. A sheep gone missing. An ox. They hunted on Carreg Du lands and pilfered from Carreg Du's fields whenever they could get away with it. Everyone knew they were not to be trusted. Still, all the Welsh shared a common enemy in the English. And with the English setting up an encampment at Rosecliffe, Uncle Clyde was right to put aside his differences with the Lloyds.

Unfortunately, Josselyn did not believe it merely an encampment. "What if they're here to stay?"

Everyone turned to stare at her. A faint flush rose in her cheeks, but she ignored it and stared earnestly at her uncle. "The group that came last winter was smaller, and they stayed only a few days. But this group is larger. And at least two men from the previous group are here again."

Uncle Clyde frowned and for a moment Josselyn feared he meant to reprimand her before the entire village, first for speaking out on a matter that was, strictly speaking, a men's issue, and second for venturing near the English encampment. After a nerve-racking silence he said, "You recognized two of them from last winter?"

Josselyn nodded. There were not many men as tall and broad-shouldered as the younger of the two. Everything about his looks and bearing proclaimed him a warrior. If he did not lead the English, he was at least central to their nefarious plans. She was certain of it.

The other man sported a heavy red beard and had more the air of a scholar. It had been he whom she'd been the most curious about. At least that was what she'd told herself. The tall man had been comely in the hard way some fighting men had. It was the attractiveness that came with absolute confidence. But that sort of confidence more often than not carried with it the unattractive specter of arrogance. So she'd turned her eyes away from him and concentrated on the smaller, portly fellow.

Was he a bard like Newlin? she'd wondered. Last winter he'd walked the length and breadth of the lands at the top of Rosecliffe, marking down his observations on a roll of parchment. How that parchment had intrigued her. Now he was back with more parchments under his arm.

Though it was only a suspicion, she felt compelled to share it. "You know how the English are—how greedy their king is. He wants our lands joined to his. Hasn't he built one of his fortresses two days' travel south of here, on land that once was Daffyd land? I think he plans to do the same thing here. I think he means to construct a castle at Rosecliffe."

"A castle? Not here—"

"Damn the godforsaken English!"

"They wouldn't dare try such a thing—"

"Yes they would," Josselyn vowed, fired up by the heated emotions rocketing around the smoky hall. "That king of theirs—Henry of Normandy—believes God has granted him the rights to our lands—"

She broke off under her uncle's dark scowl. Everyone else did the same. Only when silence once more reigned did Clyde speak. "More reason than ever to inform Madoc ap Lloyd." He stood and everyone else did the same. "Arrange for a messenger, Dewey. Now leave me to think." To his wife, Nesta, he added, "Send in the scribe when he gets here."

Josselyn filed out of the main hall along with the others. But her blood had been roused by the storm warnings of imminent warfare, and she could not simply go off to the kitchens as if nothing of consequence had taken place today. She ran to fetch parchment, ink, quill, and sand, then returned and slipped into the hall.

Her uncle stood before a painting of his brother, her father, and Josselyn knew what he was thinking. Howell ap

Carreg Du had died fighting the English nearly ten years ago. His grief-stricken wife had died giving birth not a month later, along with an infant son, both deaths also attributable to the wretched king of England. In the ensuing years the English had abandoned their efforts in northern Wales. But their successes in the south had clearly encouraged them anew, for it appeared they now had returned.

How many Welsh lives would be sacrificed to stop them this time?

She beat back a shiver of apprehension. "I have the parchment, Uncle. If you will dictate your message, I will write it down."

Slowly he turned to face her. "You have other duties. I can wait for the scribe."

She lifted her chin a notch. "I would rather write your message to Madoc ap Lloyd. My hand is as neat as any scribe's."

Clyde stared at his niece, his only brother's only heir—and his as well. She was a brave lass—that no one could dispute, least of all him. And she was smart, with an education far surpassing his own. Newlin was to be thanked for that—or blamed. Clyde often worried that the thirst for learning the bard had fired in her would lead to her unhappiness. Such knowledge made a dreamer of the most practical soul. But dreamer or no, the times would force her dreams aside. She must be practical now—as must he.

He agreed to her request with a nod. She gave him a pleased smile, but he knew it would not last.

"I bid you greeting, Madoc ap Lloyd," he began, pausing periodically as the scratching of the quill pen caught his words forever on the rare parchment. She was right, her hand was straight and true, with no ink splotches to mar its progress.

". . . time to unite against our common enemy. To ensure the peace between us endures, I would discuss a matter we have put aside in the past."

When he did not continue, Josselyn looked up. The light

cast by the single oil lamp limned her face with gold. She was as beautiful as her mother had been, he thought, not for the first time. Rich black hair. The glowing skin of robust youth. But for all her feminine beauty, she also possessed her father's soul, his daring and his impulsiveness. If any woman could tame Madoc's hot-tempered son—or at least redirect his energies—it was Josselyn.

Still, he did not relish what he must do.

"What is this matter you have put aside?" she asked, staring at him with the clear blue eyes of his brother.

"It is the matter of peace between us and the family of Lloyd."

"Yes, but how do you propose to maintain it? You know what will happen. Once the English are routed, the Lloyds will become the same thieving troublemakers they've always been. They are not to be trusted."

"I plan to marry our family to theirs," he said without elaborating.

She met his stare without blinking, and he knew to the second when she understood his meaning. Though her breathing came a little faster she showed no other emotion. "To Owain?" she said at last.

He nodded his head. "If you will agree. His time of mourning is done. He will want another wife for his son. And more children, as well."

She took a slow breath, then dipped the quill in the ink and frowned down at the neatly lettered parchment. "Do you wish to add anything?"

"No."

Josselyn watched as her uncle signed the message. Then she dated it and melted the wax so he could seal it with his signet ring. She refused to let herself react to the devastating news he'd just delivered. She refused to succumb to her fears, for she knew them to be unimportant in the greater scheme of things. But still, those fears would not go away.

Owain ap Madoc was a cruel thug, who'd been the bane

of existence for the people of Carreg Du for as long as she could recall. He was recently widowed, though, and so this should come as no surprise to her. The fact that no one would force her to wed him was beside the point. She had the freedom to turn him down. No Welsh woman could be forced to wed a man loathsome to her.

And Owain *was* loathsome to her. She knew him mainly by reputation, for she'd only laid eyes on him four times in her life. But that had sufficed. The first time had been at a harvest celebration in Carreg Du. She had been but a child and he a gangling youth, brawling with other boys. Playing cruel tricks on those younger and weaker than he. Bullying them.

The next time she'd been twelve and he'd come upon her while she was picking blueberries in Saint Cedric's Vale. She'd not understood everything he'd said, nor comprehended his innuendos. But she'd been terrified all the same.

He'd chased her like a wolf cub chases a rabbit. Not to catch her, just to see her run.

She'd never told anyone about that day. Maybe she should have. Now she understood what he'd said—about her wanting it. *It.* Josselyn shuddered in revulsion, just to remember. He'd been a disgusting youth and had become an even worse man.

She'd seen him next at the annual horse market in Holywell. By then he'd been married, and Josselyn had pitied the unfortunate girl. But the last time she'd seen him had been the worst. Six months ago he and a band of his henchmen had returned the body of Tomas, saying they'd found him along the narrow shore at the base of Rosecliffe, thrown to his death by the English said to be in the area. They'd behaved as if it were a goodwill gesture on their part to return the mangled, bloodied corpse.

Dewey had pretended that it was too, for there had been few men in Carreg Du that day and he had not wanted to provoke a fight with Owain's heavily armed band. But he'd suspected another scenario. Josselyn had overheard him saying as much to Uncle Clyde. Owain and his thugs had most likely come across Tomas on their lands, and though by law Tomas was wrong to hunt there, they'd had no cause to kill him. To murder him.

No, she need not know him personally to know he was loathsome.

But what about her duty to her family? She was her uncle's only heir. If she did not wed while he was still strong, when he died, chaos would ensue and the Lloyds would be quick to take advantage. Added to that was the pressure of this new English threat. Her family might not be able to turn so great a force away this time.

There was the increased chance of her uncle's death in the battles sure to come. She didn't like to think about it, but she knew he would want to plan for his successor in advance.

But Owain ap Madoc!

She'd as lief marry an Englishman as marry such a cut-throat!

They were being watched. Rand knew it and welcomed it. Let the people of this wretched corner of Wales spy on him and relay the news to the rest of their kin. Wales had long been claimed by King Henry. Now Rand meant to make that claim a reality—and return to London in triumph.

He stood on the pinnacle of the long hill the Welsh called Carreg Du—Black Stone. He stared down the drop-off known as Rosecliffe for its tenacious roses, then swept the horizon with his eyes. Cold sea to the north and east. Cold hills to the south and west. Yet somewhere within those dark forested hills lay a hotbed of opposition. They watched and they waited and they would do everything they could to drive him out, even unite with their enemy brothers, if need be. But he would not be driven out, and though it might take years, they would eventually come to understand that fact.

Below him the camp had begun to take shape. Already the tents were being replaced by sturdy timber huts. His workers had set to their tasks on the very day they'd landed. Sir Lovell, the master builder, supervised them using stakes and flags to mark the perimeters where the castle walls would rise, the mighty inner wall first, then the far-reaching outer wall. Even the town would have a protective wall, for Rand meant to fortify his holdings well. Every citizen under his rule would know there was safety under his pennant, whether they were English or Welsh, or something in between.

He grimaced at that thought. In between. Henry had cautioned him that a generation of children born of Welsh mothers to English fathers could as easily turn against him as fight for him. But it was not that generation that concerned him now. His men would need wives. Come the next winter, they would need the warm comfort of women in their beds. He needed to keep his men content and women were his best tool for that. Once wed, his men would be tied to this land as firmly as he now was.

Unlike them, however, he would not be tied to these lands by a woman. It was ambition that tied him here, and then only temporarily. He'd spent the whole of his life fighting for the right to own lands of his own, besides the past nine years fighting Henry's wars. Now that he had those lands, however, he faced another sort of battle.

He'd had the long months of winter to consider his situation, and as he'd assembled men and supplies, he'd also assembled his thoughts. He'd not wanted lands in Wales. But that's what he'd been granted. Now he meant to make them his—only he did not want to waste either time or effort in the process. While he was prepared to take the land by force if need be, he knew it would be faster to wage peace. But he meant to wage that peace with a powerful hand, and he meant to win.

Once the lands of northern Wales were secure for England, Henry and his advisors would be forced to acknowledge Rand's ever-increasing influence. He would make his way back to London, an even more powerful baron than before. But there was still the matter of a wife well connected to English politics. He would have to address that matter as soon as possible.

A call drew his attention, and as he watched, his burly captain, Osborn de Vere, clambered up the dark, frozen hill.

"The ship is unloaded. They sail back to England on the next tide."

"Alan has his orders, I take it."

"He does. He will return with the carpenters and stonemasons, and the rest of the food stores."

The man paused, but Rand knew what he would say next. Five years Osborn had guarded his back, and Rand had guarded his. Their thoughts had become finely attuned in the process. But that did not mean they always agreed. Rand spoke before Osborn could. "Jasper remains in England."

Osborn's eyes narrowed and his jaw jutted forward. "The hills of Wales are more likely to make a man of your brother than mincing around Henry's court. Even Jasper knows that."

"He wants the adventure with none of the responsibility," Rand retorted. "You know my feelings on this, and so does he. Until he can negotiate the twisted byways of the court and survive in that pit of vipers, he is no more than a green lad, and of no use to me. Once he has mastered Henry's court, he can come here, and I'll return to England. But enough of that," Rand continued. "What word from Sir Lovell?"

Osborn wisely abandoned the subject of Rand's younger brother. He grunted. "Faith, but I'd never have believed so mild a man could be such a taskmaster. Already his crew has marked the wall locations. The diggers have begun their tasks and two wells are being bored, one for the castle and one for the new town, just beyond the castle walls. The site is just as he had drawn out—the half-moat, the sheer cliffs.

The quarry site.'' Osborn stared around him. '' 'Tis hard to imagine a castle rising up in this very place.''

But it was not hard for Rand to imagine. He was a man who believed in setting goals: hard goals, impossible goals. So far he'd achieved them all. All but one. He'd never heard his father acknowledge his success. And now he never would. His father had died content in the belief that his heir, his eldest son, John, was the best of the lot. Randulf he had fostered to a cruel man, a man guaranteed to beat the wildness from his middle son. Jasper he'd intended for the Church. Only John had he gifted with his attention.

But Rand had defeated his foster parent's attempts to beat him into an obedient soldier, and Jasper had thrown off the shackles of holy life. As for John, he was a drunken fool who had collapsed when their father died.

Rand took a deep breath of the icy air, not fooled by every evidence of winter. Spring was near and with it would come the challenges of raising the castle defenses and appeasing an angry and suspicious populace.

''The walls will rise slowly, but they *will* rise,'' he told Osborn. ''Meanwhile, we must eat. Never doubt for a minute that the key to our triumph here lies in the success of our crops.''

''We've marked out the best fields, and once the thaw is certain, we'll begin breaking up the land. But it seems we have a problem.''

''A problem?''

Osborn grimaced. ''There's a man—if indeed you can call him such. A queer fellow, twisted and deformed. The diggers had worked their way around to that pagan altar— or whatever that pile of rocks is—when this apparition came up, right out of the stones. Scared them out of their skins. Now they won't go anywhere near the place.''

''What of the cripple?''

Osborn blew out a frustrated breath. ''He's sitting on top of the bloody altar. Won't budge from the spot.''

''So have him removed,'' Rand said, working hard to

keep a straight face. Though his captain feared no man who
came at him with a weapon, he had a superstitious bent.
Rand knew that a twisted and deformed man was bound to
raise dread in Osborn's bosom.

"Have him removed? And who's to do the removing?"

"I take it you're not volunteering."

Osborn made a quick sign of the cross. "Not bloody
likely."

"Is he bigger than you?"

"No."

"Has he mightier weapons?"

"He's got the devil with him, is what he's got! Satan
himself. Gibbering in his heathen tongue then spoutin' the
holy words of the priests!"

That drew Rand up short. "He speaks Latin?"

"Aye. And curses us in both French and English," Osborn answered. "As I said, 'tis the devil at work in him."

Rand turned for the pile of rocks, the pagan altar they'd
all assumed it to be. A crippled man who spoke four languages? Either Osborn had tapped one of the wine kegs or
he was losing his mind.

Or else this land was as possessed of faeries and wizards
and conjurers as idle gossips would have it.

But the faeries had best be forewarned and the wizards
and conjurers had better beat a hasty retreat. For Randulf
Fitz Hugh had arrived and he claimed these lands, in his
own name and in the name of Henry, King of England.

Off to his right his red wolf pennant fluttered above their
encampment. Before very long it would fly from the ram-
parts of a mighty fortress. No amount of superstition would
prevent him from reaching his goal.

Two

The one thing Osborn had neglected to tell Rand was that the man was a dwarf, not quite the height of a very small woman. Otherwise he had described the curious creature very well.

The fellow sat on a flat rock balanced on five boulders that protruded from the frozen earth. The ground beneath the flat rock was scooped away, creating a sort of small, dark cave, too low-ceilinged for a man to stand upright in, but ideal for a deformed dwarf.

Rand halted before the rock and met the odd creature's placid gaze. He was not afraid, Rand noted. That alone earned him a modicum of respect. But no more. Rand nodded at him. "I am Randulf Fitz Hugh."

One side of the man's face lifted in a smile. One of the eyes focused on Rand. "I am Newlin," he answered in perfect French.

"Are your Latin, Welsh, and English as good as your French?"

"My Latin is better than most," he answered, or so Rand translated from the holy language and hoped he was right.

"My English is also good," the man continued. "But my Welsh . . ." He finished by rattling off a sentence of which the only word Rand recognized was *Cymru,* the Welsh word for Wales. Rand had tried to learn the fundamentals of the Welsh native tongue during the months of his preparation for his journey here. Notwithstanding the king's order that the language of court be the language of the land, it was more practical to converse in the language of the people he was set to rule. But it was clear his brief lessons had left some gaping holes in his knowledge.

He addressed the man in French. "You are a native of this area?"

"I am the bard of Carreg Du. I have lived here forever."

"Where precisely is your home?"

He gestured with his good hand. "This *domen* sometimes provides my shelter. Other times the trees."

"What of the village of Carreg Du? It lies less than two miles south. Do you never live among your people?"

The twisted little man gave Rand a twisted sort of smile. "I am among my people. The people of the trees. Why have you abandoned your people?"

Rand studied the bard. His body might be twisted and misshapen, but it was clear his mind had not suffered an equivalent misfortune. "Like you, I also am among my people. I come to make my home here. To build a castle that will protect all who choose to live in peace. In peace," he reiterated.

"In peace." The bard's colorless eyes looked off in disparate directions, yet Rand knew the man watched him closely. "You English have never been wont to come to Wales in peace."

Rand crossed his arms over his chest. "That is a subject I would discuss with Clyde ap Llewelyn. Can you take a message to him?"

The bard began to rock back and forth, just a small motion but Rand noticed. "Aye," Newlin answered. "When would you meet, and where?"

"Here." Rand laid one hand on the flat slab the bard sat upon. "This is a holy place, I take it."

"A *domen*. A burial vault."

"A burial vault. And you live in it?"

"Sometimes."

Rand nodded, though he did not understand a man who lay down upon the bones of other men. "If they will come, we can talk."

"Of peace?" the bard asked.

"Of peace." Rand did not expect them to agree to the sort of peace he envisioned. Still, his position was strong. Clyde ap Llewelyn had no surviving sons to succeed him. That was one of the few bits of information Henry had provided to him. If the aging Clyde did not name a strong successor before he died, there would either be a struggle among the remaining men of the village for dominance, or another, stronger village would take them over. It had ever been so among the warring Welsh.

But if Rand could prevent the people of Carreg Du from allying themselves with any other families, he would have no significant trouble with them. And though they might despise him, his greater strength would keep them peaceful enough. It was all he wanted or expected from them.

"I will tell them," Newlin agreed.

Rand stepped back then stopped. "One more thing. I would learn your language. Welsh. *Cymraeg,*" he added. "Will you teach me?"

Newlin looked away, up toward the summit of Rosecliffe. He continued to stare at it and once again began his peculiar rocking. "I cannot. But there is another . . ." He trailed off. "Perhaps there is another."

"But I *have* to go." Josselyn met her uncle's disapproving glare with a frown of her own. "I have as much right as anyone."

"I'll not bring a woman into an enemy camp. Think on it, girl! A hundred armed men, every one of them itching for satisfaction from their enemy. No. I'll not allow it."

Josselyn expelled a sharp breath, but she was not about to give up. She tried another tack. "Have you had a reply from Madoc ap Lloyd?"

He stared at her, meeting her unblinking gaze with one equally steady. "No. I will tell you when I do."

"Why?"

A frown deepened the creases in his brow. "Because his answer and your future are tied together—" He broke off when her expression turned smug, and his frown became a scowl. " 'Tis not the same thing."

"But it is! My lands. My future. Besides," she added, "my French is far better than Dewey's, and—"

"Nay! You'll not be going!" He slammed his fist down on the table and Josselyn jumped as high as did the dishes that sat on it.

"Please, Jossy," her aunt whispered from her seat in the corner. "Please be reasonable."

If not for her aunt Nessie, Josselyn would have confronted her uncle again, if only to prove she could rouse his seldom-seen temper. How dare he treat her like a child when she was the one he meant to barter to Owain! If she was central to that plan, why could she not be an observer in this one?

But now was not the time to press her point. She forced herself to be civil. "Very well," she muttered. But as she stalked from the hall, her mind spun. She would be with the others when they marched into the English encampment. She would see her enemies firsthand and gauge their strengths and weaknesses. For she must be absolutely certain that marrying Owain was the only way to drive the English out.

God help her if she wed Owain yet lost her family's lands all the same!

They met the next afternoon, though the leaden sky gave the winter day the feel of dusk. Had Newlin known that would happen? He must have, Josselyn decided, for although the bard was nowhere to be seen, the *domen* was lit by a circle of torches that cast long, eerie shadows across the site.

Had the druids of old used the ancient *domen* in just this way? Did their spirits visit it still?

A shiver of unease marked its way down Josselyn's spine. Despite the leather tunic she wore, she was chilled by the spooky atmosphere Newlin had created. No doubt he meant to intimidate the English invaders with visions of this haunted, holy spot. Unfortunately her countrymen were equally intimidated. Even she, who should know better, was not entirely unaffected.

She followed them at a distance. Though she'd dressed as a village youth, she knew they would soon notice a stranger. She was counting on their preoccupation to aid her deception.

Her uncle halted a little beyond the reach of the torchlight, and at his signal, Dewey faced the large group of their followers. Josselyn crept nearer and cautiously slipped into the shadow cast by one tall, burly fellow.

"We come in peace, merely to talk," Dewey said, repeating the words Clyde had spoken before they'd set out for Rosecliffe. "Be alert. Stay on the ready. But keep your weapons sheathed unless ordered otherwise."

"What if they unsheathe their weapons first?" Dulas, the tanner, asked.

Josselyn's Uncle Clyde turned to face his men. "Defend yourself, of course. But do not be too ready to attack. That decision is mine to make."

"We ought to wipe them out, skewer every last one o' the bastards," the youth next to Josselyn muttered. "What d'ye say?" He elbowed her sharply.

Josselyn grunted at the unexpected blow, and it was all she could do not to double over. "Skewer the bastards," she echoed. She shot the gangly fellow a baleful glare, only to find him staring curiously at her. "Say. Who are you?" he demanded to know, lowering his brows in a suspicious frown.

Josselyn was saved answering when Dewey, her uncle, and Bower, another lieutenant, advanced on the well-lit *do-*

men. At once Josselyn slipped away from the other youth to circle around the onlookers to get a better view. Three Englishmen also advanced into the circle, and Josselyn immediately forgot about the suspicious youth, her uncle's orders, and even the heavy warrior garb she wore. The tall, broad-shouldered Englishman stood opposite the *domen* from her uncle, along with two other fierce-looking fellows. The short, red-bearded fellow she'd noticed before was nowhere in sight, unless he was among the milling crowd of Englishmen who watched, as the Welshmen did, from a slight distance away.

Josselyn studied her enemies. Though there were numerous warriors among them, knights in their mail and foot soldiers in leather, there were also others, men who served another purpose, like the red-bearded man. Her heart began to thud with dread. They were here to build a castle. She was convinced of it.

Ten years ago the English had come with their warhorses and weapons to defeat the Welsh. She had lost her parents to them, and so many others as well in those wars. Still, they had prevailed over the English, and ultimately sent them away in defeat.

But Josselyn was not comforted by that knowledge. Her gaze returned to the tall leader of the invaders. This English lord was smarter than those others had been. He came quietly. Rather than attack and take over their village, he meant to build a strong base of his own. Instead of stealing food from the Welsh, he brought his own supplies and his own workers.

He meant to build a fortress here, a castle that could support itself, and which the Welsh would not be able to breach.

Her hands tightened into fists. They must be stopped!

She studied him with narrowed gaze. He would not be easily defeated. Not this man. He seemed to come in peace, but he was nonetheless a man of war, for though he wore neither helm nor the armor and mail common to his men, there was something in his bearing that bespoke a ruthless warrior. Something in his calm expression and confident stance.

Josselyn tried to analyze just what it was. He was not overtly threatening, yet she felt threatened. But not precisely in a way she understood. She squinted across the gloomy afternoon, studying him, trying to understand why her heart had begun to pound so rapidly when all he did was stand there, staring at her uncle.

Then he spoke and her palms began to sweat.

"Welcome, Clyde ap Llewelyn. Welcome all of you from Carreg Du. I am Randulf Fitz Hugh, and I plan to make my home among you."

Dewey translated in a voice loud enough to carry back to them. Josselyn wondered why he did not also translate the rumbling timbre of the man's voice, the confident choice of words, the distressing aura of command he cast with that slow measured statement.

Nor did Dewey comment on the shape of the Englishman's lips—

She drew herself up with a gasp. The shape of his lips? With an effort she tore her gaze away from the English lord and glanced around warily. Her countrymen scowled at the man's gall. Welcoming them to their own lands! Meanwhile, she had been distracted by the shape of his lips.

Furious at the impertinent clod for diverting her so, Josselyn concentrated on him again, searching for flaws. He was too tall, very nearly a giant. And his face was scarred, once on his cheek and again on his brow. His nose was too prominent, too proud. His eyes too dark.

She huffed in righteous indignation. He had the look of a blackguard, a man with no conscience, no mercy. She'd been right the first time.

And yet when he turned his head slightly, the torchlight gleamed off his raven-dark hair, giving it the look of silk. For one ludicrous moment, Josselyn wondered if it felt as soft and sleek as it appeared.

Thankfully, her uncle's harsh response put an end to her perverse thoughts. "The welcome is ours to give, not yours."

The English lord—Randulf Fitz Hugh, she remembered his name—met her uncle's belligerent glare with a mild expression. "I accept your welcome then. These lands are claimed by Henry, king of all Britain, including Wales. I come here as his steward to protect both the land and the people who reside upon it."

"We need no protection, least of all protection provided by you," Clyde responded in steely tones. Around Josselyn her Welsh countrymen shifted restlessly, feeling nervously for the hilts of their daggers and short swords, reassuring themselves by the presence of their weapons. Mercifully, however, they did not draw them out for battle.

It suddenly occurred to her that should a battle break out, she was at a severe disadvantage, having neither the size, strength, nor skill of the men around her. Still, she had no intention of leaving. She needed to gauge the seriousness of the English presence here. She needed to decide if it warranted her marrying the awful Owain ap Madoc.

"I see that you are well able to protect yourselves, and that is good," Fitz Hugh answered her uncle's challenging words, again in a tone that was mild and yet not yielding. "I hope you will think of us as your ally against any enemies that might threaten you with harm. For you will not be so threatened by our presence."

Dewey had no sooner finished the translation than someone cried out in Welsh, "These are *our* lands!"

Dewey looked nervously at Clyde, who shook his head. Frustrated by her uncle's caution, Josselyn did not pause to think. She shouted out the translation in Norman French.

At once the mood turned ugly. Her uncle's head jerked around, searching for her, for she knew he recognized her voice. Someone's hand took a hard hold of her shoulder. For the most part, however, her Welsh compatriots agreed with the message she'd passed on to the English. This was

Welsh land. They wanted no English overlords. Least of all this most arrogant and condescending Englishman.

Josselyn glared up at the man who had grabbed her. It was Dulas, and she smirked when he recognized her and hastily let her go. Since her uncle already knew she had disobeyed him, she decided there was no reason to hide herself any longer. Squaring her shoulders, she stepped past the others and marched purposefully into the circle of light.

Later she was to recognize that brazen move as her biggest mistake. Not because her uncle would be furious; it was already too late for that. Not because the English lord would see past her disguise, for she did not think he would.

Her mistake was in drawing too near Randulf Fitz Hugh, in stepping into the circle of power that emanated from him, like a light with a life all its own. In meeting his dark, piercing eyes. She glared her defiance at him. He deflected her dislike with an amused grin. Then her uncle drew the man's attention back to the matter at hand, leaving Josselyn no recourse but to stand there, frustrated and furious. Worried.

"We have work to offer your people," the Englishman stated. "And the coin to pay for their labor."

"We have no use for English coin."

"There are those among you who may feel differently."

"I rule these people!" her uncle snapped.

The English lord paused before answering. "And who rules after you? You have no sons. But I say to you, Clyde ap Carreg Du, that I will keep the peace. I will not let your Welsh people turn on one another as a means to establish a new leader, as is their wont."

" 'Tis also our wont to unite to drive off our common enemy."

"And after that to turn on one another again. I repeat. I will keep the peace in Carreg Du, for England and for Wales."

They stared at one another, neither of them blinking. The English lord was not going to back down. Neither was her

uncle, Josselyn realized. Clyde's only son had been killed
years ago in a raid against the English, while fighting alongside Josselyn's father. She knew her uncle would rather
have a Welshman spill his blood than allow an Englishman
to rule Carreg Du.

Behind her Josselyn felt the tension rise in her countrymen. The English lord's men likewise sensed it, and the
warriors among them began to crowd forward, faces hard,
hands ready on their hilts.

In the midst of the escalating tension, a figure suddenly
emerged from beneath the *domen*. As one, the Welsh and
English soldiers gasped and fell back. An apparition? A
spirit of Cymru's druid past?

No. It was Newlin, albeit there were more than a few
who believed him an apparition in his own right.

But not Josselyn, and apparently not the English lord
either. He did not flinch when Newlin, casting long shadows with his beribboned cloak and sideways gait, clambered up on the top stone that covered the *domen*.

"This discussion is done. 'Tis time for meditation. But
know you this, English and Welsh alike," he intoned in
Norman French which Dewey translated from a safe distance. "There is a fate oft recited. A lullaby. A prediction.
A truth we cannot escape." He lapsed into Welsh, into the
child's song every son and daughter of the Welsh hills
knew.

This time Josselyn translated it for the English lord and
his men to hear—and to heed.

> *When stones shall grow, and trees shall no',*
> *When noon comes black as beetle's back,*
> *When winter's heat shall cold defeat,*
> *Shall see them all ere Cymru falls.*

When he was done, when his voice was merely an echo
resounding in the chill, the bard subsided into a squat lump
upon the *domen*, an ancient swaying figure that seemed to

draw all the light to himself. An early nightfall had thrust the countryside into darkness. But still within the brave circle of torchlight, Josselyn's uncle faced the English lord.

"You will never rule Cymru," Clyde said, not reacting when Josselyn did the translating. "Henry will never rule Cymru. These stones will grow before that happens. The day will turn to night, and winter to summer before any Englishman rules here."

So saying, he turned and strode away, back to his men, with Dewey and Bower trailing in his wake. Josselyn was slower to react. For some reason she was not reassured by the age-old rhyme. Frowning, she stared at Randulf Fitz Hugh.

He was frowning too. Just a slight crease in his brow that caused the scar there to pucker. He did not like what he'd heard. Her doubts began to recede. But then his dark, assessing gaze turned on her, and a feeling very near panic overwhelmed her.

"I am in need of someone to teach me your language. Will you?"

She'd not expected that, and for a moment she could not find words to respond. Neither French ones, Welsh ones, nor English. Something about the man—or something perverse in her own nature—turned her mouth dry, and her brain to mush.

She shook her head no. It was the best she could manage. Then, fearing to linger a moment longer in his disturbing presence, Josselyn turned and fled to the safety of her countrymen.

So much for bravery, she chastised herself as they made their long, silent march home. So much for her foolish hope that the English would be easily routed and she could be spared a marriage to Owain.

She hated Owain. She hated Randulf Fitz Hugh. At the moment she hated Newlin too. What was his role in all this? Where did his loyalties lie?

Then Dewey fell into step beside her and her spirits fell

lower still. "Your uncle wishes a word with you when we reach the village. And I'll thank you not to try and take over my role as translator in the future. Interferin' wench," he added under his breath.

Josselyn did not honor him with a reply. At that moment she hated him too, and every other man who'd ever crossed her path. Interfering wench, indeed! Wales would be a far better place if women ran things. Any country would be. No fighting. No need for weapons or shields or war animals. Just peace and prosperity and enough food for everyone.

Men! Who needed them at all?

Three

Josselyn was not so glum come morning. The temperature had plummeted and a late snow had fallen. Despite the stern lecture she'd received from her uncle the night before—or perhaps because of it—she now felt cleansed and renewed. The world was fresh and pristine, its blanket of white unmarred by either man or beast. Likewise, her transgressions were behind her. She could start anew.

After briskly assembling a breakfast of hot mush and bread soaked in milk, she volunteered to distribute the previous day's leftover bread to the needy. Aunt Ness's joints ached in the cold so she never minded yielding outdoor tasks to her niece when the wind was this cruel and the cold this bitter. Today, however, Nessie watched Josselyn with unusual intensity.

"You'll be a good girl, won't you? You'll do as your uncle asks, him bein' like a father to you all these years."

Josselyn smiled apologetically. "I'm mindful of my responsibilities, Aunt Ness. But I've a need to be outside for a while. I'll be back by midday."

Now, with only one more stop to make, Josselyn let her mind roam free. The snow crunched beneath her heavy boots. The air was sharp, freezing its way into her lungs. But the sun had burned away the clouds. The snow would probably not last the week. She squinted against the glare, looking across the narrow valley, marking the path of the River Gyffin by its edging of white-fringed shrubs and heavily laden spruce trees.

How beautiful this valley was. In every season, whether cloaked in white, bursting with green, or emblazoned with gold and red, it was a magical place. Their place. She would never yield it to the English.

But what could she do, short of marrying Owain ap Madoc? She stood in the shadow of an ancient yew, letting the stillness seep over her. Into her. Then she blinked. The Englishman wanted workers, men to help build his castle. He also wanted a translator, she recalled, someone to teach him to speak the native tongue. Perhaps he had work for women as well, women to cook and do laundry, and mend both man and beast. Her breath quickened. What better way to undermine their enemy than from within?

She threw back her woolen hood and took a deep breath, then studied the path that led to Rosecliffe. She was dressed as a woman today. He would not connect her with the outspoken lad from last night.

Besides, she didn't mean to converse with anyone right away. Most especially not with him. Today she would only observe them, and perhaps speak with Newlin, if she could get his attention.

Resolved, Josselyn hurried to the last cottage in the loose scatter of buildings that made up Carreg Du. The widow Gladys lived there with her three children, but no smoke wafted from the chimney. The place was little more than a hovel, a stone structure with a slanted roof. But its cramped size provided one benefit: it was easy to keep warm. So why was the fire out?

The answer lay sprawled across the single pallet. Gladys, widow of Tomas, was drunk, snoring in great frosty puffs, while her children huddled beneath a pair of ragged blankets. At Josselyn's noisy entrance the eldest child peered out at her.

"Our mam is sick," the girl explained. "She's sick, that's all."

"Sick," Josselyn muttered, laying the bread on the scarred table, the only piece of furniture in the frigid hut. She turned toward the fire. Thankfully a few embers yet glowed. "Did you bank this fire, Rhonwen?"

"Aye," the child said. "But there's no firewood left to keep it goin'."

No firewood. No food. Of course, there had been enough spirits to make a grown woman neglect her poor, fatherless children. Furious with Gladys, yet mindful that the woman still mourned the loss of her husband, Josselyn funneled her anger into action. "Come along. I'm taking you home with me. Leave the bread for your mother," she added when Rhonwen stared hungrily at it. "Aunt Ness will give you warm mush and cheese."

Rhonwen shoved her tangled hair from her brow. The promise of a warm meal was enough for her. With a deftness a nine-year-old should not possess, she scooped up her three-year-old sister with one arm and her infant brother with the other. When the baby began to wail, the girl looked up at Josselyn and shrugged. "He's wet. And hungry. D'ye have any milk?"

Josselyn's lips pinched together in frustration. "We'll find something to satisfy him. Come along, now."

When the child sent a worried glance back at her snoring parent, however, Josselyn's frustration dissolved. Poor motherless child. Rhonwen's mother neglected her, yet she hesitated to abandon the woman. Before she could change her mind, Josselyn flung the blankets over Gladys. Then she herded the children out of the cottage, slamming the door as she went.

Aunt Ness would take them in, at least for the duration of this cold spell. After that they'd have to parcel the children out among their relatives. Someone had to mind them until their mother was once more up to the task.

The morning was almost gone before Josselyn could slip

away again. Aunt Ness had gathered the forlorn little brood into her arms like a mother hen too long without chicks of her own. The baby quieted under her ministrations, and the younger girl trundled along in her wake like a tiny, thumb-sucking shadow. Rhonwen, however, clung to Josselyn. She followed her now outside into the fenced courtyard.

"Where are you goin'? Can I come too?" the child begged.

"Not today," Josselyn said. When the hollow-eyed little girl stared longingly at her, however, she almost relented. Then she reminded herself of her destination. The English encampment was no place for a child. "Not today," she repeated, frowning to emphasize her words. "Mind little Cordula and Davit. I'll return before long. And I'll tell you a story after supper," she added when the girl did not budge.

That got a response. Rhonwen's eyes brightened and she backed toward the house. "A story. I like stories. Are there dragons in it? And faeries? And a handsome warrior to slay the dragon?"

"Of course there are."

Satisfied, Rhonwen ran into the house without further comment. As Josselyn turned toward the path that led to Rosecliffe she was smiling. Dragons and faeries and a handsome warrior. How like a child. Now she'd have to think up some story to satisfy the girl.

Once beyond the village, however, and on the snow-shrouded path to Rosecliffe, she was struck by an unhappy thought. She was off to spy on a dragon even now, the English king's castle-building invader. The faerie bard Newlin might help her. Or he might not.

But who was to play the part of her handsome warrior?

Randulf Fitz Hugh's face flashed in her mind. A rugged face, scarred and limned by torchlight. Some might call him handsome. She might, were he not a hated Englishman. But he was English, an English dragon come to do her people harm. She would not call him handsome. So who did that leave? Owain?

Frowning, she pushed on, climbing the hills, maneuvering up the slippery slope. Owain ap Madoc was not ugly to look at, but that was the only good thing she could say of him. He'd married young and sired a son, and had been widowed now almost a year. That much she knew—and also that he scared her to death. Had he killed poor Tomas? It could never be proven, but in her heart, she believed he had. She shuddered in horror and paused to catch her breath, leaning against the peeling trunk of a towering sycamore tree. The image of sad, drunken Gladys and her hapless brood preyed upon her mind. No, Owain was no handsome warrior to save Josselyn or anybody else from the threat of the dragon. If anything, he was worse than the dragon itself. So what was she to do? She was caught between the enemy English and the enemy Welsh.

She would simply have to be her own warrior, she decided. She would have to find a way to undermine the English presence in their part of Wales. Uncle Clyde might disapprove, but he could not stop her. And in the end he would thank her—and she would not have to ensure the safety of Carreg Du and her people through a marriage to Owain.

She pulled her shawl over her head and shivered with the cold. Or was it fear that sent an icy chill racing down her back? She stamped her feet, chasing away both the cold and her fear. She was almost there. She would not turn back now. She would spy on the English and plot a way to gain entrance to their camp. And somehow—somehow—she would rid herself of their presence on her lands.

And save herself from the Welsh bully as well.

When she reached the edge of the forest below Rosecliffe, the Englishmen were working despite the snow. Not digging though. The ground was probably too hard. Instead several gangs of men cut down trees, cleaned them of their limbs, and dragged them up the hill.

Josselyn settled herself behind a tree with a split trunk and studied the scene before her. Five stakes with red flags tied to them seemed to mark the corners of an immense structure. Surely that Fitz Hugh fellow did not mean to build a stone keep so large!

She'd seen two castles in her life, both of them heavily fortified keeps three stories tall. But they had not been one-tenth the size of this structure marked out on the crest of Rosecliffe.

And why had they begun another ditch so far from the castle? She'd heard of a moated castle but she'd not pictured anything remotely this big. Her gaze returned to the nearest knot of men. They'd cleaned a log near the edge of the forest and one of them now hitched a pair of draft horses to it. Another man knelt on one knee beyond the far horse.

When he stood, however, Josselyn's breath caught in her chest. Randulf Fitz Hugh himself. And he labored beside his men. Were it not for his excessive height, Josselyn would not have recognized him at all, because he had shed any symbols of his rank and, like the others, wore rough hose and braies, and a plain chainse and sleeveless tunic.

She strained forward, trying to see what he did. Struggling to hear what he said. But the glare on the snow was too bright, and their voices muffled by the distance. He patted the horse once, then when someone hailed him, looked over his shoulder.

The red-bearded man was hurrying over to him, hunched into his flapping cloak, gripping a rolled parchment in his hand. At once Josselyn's focus shifted to that parchment. If only she could see it.

If only she could steal it!

The two men walked apart from the others, and while the work crew urged the horses up the hill with their load, Fitz Hugh and Redbeard bent over the parchment. They were so intent on their discussion that Josselyn took a chance. There was a shrubby stand of hollies to her left, forward of where she now hid. Perhaps from there she'd be better able to hear.

Slowly she crept forward, watching them all the time.

Redbeard pointed down the hill and Fitz Hugh gestured in Josselyn's direction. At once she dropped to her knees, holding her breath while her heart beat a deafening rhythm in her ears. Both men stared. Did they see her? Then Redbeard made a sweeping gesture with his hand and stabbed the parchment once more with his mittened finger.

Josselyn was almost too frightened to move. Almost. Slowly she gathered her feet beneath her. Slowly she inched forward again.

". . . harder to dig. But the stones are better . . ." The wind carried Redbeard's voice briefly to her, then away.

"How is the second well coming?"

That she heard clearly, in a voice she recognized well, though she'd heard it but one other time. Two wells? Her village used river water, but that was not good enough for the English. They needed two wells for their water. If only there was a way for her to sabotage their plans!

Then a shriek rent the winter quiet, a shrill child's cry that made Josselyn's blood run cold. Her head jerked around, searching for its source. She hadn't seen any children among the English.

No sooner was that thought formed than she realized how stupid it was. And how dangerous matters had just become. For it was panicked Welsh cries that she heard. *"No! Let me go! Help. Help!"*

It was a Welsh child they'd captured!

As one Fitz Hugh and Redbeard whirled about. The shorter man frowned at something beyond Josselyn's right shoulder, while Fitz Hugh strode purposefully toward the contretemps.

Josselyn shrank deeper into the dubious protection of the hollies. What had happened? What should she do?

From somewhere behind her a man laughed, then let out a cry of pain. "The bloody brat bit me!"

"Keep your hand out of his mouth then," Fitz Hugh replied as he passed not ten paces from Josselyn's hiding spot.

"It's a girl," the other Englishman responded peevishly. "Too bad she's not a mite older," he added. "I could think of a good use for her if she was."

Josselyn knew what that meant, and her fear trebled. English warriors had only one use for Welsh women. Everyone knew that. Then the child shrieked again and let out a string of curse words no child should know.

Josselyn recognized that voice. Rhonwen! The child had followed her!

"Give me the saucy little wench," Fitz Hugh growled.

Without pausing to think of the consequences, Josselyn shot out of the holly stand. She would not let them hurt a child!

"Behind you, m'lord!" somebody shouted.

Everything happened too fast. Fitz Hugh ducked and spun around. Beyond him Josselyn saw Rhonwen struggling to escape a stocky fellow. But before she could reach the child, Josselyn was tackled, thrown to the frigid earth, and crushed beneath Fitz Hugh's hard, unyielding weight.

For the first few seconds afterward Josselyn couldn't breathe. Stars swam before her eyes and she had the oddest sense of sinking into a dark, shadowy hole. Even her vision began to fade. She was going to faint.

But a part of her knew she could not let that happen, and somehow she fought her way back to the light.

The weight above her shifted, but still she could not catch her breath. Then she was rudely hauled upright, bent over a man's brawny arm, and struck sharply on her back.

At once she gasped and was rewarded by a huge rush of cold air into her chest. With the air came also her reason—and the realization that she was bent over the arm of the English leader himself. The enemy she'd come to spy on held her like an armful of wet laundry. She would kill

Rhonwen for getting them into this predicament. That is, assuming they survived it.

"Now that 'un's more of an age to be useful," the man who held Rhonwen remarked with a chortle. "What d'ye say, milord? Will you trade wenches with me?"

Josselyn struggled to regain her balance and tried to twist out of Fitz Hugh's grip, but it was impossible.

"I don't think so. This one has too much spirit for the likes of you, Harry." With one hand Fitz Hugh clamped Josselyn's arms to her sides; with the other he pushed her unbound hair out of her face.

All at once she was face-to-face with him, and held so tightly that her legs and belly pressed intimately against his. The shock of his nearness, of having his dark eyes run over her face, silenced her for a moment. His eyes were such a dark gray they could have been mistaken for black. The black of midnight. The black of a mountain wolf.

Then his hand moved down the back of her head, tangling in her hair as he ran his fingers through it, and he gave her a wolfish grin. "She's too fair for the likes of you as well," he added, though in a lower tone, one the other man probably did not hear.

Josselyn shivered with fear and also a disturbing sort of awareness. No man had ever held her so, least of all against her will. He had no right.

Brutally she repressed her fear. "I'm too fair for the likes of you also," she snapped in his native tongue. "If you have any honor whatsoever, you will release me at once. The child also."

His brow arched in surprise, and Josselyn took a small satisfaction from that. While she had the advantage she must make use of it. "If you would be so kind as to release me?" she added, knowing that she must not show her fear.

"You speak like an English aristocrat," he replied, but without loosening his hold in the least. "How is that?"

She tilted her chin up. "We Welsh are a brilliant people."

"No more brilliant, I'm sure, than any other. I'll ask you again," he said, letting his hand slide farther down the length of her hair to rest at the small of her back. "How do you come to speak my language so well?"

Josselyn trembled. There was no harm in revealing the truth, and perhaps a great harm—to herself and Rhonwen—in hiding it. "Newlin taught me," she bit out. "There. Now will you release me and the child?"

To her surprise he did release her. She backed away, hugging her arms about her. She gestured to Rhonwen. "Have your man let her go too."

With one nod of his head it was done. Rhonwen bolted from her captor, then halted behind a bare-limbed elm tree. *"Josselyn, come. Run!"*

But Josselyn knew running was the wrong reaction. She'd wanted to spy on the English. What better way to do it than by ingratiating herself with their leader, the fierce Randulf Fitz Hugh? She faced him, conscious that even without his knightly trappings, he exuded a raw power that was intimidating. She had to remind herself that he'd approached her uncle in peace last night. Surely he would not try to destroy that peace now.

"I thank you," she said, though not with much sincerity. "The child meant no harm. She was merely curious."

"And you? Is that what drew you here as well? Curiosity?"

This was our land long before you claimed it for your campsite. That's what Josselyn wanted to say. Instead she answered, "I suppose I am curious. But I have another reason."

Their eyes met and held, and she felt his awareness of her as a woman. It was no compliment, she told herself when his gaze moved over her in a slow, assessing fashion. These were men without women. Anything with breasts would satisfy them. When she self-consciously crossed her arms across her chest, he grinned again.

"What is this other reason that brings you here?"

She lifted her chin a notch. "You said you have jobs to offer. Well, I find myself in need of employment."

"I'll hire her meself," the man called Harry chortled, swaggering across the snow-covered ground. "I can keep 'er busy—and happy too."

Josselyn's eyes narrowed to slits. *"Asyn,"* she spat at the crude oaf.

"Asyn," Fitz Hugh mocked. "I wonder what that could mean."

Josselyn's glare shifted back to him. "It means that Welshwomen are not the meek and spineless creatures you lowlanders breed. It means that a man who tries to—" She broke off, only belatedly realizing that her anger could swiftly trip her up.

"It means that you all carry daggers." Fitz Hugh's amused gaze fell to the hip sheath that held her short-bladed weapon.

Josselyn moved her hand to the hilt of it, then gasped when it was not there. She glowered at him, infuriated all the more by his insolent grin.

He extended his hand with her small dagger in it. "Here. Take it."

Unaccountably, her heart began to race. He held his arm steady, daring her to approach him and take back the weapon. Josselyn glared at him. If she'd disliked and mistrusted him before, now she truly hated him. He was a bully, brother under the skin to Owain and all men of that ilk. They thought they could take whatever they wanted, no matter the cost to others.

But they succeeded only if their prey panicked, only if their target was impetuous and unwise. He could only bully her if she allowed him to.

She refused to do so.

"Do you have employment to offer, or was your claim a false one?"

"My claim," he echoed. "What have you heard of my claim? You were not there last night—" He broke off and his perusal of her became more intense. Then he grinned. "You *were* there. The second translator. That's why your voice sounded familiar. You were dressed as a boy."

It was Josselyn's turn to give him an arch smile. "That was my brother," she lied, just to spite him.

"Your brother. And is this your brother's dagger?"

Steeling herself, Josselyn strode up to him. "No. It's mine." She calmly took it from him, then forced herself not to back away as she slid the weapon down into its sheath. Then she looked up at him.

He was too close to her. He could grab her again, although somehow she knew he would not. Still, he was too close.

"What sort of employment are you offering?" she asked in a voice she feared was not so nonchalant as she would like. "Respectable employment," she added when the other Englishman edged into her line of vision.

"I would respect you," Harry offered, leering at her. "I respect ev'ry wench I ever gave it to, and you would—"

"Enough!"

Harry broke off at Fitz Hugh's sharp command, and it was a good thing. If he hadn't ceased his vile remarks, Josselyn feared she would have had to slit the vermin's throat.

"Get back to work," Fitz Hugh ordered the man. "Tell Sir Lovell that I'll be with him directly."

He turned his attention back to Josselyn, but she made the mental note. Sir Lovell. Was that Redbeard's name?

"So you wish to work for English coin. What's your name?"

Josselyn's thoughts spun. There was no harm in the truth, was there? "Josselyn. Josselyn ap Carreg Du."

"Josselyn. What work do you propose to do for me, Josselyn?"

He was still too close, but she deemed it not unreasonable for her to step back now. She'd shown him she wasn't afraid. "I can cook. I'm known for my stews and roasted meats. I also sew, mend clothing, and do laundry.''

''Can you teach me to speak Welsh? *Cymraeg?*'' he added.

She hesitated before answering. ''I can.'' *That's not to say you are bright enough to learn it though.*

He stuck his hand out and, to Josselyn's shame, she flinched back as if struck. In the background she heard Rhonwen's fearful cry: *''Come away from him, Josselyn. He's an evil man. He will hurt you!''* But he only held his hand out to her.

''I will pay you one denier every week. When I am fluent in your language, there will be a bonus of three deniers. Are we agreed?''

Josselyn stared at his hand, then raised her gaze reluctantly to his hard, lean face. Despite the scars she'd noted on it last night, his face was strong and manly. Handsome, in its own harsh way.

But handsome or no, she didn't want to touch him. She was afraid to seal their agreement by taking his hand. It was purely illogical, she knew. But knowing that changed nothing. Unfortunately, there was no other way.

She extended her hand and tried to grip his with the same, impersonal force he used. It was impossible. His hand enveloped hers. The warmth of it banished the cold that made her fingers numb. How could he be so warm?

''We are agreed,'' she muttered, then promptly yanked her hand back.

''Good. So, tell me. What does *carreg du* mean?''

''It means 'black stone.' I cannot begin working for you this very minute,'' she added in an irritated tone.

''Why is that?''

She gestured to Rhonwen, who lingered nervously at the edge of the woodland. ''I must see the child back to the village.''

He shrugged. ''She can join us.''

''Her mother will worry,'' Josselyn countered. ''I will come tomorrow.''

He grimaced and rubbed his chin, all the while staring thoughtfully at her. "So be it. Tomorrow."

Josselyn stared at him another long moment, then without comment turned toward Rhonwen. Tomorrow would come soon enough. Between now and then she must tell her uncle what she was up to, weather the explosion that was bound to follow, then restore his calm sufficiently to discuss the precise nature of the information she should try to uncover about the English lord and his plans.

All in all, she'd had a very good day, she decided when she reached Rhonwen's side. It hadn't gone as she'd expected, but then, whatever did?

"Let us begone from here," she said, taking the child by the hand.

"Bloody English bastards!" the girl spat back at the Englishmen.

"Rhonwen! That is not proper language for a child, nor for a lady."

"My mother says it all the time. I hate the English. They killed my father; now I wish they were all dead." She pulled her hand from Josselyn's and stared suspiciously at her. "Why were you talkin' to him so long?"

Josselyn stared into the girl's face. She was so young and yet, somehow, so old. "I'm going to work for him. Spy on him," she added before Rhonwen could protest. She caught the girl by the shoulders and crouched down so that they were face-to-face. "I know he's our enemy, Rhonwen. But I also know he's stronger than I am. If we are to defeat him and all the others that Henry will send to replace him, we must do it with cunning and stealth.

"I am a woman, as you soon will be, and weaker than a man. But if I am smarter, I can defeat him just the same. And I do plan to defeat this particular man."

She looked back, following the line of their footprints in the snow toward the place where Randulf Fitz Hugh had been. "Mark my word on it. I plan to defeat him."

Four

"And just what is it you think that cursed parchment can tell you?"

Josselyn heaved a sigh of relief. For the past hour her uncle had railed at her, threatening to confine her to the hall—anything to prevent her from returning to the English encampment on the morrow. Aunt Ness had despaired, wringing her hands together, then throwing her apron over her head and running from the hall when she could bear no more.

But Josselyn had stood her ground and eventually her uncle's temper had eased—and not a moment too soon. Between her outrage over the irresponsible Gladys, her fury at that cocksure English lord, and this heated confrontation with her normally taciturn uncle, Josselyn was utterly worn out.

She wanted nothing more than to retreat to her chamber, crawl beneath the heavy sheepskin, and give herself up to sleep. But that was not to be. Now that her uncle Clyde had capitulated, they needed to plan.

She rubbed an aching knot at the back of her neck. "I suspect that parchment depicts the arrangement of the castle they plan to construct. I'm sure Redbeard—Sir Lovell—is the master builder."

"A castle takes years to build. Knowing their final plan

is of no import. We must drive them out before the first walls go up.''

''And how are we to do that?''

He met her gaze only a moment before looking away. ''You know how,'' he muttered.

''Owain ap Madoc is a pig,'' she spat, unable to be tactful. ''He may be a Welshman, but he is a pig nonetheless.'' She leaned forward and placed a hand on his arm, imploring him to understand and support her plan. ''I understand the predicament we are in. Without his aid we cannot defend ourselves against the English, let alone drive them out. They are too many. But before I sacrifice myself to the likes of Owain, don't I deserve a chance to find some other way to defeat the English?''

He shrugged off her touch, then scrubbed his hands over his face. ''Enough. I have agreed. What else would you have of me?'' He glared at her as he picked up a half-filled cup of wine and quaffed the contents.

''Tell me what to look for, what signs to observe. How to know what will be helpful to our cause. I know nothing of castles and warfare.''

He sighed, then shoved his cup away and leaned across the table. ''Very well. Let me think.'' His heavy brows knit together in a frown. ''The dimension of the storerooms and stables—and the barracks. That will give us an inkling of the size of the garrison they expect to house in our midst. Also the system of guards, the rotation. We need to know their weakest points, their least guarded moment.'' He looked her straight in the eye. ''Also, where their leader sleeps. How well he is guarded.''

Josselyn did not blink at the implication that the English lord might be killed. If she had, she knew her uncle would have resumed his objections, for there was no room for softness in war. And this was a war, she realized. She must help vanquish Randulf Fitz Hugh if she were to avoid a hellish union with Owain ap Madoc. The unadorned truth was that many would die.

But though she did not blink, something inside her rebelled at the idea of Randulf Fitz Hugh dead.

She and her uncle talked into the night. Ness returned, peeking warily into the main hall, then bustling about in relief when she saw that calm had returned. She and Rhonwen prepared the two younger children for bed, then they too said their good-nights and made their way to their beds.

But as Josselyn and Clyde spoke of wheat stores and armorers, of warhorses and stock cattle, Rhonwen sat at the top of the freshly swept stairs, huddled in a shadow and listening. She listened and she vowed to be just as brave as Josselyn was. Just as daring.

She'd been so scared when that man had captured her. Then Josselyn had rushed to her defense, brave despite her fear. For those long, awful minutes, Rhonwen had been sure they would both be killed. Or worse.

She didn't think anything could be worse than death, but her mother had once sworn that there was indeed a fate even worse than death.

But Josselyn had managed to get them safely away from the English camp and her words were now forever imprinted in Rhonwen's mind. No matter that a man was bigger and stronger than a woman. If the woman were smarter, she could still defeat him.

Sitting there in the cold, dark stair hall, listening to the low murmur of Josselyn plotting revenge on the English, Rhonwen vowed to make herself smarter than any man could ever be. She would never let herself be dependent on a man for her safety or her well-being. She would never be like her mother. Instead she would be smart and brave, a warrior in her own right.

She would be like Josselyn.

Rand anticipated Josselyn's arrival at his encampment. Last night he'd given strict orders that the local women were not to be threatened in any way. He'd outlined harsh punitive repercussions for anyone who disobeyed that order.

Most particularly, the Welshwomen were not to be raped or threatened into having sex. They could be bribed, of course, with coin or trinkets or food. He would not begrudge his men that much. But the women had to be willing. Their wishes had to be respected.

Then he'd lain awake half the night wondering whether Josselyn of the midnight hair and flashing blue eyes would sell her charms to him for the price of a coin or two.

Osborn had questioned the wisdom of allowing one of their enemies access to their camp. But Rand was not worried. She was just a woman, curious enough to spy on them from afar and brave enough to leap to the defense of a child, but still only a woman and not to be feared.

And such a woman. Her breasts were soft and full, and her waist was slender. No doubt he could span it with his two hands. Her legs were long and, in his imagination at least, shapely and strong. Visions of those legs wrapped around his thrusting hips had haunted his dreams all night.

That she was fluent in French was an added blessing. It gave him reason to spend time with her. As important as he considered learning Welsh, however, at the moment what he most wanted to hear had nothing to do with politics, castle building, or even survival. He wanted whimpers of desire, moans of passion, and cries of completion.

Rand rubbed the back of his neck in frustration. It was bitterly cold in this godforsaken place, but the thought of that raven-haired wench had him as randy as a boar in rut.

He looked around, trying to banish Josselyn from his mind. His tent was pitched on the site where the great hall would eventually rise. The land was reasonably flat there. The inner wall would be built where the downward slope of the hill increased, with the outer wall below it, following at least partially a natural outcropping of stone. Beyond that a town would someday crowd up to the castle walls, filled with people of both English and Welsh descent. And his red wolf pennant would wave over all.

Not that he meant to linger in this place that long. He

would build Henry's castle for him. He would give the king a mighty fortress to protect his interests in the cold, frozen place. But he would not live out his life here, not so long as the center of power resided in London—as it always would.

"Power is a fey creature," a voice spoke as if from the depths of Rand's own mind. But it wasn't his mind. Something moved to his left, and even as Rand jerked and spun to face this silent-footed creature, he knew he'd overreacted.

Newlin stood there, staring at him with his strange, unfocused eyes. A chill ran down Rand's backbone and his right hand twitched with the urge to grasp the hilt of his sword. The bard was strange enough as it was. The last thing Rand's edgy band of men needed to believe was that the spooky little character could read minds.

"There's not a man alive who doesn't lust for more power than he already possesses," Rand said when the bard only stared at him.

Newlin gave a one-sided shrug. "A man controls his lusts. He does not allow his lusts to control him."

Rand's eyes narrowed. Were it not for his wish to keep peace with the Welsh, he would send Newlin and his irritating observations on his way. But the man was an honored bard among the Welsh. The fact that most of Rand's men were afraid of the odd fellow made it even more important that Rand appear unaffected by him. In short, he had to endure the bard's presence.

But Rand would be damned if he'd let the man disconcert him.

"Tell me about the woman Josselyn," he demanded, changing the subject. "She has agreed to teach me your language. Why did she disguise herself as a lad the other night?"

Newlin smiled. "Josselyn. Yes, she is a woman now. But she is not far removed from the orphaned child I found crying, lying atop the *domen*."

"You took her in?"

"We all took her in. From me she learned language. From Dewey how to use a dagger. From Ness how to cook. From old Mina how to sew."

Rand considered his next question.

"No, she has no husband," the twisted little man answered before Rand could phrase the question.

Rand clenched his jaw and beat down the irrational notion that the bard really could read minds. The woman was comely. Any right-thinking man would wonder if she were already wed. It was no great feat for Newlin to deduce that. "Why did she disguise herself as a lad the other night?" he persisted.

Newlin was slow to answer. "We men of *Cymru* allow our women many freedoms. But we are no different than you English when it comes to war. 'Tis men that fight, not women. She was told not to come but she hid her true identity beneath the garb of a warrior youth."

"She revealed herself when she spoke. Was she punished for her deception?"

Newlin smiled and his odd gaze drifted away from Rand to focus somewhere down the hill. This time it was Rand who deduced Newlin's thoughts. "She comes," Newlin said, even as Rand spied her silhouette.

She strode up the hill without hesitation. The workers paused as she passed, staring after her as men deprived of women are wont to do. If those hungry stares bothered her, it did not show. She moved swiftly, straight toward him, and though she was covered in the same heavy green cloak, with a *couvrechef* knotted over her head, Rand felt the unmistakable rise of lust.

He was no better than his men, he berated himself. And yet why should he be any different? He was a man gone three weeks without a wench. Were Josselyn a toothless hag, his surging manhood would be no less demanding. He tamed the beast in his braies with a stern exercise of willpower.

She stopped before him, but after a brief glance, turned to Newlin. *"Dydd da,"* she said, giving the man a smile. Then she looked back at Rand and her smile disappeared. "That means 'I bid you a good day.' "

"Dydd da," Rand repeated.

"Chwithau," she responded, giving no indication of either approval or disapproval of his pronunciation. "The same to you."

"When I taught you," Newlin said, "I began with the world around us. The stones and trees. The sky and sea."

"So you did." She stared at the bard as if trying to decipher some further meaning in his words.

Meanwhile, Rand made his own interpretation. Josselyn didn't really want to teach him her language. She'd rather cook or clean to earn her coin. But since she'd agreed to teach him Welsh, Newlin was advising her to do her task well, even if it were not what she preferred.

A good man, that Newlin. Good, but odd. Rand decided to take control of the situation before Josselyn could.

"You can follow me around and teach me as Newlin advised. Once I've mastered the important words, you can explain how to put them together."

"As you wish," she replied in a bland tone.

But though Josselyn's voice displayed no emotion, inside she seethed. Follow him around! She was no cur dog to trot at his heels! But she would let him think she was, if that's what it took to lull him to complacency. She would be mild and pliable and as earnest an instructor as he'd ever had—if indeed he'd ever been instructed in anything beyond murder and mayhem.

She turned to Newlin. "Nessie sends word that she is cooking crust rolls today. Your favorite, I believe. You are welcome to the evening meal."

He nodded to her then to the Englishman, and without further comment, meandered away. Josselyn watched him depart, comforted by his brief presence and the familiar dip and sway of his gait, even though he was leaving her alone

with the English lord. But then, it had been her decision to
come here yesterday, and her decision to seek employment
from him. If she did not want to be here, she could have
stayed away.

She took a fortifying breath, then turned to face her new
employer. Her ancient enemy. "Shall we begin?"

He studied her with a gaze far too intense for her liking.
"Have you had breakfast?"

"*Brecwast*. Breakfast. Yes. *Do*."

"Very well." He continued to stare, as if challenging
her, and Josselyn was hard-pressed to restrain her temper.

"You are building a ditch there. *Ffos*," she said, pointing to where a crew of men with picks and shovels labored
in a long trough.

"It's for the foundation of a wall."

"*Gwal*." She said the Welsh word. "To keep my people
out or your people in?"

"To keep my allies safe, whoever they may be. And to
keep my enemies out. Whoever *they* may be," he added.

"Don't you know who they are?"

A slight grin curved up half of his mouth. A taunting
grin, she noticed. "I hope to make everyone my ally. Especially you."

That bold remark should not have flustered her, but it
did. She, his ally? No, that would never be. But she must
not reveal that to him. She met his amused gaze. "Mayhap
it shall be *you* who becomes *our* ally."

" 'Tis the same thing."

"No." She stared steadily at him. "It is not the same
thing at all."

Across the short space between them some tension
hummed, something that was more than her Welsh defiance
and his English aggression. She must not look away from
him, she told herself, for to do so would appear an act of
cowardice. Yet even had she wanted to, she could not have
torn her gaze from him. He was that compelling.

Her salvation came in the unlikely form of Redbeard.

The master builder barreled up the hill, Fitz Hugh looked away, and Josselyn expelled the breath she'd not known she'd been holding.

By the blood of Saint David! What had just happened? The surface of her skin fairly crackled from the intensity of the moment. She took a step backward, rubbing her arms to erase the prickle. She needed distance from him. Thankfully he now focused on Sir Lovell's words.

". . . a soft spot. It will require a deeper foundation."

"Which will take longer?" Fitz Hugh asked, frowning.

"Aye, it will. But changing the inner wall to skirt that soft vein will create a blind spot. The tower would have to be extended. See?" He spread the parchment he carried on the ground and both men squatted before it.

Josselyn stood very still. She wanted them to forget she was here. She wanted to listen and learn. But mostly she wanted to see what was drawn on that parchment. She squinted, trying to see past the glare of morning sun on the pale parchment. She must have leaned nearer, or tilted her head. Something drew a sharp look from Sir Lovell, for he halted in mid-sentence and nudged Fitz Hugh.

"Is this your new translator?"

Fitz Hugh turned to look at her. "It is."

"Good day, Sir Lovell," she said, determined to win the older man's confidence. "Will you also be wanting to learn *Cymraeg*?" She smiled determinedly at him and after a moment the suspicion on his face eased.

"If I'm to spend the next ten years of my life working here, t'would seem a wise thing to do. Bless you, lass, for offering."

" 'Lass' is *lances*," she responded.

"Llances," he repeated, this time smiling. "You're a bonny *llances*. I've two daughters, you know, though both younger than you."

"Shall they be coming to join you here?"

"Eventually," Fitz Hugh cut in before Sir Lovell could answer. "Eventually we shall all bring our families here.

But first we have work to do. Come, Lovell, show me the area you referred to.''

The two of them walked off, angling down the hill and leaving Josselyn to follow in their wake. But for a moment Josselyn simply stared at them. These Englishmen were unlike any men she'd known before. The one, tall and arrogant, both drew her and terrified her. The other, stout and affable, reminded her unaccountably of her father. He looked nothing like him, of course. She recalled little of her father, save that he was dark-haired and tall, with a deep, rumbling voice. More like Fitz Hugh in appearance than Sir Lovell. But something in Sir Lovell's expression, something in his voice when he spoke of his two daughters . . .

With an effort she shook off those maudlin thoughts. He was a man who felt affection for his daughters. That was all. The similarity went no further. But if he wanted to befriend her and treat her as he might one of his own daughters, she would be the fool not to take advantage of the situation. After all, that was why she was here.

Admonishing herself not to be overly concerned with anything save gathering information about her English enemies, Josselyn hurried to catch up with them.

''What is the word for 'mud'?'' Josselyn asked as she toyed with a piece of stale brown bread.

Rand tried to keep his gaze on her eyes and not let it wander down to her rosy lips or, worse, to her firm breasts. ''Mud? *Llacs*,'' he answered.

''How about 'bread'?''

''*Carreg*.''

''No. *Carreg* means 'stone.' ''

Rand grinned at her and held up a piece of rock-hard bread. ''*Bara. Carreg*. At the moment I see no difference.'' He tossed the bread into her lap and then a handful of pebbles as well.

It was a lighthearted gesture. Flirtatious, even. But she

obviously didn't like it, for she shoved both bread and stones aside, then stood, shaking her skirts out.

After a long morning leading Josselyn around the castle site, pointing out everything—horses, tools, trees, carts— and having her give him their Welsh names, Rand had sent her to fetch bread, ale, and cheese for their midday repast. They sat apart from the others in a sunny patch of ground where a few early plants showed the beginnings of their spring green. Now, as she moved away to sit on a flat boulder projecting up from the ground, the sun shot sparks off her waist-length hair, and brought a pretty flush to her cheeks.

Or was it his flirtation that had caused her color to rise?

He decided to find out. "How do you say 'your hair is as shiny as a raven's wings'?"

She shot him an irritated look, but her cheeks grew pinker still. "You don't," she snapped.

He lolled on his side, propping his head on one hand. "Why not? One day I may be wooing a black-haired maiden. I'll need to know such words."

"Speak them in English, then. I doubt any Welshwoman would be unwise enough to listen to such drivel."

"Drivel?" Rand laughed out loud, something he realized he hadn't done in months. "Do you suggest that no Welsh-woman can be successfully wooed by an Englishman?"

She sent him a cold glare. "I do. If you come here seek-ing women, you are destined to be disappointed. You may find a whore or two. But no respectable woman would be-tray her country with you."

Her haughty tone killed Rand's good humor. He sat up. "I find your attitude curious, considering how swiftly you agreed to work for me."

"That was for coin. Nothing else."

"For coin. That's what whores work for too."

"So they do. The difference is, I am not a whore!" She pushed off the boulder and snatched up her cloak. "Your lesson is over."

Rand caught her by the wrist, and spun her around to face him. His temper had flared at her disdain—until he touched her. Now he stared at her wary face and cursed himself for being a fool.

He needed a woman, yes, but a whore. Not this woman. Not in that way. She was willing to teach him her language, a crucial skill if he were to control these lands without bloodshed. He needed Josselyn ap Carreg Du. No matter her reasons for teaching him, he could not risk frightening her away. And that meant steeling himself against her charms. Her considerable charms.

Beneath his fingers her pulse raced. Her skin was smooth and warm. It would be that way everywhere—

Bloody hell! He could not allow himself to think about that!

" 'Twas not my intent to insult you, Josselyn. You need not run away. I won't hurt you." He released her hand, but kept his eyes locked with hers.

She stepped back a pace, breathing hard, he noticed. Her chest rose and fell against the shawl crisscrossed over her dress and tucked at her waist. Her breasts were not large, but neither were they small—

He grimaced inside. He had to cease looking at her in that way. He had to find another woman to appease his lusty appetites.

"I'm not running away," she snapped. "I have other responsibilities, that's all. You've learned enough for one day." She bit her lower lip a moment then said, "Goodbye."

"Wait." He caught the edge of her cloak. "When will you return?"

She tugged the cloak free. "On the morrow, perhaps. Or the next day."

She turned to leave, but he stopped her with another question. "Can you find me a cook? Someone who can bake good bread? *Da bara?*"

"*Bara da,*" she corrected. She studied him in silence.

"Perhaps there is a woman who might agree. But for baking only," she added. "I will supply you with no whores. Those you will have to procure without my aid."

Rand grinned and nodded. "Agreed. Until tomorrow then. And Josselyn," he added. "You have my thanks."

You have my thanks.

Josselyn stormed all the way home, irritated beyond all reason by that simple statement. *You have my thanks.*

It was not his words that angered her, though, but her reaction to them. She'd smiled at him—not in a calculated effort to lull him into complacency, but in honest response. A stupid, exceedingly foolish response.

She paused now at the river ford and looked back along the woodland track, but she could see no sign of Rosecliffe or the Englishman who would be lord there. What on earth was wrong with her? The whole day she'd been fighting a perverse reaction to him. She was behaving as if she'd never seen a comely man before.

Unfortunately, she never had seen one who attracted her so powerfully as did this one.

Five

Josselyn did not make the trek to Rosecliffe the next day. Her uncle Clyde questioned her about what she'd seen and heard, about the Englishman, Fitz Hugh, and the parchment Sir Lovell carried everywhere. Dewey and the others listened too, but once done, she was dismissed while they debated what action they should take regarding this latest wave of English invaders.

She debated also what she should do, but it was not warfare that consumed her. She had an idea, but wasn't certain how best to achieve her aim, so she went looking for Rhonwen.

She found her in the kitchen. "Is your mother a skilled cook?"

The skinny little girl was playing with a half-grown pup from Uncle Clyde's favorite hunting hound. "I s'pose," she answered slowly. "But I don't want to go back to her. She came yesterday, but I told her to go away." Her pointed chin jutted out defiantly. "I won't go back. You can't make me."

It tore at Josselyn's heart to see the child's animosity toward her only parent. "I will not send you back to her if you do not wish to go."

"Then why should you care if she's a good cook?"

"The English need a cook."

Rhonwen's face screwed up in a frown. "Why d'you want to help those evil English? Let them starve. Maybe then they'll go back to their own country," she finished heatedly.

"It's not them I want to help, Rhonwen. It's your mother. Come here. Let me fix your hair."

Though the child hesitated, she finally crossed over to her, as Josselyn knew she would. Rhonwen was a brave little girl, but also a frightened one. She kept herself a little apart from everyone, but it seemed she liked to have her hair brushed. Now she seated herself before Josselyn and submitted to the long strokes of the horn comb.

"Your mother has lost her way since your father died. She needs a little push, something to do with her life."

"She has us—She *had* us. There was plenty for her to do with me and Cordula and Davit. Only she wouldn't. She wouldn't even take care of her own children."

The quiver in Rhonwen's voice was painful to hear. On impulse Josselyn wrapped her arms about the child and hugged her close. "I know you're angry with her, Rhonwen. I'm angry at her too. But I want to help her to be a good mother again, and—"

"Then send her to those English soldiers!" Rhonwen cried, tearing out of Josselyn's embrace. "Send her to them. Maybe they'll kill her!" She stopped before the low-beamed kitchen doorway. "And if they do, I won't be sad at all. I'll be happy when she's dead. I will!" Then she threw her skinny body against the door, flung it open, and dashed away.

"Rhonwen! Wait!" But it was too late. Josselyn watched from the open doorway as Rhonwen disappeared behind the woodshed, into the forest beyond.

She would be back, Josselyn reassured herself. The child would be back before dark, before the evening meal was over and the food cleared away. Meanwhile, she must approach Gladys and see whether this plan of hers had any merit.

"Cook for the English? Are you mad?" Gladys exclaimed when Josselyn found her. "They killed my Tomas. Mayhap one of this very group did the foul deed. Cook for them? Never! I hate the English," she finished vehemently.

At least the woman was not drunk, Josselyn decided. But that was more likely due to lack of access to strong spirits than to any higher motive. The mean cottage was still a shambles, and the woman positively stank.

Josselyn planted her fists on her hips. "You hate the English? Well, your daughter hates you. What do you plan to do about that?"

It was shocking how swiftly the fire went out of the woman. Her whole body sagged, as if Josselyn had struck her a mortal blow. Rather than feel guilty, though, Josselyn pressed her advantage. " 'Tis well past time for you to rise above your own misery, Gladys. Your children need their mother to look after them."

"But Rhonwen hates me." A tear spilled past the woman's bloodshot eyes. "What good will it do—"

"She says she hates you, but it's only because she needs you and you've failed her. How else is she to react? But you can earn her respect again. Help me fight the English."

"Fight them? But . . ." Gladys wiped her eyes with the back of her wrist. "Do you mean for me to poison them?"

Feeling the first glimmer of hope, Josselyn grinned. "At some point it may well come to that. For now, however, I want to earn their trust. We shall not rout them right away. They are too many. But if they continue to construct this castle and they begin to trust a few of us, the day will come when we can attack them from inside their own defenses. Once we drive them out of their fortress, they will not be able to take it back from us."

Josselyn leaned forward earnestly. "Right now they need a cook, someone who can make better bread than this." She fished in her pocket and tossed a piece of the awful stuff to Gladys.

Gladys caught it and sniffed. " 'Tis rye flour, and stale."

" 'Twas no better on the day it was baked."

"Have they built any ovens?"

"Just one. But they're to begin the kitchen building directly. You know how men are. They'll do anything for the promise of tasty victuals. And they pay in coin."

Gladys peered at her. "How d'you know all this?"

Josselyn straightened. "I'm teaching the English lord to speak our language. He pays me a silver denier every week."

Their eyes met and held. Josselyn could see the thoughts whirling in Gladys's head. "So I would not truly be helping the English. I would be spying on them—and getting paid by them for doing so."

"That's precisely right."

"What if one of them should try to . . . You know . . . Make lewd advances?"

"I've already discussed that with their leader, Fitz Hugh. He promises to keep his men orderly and respectful."

"And you believe him?"

"He has been true to his word so far," Josselyn vowed. But she wondered, was it lewd the way his touch made her heart pound? Ruthlessly she quashed the very idea. "Will you do it?" she asked.

Gladys stared at her a long time. Finally she nodded. "Aye. But will you explain to Rhonwen? I don't want her to hate me."

Josselyn leaned forward and placed a reassuring hand on the other woman's arm. "I shall. It may take some time, Gladys, but the day will come when you are reunited with your children."

Gladys's eyes welled once again with tears, and when she spoke, her voice was thick with emotion. "I've been a poor mother these past months. You were right to take the children away from me. But I want them back. I want them back. If I must fatten every one of those Englishmen to prove my worth, then so be it. When will you be wanting me to begin?"

"We'll go there together, tomorrow," Josselyn answered, relieved beyond measure. "Be ready at dawn, and make yourself presentable. No one wants a cook with filthy hands." Especially Fitz Hugh, whom she'd noticed kept himself cleaner than most men did.

He would be even further in her debt after this, Josselyn gloated on her way back to her aunt and uncle's house. Better yet, however, she would have someone else for support while she was in his camp, someone who was Welsh and a woman. For the sobering truth was, she did not entirely trust Randulf Fitz Hugh.

Nor did she entirely trust herself when she was around him.

The next day threatened rain. But it was not so cold, and Josselyn smelled spring on the air. The English workers were hard at their labor by the time she and Gladys arrived. Josselyn was amazed at the progress they'd already made. The walls for two wooden structures had been raised and a swarm of men now hurried to finish the roofs.

Likewise, the soft spot along the base of the wall that Sir Lovell had spoken of was already dug out. A road from the quarry area to the walls had been cleared with four carts pulled by double teams of oxen hard at work.

"Sweet Jesu, but they waste no time, do they?" Gladys muttered.

"I suspect their master is an ambitious man," Josselyn answered.

"Aye, but we shall trip him up."

"That we will. But do not say such things around here, even to me," Josselyn cautioned. Searching for Fitz Hugh, she scanned the busy site that had so recently been an austere hillside, inhabited only by the thorny roses that gave it its name. To her surprise, she spied him near the *domen*, speaking with Newlin. She had seen Newlin but briefly the day she'd been here, and she'd wondered if he would leave his odd home for a more solitary locale. But here he was, conversing with the enemy as easy as you please.

Feeling an unexpected spurt of jealousy, she hurried toward the incongruous pair.

". . . great beasts once roamed these hills. I've seen their bones—and felt their energy," Newlin was saying when Josselyn and Gladys reached them. "Ah, Josselyn," he said when one of his wandering eyes landed on her. "Do I smell fresh bread?"

Though Josselyn was not surprised by his astuteness, Gladys was. She came to a skidding halt and her startled gaze flitted from the strange-looking bard to the forbidding-looking Englishman. Before she could bolt, however, Josselyn grabbed her by the arm.

"You get ahead of us, Newlin. Sir Randulf, I bring you Gladys. She has agreed to bake and cook for you and your men." She sent him a challenging look. "I told her you would pay her in coins, as you pay me, and also that you would ensure her safety, here and on the path to Carreg Du."

His dark gaze landed only briefly on Josselyn before moving to Gladys. He gave the fidgeting woman a slight smile. "Welcome to Rosecliffe Castle. Whatever you need to make the kitchens functional, you shall have."

Josselyn interpreted his French words for Gladys, and beneath her hand she felt the woman's tension ease a bit. When Gladys whispered to her, she turned back to Fitz Hugh. "She wants to know how your present cook will feel about her presence here."

He grimaced. "We have no real cook. On the journey here the man we hired to cook broke his arm. It became infected and we had to send him back with the ship." He shrugged. "Anything you cook is bound to be better than Odo's efforts. You need not worry that he will resent your presence here. Even he does not like the food he prepares."

Gladys nodded when Josselyn explained his words. But she did not smile, and that made Josselyn a little nervous.

It was important that Gladys conceal her animosity toward these English.

She cleared her throat and addressed Fitz Hugh. "If you like, I'll work with her today, just until she gets her bearings."

"What of my Welsh instruction?"

"We can continue in the afternoon," she suggested. "Where is your kitchen? *Dy cegin?*" she asked.

The kitchen and storeroom were the two buildings being completed. The oven had been constructed first, and though the roof was still open sky, Gladys and Josselyn decided to fire it up. As Fitz Hugh had predicted, Odo was glad to relinquish his duties. When Josselyn asked him to stay and help in the kitchen, however, he agreed.

" 'Druther cart around ale and victuals than mud and rocks," he said with a good-natured bob of his head.

"I will not have an Englishman in my kitchen," Gladys muttered when Josselyn explained Odo's presence.

"You will work with him and be happy to have him," Josselyn hissed right back in Welsh. "If you cannot deceive *him* about your true reason for being here, how can you expect to deceive anyone else?"

Gladys worked her jaw back and forth a moment. "Very well, then. But how'm I to explain to him what he is to do?"

"Learn his language. It will only help our cause. Point, like this. *Blawd,*" she said, looking expectantly at Odo. "*Blawd,*" she repeated, patting a heavy sack.

"What? Oh, I see. Flour. That's flour," he repeated, beaming.

"You see?" Josselyn said to Gladys. "Their word for *blawd* is 'flour.' Learn it and remember."

Gladys's reluctance diminished as they set to their new task. She started Odo chopping vegetables and scaling a basketful of mackerel and whiting, while she and Josselyn began the lengthy process of making bread.

By midday a hearty fish stew simmered in a massive pot

in the brand-new hearth. A dozen fragrant loaves cooled on the kitchen table. Another dozen baked in the oven, and two dozen further sat rising before the hearth.

Josselyn, Gladys, and Odo were sweating profusely, for the day was mild and the kitchen warm. When Odo rang the dinner bell and the workers dropped their tools and hurried toward the kitchen, the two women shared a look of pride. One meal for nearly a hundred men was perhaps not so great a feat. Three meals a day for that many, day after day—now that would be an accomplishment. But Gladys was up to it; Josselyn was certain of it.

"My compliments to the cook," Sir Lovell said, smiling and bowing to the older woman. There was no reason to translate that, Josselyn saw when Gladys smiled. Then realizing she had smiled at an Englishman, Gladys ducked her head and turned away.

"You've done me a great service, bringing her here," a familiar voice said in Josselyn's ear.

"She needs the coin," Josselyn replied offhandedly. She sidled away from him, disconcerted by his nearness and the husky quality of his voice.

"As, I gather, do you. Today I would learn the trees and creatures of the forest."

"Very well." She removed the length of toweling she'd tied about her waist and set it aside. "I shall leave you and Odo to manage the rest," she told Gladys in Welsh. "Don't leave for the village until I return."

Gladys gave her a long, steady look. "Be wary of him," she replied, indicating Randulf Fitz Hugh. "He wants more from you than merely to learn our language."

It was Josselyn's turn to duck her head and turn away. He might want more, but he would not get it. Still, to have someone else express her fears out loud made his threat so much more potent. Though she was still warm from her work, she snatched up her cloak and flung it around her shoulders.

"*Derwen*," she said, pointing out the solitary oak that

stood just beyond the stout wall the English were building. *"Hebog,"* she said, gesturing at a falcon that was startled away from the tree when they drew too near.

"Slow down," Fitz Hugh ordered when she would have continued down the hill. "There's no need to hurry. You've worked hard; you deserve a rest. Besides," he added, patting his stomach. "I devoured more of your delicious stew than I should have. Come, stroll with me a while, Josselyn."

Stroll with me a while.

Like the signal bells in the village, alarm sounded an immediate warning in Josselyn's head. Stroll with me. Lovers strolled, not enemies.

"I do not stroll. *Mynd araf fi nag,*" she translated for him. She hesitated only a moment before continuing. "I will not pretend a friendliness I do not feel, Fitz Hugh. It would be best if we both understand that."

He studied her, his hands on his hips. "You make too much of my suggestion, Josselyn. Perhaps you do not completely understand the meaning of the word 'stroll.' It means 'to walk slowly.' "

"I know what it means."

"Then walk more slowly."

Josselyn stared uneasily at him. Then she started forward again, albeit at an easier pace. But her heart pounded even more rapidly than before.

"Why don't you point out what you wish to learn," she suggested as they angled toward the strip of wildwood that sheltered the river from view.

"What I wish to learn," he echoed. She felt his gaze upon her, but she kept her eyes fixed on the path before them.

"What I want to learn," he repeated as she braced herself to repel an untoward solicitation from him. "Is how I can best maintain peace with my Welsh neighbors."

She hadn't expected that, and for a moment Josselyn's

mind was blank. Maintain peace? "Go back whence you came," she blurted out.

He gave a humorless chuckle. "I hope that is not your only suggestion."

"If you seek to gain my support, you waste both your time and mine. I will teach you to speak *Cymraeg,* but I will not abandon my people."

"I do not ask that you abandon your people. I wish only to live here in peace with the Welsh. Is that so difficult a thing?"

"The Welsh and English have never managed well together."

"You and I manage well together."

"Only because you are a man and I a woman . . ." She trailed off, unsettled by the vast implications of those few words. She'd meant to imply that two men would not get along so easily.

"Yes," he said, coming to a halt. "I *am* a man and you *are* a woman."

In the dappled shade of the bare sycamore trees they faced one another. The forest was still, not yet alive with the noisy exuberance of spring. But Josselyn was deafened by the blood roaring in her ears. This was not supposed to happen! She was not supposed to react to him this way.

"I . . . I . . ." She closed her mouth with a snap and tried to compose her thoughts. But it was hard with his eyes moving over her like a caress, gathering her up as if she were his to possess. "I am a translator, your teacher. That is why we get along. Were I a man, a soldier of *Cymru,* we would not be so peaceable."

"Mayhap I should press my suit with the women of Carreg Du."

"All of them?" she sputtered, aghast with the quick image of him passing that heated glance over every woman of her village, plying every woman she knew with his husky voice and seductive words.

"My men will need wives," he answered. "They will

want families. In that regard we English are no different from you Welsh.''

Wives. Families. Josselyn realized abruptly how foolish her thoughts had been. He meant women for all his men, not just him. ''You would have your men seek Welsh wives?''

''I would. How would their Welsh fathers respond to that?''

Josselyn shook her head. Was he serious? '' 'Tis not so much the fathers as the women you must convince. We Welsh do not force our women to marry against their wishes.''

''I've heard as much. But surely there are those fathers who pressure their daughters to marry as *they* wish, to make the alliances *they* desire.''

Josselyn thought of the pressures on her to wed Owain ap Madoc and it brought her up abruptly. This was not a subject she wished to discuss with an Englishman. Especially not this Englishman.

She turned onto the path once more, acutely aware that he trailed her closely. ''Welshwomen are every bit as loyal as Welshmen. They will not take up with your English workers.''

''But they will take my English coins. As Gladys does. As you do.''

They had reached the river's edge. Josselyn turned to face him, composed now, staunch in her ability to resist him. ''We will take your coin,'' she admitted. ''But that is all. You will not live out your life among us, Englishman. You delude yourself and your people if you think you will.''

She expected her words to rouse his anger, but to her surprise he gave a tolerant half-smile. ''I have no intentions of living out my life here, my hot-blooded Welsh maiden. *Llances Cymry,*'' he echoed in Welsh. ''But before I leave here there will be a towering fortress, a thriving town, and nurseries full of babes born of Welsh women to English men.''

She scowled at him. "English bastards, more than like."

He shook his head at her angry reply. "The next ship brings a priest. I would see my men wed. I would see them anchored to this place. To this soil."

Josselyn turned away from him, for something akin to panic had seeped beneath her skin. Anchored to this place ... this soil. This man would not go easily, she realized. He did not care if she or any other Welsh workers knew what he meant to build here. He did not fear their knowledge of his plans. If anything, he wanted them to know. He wanted them to understand that he and his people meant to stay. He offered them peace, but the massive fortress he planned threatened war if they opposed him.

The choice was theirs to make—or rather, hers. If she wed Owain, they might be able to drive him out. If she did not wed Owain . . . What would happen then?

She needed to think, to talk to her uncle, or better still, to Newlin.

That thought had not yet left her head when a shout and a splash startled her. "Wily wretch!" A squat figure trundled through the shallows of the river. Newlin, she realized, both amazed and relieved. Newlin, with his fishing pole and his hook. Blessed be, but he was the answer to her prayers.

Rand did not share Josselyn's feelings about the bard's untimely interruption. By rights he should have been relieved to have someone break the thread of tension building between him and the skittish Josselyn. He should not risk losing an interpreter of her skills simply because he desired her in his bed. He should control himself.

He should seek out some other woman.

But he did not want to control himself or find another woman. When she'd thrown in his face the fact that she was a woman and he a man, he'd come perilously close to showing her how right she was.

Would she have responded to his rough caress? Would she have arched into his embrace? Would she have lain back and wrapped her long legs around his hips—

He broke off with a muttered curse and beat down an unseemly arousal. It didn't matter how she would have responded. The moment had passed and now Newlin was here.

"Have you had much success?" Josselyn asked the bard. It was obvious to Rand that she was much relieved by the other man's presence.

"We play a game, he and I." One of the bard's eyes wandered to Rand. "Today he has won."

Was the man speaking of a fish, or did he refer to him? Rand wondered. "There is stew left. Fish stew," he added. "If you go down to the kitchen, Gladys will serve you a portion."

Newlin nodded his thanks. "I will try my watery friend once more, then perhaps I will be forced to concede his triumph. But I will try. So," he added. "Are the victuals Gladys prepares to your liking?"

Rand nodded. "They are. And I have Josselyn to thank for that. My men will be more content with their appetites satisfied."

The bard gave a vague smile. "A man's appetite can be a worrisome creature, if he cannot control it."

Now what was Rand to make of that? Were Josselyn and Gladys planning to poison him? Or did the bard refer to Rand's lust for Josselyn—or to his lust for land and the power it would bring him?

"Do you speak in parables?" he asked, deciding to be blunt. "Is this a warning you give me?"

Josselyn moved nearer the bard, a protective gesture Rand did not miss. Newlin looked up at her. "Your skirt will get wet." Then he replied to Rand. "I am not one given to warnings. What happens to you, to me—to anyone—is neither right nor wrong. There is no need for warnings. We each of us make our decisions—or react on impulse or instinct—and our future is altered. Who is to say whether that future will be better or worse than another future? Certainly not I.''

He paused and began to rock forward and back. ''Then again, I do advocate caution. I believe thoughtful contemplation and wise decision-making can ease each of us into our particular future. 'Tis impulse—and malice—that heap misery upon us all.''

There was more to the bard's enigmatic words than that, Rand suspected. But the bard had no intention of revealing it. The infuriating thing was that Rand did not believe in superstition, nor did he place any faith in the warnings of seers, mystics, or bards such as Newlin was said to be. Yet there was something about the man . . .

He switched his gaze to Josselyn. She was staring at Newlin, a small frown between her eyes, as if she too sought to decipher the man's strange words. It was plain she held him in high esteem.

What part the bard would play in the struggles to come, Rand was not certain. Her role was even less so. That she opposed his presence here was plain. Whether that would change he did not know. The only thing certain was that he would not be able to control himself around her for long. The day would come when he would possess her—or send her fleeing from his efforts to do so.

For now, however, he would bide his time, learn to speak her language, and raise the walls of his castle as swiftly as he could.

Six

During the week that followed, the English ate very well. Roasted boar. Venison stew. Grilled fish. And loaves and loaves of delicious fresh bread. Two other women joined Gladys at her labors, and Josselyn took great satisfaction in watching Gladys direct them. So far as she could tell, the woman had not succumbed to the lure of strong spirits.

But as the meals improved, so did the men's work. The kitchen and storehouse roofs went up in a single day. One of the wells began to yield clear water, and the inner wall of the castle began to rise.

It was that last event which most incited the people of Carreg Du. Although the English kept strictly to themselves, only hunting in the forest, and fishing where the river met with the sea, they were a presence the Welsh could not ignore. Every Welsh blade, from dagger to long sword, was honed to a vicious edge that week. Every leather hauberk was patched, every helm polished, and ready stores of dried provisions were packed. The call to arms could come anytime, and no one wanted to be unprepared.

That the week dragged by without incident was testament to her uncle's caution—and his commitment to his niece.

On the Sabbath as they left for the gathering at the shrine to Saint Aiden, Josselyn walked at his side.

"Here is the coin I was paid." She handed him the small silver piece with its profile of the British king and his long, pointed nose.

He glanced down at it, then straight ahead. "What am I to do with it?"

"Use it for whatever you deem best. Something that will help us all."

He didn't reply for so long it was all Josselyn could do not to pinch him. "Better you save it to bring to your husband."

So. There it was. Josselyn knew the decision she must make. And she knew now how her uncle wanted her to decide.

"What would happen if I did not agree to marry?"

"We do not have enough men to defeat these English."

"Perhaps we should remind Owain and his father that they will not like having the English as their neighbors. To help us now is to help themselves."

Clyde stopped and drew her aside, gesturing for Ness and the others to continue on. Only when they were alone did he address Josselyn again.

"Owain wants you to wife. He wants *you*. I believe that in the end the Lloyds will help us, with or without the marriage. Madoc will see to it, albeit grudgingly. But Owain will watch and he will wait. And he will remember that his offer was rebuffed. Though Madoc has many years left, the day will come when his son will wrest power from him. Then, when the time is right, Owain will strike at our backs. If he cannot have our lands legally, he will take them in another manner." His eyes burned into hers. "The results will be bitter. Many will be killed, like Tomas. And many more will suffer."

Josselyn looked away, unable to face the truth of his terrible words. Whether she wed Owain or not, Carreg Du would succumb to his greedy ambitions. But one way many would suffer. The other way only she would.

She sucked in a breath and battled the sting of tears.
"How soon must I decide?" She looked back at him,
though she knew fear showed in her eyes. "How long?"

Her uncle sighed. " 'Tis hard to say. So long as I live
you have time. But if the English should force a conflict . . ." He shrugged. "And then, there is the chance that
Owain could wed another."

That was the remark that stayed with her throughout the
Sabbath services. Owain could wed another, and much as
she wished he would, Josselyn knew that would seal her
people's fate. Owain was a bully and he would be quick to
overrun Carreg Du if he thought no one was strong enough
to stop him. For now his father kept him in line, but Madoc
would not be able to do so forever. As for her Uncle Clyde,
he had never been a man of war. That was why they had
not responded to the English threat more aggressively. How
much slower would he be to respond to a Welsh threat?

Josselyn prayed with a devoutness she had not felt in
months. She prayed for her uncle's continued good health,
for Owain's patience, and for an idea—any idea of what
she could do.

The only idea that came to her, however, was to seek
out Newlin, and after the service ended, she did just that.

But she did not find him. He was not at the river fishing.
He was not at the *domen*. She did not want to approach the
English encampment, especially since she suspected Rhonwen trailed somewhere behind her. But near the edge of
the forest Sir Lovell spied her and, much to her dismay,
called out for her to wait.

His cheeks were ruddy as he hurried up to her, for the
day was the warmest they'd yet had. "What brings you
here on the Sabbath, Josselyn?"

"I look for Newlin. Have you seen him?"

"He and Rand sat up conversing late into the night. But
I have not seen him today." He paused, then went on. "I

am glad I spied you, for I would speak to you on a matter of some . . . some importance to me.''

"What matter is that?" Josselyn asked, her curiosity piqued. She saw the master builder daily but he seldom singled her out, save to greet her in the same courteous manner he used with all the Welsh women. As she studied him, his face grew redder still.

" 'Tis . . .'Tis the matter of . . . Gladys.''

Gladys? It took a few seconds before Josselyn divined the true import of what he'd just revealed. Gladys! A stroke of lightning could not have startled her half so much. Sir Lovell was interested in Gladys—Gladys, the widow of Tomas.

She turned away and fiddled with her skirt while she tried to compose herself. But it was hard. Fitz Hugh had hoped for this. He'd planned for it. English men and Welsh women. And she'd inadvertently helped him.

But she must not let it go any further. It would undermine her plans if romance bloomed between these two. She had to stop it before it began.

She cleared her throat. "Gladys has had a difficult enough time since her husband's death without you making things worse for her.''

He stepped back, a stricken look on his guileless face. "But I want only to help her, not to make her life harder still. My wife is gone, as is her husband. Besides, she has children she should be tending to, not our kitchens.''

"Her children are well tended, now. Gladys took her husband's death hard,'' Josselyn said, forcing herself to be cruel. "In the aftermath she was a poor parent, and her children were taken from her. She wants them back and every day she comes nearer that goal. How do you think her people would feel if she took up with an Englishman? How quickly do you think they would return her children to her? And even if they did, her eldest child would never forgive her. Look behind me, Sir Lovell. Search the forests for a little girl. She is Gladys's eldest and she hates that her mother works here. She worries, and can you blame her? 'Tis said her father—Gladys's husband—was killed by the English.'' *Though it is more likely Owain did it.*

But Josselyn could not concern herself so strictly with the truth, not when Sir Lovell desired Gladys—not when Randulf Fitz Hugh's plan was working, and after only two weeks' time! She pressed on before he could reply. ''If you care for Gladys, you will let her be. You will not force her to choose between you and her own people. Between you and her children.''

He nodded and backed away, mumbling. But his shoulders sagged and his head was bowed. As he departed, Josselyn beat back an awful wave of guilt. He cared for Gladys; that was clear. But did he care enough to do what was right for her, or would he be selfish and think only of himself?

She watched him angle across the long slope of the hill, a lonely figure heading back to Rosecliffe. She turned in the opposite direction. She'd done the right thing. It seemed cruel, but in truth, it was a kindness. There was no hope for a match between those two. Perhaps if Gladys did not already have children. Perhaps a Welshwoman with no family of her own might find contentment with an Englishman. But even then there were too many years of animosity between their people.

Like the enduring animosity between Owain's family and her own, a niggling voice whispered from the depths of her mind. The fact was, waging peace through intermarriage was a common practice in Wales, as in all of Britain. Randulf Fitz Hugh sought to do no more than her own uncle did.

''Taran,'' she swore. She turned her back on Sir Lovell's distant figure and headed north, toward the bay and the sea beyond it. If only her father were here. She would not be so beset by troubles if Howell ap Carreg Du were still alive. He would chase the English away and cow Owain and his

thugs as well. And he would help her find a good, strong man to wed.

"Your father loved this spot."

Josselyn jumped in alarm. "Newlin!" She pressed a hand to her racing heart. "You startled me. How did you know I was thinking of my father?"

The bard smiled. "He often brought you here. Do you not remember?"

Josselyn stared around her. "I remember sitting in a tree with him. That tree." She pointed at a gnarled oak that looked older than time itself. "I remember him climbing to the top while I clung to his back. He called me his little squirrel."

" 'Tis the tallest tree in these forests. From its topmost branches you can see the horizon."

"The horizon is always visible," she reminded him. "From wherever a body stands, she may see some sort of horizon. You taught me that."

His warped face turned up in a grin. "So it is. But is it the horizon she wishes to see?"

That sobered her. What horizon did she wish to see now? What future did she want? Despair settled heavily upon her. "I don't know what to do," she confessed. "I am sore beset and caught between two enemies, the English and Owain ap Madoc."

He nodded, then turned and continued walking in the direction she'd been heading. "You have considered all your choices." He did not term it as a question.

"I have. If I marry Owain I encourage a battle with the English. If I do not marry him I put off that battle, but I cannot avoid it forever. Why must we ever be forced to fight for our own lands?"

"There is another choice," Newlin replied, ignoring her frustrated words.

"Another choice? Yes, to battle the English alone, without the aid of any allies, or with reluctant ones," she added, recalling her uncle's words. "That choice is not much better, for Owain will ultimately exact his revenge on us.''

The bard stared steadily at her. ''You could join forces with the English.''

That was such a ludicrous idea, such a thoroughly ridiculous thought, that Josselyn laughed out loud. ''Join forces with the English? Surrender to them, you mean. Give up our lands, our independence. Our way of life. No, that will never happen.''

''You are thinking like a man. Think like a woman, Josselyn.''

''What is that supposed to mean?''

Newlin gave his one-shouldered shrug. ''Sir Lovell admires our Gladys.''

''Oh, no. Not you too!'' she cried. ''You want Welshwomen to marry these Englishmen? Where is your loyalty? Gladys deserves better than an Englishman. She deserves a good Welshman to serve as father to her Welsh children. To give her more Welsh babies.''

''Gladys's future is for Gladys to live. Her horizons are for her to seek.''

Josselyn had never felt more confused. ''Are you telling me she should marry Sir Lovell? That cannot help but lead to disaster.''

They had reached the place where the hill fell away to the sea, where the forest gave way to gorse and heather. She could see the bay, enclosed by the two arms of land, and beyond, the gray churning sea. Somewhere to her right was the black stone outcropping with its tangle of wild roses, where the English raised the walls of their fortress. She sucked in great drafts of cold sea air and tried to think clearly.

''Even if I leave Gladys to her own devices, there is still the matter of what I should do—and don't say that I should marry an Englishman. Help me, Newlin.'' She raised her arms then let them fall to her sides in a helpless gesture. ''Help me, for I am much confused.''

She thought he would not answer, he stared into the distance so long. He began the subtle rocking typical to him, then stopped and turned his odd gaze upon her. "Yon English lord asks many questions."

The English lord? Josselyn didn't want to talk about Randulf Fitz Hugh. She wanted to forget he existed at all. Only she couldn't. Indeed, he was the source of her current misery. If he hadn't come to Carreg Du she would not be in this dilemma. She sighed. "What sort of questions is he asking?"

"Questions about the niece of Clyde ap Llewelyn."

Josselyn gasped and every one of her emotions focused on that remark. Alarm. Outrage. Panic. Then a perverse sort of thrill. He was asking about her. Then panic returned. There was only one reason he would care about Clyde's niece: because she was the lone heir to these lands he wished to claim. "Does he know that *I* am that niece?"

"It would seem he does not," Newlin answered. "But eventually he must find out. As he learns our language he has but to ask any of the women who work for him." Left unsaid were two facts: she was the one teaching him their language; and she was the one who'd brought other women to work in his camp.

As if one of the black clouds out of the west had settled over her, the weight of Josselyn's responsibilities pressed even more heavily upon her. "If he finds out, he will want to prevent any marriage I might make which could be detrimental to his interests."

"That is likely."

"Then I must . . . I must cease my role as his teacher. And stay well away from his encampment."

"Your uncle will want you to make your decision about Owain."

Josselyn looked away. "Yes. I know."

They sat in silence a long while. The wind blew in cold, erratic bursts, chilling her to the bone. Depressing her further still. Despite the cold, spring had arrived. The seasons changed, often with much struggle between them. So were the seasons of her life changing. She'd remained a child, an innocent, for far longer than most. But now she must make the painful transition to womanhood.

She must do what she knew was right.

"I shall leave you now," Newlin said. In a moment he was gone and she was alone—and colder even than before. She sat down, huddled, actually, with her arms wrapped around her legs and her chin resting on her knees. She stared out at the sea and thought about Owain.

Perhaps time had softened him. Perhaps, despite the bad temper of his youth, he had matured into a better sort of man.

But then, there was still Tomas's death to explain. While no one could prove Owain had been involved, she'd heard Dewey's suspicions and seen her uncle's grim expression. How could she possibly marry a man she suspected to be a murderer?

"Josselyn?"

For the second time that afternoon Josselyn jumped in alarm. But this time it truly was cause for alarm, for this time it was not Newlin. The voice was too low. The shadow that fell across her was too long. Fearful—aware—she lifted her head to find Randulf Fitz Hugh standing but three paces to her right. How had he come so near without her hearing him?

"Is aught amiss with you?" he asked, while his eyes devoured her. She shivered with sudden awareness. She'd glimpsed that look in his eyes before, the hungry look of a man wanting a woman. Those other times, however, he'd quickly quashed it, and they'd gone on to speak of nouns and verbs, of adjectives and sentence structure. *Cymraeg* was a complex language and, to his credit, he seemed intent on mastering it. Whatever desires he might have for a woman—for her—he'd kept reasonably well hidden.

But he wasn't hiding it now.

She stood, her knees shaking, her heart racing. "I am fine. I thought I was alone."

"As did I," he answered, stepping closer.

Josselyn moved back a pace, then two. Tension fairly crackled in the air between them, and she knew she must get away before it erupted. The worst part of it, however, was that the tension was not solely of his making. That was what terrified her most.

For his part, Rand felt anything but terrified. And though he recognized the fear in Josselyn's eyes, he saw also her awareness of him. Had it been only fear she felt, he could have controlled the lust that surged within him. But that awareness, that spark that stretched to the breaking point between them, was too compelling. Too powerful. So he stepped forward, caught her by the arms, and held her still before him. He would not let her flee, not until they explored the source of this awareness they shared.

"What—What do you think you're doing?"

She tried to shrug out of his grasp but he wouldn't let her. Beneath his hands her arms were slender and strong. And warm. His gloves and her wool garments could not disguise that fact.

"I wish to learn a new facet of your language, Josselyn. Teach me the words a man says to a woman." He pulled her a little nearer. "How does a man say 'your eyes are bluer than the sky'?"

She stared up at him with those huge blue eyes, stared up at him as if he were a madman. And indeed, he was behaving like one. Where did those words come from? He sounded like a lovesick lad, gushing poetic nonsense when all he really wanted was a quick tumble with a pretty wench. He must still be in the grip of the prodigious quantity of wine he'd consumed last night.

But her eyes *were* bluer than the sky. And her hair . . . "Your hair smells of sunshine. Sunshine and snow."

He bent his head and nuzzled her thick, raven-wing locks. "Teach me those words, Josselyn. How do I say 'I want you'?"

He heard her soft gasp. He felt the quiver that vibrated

up through her body and sent a responding quiver through his. He knew she considered him her enemy. He knew she had her own secret reasons for working for him. But she wanted him nevertheless. He had not been wrong in that.

He pulled her up against him so that her thighs bumped against his, her breasts flattened against his chest, and her belly pressed warm and womanly against his arousal.

He groaned against her fragrant hair. "I want you, Josselyn. How do I say the words so you will understand how much? I want to make you mine. Here. Now."

Seven

She didn't know the words. That's what Josselyn tried to tell herself.

I want you.

She'd never said those words to anyone—at least not with the particular meaning he implied. And no one had said them to her. Most certainly not in Norman French.

But Randulf Fitz Hugh was saying them to her now, and like a green girl, she was succumbing to the seductive lure of them. The seductive lure of *him*.

Then again, she *was* a green girl, a voice in her head reminded her. If she was succumbing to him, it was because she had no experience with men.

Perhaps it was time she gained some.

"Admit that you want me too." His words were a slow, hot whisper in her ear, a thrilling caress against her neck.

Josselyn let out a little moan in spite of herself. *"Fi dymuno ti,"* she said, in Welsh.

"Fi dymuno ti." His arms circled her, fitting her even more intimately against him, and to her shame, she did not protest.

This was so wrong, and yet she could not stop herself. She was curious. The fact that he was her enemy did not matter. Soon enough she would be wed to Owain and forced to suffer his repulsive touch. Was she not entitled to at least one encounter of her own choosing before she submitted to a man she despised? Could she not just one time embrace a man she also desired?

But she should not desire him. He was English, and an enemy of the Welsh people. Added to that, there was no affection between them. How could she be so drawn to him? How could she desire him?

But she did desire him. So she arched into his embrace and wound her arms about his neck. And when his mouth sought hers, she rose to his kiss and surrendered herself to the fearful thrill he roused in her.

It was not what she expected, but then, she did not truly know what to expect. He was big and broad and hard with muscle. But his lips, though demanding, were warm. He was forceful and possessive, the most dangerous man she knew. And yet it was that very danger that drew her. He was forbidden to her and yet she wanted him. And he wanted her.

His mouth moved over hers and compelled her to respond. His tongue traced the curve of her lips, the seams where they joined, and she let out a hungry little sigh. Then one of his hands cupped her face and he somehow teased her lips apart. Without warning, his tongue slid inside her mouth and at once everything spun out of control. Every least portion of her body came alive in a way she'd never before experienced. Her blood ran faster, her skin burned hotter. With every stroke of his tongue, something leapt to life in her belly, something terrifying and intriguing and completely illogical. He was devouring her and, heaven help her, she wanted to be devoured.

There was little she was conscious of, save the erotic play of his mouth upon hers. But she felt his one hand tangle in her hair, freeing it of its Sabbath coiffure and releasing it to the caprice of the winds off the sea. She felt the movement of his other hand down past her waist, to curve over her derriere and press her almost violently against his thickened maleness.

She knew about arousals, about how mating occurred between animals and how it must occur between men and women as well. But the hard length of it burning against her belly was nevertheless a shock. For a moment she faltered and turned her face away from his.

"Ah, Josselyn. You are sweet. Sweeter even than I had guessed." He tilted her head back so that their eyes met. "*Fi dymuno ti.* I must have you."

She was drowning. This was how it must feel to sink down, to know you were going under. To not be able to help yourself. His eyes were so dark—the color of the night sky, nearly black and yet with enough light in them to make them gray. The jagged scar on his cheek fascinated her. The arrogant slant of his brows, the proud line of his nose . . . The husky demand in his voice when he said he wanted her.

A sensible woman would stop. A wise woman would take this new wealth of emotions and consider them a while; she would try to understand them and comprehend why this particular man roused them in her. But at the moment she was unable to be sensible, and she'd never been terribly wise.

"You taste like honey, sweet and warm," he murmured. He caught her lower lip between his teeth and gave a gentle tug. When Josselyn opened for his kiss, however, he slid his mouth instead along her cheekbone, trailing kisses up to her ear, then down the side of her neck.

She'd never known how sensitive she was there, she realized as she gave herself up to the exquisite pleasure of that simple little caress. She swallowed and he immediately moved the kiss to the hollow of her throat. She swallowed again and felt as if he drew some portion of her up into himself when she did. It was astounding. He but touched the surface of her skin, and yet it connected to something so much deeper. She felt as if she were just now discovering the most basic knowledge about herself.

"Wait," she breathed when he tilted her back in his

arms. Her whole world was off balance, tilted away, spinning out of control. She knew he would not actually let her fall, but she feared at the same time that she would never quite regain her balance again.

"I don't think I can wait."

"But . . . But you must." A small bit of reason returned. She was in the arms of her enemy, behaving in a way she'd done with no man before. Like a wanton. Like a harlot. "No, I cannot—"

He silenced her protests with a kiss, and though she struggled, she was crushed by the wave of desire he summoned. One of his legs insinuated between her knees and she felt the new sensation of his leg abrading her thighs and pressing erotically against the secret place between her legs.

Meanwhile his kisses grew bolder and his tongue delved deeper until she responded with an equal boldness. She kissed him back, discovering the pleasures of possessing a man's mouth—this man's mouth. She withdrew her tongue, then he thrust his in. Like a duel. Like a dance. They teased and roused one another until Josselyn was on fire with a desire for more.

Even so, she was not prepared for the touch of his hand to her breast.

"Oh!" She squirmed against him, trying to pull away and yet not pull away.

"Do you like that?" He whispered the hot words in her ear as he thumbed across the peak of her incredibly aroused nipple.

"I . . . I don't know," she gasped.

He laughed at her candor. "Has no other man taken the time to rouse you there?"

She shook her head. "No. No man has ever touched me there."

He started to laugh again, then stopped. His hand stilled as well. When she looked up at him his brows had lowered in a faint frown. "Do not say that you are a virgin."

His words were like cold water, cooling the quick flare of her desire, chilling her with a sudden dose of reality. What was she doing with him?

"Let me go."

"Answer me first. Are you a virgin, Josselyn, untried by any other man?"

She glared at him. Her foolish passion turned blessedly to fury. "Of course I am. I am not yet wed. Do you think all Welshwomen whores?" She tried to twist away, but his hands were like steel, holding her in place.

"In England a man keeps a close eye on his virgin daughter. He does not allow her to wander the fields and forests, alone and unprotected."

"Unfortunately, my father is ten years dead," she cried. "And at the hand of an Englishman like you. But even were he alive, I would have the freedom of these hills. Until you English came, a Welshwoman had nothing to fear on her own lands. Now let me go!"

"Why? Because you fear me?"

Fear him? She'd be a fool not to fear a man who, beyond being her enemy, could also render her a mindless fool with merely the strength of one kiss. She stared up at him, unnerved, but determined not to reveal it to him.

"I have not thought you a man to force an unwilling woman."

He considered her words. "I am glad for your high regard. You are right, I take no pleasure in rape. But you, sweetling, are hardly unwilling."

"Perhaps . . . perhaps before I was not. But now I am. Let me go!" she demanded once more.

"And if I do not?"

He pulled her a little nearer and she had to beat back a wave of panic. "If you force me I will fight you. And I will hate you."

"You already hate me," he reminded her.

"But I will hate you more. Much more." She broke off, for she knew her threat sounded worse than ridiculous. He did not care how she felt about him. To her surprise, however, he released her and took a step backward.

"I would not have you hate me, Josselyn. Anything but that."

Josselyn stumbled back a pace also, confused. Relieved. Uncertain now how to behave. "What happened just now . . . It was a mistake," she finally said.

"And you are sorry it happened?" When she did not immediately respond, he laughed. "If there was any mistake, it was only that I assumed you were more experienced than you are."

Josselyn stared at him across the space of the little glen. Did that mean he would not have taken such liberties with her had he known her an innocent? Did it mean he could no longer desire her because she had not the experience to adequately sate his hunger? A profound disappointment settled over her. No, a *perverse* disappointment. Why should she care *what* he thought or *why* he'd stopped?

"I must return home," she muttered, needing to be alone, to think on what had just happened.

"Wait. You said your father was killed. What of the rest of your family?"

A prickle of unease crept over Josselyn. She had already revealed too much. He did not need to learn anything further about her, most especially that she was the niece of Clyde ap Llewelyn.

"I live with my mother—and my brothers and sisters," she lied.

"The little girl Harold caught. Is she your sister?"

"Yes. Now I must go."

"Will you come on the morrow to continue my lessons?"

His gaze was dark and warm upon hers and she understood at once that her innocence was not a complete impediment for him. The tiny thrill that knowledge gave her confused her further still. "I cannot say," she answered.

"I cannot say." Then she turned and fled, never looking back.

She felt his gaze follow her though. Even when she was far from his view, she still felt the imprint of his gaze.

How could she ever have let matters get so out of hand? she chastised herself as she hurried home. Now she could never return to the English encampment. Most certainly she could not continue to teach Randulf Fitz Hugh her language. She must stay strictly out of his path.

For if she did not stay out of his path, she feared she might fall straightaway into his bed.

Rand was amused—and frustrated. What a sweet armful of a wench. To find her to be a virgin had been a sore disappointment—at first. The more he thought on it, however, the better pleased he became. Josselyn was a virgin. He would be the first man to taste of her sweetness.

The very thought sent blood surging to his loins.

"Bloody hell," he swore.

Osborn looked up from the sword he honed to a razor's sharpness. "What ails you?" Then he laughed. " 'Tis the wench, is it not? We've all of us been restless in our sleep of late. But at least we do not spend the day in the company of so fair a lass as that Josselyn." He chuckled at Rand's silence. "Have you offered her coin?"

"She's not a whore."

"She consorts with the enemy for coin."

" 'Tis a different thing entirely. She's teaching me Welsh," Rand grunted.

"And patience as well, it would seem. But have you never wondered why she's teaching you her tongue?"

Rand shot him a warning look. "No doubt she hopes to spy on us, to tell Clyde ap Llewelyn what we plan."

Osborn snorted. "If that's so, then these Welsh are a branch of coward I've never seen before. Sending their women to spy on their enemies. Who is she that they would value her so poorly—or else trust her so well?"

Who indeed? Rand had no answer for his captain's troubling question, and it preyed on his mind the remainder of the cheerless day. When Josselyn did not appear in camp the next morn it disturbed him even more. Gladys came, as did the two other women who now worked in the kitchen with her. But Josselyn stayed away.

It was just as well, he told himself. He would not question Gladys about her, for Gladys would carry those questions back to Josselyn and she would be even further alarmed. But he meant to learn more of this Josselyn ap Carreg Du. What they'd begun in the quiet wildwood would not be ended so easily as this. Not so easily at all.

Josselyn folded her best wool gown, a finely woven shawl, and an extra kirtle, and rolled them together into a neat bundle. As she rolled, she tucked her comb, stockings, indoor slippers, and a length of embroidered cloth between the garments.

The cloth, elaborately worked with hawks and foxes, squirrels and otter, was a gift for her bridegroom. It was the first project she'd undertaken in anticipation of her eventual marriage, begun when she'd first become a woman—when she'd first experienced her monthly courses. There had been many other such projects. They were supposed to demonstrate to a future husband that she would make a superior wife.

To her mind now, however, the more important question was, what sort of husband would Owain ap Madoc make?

She would know soon, for once the rain relented, she and her uncle, accompanied by a select band of men, would set off for the Lloyd stronghold.

She had thought long and hard about what she should do ever since she'd fled from the Englishman and his unnerving embrace. Before now, her dread of Owain had kept her from making the decision. Perversely, it was her attraction to Randulf Fitz Hugh that now compelled her to agree to her uncle's plea. She could not stay near the Englishman. She must wed and take herself off to her husband's home. Only then would her family's lands be safe from the threat of the English.

Only then would she be safe from the threat of that one particular Englishman.

"Now you mean only to sign the contract. Isn't that so?" Aunt Nessie asked her husband for the third time. "You will not wed my niece away from Carreg Du without my presence at her side." She wrung her hands together and her anxious eyes darted from her husband to Josselyn, then back to Clyde. "She will want another woman with her when she finally weds."

"I will refuse to marry anyone unless you are there," Josselyn vowed, sending her aunt a reassuring smile. Inside, however, Josselyn was anything but reassured. She stared around the low-ceilinged hall she'd lived in all her life. What would it be like to be away from this place, from her family and all the people who cared for her?

As always, her uncle's home teemed with people. Two boys worked the spit, turning a boar for the evening meal. One maid scrubbed the walls while two others stitched by torchlight. Gladys sat near the fire, telling Davit and Cordula a story. Everyone was busy except Rhonwen.

The young girl sat apart from the others. She had not forgiven her mother and did not trust her yet. And though she said she understood why Josselyn must marry one of the Lloyds, it was clear the child felt betrayed. She'd withdrawn from everyone and sat aloof in a corner, staring sullenly at Josselyn when she thought Josselyn did not see, and feigning interest elsewhere whenever Josselyn glanced in her direction.

A world of misery awaited poor Rhonwen, Josselyn fretted. And probably herself as well. But what choices did either of them have?

Josselyn sighed and stared blindly at the neatly rolled bundle of her possessions. With another sigh she tied her apron around it. There was no reason to delay. The rain had reduced to a drizzle. Dewey brought the horses and, under a heavily laden sky, the small party finally set off.

"We'll be home before Saint Rupert's feast day," Clyde told Nesta. "Keep a sharp watch posted," he instructed Dewey. "I do not trust these English should they discover what we are about."

Nor did Josselyn, though she kept silent. She'd not told him of her encounter with Randulf Fitz Hugh. It was too humilating. If he wondered at her abrupt change of heart about Owain, he did not mention it.

But as they progressed south, through the forested valley that lined the narrow Gyffin River, along a rocky track barely wide enough to accommodate a cart, her spirits fell further still. She would have to leave this valley and live among her husband's people. She would be torn from her home and family and thrust among a people she'd never liked or trusted.

A wave of panic rushed suddenly over her. She could not do this. It was impossible!

She reined in her placid mare and, alarmed, the poor creature stamped a tight, nervous circle. Josselyn stared wildly about. Somewhere behind her was home. Somewhere behind her were family and friends and the familiar haunts of her childhood.

But there was also an Englishman come to build his castle and claim their land. He would claim her, too, were she not exceedingly careful.

"Josselyn? What ails you, girl? It canna be that mare."

In the dense, damp forest, her uncle's voice was startlingly loud. Yet it gave her an anchor against the sucking panic that tore at her.

"The mare . . . is fine. It's just that . . . I haven't ridden in a goodly while." She looked over at him, knowing her fear must show in her face. Their eyes met and held. Then he gestured with his hand.

"Come ride beside me. You will grow more easy as time goes on." He referred to the riding, of course. Yet as they proceeded forward, Josselyn wondered if he meant more. And if he did, she prayed he was right.

Rand listened to the report from the watch with a rising temper.

". . . six men and one woman, with two packhorses accompanying them. They left shortly after the weather eased." Osborn paused. "They headed south."

"To the Lloyds."

"So it would seem."

Rand clenched his fists, then forced himself to relax his tensed hands. He'd hoped to avoid outright battle with the Welsh. He'd hoped their well-known distrust of one another would delay a confrontation long enough for him to prove that he did not plan to disrupt their lives.

He was prepared to deal with an occasional skirmish, a hog stolen, a storehouse fired. But he did not want to engage them on the field of combat, for then he'd be obliged to crush them. And the wounds formed from such a battle might never be healed.

Unfortunately, today's turn of events could mean only one thing: Clyde ap Llewelyn meant to wed his niece to Madoc ap Lloyd's family—probably to his son. Unified, the two families posed a much greater threat than did either of them alone. And they knew it.

Rand stood and began to pace the length of his newly constructed quarters, which functioned also as the main hall. "Select a party of five men to accompany us—you and I. We ride into Carreg Du."

"To what end?" Osborn asked.

"To ask a few questions. And receive a few answers," he tersely added.

"But who's to translate? The wench hasn't been here in three days."

Rand didn't bother to answer that. He was well aware that Josselyn had been absent these several days—acutely aware—and that was what bothered him. He needed to know if she was merely frightened by what had passed between them in the forest glade, or if there was something more involved in her absence.

One woman had accompanied the party heading south. One woman, no doubt Clyde's niece. But what if that woman were Josselyn? What if she'd deceived him, diverting him with her comely face and alluring body?

What if the orphaned Josselyn ap Carreg Du was in reality Clyde's niece and heir to the wildwoods of Carreg Du and Rosecliffe?

Once more his fingers curled into fists, and this time he could not shake them out. Had the brazen wench made a fool of him? Had she come into his camp, worked for him, aroused him—and finally kissed him—knowing she would be the one to ally two warring families against him?

"God's bones!" He kicked over a stool, then flung open the door and stormed out into the blustery afternoon. The bitch had him tied in knots. Was he mad not to have seen the connection sooner? Or was he mad now to imagine a woman could fool him so easily?

He no longer knew what to think. Mayhap she was no virgin at all, but a practiced seducer bent on twisting him for her own purposes.

And now she no doubt meant to seduce this Owain ap Madoc in the same manner. Lure him with her sparkling eyes. Entice him with her pouting lips. Blind him to everything but her sweetly rounded body. She would buy the man's loyalty with her female lures, then send him and his brethren into war against Rand.

Behind him Osborn cleared his throat. "D'ye think *she's* the niece, that Josselyn is Clyde's niece—and the bait for the Lloyds?"

Rand clenched his jaw reflexively. "There's only one way to find out for sure."

Eight

The Welsh village was nothing like an English one, for it was anchored by neither a castle nor a church. A wide muddy track rambled between a few stone buildings, some with slate roofs, others with thatch. But most of the houses were tucked back behind trees and boulders, spread apart, not clustered together as was the way in England. Here and there borders of stones marked the edges of what must be kitchen gardens. A few were already being worked in preparation for the spring planting.

Rand paused at one end of the village and the rest of his men did the same. He didn't see a single villager—neither man, woman, nor child. A cat preened on a windowsill, then disappeared on silent feet. A dog snuffled at a door. When it saw the riders, its hackles raised and it began to bark. But when Rand urged his horse forward, the skinny hound backed away, then slunk behind a lean-to shed. It kept barking though, and Rand had no doubt every Welsh villager was well aware of the English presence in their midst.

He rode toward the largest structure in the village. It was a fine two-story house, plastered on the lower story and whitewashed as well. Elaborately knotted motifs decorated the lintels above the window openings, and a lenten rose bloomed on either side of the carved entry door.

A curtain moved in one of the upper windows, but Rand did not flinch. He came in peace—at least for now. He dismounted and signaled his men to do the same. Then he handed his horse's reins to one of his men and approached the door.

Before he reached that portal, it opened and the man named Dewey stepped over the threshold. The Welshman spread his legs and crossed his arms. Though a full head shorter than Rand, he did not appear likely to give ground even were a bull charging him.

Rand halted and met the man's suspicious stare. At least with Dewey there would be no language difficulties.

"I bid you a good day."

"Good day," came the clipped response.

Rand kept his gaze steady. "I understand Clyde ap Llewelyn has departed for the south." The man's eyes flickered a faint surprise, but otherwise he did not respond. Rand continued. "I would speak with Josselyn."

"She is not here."

"Is she the woman who rides with your master?"

"We have no masters in Wales," Dewey countered in a superior tone.

"Is she his niece?"

This time the man gave a small smug smile. "She is."

The sly bitch! Though it made no sense, Rand felt an undeniable sense of betrayal. He struggled to tamp down his fury. "Does this mean she will no longer teach me your language?"

"I wouldn't know about that."

"Perhaps you will take over that task," Rand said, just to annoy him.

As he'd expected, Dewey bristled. "I've more important duties than to waste my time trying to teach an Englishman to speak as a Welshman."

Rand's eyes narrowed. "Important duties or foolish ones? For if you and Clyde and the Lloyds think to raise an army against me, 'tis a foolish task you undertake. Foolish and deadly.''

Dewey stiffened and a mulish light glittered in his eyes. But he did not respond, and after a long tense moment Rand gave a curt nod and took his leave. This time as the English riders made their way through the village, faces appeared in the window openings. Heads peeped around doors.

They saw the English departing, so they did not fear, Rand supposed. But the English were not departing. Not hardly. Nor would Josselyn's marriage to Owain ap Lloyd change anything, save that he needed to find some other halfway comely wench to ease the lust Josselyn had roused in him. Some other wench to pant erotic Welsh words in his ear.

He kicked his horse and leaned over the animal's thick neck when it surged forward. But he couldn't outrun his thoughts. For while he found some other woman to ease his lusts upon, this Owain would be easing his lusts upon Josselyn. Josselyn, who was still a virgin—or was she?

Virgin or no, however, Rand had thought to claim the wench for himself.

"Damn her!" he swore as he urged the gallant animal on to a reckless speed. Stones scattered behind him. Osborn's call was but a faint echo. The bitch had played him for a fool.

None of her people would do so again.

Josselyn hunched into her sodden cloak. It had rained the last two hours and the heavy sky had brought an early dusk upon them. It was nearly dark when they finally rode into Afon Bryn. She was cold and wet and hungry—as were they all. She did not think, however, that the others were frightened. Though she tried not to show it, she was as frightened as she'd ever been.

Torches flickered in the drizzle, marking their route through the dreary village. The few houses circled a larger building, and it was that well-lighted structure to which they made their way. As they progressed, they gathered a crowd of curious onlookers, mostly women and children, for the men had already gathered outside the main hall.

Josselyn and the others dismounted and the door to the hall swung wide. A tall, muscular man with graying hair stepped outside—Madoc ap Lloyd, Josselyn assumed, for he was an older version of the man who trailed him, Owain.

She studied Owain closely. He was as handsome as ever, she supposed, with smooth skin and even features. But the cruelty of his soul outweighed any comeliness he might possess. Even now his eyes moved over her as if he saw past her cloak and gown, to the pale, shivering skin beneath her damp clothes. She shuddered and knew it was not on account of the cold.

"Welcome, Clyde ap Llewelyn. Come," the older man said. "Warm yourself at the fire. Share our food and wine. We have much to speak of."

Clyde met this affable welcome with an equal cordiality, and the two men entered the building together. Then it was Josselyn's turn to advance to where Owain awaited her.

"You have grown up. And filled out," he murmured, running hard but appreciative eyes over her.

Josselyn raised her chin a notch. "I am not the frightened little girl you tormented so many years ago."

He grinned, plainly unperturbed by her accusation. His eyes focused on her breasts. "No. I see you are not." He met her gaze and extended an arm to her. "May I escort you?"

"That will not be necessary," she snapped. When she tried to sidle past him, however, he caught her by the arm and tightened his hold until she knew she would bruise.

"I insist."

Behind her Josselyn heard Bower mutter and step forward. In response one of Owain's men did the same. " 'Tis all right," she interjected into the tense silence. She looked up into Owain's smug face. "You're hurting me," she stated, slowly and clearly.

He waited one long moment before releasing her arm. "My pardon, Josselyn. I sometimes forget my own strength."

Josselyn said nothing. What would be the point? But as she swept past him she felt a cold dread like nothing she'd ever before known. For an instant Randulf Fitz Hugh's image rose in her mind's eye. He was her enemy and Owain her ally. Yet could she but choose between them, it was the enemy she would run to, the enemy whom she feared less.

But her wishes didn't matter, she reminded herself as she entered the smoky, torchlit hall. Her future was of lesser import than that of her Welsh people, her Welsh lands. It was Owain she must wed if she were to save her lands from the English. Owain she must give her body to. Owain she must provide sons for. Sweet Mary, but it would take all her strength and prayers to go through with her wifely duties to him when the time came!

She slept badly, in a small room opposite the one given her uncle. Bower slept on the floor outside her door—a symbolic gesture, her uncle had said. But Josselyn had wondered. Her uncle had watched Owain all evening, and though he'd said little, Josselyn knew his moods well. He was not pleased with Owain. He was not pleased with this situation.

The menfolk were still abed when she rose. In the main hall three servants worked to prepare the morning meal. They were supervised by an older woman, Madoc's widowed cousin Meriel, who ran the man's household. Though last night Meriel had said nothing in the men's presence, this morning she welcomed Josselyn with a thin smile. "Take a seat near to the fire. I'll bring ye somethin' to warm yer bones."

"Thank you, but you needn't wait upon me."

The other woman tilted her head and gave her a shrewd look. "I'd be a fool not to give you good welcome. I'm in sore need of another woman's company in this household. A house of widows and widowers,'' she continued, as if last night's silence was now finally being relieved. ''We've been that too long, the three of us. One of us needs to marry again, and Owain is the likeliest. Have you met his boy yet?''

''His boy? No, but—''

''No need to fret over that one. He'll come around.''

''Come around? Does that mean—''

''He don't want his da to wed again,'' Meriel interrupted. She lowered her voice to a confidential whisper. ''Not that Owain cares what the boy thinks. Mostly Rhys is off in the hills by hisself. He's a solitary lad, he is. But already a wonder with his little bow, and an amazing fisherman.''

''How old is he?'' Josselyn asked when the woman paused for breath.

''How old? How old. Well, let's see. 'Twas that cold winter. That terrible one when the ice storm broke the branches off all the trees.'' She counted on her fingers. ''The ice storm. The year Meghan died—that's Owain's wife. The year Toff took sick. The year of the fever. The year Gaenor lost her baby. The next year she died too— she was Madoc's daughter.'' Meriel paused. ''He's seven years old, or thereabouts.''

''Seven? And off in the hills alone? Where does he sleep?''

Meriel shrugged. ''Sometimes here, next to the fire. Other times in the stable with the horses.'' She shook her head. ''Don't be worryin' about that one. 'Tis the father you'd best concern yourself with.''

A shiver ran unbidden down Josselyn's spine. ''Yes,'' she murmured. ''Owain is the reason I'm here.'' She studied the other woman. Could she trust her? She picked her words carefully. ''Have you any advice for me that will make marriage to him . . . easier?''

The woman drew back, and she took an uncharacteristically long time to respond. ''I'll not be deceiving you.

Marriage to Owain will never be easy. Nay, that's not true. He's not a bad sort. But he can be a bully. His first wife was too meek, you see. He's a man like his father and his grandfather before him, a man who needs a strong woman to stand up to his temper. A woman with a nature as lusty as his own," she added with a sly look in her eyes.

Another shudder, this time of revulsion, coursed through Josselyn. She knew, with unshakable certainty, that she would never feel lust for Owain ap Madoc. Never.

Meriel must have read Josselyn's emotions, for her lined face grew stern. "A wife's lot comes easier if she resigns herself to the rigors of the marriage bed. After a while you will learn to like it, at least somewhat. There are even those women who lust after their men," she added with a sly look. "Every bride feels as you presently feel. But in time—"

Meriel broke off at the measured tread of booted feet upon the narrow stairs. When Madoc ap Lloyd entered the room she hurried to pull out his chair, then carried a steaming cup of heated ale to him.

He thanked her with a nod and a grunt, then fixed his piercing brown eyes on Josselyn. " 'Tis a good thing for a woman to rise early."

Josselyn decided to be blunt. "That is not why your son will wed me, because I rise early or late."

He chuckled in amusement. "No, 'tis not. He wants a comely wench in his bed, one who will give him many sons."

"And in return he will help us fight the English who threaten our land."

"*We* will help fight them," Madoc amended. "I am the leader of this family, not my son. But understand this, Josselyn: we will fight the English with or without this marriage between our families. Eventually every Welshman must fight them, for they will spread like a plague upon our land if we do not. When you wed Owain, you ensure a peaceable bond between our families, one that will help us work together with more trust than in the past, one that will endure and bring peace and prosperity to us all.''

Josselyn's brows drew together in a frown. It was no more than she already knew, yet it made her decision to wed Owain harder still. "I do not anticipate my marriage to your son with much joy," she admitted.

He speared her with his sharp gaze. "Have you another lover?"

"No!" But she knew that was not entirely true. Still, Englishmen did not count, especially an Englishman who did not offer anything more than a brief, lusty encounter. And he'd not truly become her lover.

Madoc studied her. "I will keep my son under control. Though he has a temper, he never hurt Meghan. He will not hurt you."

That was little enough reassurance, yet it was clear to Josselyn that it was the most reassurance she would get. Clyde descended into the main hall and Madoc turned to greet him. Slowly the room filled with people—men who broke their fast, and women and servants who waited upon them.

When Owain entered the room, however, he sought out Josselyn. "Come and sit with me, and eat," he said, catching her by the arm.

His touch was gentle, his smile sincere. Even his words sounded more a request than an order. Though she did not desire his company, Josselyn deemed it best to comply. Under the watchful eye of everyone in the smoky room, he escorted her to the head table and signaled for food and drink.

Josselyn sat on the bench and he sat beside her. A full plate and full mug were immediately set before her. Then he offered her his knife and she knew she must take it. "Thank you," she murmured.

"When we wed, all that is mine will be yours. From this knife to this hall," he said, gesturing with one hand while he drank with another.

You are not the leader of this family yet, Josselyn thought, echoing the words his father had spoken but minutes ago. Owain was nothing if not ambitious and cocksure. And yet that should not be a criticism, for wasn't the English lord even more steeped in those masculine traits? Those traits had not repulsed Josselyn then, why did they repulse her now? It must be something else about Owain.

Perhaps it was only the threat of forced marriage, she reasoned, willing herself to eat. Perhaps if she did not feel trapped into this marriage, she could find something in Owain to admire. She put down the knife with a clatter. She owed it to both of them to try and find it.

"Might we walk apart from here? I would speak to you privately," she said, peering cautiously at him.

A smug grin curved his lips. "As you wish." He rose and took her arm.

"I want *only* to talk," she stated, needing to make herself very clear. "I want to ease the tension between us. Nothing more."

He considered her a long moment. When they stood a silence had fallen, and now everyone stared at them. "Very well," he agreed. "We will walk and talk. That is all. For now."

Outside the air was sharp and cold. He led her down a rutted path, away from the smoky hall and crowded village. When they reached a stand of beechwood, she halted. He turned to face her and reached for her hand, but she shied away. A flash of irritation showed in his eyes, but he swiftly banished it. He gave her a bland smile. "What did you wish to speak of?"

Josselyn cleared her throat. This was so awkward. "We are being thrust at one another. Do you feel the pressure to wed with me?"

He shrugged. "I am in need of a wife."

"And one woman will do as well as another?"

He must have heard the edge in her voice for he grinned. "A wife is not just any woman. She must be comely and soft, an enticement to keep me night after night in her bed.''

''I see.'' Her face grew crimson at his frank words. ''Do you imply you will seek other beds if she does not entice you sufficiently?''

''You needn't fear, fair Josselyn. You entice me very well. Shall I show you just how well?'' he added, stroking beneath the front of his tunic.

Josselyn's nostrils flared in distaste. She started to turn away, but he grabbed her by the arm, laughing. ''Your squeamishness befits the virgin you are said to be. Never fear, Josselyn. I shall ease you into the ways of marriage. Before long you will be more than content to be my wife.''

So Meriel had said, and yet Josselyn could not believe it. She needed to speak to someone else, a married woman like Nesta or Gladys. ''Perhaps you are right in this,'' she muttered, wanting only to escape his loathsome presence.

But Owain was not ready to release her. He forced her to face him. '' 'Tis only right that we share a kiss to seal our betrothal.''

''I have not yet agreed—''

''But you will. You have no choice. Otherwise the English will take over your lands.''

''So I am constantly reminded. But your own father believes all the Welsh families will have to join together to fight the English. Whether we wed or not, your family will eventually come to our aid.''

''Eventually, perhaps. By that time, however, there will be nothing left of Carreg Du. Its men will be dead, its women raped, and its children starving. And all on account of a virgin's squeamishness.''

The picture he painted was terrifyingly real. And yet it did not have to be so. ''You could agree to help us now, before it comes to that.''

''To what end? It would gain me nothing to risk my life for Carreg Du. But if I knew you awaited me in my bed . . . If I knew you would bear me strong sons to unite our

families and end the animosity between our people . . .
Then I would have a reason to fight.''

He pulled her closer. She could feel the heat of his body,
it was that near to hers. But despite his heat, she'd never
felt so cold.

Then his head bent closer to hers. ''Kiss me, Josselyn.
Abandon the little girl you have been and become a woman
in my arms. Just one kiss,'' he urged her. ''That's all I
want for now.''

If it were only him trapping her there, she would have
turned away. She could have called out for help and fought
him with all her might. But it was more than his greater
strength that held her frozen before him. It was her responsibility to her people, the men, women, and children who
would suffer under British rule. So she stilled in his arms,
and when he smiled the smile of a triumphant predator, she
closed her eyes.

There was a pause, long and fearful, and finally she
opened her eyes. Only then did he move. He drew her hard
against him and thrust his hips against hers. She felt his
arousal, stiff and repugnant against her belly, and panic rose
like a bilious wave in her. Only when that panic showed
in her eyes did he at last lower his head. Only when she
trembled with unreasoning fear did he take her mouth in a
grotesque parody of a kiss.

Rand had kissed her, and though it had frightened her,
it had melted something inside of her too. What Owain did
was turn her rigid with fear, and cold with outrage. Sick
with dread.

He was not brutal, but that was the only thing she could
say to his credit. He did not physically hurt her. But he
was greedy and relentless, and when he forced his tongue
into her mouth, he ground his loins crudely against her once
more.

She struck out at his head, and she heard his grunt of
surprise. ''At least you have spirit,'' he said when he let
her go. ''At least I will know you are alive in my bed.''

Josselyn glared at him as she wiped her mouth on her sleeve. She didn't want his taste in her mouth, but feared she would never be rid of it.

"You are a pig," she swore. "I may be a virgin, but what you know of pleasing a woman is dwarfed by the seed of a mustard!"

His smug grin disappeared. "In time you will come to crave my touch."

From somewhere the children's rhyme came to her. *When stones shall grow and trees shall no'* . . .

She stepped backward, keeping wary eyes on him. "You are a pig," she repeated. Then she turned and ran—not for the safety of the village, for it was Owain's village, but for the safety of her uncle's presence. She could not go through with this abhorrent marriage. She could not do it!

In the end, she had no choice. Clyde and Madoc had already agreed on the marriage between their people, and the particulars of the marriage contract. Unless Josselyn wished to stand up and refuse Owain, and thereby subject her people to even more animosity from the Lloyds, she must marry Owain.

But not now. Not yet.

"Then when?" Owain glowered at Clyde, challenging the man with his eyes. "I need a wife now."

"Saint George's day will give Josselyn and her aunt time to prepare," Clyde retorted, not flinching away from the younger man's threatening manner.

" 'Tis a reasonable request, little more than a fortnight," Madoc said.

"You will come to Carreg Du for the ceremony—and live there at least until fall."

"That I will not do!" Owain snarled.

"If there is to be peace between us, you will do this," Clyde stated in a steady voice.

"We are agreed on that as well," Madoc stated. "Besides, 'twill be a better base for our attack on the English,'' he reminded his angry son.

Owain stared at Clyde a long, hard while. Josselyn watched the war of emotions play across his face, the struggle for control in his pale eyes. Then he smiled, a terrible, placid sort of smile, and she shivered with fear. ''Very well,'' he agreed. ''We will make our home at Carreg Du— until the English are routed. But after that neither of you will interfere in my marriage again.''

They departed with that ominous threat echoing in Josselyn's head. Once wed to him she would be at his mercy. Once she became his wife, his word became her law.

There were some safeguards, of course. He could not beat her, nor abandon his responsibilities to her. But he could make her life miserable. There were ways, she feared, that he could make it unbearable.

The sky hung gray and somber above them as they set out from the Lloyd stronghold. They rode silently, in single file, with Josselyn in the middle. A grim departure from a grim place—with a grim future awaiting her. She shivered beneath her heavy cloak, but her chill came from within. The cloak did not exist that could warm the bitter cold that had seized her heart.

Her uncle must have sensed her mood, for once they entered the enclosing forest, he dropped back to ride beside her. ''Is aught troubling you?'' he asked in a gruff voice.

She shook her head. ''I am all right,'' she lied. *I will never be all right again. How can you think I will?* ''I will be fine.''

The sounds of the wildwood filled the silence between them. The birds and squirrels had begun the spring routine, the seasonal work of building and breeding. Josselyn looked up into the trees, the alder that were bare of anything but swelling buds, and the oaks that retained a small portion of their leaves through even the bitterest of winters. A lone squirrel chattered down at the passing line of horses. A chough preened itself then flitted higher and then away.

In a low fork of a hazel tree something moved and Josselyn stared. A polecat? Not in a tree. A bear cub? Not this early in the year.

Then it peeped down at them and she smiled to herself. A child, a little boy with a dirty face and ragged sleeves. And a swollen, discolored eye. She reined in, drawing her uncle's attention.

"Is aught amiss?" he asked.

"Look at that child. There, in that tree." She pointed. "He is hurt. Something has struck him in the face."

Behind her Bower drew up. "That's Owain's whelp. Rhys, his name is. I saw 'im in the yard near to the kitchens yesterday. His father cuffed him one. I dunno why. But he wasn't hurt bad. Little as he is, he didn't even let out a whimper."

The boy scowled at their discussion of him and climbed higher. Josselyn gasped when he slipped and nearly fell. Once he safely straddled a sturdy branch, however, he turned his dirty face back toward them.

"Get away from here, you thievin' asses!" he cried. He dug in his ragtag cloak, then flung a rock at them. "Get away, you bloodless bitch!"

"Hey, there!" Bower yelled up at him, shaking his fist. "Watch your tongue else I'll rip it out of your head, you nasty little beggar!"

"Just try it and my father will slice your balls off. And I'll eat 'em for my supper!"

"The bloody hell you will!" Bower started to dismount, but Clyde stayed him with a gesture.

"Leave him be. We've a long journey yet ahead of us."

"The cheeky brat deserves a sound thrashing for his disrespect. Especially toward the woman who's to take over the motherin' of him."

"What d'ye expect of the son of Owain ap Madoc?" one of the other men muttered.

What indeed? Josselyn wondered.

They started forward again. The child threw his remaining stones, but they fell harmlessly short of the riders. Josselyn turned to get one last glimpse of him, a last look at the child she would soon have the care of. As if he sensed her thoughts he heaved one final stone at her. Though it did not reach its mark, his words did.

"I hate you!" he screamed down at her in his high-pitched childish voice. "I hate you. You'll never be my mother!"

Nine

Rand watched and he waited. His network of men relayed the word: Josselyn traveled with the rest of the party back to Carreg Du. It appeared she had not been wed to Owain ap Madoc. At least not yet.

Nor would she ever be, Rand vowed.

His hands tightened on the reins and his heavy mount tossed its head in anticipation. What would he have done if she had already been wed to the man, sealing a union of Welsh forces against him?

He would have increased the guard around his encampment, and exhorted his workers to labor even more swiftly than they now did. He'd already bribed them with a series of rewards. If the first level of the castle wall was erected by winter, he promised them two years of no taxes and only half the annual days required laboring in his behalf. Already he saw the results of his generous offer. The men worked long and hard with no bickering and one common goal: to raise the entire inner wall to a height of eight feet before winter's onset.

He needed that wall to keep the Welsh at bay, but if Josselyn had wed Owain, he would not have had it, not by several long months of labor. But Josselyn hadn't wed Owain yet, and as a result he had a chance to hold the

Welsh at bay while he rushed to raise the walls of his castle. Henry's castle.

Rand watched from his sheltered position on a thickly grown hillside above the narrow track. She rode fourth from the back, and he approved. That was the safest place for a woman in a line of six men. But as they neared their homelands, the Welsh relaxed their guard. Rand watched one of the rear guards pass Josselyn on a wider part of the track and make his way up toward the front of the line. At the same time, the last man in the line reined his horse in and dismounted—probably to relieve himself.

Again Rand's fist tightened on the reins. With a nod to one of his men, he gave the signal to take the straggler. In a moment only one solitary rider would stand between him and Josselyn, and once he had her, there could be no union of Welsh against him. Once she was his hostage, her uncle would not dare attack the English stronghold, either with or without aid from others.

Once she was his captive, Rand would have the deceitful wench in his power and he would find out just how honest her attraction to him was.

He heard the cry of a bird—his man's signal for success. Below him the careless Welshman's mount disappeared into the forest. Josselyn and the last rider were beyond his view now, but he and Osborn knew what they each must do. Ahead of them the path turned once, then again. It was there they would strike. Osborn would disarm the Welsh soldier; Rand would capture Josselyn ap Carreg Du.

He urged his able steed over the low hill, through the thick growth that was not so much a forest as dense scrubland. He dismounted and crept forward. With a single look he and Osborn coordinated their attack. Then she was below him, slender and straight in her green cloak, a warm sight on a cold afternoon. In a moment she would be his. The thought sent blood rushing to his loins.

That was *not* why he wanted her, he sternly reprimanded himself. This was politics, nothing more. A way to safeguard his workers against any threat of Welsh interference.

But that fact didn't change anything. He wanted her, and short of forcing her, he meant to have the unruly wench in his bed. First, however, he had to capture her.

To his right he saw Osborn tense. The time was now!

Silent as a cat and just as confident, Rand sprang from his hiding place. Over her horse's haunches he vaulted and landed behind her. With one hand he snatched the reins. With the other he muffled her cry. Then he dug his heels into the startled mare's sides and forced her into the shielding forest.

Josselyn screamed, then choked on it. A hard, callused hand trapped the very breath in her throat. A hard, intent body wrapped itself around hers. Her horse half reared and nearly toppled over when the man's full weight landed. But it was as if the man would not allow the animal to fall. With a swift twist of the reins he launched the horse into the woods, plunging down a sharp incline, then around a boulder before beginning to climb again. And all the time his hand stayed, a vise across her mouth and cheeks.

She fought him. Though petrified with fear, she fought him, clawing at his hand on the rein, struggling desperately to escape his brutal grip. Her heart raced with terror, but still she bared her teeth and tried to bite him.

His reaction was to pull her harder against him. "Don't attempt it, Josselyn. For I vow, you will regret it."

Randulf Fitz Hugh! Josselyn's first reaction was relief.

Her second was acute shame. She had thought him Owain, come to claim her now for his wife. She would not put such a vile deed past him. That it was Rand meant she was safe from Owain a while longer.

Except that she was not safe at all, and she was a fool to think she was. A perverse fool!

In silence he guided the horse deeper into the low-hanging forest. She felt the tensing of his muscular thighs against hers and knew the horse felt it too. Like the well-behaved mount she was, the mare settled down and picked her way surefootedly through the heavy undergrowth, taking Josselyn farther and farther from safety, and deeper into the lair of this newest predator of the wildwood.

Only when she was exhausted and unable to fight him any longer did his rigid hold on her ease. Only when they were met by another man leading a powerful horse—*his* horse—did the English lord loosen his grip on her mouth. Even then, however, he did not entirely release her.

"Call out and my man will slit your countryman's throat." He twisted her head to the side so she could see his Captain Osborn leading Bower on his horse. Bower's mouth had been covered with a length of cloth and his hands knotted behind his back. His eyes showed his fury, but also his fear.

Would he truly slit a helpless man's throat? Josselyn was afraid to find out. As if he read her thoughts Rand whispered roughly in her ear. "So we are agreed?"

Reluctantly Josselyn nodded. What other choice was left to her?

"Good." He took his hand away and she sucked in great gasps of air.

"What do you think to accomplish—" A strip of bunched linen cut off her words. When she tried to snatch the gag away, he caught her hands and, with a practiced move, bound them behind her with more of the linen. Then he dismounted, hauled her kicking and wriggling from the mare, and as if her rage and struggles were of no consequence at all, mounted his own horse with her slung under his arm and planted her firmly in front of him.

"Enough of this!" he growled in her ear. "It avails you nothing to fight me. You cannot win."

The gall of the man! Though her scream was contained by the bindings across her mouth, her rage was not. Determined to wreak some damage on him, she kicked backward, at first wildly, then deliberately. When her leather-shod heel caught him just below the knee, it jarred her enough to hurt. But it hurt him more.

"Damnation, wench! Be still or I'll sling you over my lap like a sack of flour."

She kicked again, but he evaded her foot, then trapped it between his leg and the horse's side. "You cannot win," he repeated, only this time he wrapped both his hands around her and pressed her flat against him. One of his hands splayed wide across her stomach, and she felt the hard palm and long fingers as distinct entities, as distinct threats. She was so vulnerable with her hands bound behind her and her legs wide, straddling his mighty horse. She was at his complete mercy.

His other hand curved around her neck. His fingers threaded through her tangled hair and his thumb caressed the hollow of her throat. She swallowed and knew he felt her fear. She knew also that he felt her awareness of him.

By the Blessed Virgin! She was not supposed to react this way to him.

"That's better," he murmured when she stilled. He paused as if he meant to speak again. She felt his hand move on her stomach, just a tiny shift, but it sent quivers racing through her that she surely must feel. For a long suspended moment neither of them moved. Then with a muffled oath, he picked up the reins, kicked his horse, and it surged forward with his men and the trussed-up Bower just behind them.

The ride took nearly an hour, an hour that tested the big horse sorely. But the animal was game and its pace did not falter under its double load.

Rand did not speak to her once during the ride, which suited Josselyn very well. She was angry and frightened and sore confused. Until she had her emotions under better control, she did not want to engage in any discourse with him.

The early dusk crept over them but he pressed on. Beneath her the horse labored. Rand curved around her—his legs around her legs, his arms around her shoulders and sides—and she was excruciatingly aware of his warrior's body. Even worse, her bound hands were trapped between her back and his stomach. His lower stomach.

On a level stretch of ground, as the horses cantered a steady pace toward the English encampment, she twisted her wrists back and forth and tried to stretch her cramped fingers. She froze when her fingertips brushed something hard and growing.

Knotting her fists, she groaned and leaned forward. He was aroused! Worse, the fact that she could arouse him started the strangest reaction in her.

"Unfortunate situation, isn't it?" he murmured, breaking his silence at last. She felt him fumble with the cloth over her mouth and in a moment she was free to speak once more.

"Unfortunate indeed," she snapped, working her stiff jaw back and forth. "Unfortunate that you have just brought down the wrath of Wales upon your head and that of your workers."

"I see you are not well versed in the art of warfare. Consider. So long as I hold such a valuable captive as you, there will be no outright attacks on me or my people. But that's not what I was speaking of." He leaned into her back and once more her hands felt the rigid power of his maleness. With every stride of his powerful steed, it was thrust against her tensely knotted fingers. "It's unfortunate that we are enemies, for we would make very good lovers. Mayhap we still will."

"Never!" she swore. "I'd choose death before agreeing to that!"

"I doubt it will come to so difficult a decision as that, Josselyn." His tone was smug, so much so that had her hands been free she would have slapped him. As it was, she had to swallow her fury and try to change the subject.

"How long do you plan to keep us captive?"

She felt his chuckle, his chest moving against her back. With a gesture of his head he indicated Bower. "He will go back tonight, with a message for your uncle—and for your betrothed. You . . . You I will keep for a while.''

Josselyn prayed he could not feel the wild thumping of her heart, or the uncontrolled shiver of awareness that streaked once more up her back. Her skin lifted in prickles all over her body. He meant to keep her. But for how long, and to what end?

They arrived at the English encampment on Rosecliffe after dark, coming in up the narrow coast path. Josselyn was exhausted. The journey to Afon Bryn and her dread of a union with Owain had been taxing enough. But this capture by Rand Fitz Hugh attacked her on another level entirely. She could not be rigid in his grasp forever. She could not deny her attraction to him, at least to herself, nor her relief to be saved from Owain's vile clutches.

But this was all temporary. It had to be, for he was her enemy and she was committed to banishing him from Welsh lands. From her lands.

Still, when they wended their way into the well-guarded campsite, when he slid over his horse's rump then caught her around the waist, lifted her safely to the ground, and led her toward the sturdy structure that served as both the main hall and his personal quarters, she knew one thing clearly. He would not hurt her, at least not in the same way Owain might. He might prevent her from leaving his camp. He might fight her family to the death—his or theirs or both. However, he would not deliberately hurt her.

But he might seduce her.

She swallowed hard at the thought. He might not force her because he might not have to. He could very well decide to seduce her—and succeed. Somehow she knew that giving in to him willingly could, in its own way, hurt her far more than being forced.

''You'll stay here.'' He swung the roughly planed door back on its leather hinges and gestured for her to enter.

She halted just outside the door and peered into the room, lit by a small fire burning in the hearth and a brace of candles mounted on the wall. It appeared cozy and warm, far too appealing when she was so cold and tired. "I'm to go in there with you? The two of us alone?"

He gave her a slow smile. With one hand at the small of her back he propelled her inside. Before the door thumped closed she had scurried to the far side of the open space. It was a useless effort, she knew, as was her determination to keep the massive table and ornately carved chair between him and her. She had no real defense against him save her own wits. Unfortunately, he possessed the singular ability to scramble them at will, especially when he grinned at her as he was doing now.

"Be at ease, Josselyn. You have nothing to fear from me."

She could not believe her ears. "You dare to say such things to me when you have taken me against my will, gagged me, tied me like a sheep for the shearing! And now you would—"

"Now I would like to untie you," he said, breaking into her tirade. "That is, assuming you will come close enough for me to do so."

When she only stood there, staring suspiciously at him, he shrugged off his leather hauberk and untied the sheath that held his short sword. Then he pulled back the chair, flung himself in it, and signaled with his fingers for her to approach. "Come, Josselyn. If you would be freed from your bindings, you must find the courage to approach me."

" 'Tis not courage I lack. That I possess in abundance, as do all the people of *Cymru*. But I also possess an abundance of mistrust of you."

He bent down and removed one boot, then the other. "Suit yourself," he said when he once again sprawled back on the big, rug-draped chair. As she watched he untied the knife sheath on his thigh and set it on the table. Then he reached for an ornate ewer that stood on the table and poured himself a mug of ale. He drank a long time, then set down the mug, gave a great satisfied sigh, and studied her with a half-grin playing on his lips.

"Would you like ale? Or do you prefer wine?" The grin increased. "Or perhaps you are hungry. I know I am."

Josselyn looked away. She didn't want to see the expression in his eyes. She didn't want to know what he was hungry for. Then her stomach gave an embarrassing rumble, and she knew it was pointless to defy him. She needed to have her arms freed, and he was the only one who could do it.

She gritted her teeth and glared at him. Then without speaking, she marched up to him, turned around, and waited.

It seemed to take forever, though it was only a few seconds. He caught her bound wrists and gave a quick unexpected tug so that she had to take an awkward step backward. Just one step, but it threw her off balance and too near him. Her equanimity—what little she had left—began to slip.

His fingers were warm and strong, but they fumbled over the linen, drawn now into a taut, stringy knot. "I'll have to cut you free," he said, leaning past her to reach his knife.

His knee brushed her leg. His hand rested on her waist, just above the curve of her hips. She held her breath. Then he caught the twisted linen with the well-honed tip of the blade and she was free.

But not entirely.

Before she could escape he caught her by one wrist. She spun away, but he was too fast and too strong. He tossed the dagger on the table and caught her other hand and forced her to stand before him. "Let me see your wrists, to see if you're hurt," he explained.

"I'm not hurt. Let me go."

But he ignored her and drew her arms up so he could inspect them. "You're chafed."

"What do you expect?" she snapped.

He looked up at her, his face serious. "I don't want to hurt you, Josselyn. But I can't let you go. You need to understand that."

She glared at him, mutinous and yet shaken too. He meant what he said and she should hate him. But he was massaging her sore wrists with the gentlest of touches.

She forced herself to sound stern. "And you need to understand that I cannot be your willing prisoner."

"Then you will be my unwilling prisoner." His thumbs moved soothingly over her reddened skin, reviving her, stimulating her. She stood there between his outstretched legs, looking down into his dark opaque eyes, which glinted the flickering firelight back at her. When he spoke again, the low timbre of his voice seemed to vibrate through her. "I wonder just how unwilling a prisoner you will finally prove to be."

Their eyes held and some communication passed between them. Words were not a part of it, nor was understanding, for they did not speak and she surely did not understand this attraction between them. But a connection was forged every time they touched. Every time their eyes met.

Every time she was in his presence.

Her heart began to pound, like surf booming on the rocks, like thunder rattling the heavens. Her heart pounded, her body trembled, and she knew she was in grave danger of succumbing to this enemy she wanted to despise.

Slowly she drew her wrists out of his hold, and he let her. She backed away, bumped into the table, then sidled around it. Only when she was across the room was she able to drag her gaze away from his mesmerizing one.

"I'm hungry—for food," she quickly added.

He stood and crossed to a cupboard, removing another mug as well as a loaf of bread wrapped in cloth and a small, wax-coated wheel of cheese. He set them on the table, then stuck his dagger into the cheese. "Eat your fill. Then you can sleep. There." He pointed at a bed in a curtained alcove.

She chanced another glance at him. "And where will you sleep?"

His glance held her captive. "Are you willing to share?"

Unnerved, she shook her head and hugged her arms around herself. "No."

"Then eat," he said with a sweep of his hand. "Eat so that at least one of us will not go to bed starving this night."

She reached for the knife and when her fingers wrapped around it she felt a secret surge of power. She held a weapon. He did not. But when she peered sidelong at him, she knew that was no advantage. Even had she wielded a sword, he would still have the advantage. For even had she the skill to overpower him, she was not certain she had the strength of will to plunge any length of hardened steel into his flesh. If he were threatening her life or the lives of others, she could. But he was offering her food, giving her his bed to sleep in. She should try to escape him, and eventually she would. But she could not do so by cutting him with his own knife.

Appalled at her own perversity—after all, he was her enemy—she sliced off a hunk of cheese, then a generous piece of bread. Giving him a deliberate, narrow-eyed look, she thrust the knife back into the cheese, then poured a mug of ale and retreated with her supper to the far side of the room.

She was famished and ate swiftly, but still it was the worst meal of her life. No, she realized after a moment. The meal with Owain at her side had been just as awful. Given the choice, however, she'd rather be in Randulf Fitz Hugh's presence than Owain ap Madoc's. It should be the other way around, but she could not lie—at least not to herself.

That did not mean she wanted to be in this predicament, however. Anything but. Still, given a choice, the English lord appeared more and more to be the lesser of two evils.

She quaffed the last of her ale. Rand did not speak while she ate, nor did he eat. Now, he refilled his goblet and settled back in his chair, still observing her. It wore on her nerves until she couldn't restrain herself.

"Well? Aren't you going to explain why you have kidnapped me? Because if you're not, I am much wearied by this day's work and would prefer to sleep rather than suffer your unrelentingly rude stare." She crossed her arms and glowered at him.

"Tell me why you hid your identity from me."

"I hid nothing. My name is Josselyn ap Carreg Du."

"You are Clyde's niece. His only heir. You hid that."

"I did not hide it. I simply chose not to reveal it, and with good reason. I feared this very thing happening, and clearly I was wise to do so. But not wise enough," she added bitterly.

As if on cue a knock sounded at the door, drawing his attention. "We have a little business to attend to," he said. At his call to enter, the door swung open, and Bower, still bound, advanced into the room, followed by the two Englishmen, Osborn and Alan. Josselyn crossed to her countryman at once. Alan would have blocked her path but for Rand. "Let her be."

"Are you all right?" she whispered in Welsh.

"Aye, lass. But what of you?" Bower asked, examining her with anxious eyes. *"He hasn't . . ."* He let the rest trail off, but Josselyn knew what he meant.

"No, he has not," she muttered. But color rose hot in her face as she focused on untying his hands. When she could not she glanced at the dagger still standing in the wheel of cheese, then over at Rand. With a slow nod he answered her unspoken question.

In a moment she had Bower free. But when he would have grabbed for the dagger, she pulled it away. " *'Twill do no good,"* she said, sticking the dagger back into the table this time. "Now," she continued in English, turning to face Rand. "Will you explain what you expect to gain from this mad scheme of yours?"

Ten

Rand watched the Welshman melt into the darkness. It was too late to undo what he'd set in motion. But that didn't stop him from wondering if he'd made a colossal error in judgment. Would his daring move prevent the Welsh from attacking Rosecliffe? Or would it unify them further against him?

He scrubbed his hands across his face and tried to think rationally. Clyde ap Llewelyn would not risk Josselyn's life. Rand was certain of that. But where was the man? Why was he or his messenger not already here, demanding in outraged tones the return of his niece? The village was not so far away. Why was he the one sending a message to the Welsh and not the other way around? Didn't the man care about his niece's well-being?

Perhaps she wasn't his niece after all.

"Bloody hell," he swore into the night sky. Could Josselyn be merely bait, not the real niece at all, but only a spy sent to dupe him?

But then, why would the Welsh do that?

"Damnation!" He was not a man used to self-doubt, and he didn't like it. Unfortunately that accursed wench, curled now in his bed, was driving him mad.

He wanted her, even though he knew he ought to leave her untouched.

He was certain she was the right woman, yet she made him worry that she'd duped him once more.

He couldn't make up his mind.

Stifling a frustrated groan, he frowned at the sturdy building where she waited. A guard stood at the door. Smoke wafted from the new chimney. A faint glow showed at the edges of the shuttered window. Inside it was warm.

She was warm.

With a curse he turned away and stared blindly down the long slope of the hill. He saw the white puffs of his own frozen breath. The moon cast just enough shadow that he could make out the dark outline of both the inner and outer walls that Sir Lovell had laid out. The inner wall progressed swiftly, but not swiftly enough. With this new tension between him and his neighbors, he would have to temporarily abandon the outer wall and concentrate all the workers on raising the inner wall to a level higher than a man's head. Only then would he return Josselyn to her uncle.

And to Owain.

He scowled. God's bones, but the thought of her in another man's bed was maddening.

"A man's will is a strange creature, sometimes even to himself."

Rand's hand flew to the hilt of his dagger. Then he recognized the lumpy shadow that emerged from the darkness. Damn that Newlin!

"Do you speak of yourself, or pass judgment on me?" Rand growled.

" 'Tis not for me to pass judgment on anyone. God gives us a will to do with what we please. Whether it will please Him, however . . ." He trailed off with a one-shouldered shrug.

Rand was in no mood for evasive words. Not tonight. "Where is Clyde? If Josselyn is his niece, why is he not here, demanding her release?"

He thought the old bard would not reply. Then Newlin

chuckled. "She is his niece and he will be here soon enough. But consider: a woman with the power to start a war has also the power to forge peace. I would speak with her," he added abruptly.

Without waiting for an answer, he started toward the guarded building and after a moment Rand followed, shaking his head. The woman had him doubting his own judgment. But his judgment had been sound and he vowed not to allow her to affect him like that again.

That decided, he assessed the situation. He trusted Newlin, but only up to a point. Josselyn he did not trust at all— except for her physical response to him. He trusted her passions. But the passions of the flesh were a new thing for her. Her passionate feelings for her people and lands had always been a part of her. He would put nothing past her when it came to her desire to escape and wed Owain.

"Newlin!" she gasped when the bard entered. She lay on Rand's bed, but fully clothed. When she spied him behind the bard, her expression of relief changed to one of suspicion. She scrambled off the high bed. "Will you grant me no privacy at all? Can I not even converse with a friend?"

"Be glad I allow you to see him at all. You are my prisoner, not my guest."

Her glare was lethal. Had she access to the dagger she'd used on the cheese, Rand was certain she would have lunged furiously at him. As it was, she skewered him with her eyes, making it more than clear that she'd like to tear him to shreds and spread his entrails across the tamped earth floor.

In return he gave her a bland smile, settled himself in his chair, and gestured with one hand. "Proceed with your visit—but in English only, else I shall be forced to ask Newlin to leave. Go ahead. Talk. The hour grows late and I am weary. It has been a long day," he added, broadening his smile.

She turned away from him, but he saw anger in her stiff

posture and the rigid set of her jaw. When she spoke to Newlin, however, her voice was low and carefully modulated.

"Does my uncle know where I am?"

The bard had been shuffling slowly around the room, observing the newly built structure, running a hand over the rough stone surface, sniffing the wood of the door and window frame. " 'Tis English oak. You brought it with you?" he asked Rand.

"If I must build here in this land of stone, I can at least bring the finest wood with me."

"If you *must* build here?" Josselyn interjected. "Didn't you *want* to build here? Isn't that why you came here, to claim lands that are rightfully ours?"

He hadn't meant to reveal his reluctance to come to Wales, but as he studied her he decided it did not matter if she knew the truth. Perhaps it was for the best. "Henry sent me. Once I secure these lands—build a castle and bring peace to my people and yours—I will return to London."

"So you don't intend to stay."

"No." But although Rand was certain of his answer, he was less certain how he felt about it. Josselyn ap Carreg Du undoubtedly was thrilled to know he would someday depart her lands. What she did not yet understand was that he might leave, but the English presence never would. Eventually he would send for his brother to take his place. Even Jasper would be able to keep the peace in these hills once the walls of Rosecliffe Castle were complete.

Then an unexpected thought occurred to him—a logical yet repugnant thought. What if he made Jasper marry Josselyn?

There was much to be said for such a match. It would aid him in achieving the peace he sought, and they would undoubtedly be attracted to one another. After all, Jasper was not particular when it came to women. In truth, the randy lad stuck his prick in anything that moved—no doubt to compensate for the celibate years he'd spent preparing for a life in the Church. As for Josselyn, she was passionate enough to find contentment with Jasper. Women fawned over the half-grown pup as if he were a deity.

Yes, it would be a wise match and he should have thought of it sooner. But the very idea set Rand's teeth on edge. He glared at Josselyn, angry at her, at Jasper, and even the king for putting him in so untenable a situation.

"Get on with your visit," he ordered. "As you can see, she's not been harmed, nor will she be, so long as she does as she is told."

"As I am told? I wonder just what it is you will *tell* me to do," she sneered right back at him. She turned, appealing to Newlin. "He has locked me in his private chamber. How safe can that be? My uncle will never stand for it," she swore, aiming her venom once more at Rand.

"He has no choice," Rand retorted. "Answer me, Newlin. Does Clyde miss his niece yet? Why has he not approached me—or are you sent here tonight as his messenger?"

"I cannot speak for him, for he has not yet returned to the village."

"Not returned?" Josselyn swung back to face Rand. "What have you done to him?"

"Me? I've done nothing—"

"You've stolen me from the safety of my family and dispatched at least two of the guards in the process. Oh, Newlin." She spun back to the bard and took his hands in hers. "Tell me he has not been harmed. That no one has been harmed!"

Newlin managed somehow to circle her smaller hands with his. "No *Cymry* have died this day."

"Then where is he?"

Rand stood there, frowning. Then in a rush, understanding came. "He thinks Owain has stolen you! He's gone to seek you at Afon Bryn."

Josselyn opened her mouth as if to deny such a ridiculous

accusation, then immediately closed it. She stared balefully at Rand but he could see the truth dawn in her face.

Henry had advised him that the Welsh were a fractious lot, always at odds with one another. But he had not suspected the alliance between the Lloyds and the people of Carreg Du to be so tenuous that they would suspect one another before suspecting an enemy common to them both. He grinned at the irony of the situation.

"I'm right, aren't I, Newlin? Aren't I, Josselyn?" he added in a smug tone. Then he laughed, enjoying her stony silence. "I'll leave the two of you now. Send whatever messages you wish, Josselyn. It will change naught. You are my hostage against any Welsh attacks on my men. I've already sent that message to Clyde, but you can confirm it to him, Newlin. So long as he does not harm my people, I will not harm his."

The diminutive bard fastened his one good eye first on Josselyn, then on Rand. "When I speak with Clyde it will be of my own observations. He will ask me how his niece fares, and I will tell him. He will ask your true intentions." The ageless fellow paused. "I will tell him that as well."

Rand met the bard's unblinking gaze. "And just what do you think my true intentions are?"

It was Josselyn who answered. "That you seek to rule us and force your vile English ways on us despite the fact that you hate our lands and can hardly wait to leave here." She stood, eyes flashing in the candlelight, her hair wild about her shoulders, her fists planted belligerently on her hips.

She would never be content in London. That aberrant thought struck painfully in Rand's consciousness. She was too wild, too passionate in her convictions. Too much a part of her beloved wildwood. She would make an apt wife for the Lord of Rosecliffe, but she would be like a tethered bird in the smelly sprawl of London. He'd captured her, but with a sinking feeling he knew he would never possess her nor have the true pleasure of her.

Swallowing an oath, he forced that last absurd thought away. The only pleasure he'd ever wanted of her was the use of her body, which possibility was not yet fully thwarted. Unless, of course, he did wed her to Jasper.

This time he cursed out loud. "Make it brief," he snapped to Newlin. "'Tis late and I do not relish sleeping outside. I caution you, wench. Do not make me sorry I have offered you the comfort of my quarters." Then angry at Josselyn, at Newlin, and especially at himself, he strode from the room and slammed the door with what he meant to be authority, but which he suspected sounded more like pique.

In the wake of his stormy departure, Josselyn wilted, like a sail bereft suddenly of the winds needed to power it forward. She slumped onto the bed and raised mournful eyes to the bard. "Oh, Newlin. What am I to do now?"

"I do not believe he means you any harm, child."

"Just because he hasn't shackled me to a wall or denied me food and water doesn't mean he will not harm me," she muttered.

Newlin smiled his sweet, one-sided smile. "He would cut off his own hand before allowing any harm to befall you."

She grimaced. "You mistake him for a man of honor."

"I see what I see."

"You see more than the rest of us." She crossed the room and knelt before him. "Tell me what to do, how to escape and best help our people."

"If you escape there will be war. Does that help your people?"

"They are not just my people, they are your people too. And yes. To be free of English rule—is that so bad a thing?"

He was quiet a long, somber moment. Then he roused as if from a place only he could visit. "The stones do grow."

"What?"

"Yonder. All around us." He gestured wide with his shriveled arm.

"The walls he builds? Is that what you mean?" Josselyn asked with a sinking heart. "Is that what the prediction means?"

" 'When stones shall grow and trees shall no'.' "

Josselyn sprang to her feet, frightened now as she'd not been before. "Then we must tumble these walls of his before they can grow. I must escape, Newlin. I must! Will you help me?" she pleaded. "Will you?"

He patted her hand. That was the only reassurance he gave her. "Listen and learn, my child. I will speak with your uncle when he returns. We will see what we will see. Do not trouble yourself with matters you cannot control."

"But what of those matters I can control, or at least influence for the better? 'Tis those matters I *must* trouble myself with."

"Listen and learn," he repeated. "And do not fret."

Do not fret.

Josselyn sat on the floor after the old bard left. She wrapped her arms around her knees and heard the echo of Newlin's last words. Do not fret. How could she possibly not fret?

She raised her head and stared around her. Her prison was sturdy and strong. And snug. Though new and without the softening effect of plaster and painted walls, or of rugs and tapestries, it was nevertheless a pleasing space with high ceilings and a good chimney. But pleasing or no, it was still a prison.

She searched it with her eyes, seeking a weak spot, a way to escape. The wind rattled the shutter as if it battled to get in, just as she battled to get out, and she rose and crossed to it.

Locked from without.

Frustrated, she banged on the solid wood, hurting her fists but not caring. "*Mochyn ofnadwy!* Disgusting pig!"

"Go to sleep," a low voice growled from just beyond the shutter.

She leapt back as if stung, then glared at the wood, imagining Randulf Fitz Hugh's smug face just beyond it. *"Cil lwfr,"* she spat.

"Hmm. *Ci.* That means dog. I'll hazard a guess. I'm some sort of lowly dog. Am I right?"

"Mochyn! I despise you, you coward. You're a snake. *Sarff y."* Her chest heaved with emotion. In that moment she wanted nothing more than to kill him with her own hands.

The shutter creaked. "I desire you. *Fi dymuno ti."*

Josselyn gasped and jerked away from the window. From anger to confusion to panic—her heart pounded a painful rhythm beyond her control. "Well, I . . . I do *not* desire you. I hate you. You . . . you repulse me."

"Shall we put your words to the test?"

Rand rattled the shutter. When there was no response he rattled it again. Damn, but he desired the feisty wench! He was hard, just standing outside the window, knowing she was alone inside his private quarters. He took two hefty gulps from the wineskin he held.

"What's wrong, Josselyn? Have you no quick retort to that?" He settled his shoulder against the stone wall and placed his hand flat against the shutter. He had but to remove the hastily added latch to open the shutter. She would not be so tart-tongued once reminded of her easy capitulation to him in the forest. And she still a virgin.

He groaned at the painful surge of blood to his loins. Why did no woman of the English court affect him this way? Even DeLisle's daughter whom he'd hoped to wed had done little to arouse his lust. But this Welsh wench—

"What ho? Denied entrance to your own quarters, are you?" a cheerful voice called out from behind him.

Rand pushed away from the wall, cursing himself for a fool—and cursing Osborn for pointing it out. Behind Osborn he saw the shadow of another man. Alan. And both had celebrated the day's success with more than a little wine.

"Methinks she has a hold of his balls, Alan. What say you?"

Alan grinned. He was not normally so familiar with his liege lord, but Osborn's good humor, together with the wine, conspired to banish his caution. "She has small, slender hands. But they look strong."

"Strong enough to bring the mighty Fitz Hugh to heel?" Osborn pressed.

"Enough!" Rand growled. Bad enough they jested at his expense. For Josselyn to overhear them would be even worse.

"I say take the wench and have done with it," Alan announced, then belched.

Rand shouldered past the two, shoving Alan flat onto his back. "Enough!"

But Osborn was not intimidated by Rand's foul mood. He strolled along behind him, just out of reach. "Is the lad's suggestion such a poor one? Methinks 'tis precisely to your liking. So why not relieve your discomfort? Unless you fear she will refuse you."

"She will not refuse me." Rand swung around to face his tormentors. "She will not refuse me. But I have other plans for her."

"Other plans? What other plans?" Osborn laughed.

"Jasper."

He should not have spoken his half-formed thoughts. But once said, it could not be taken back, and now his brother's name hung in the darkness between them, a word—an idea—that would not go away.

"Jasper?" Alan pushed to his feet and again belched. "You're givin' that armful to Jasper? Why should he—" He broke off when Osborn elbowed him in the ribs.

"What about Jasper?" Osborn asked. His jocularity had turned serious. "D'ye mean you will marry the Welsh-woman to Jasper?"

Rand clenched his fists. It made perfect sense, and yet some part of him was loath to commit himself to the idea.

When he did not answer, Osborn approached him, a curious look on his face. " 'Tis a wise plan. Wise, indeed."

"At the moment it doesn't feel wise," Rand grunted. He wanted her. Everyone knew it. But if she *were* to be Jasper's wife someday . . . "Bloody hell," he muttered, struggling to quell his unreasonable desire for her. Marrying her to Jasper would solve a mountain of problems. He refused to lose a political opportunity over a woman. He'd made that mistake with Marianne. He would not do so again. He could resolve his physical needs with someone else. Anyone else.

Steeling himself, he met his old friend's eye. "Jasper has proven good for little beyond wenching. He failed as a man of God. He sees Henry's court not as a political opportunity, but as a royal brothel. The boy's only talent is women. He should be able to tame this one easily enough."

Osborn considered that a long, silent moment. "Will he agree?"

Jasper had pleaded eloquently to be allowed to accompany Rand to Wales, to have a part in quelling the difficult Welsh. But Rand had denied him that chance. To offer it now, sweetened by a woman . . .

"He'll agree," Rand muttered.

"Will you send a messenger to him, then?"

Rand tilted his wineskin up to his lips and took a long pull before answering. "Come the morn I'll prepare a letter." Then unwilling to discuss the matter further, he turned and strode away.

Osborn watched him go, not as pleased with this turn of events as he'd thought he'd be. "He's givin' his brother the woman he wants."

Alan took that as a signal Osborn wanted to discuss the matter further. "He don't plan to stay here forever, you know. What would he do with a Welsh wife at court?"

Osborn didn't bother to answer.

In her stone prison Josselyn sank down from the shut-tered window and leaned heavily against the cold, rough wall. Osborn had not answered Alan because the answer was so obvious. Randulf Fitz Hugh would not marry a Welshwoman, but he'd thrust her at his brother, this man they called Jasper. This man who was good for little beyond wenching, it seemed.

A sob rose in her throat but she ruthlessly quelled it. From one unwelcome marriage to the next she was thrust. A cruel Welshman. A womanizing Englishman. Mean-while, the one man she might consider would not consider her—

No! she told herself. No. She would never consider wed-ding herself to the likes of Randulf Fitz Hugh. Even if he begged her. He was her enemy. That was all he ever could be.

She had to escape, she told herself, staring wildly about. She could not resign herself to the unhappy fate Rand planned for her. Perhaps if she used the candle to fire the roof. They would rush in to save her and in the confusion she could escape.

Then she sighed and looked instead at the bed that stood in the alcove. She was weary beyond the telling, and drained by the extremes of her emotions. Tomorrow would be soon enough to escape. Tomorrow she would come up with a better plan.

Tomorrow she would wreak havoc on Rand's devious plotting. But for tonight, she would sleep.

Eleven

Sleep brought Josselyn little solace, for she dreamed of stones sprouting in the fields, of stones growing around her as she sat or ate or slept. Of stones that encircled her and would not let her go. Then she was jolted from those dreams by the shout of a guard and a rude banging at the door.

"Rouse yourself, Mistress Josselyn. Your uncle's come a-callin'."

She flew from the bed and across the still dark room to the door. "He's coming here?"

"Aye." She recognized the voice as belonging to Alan. "Make yourself pretty, love. There's an ewer of water and a bucket for your other needs."

Other needs, indeed! Men were all pigs! She tried the latch. "Unlock the door."

She heard him laugh. "What? And risk havin' my head bit off? Not likely. Unlockin' this door is a chore Rand reserves for himself alone. Go on, now. Get yourself ready. They should be here directly."

Josselyn bathed her face and arms and rinsed her mouth only because she could not sit still as she waited. She spied a bone comb but refused to use it. Bad enough she'd dozed in his bed; she would not use his personal articles, for it implied an intimacy they would never share. Never, she swore.

So she finger-combed her tangled hair and nervously plaited and replaited the heavy length of it as she waited. And all the while she strained to hear.

From a distance she caught the sound of men's voices, an angry hum, a word here and there accented with threat. But no clash of weapons. No ring of steel on steel, thank God.

The room was still and dim. She'd left one candle burning and it bravely fought back the dark. Dawn was still a long way off. Then the guard outside scrambled to his feet and the sound of boots on the gravelly hillside sounded an alarm in her head. Rand had come for her!

The lock rattled; the door swung wide. But it was only Osborn. In the circle of light cast by his lantern he gave her a frankly curious look. "Your uncle wants a look at you, to make sure you've not been harmed."

"Am I to be allowed to speak to him?" she asked in chilly tones.

"I don't expect so. Of course, if you were to try, there's no tellin' what you might be able to wheedle out of Rand. But I suppose you know that."

He had a hold of her arm and he looked straight ahead as they walked across the encampment, so Josselyn could not make out his expression any better than she could decipher his words. Was he advising her to be nicer to Rand? To seduce him?

But that made no sense. Why would he want her to do such a thing?

There was no time to ponder the inconsistencies of Randulf Fitz Hugh's captain, however, for ahead of them two groups of warriors faced one another across the wide footing where the wall had begun to rise. The rest of the English contingent spread along the curving inside length of the fledgling wall. They bristled with swords and axes and pikes. Warrior and stonemason alike, they all looked fierce and ready to fight to the death for this small piece of Wales they'd laid claim to.

By contrast, her uncle's band posed no real threat. A dozen men. Not as many even as the first time they'd approached the English camp.

Josselyn did not understand his subdued show of strength. He should have everyone here. He should put on as fierce a front as Randulf Fitz Hugh did. Not that she wanted them to fight. In truth, that was the last thing she wanted.

"He must be a wise man, your uncle," Osborn observed when he bade her stop a good twenty paces back from the wall. She glanced up at him and he grinned. " 'Tis clear he came to talk, not to fight. You must be very important to him."

Josselyn stared across the darkness to where her uncle stood. He looked weary. He looked old. The palaver with Owain and his father had been strain enough for Clyde. How much worse this new turn of events must weigh upon him. He'd never wanted to lead their family, but he'd stepped up to the responsibility when his brother had been killed. Always he had led them as much as possible toward peace, sometimes to the frustration of hotter heads than his own. He'd also played the role of father to the angry and confused young girl she'd been.

Her gaze swept over her aging uncle with an affection she seldom acknowledged. He was a good man caught in the midst of a terrible dilemma. There was no one right choice to make. Every decision carried some promise of success and some threat of disaster. The least she could do was make this situation easier for him.

She raised her hand in salute and he acknowledged the gesture with a nod. He started toward her until Rand blocked his way. At the sight of her captor Josselyn sucked in a breath—half fear for her uncle, half another, darker emotion. The English lord was so tall, so broad of shoulder. In a battle he would do grave harm to her uncle or to any other man he faced. He could hurt her too, if he chose to. But she didn't think he meant her any harm.

An echo of Osborn's amused remark sounded in her ear. *There's no tellin' what you might be able to wheedle out of Rand.* Was that true?

She looked sidelong at Osborn. "I don't want anyone to fight on account of me."

"It may be too late for that, love," he answered, without removing his eyes from the two men in the circle of light.

Josselyn caught him by the arm. "No. You misunderstand me. I am willing to stay as a hostage to peace. You must tell my uncle that. Or let me tell him."

Osborn swung his head around and studied her. "What accounts for this meekness? To hear Rand tell it, you are a termagant, a wild Welsh wench. But here you are, mild as a lamb."

"Lamb or termagant, it matters not! You must tell my uncle I consent to this situation—odious as it is," she added, bristling at his amusement.

Osborn laughed then signaled Alan. "Keep a tight hold on the wily wench. I've a message to deliver."

In the cold circle of flickering torchlight Rand met Clyde's cold glare. "So long as you keep peace with me, she shall be treated well."

"And I have your word on that," Clyde scoffed after the translator spoke. "The word of a thievin' Englishman."

Rand stiffened at the insult but he did not rise to it. The man was entitled to a certain amount of anger. If Rand expected the Welsh not to strike back at him when he kidnapped one of their own, the least he could do was restrain his temper in the face of their insult.

"She will be treated as well as any lady could hope for."

"If you think to keep peace in this way, you are a fool. She is betrothed to Owain ap Madoc, and he will not stand for this. Nor will the rest of his kin. They will join me in opposing you."

"And thereby risk her safety?" Rand shook his head. "So long as there is peace she is safe. But if you rally your forces against me, you will lose her—and lose the battle as well." Rand stopped when Osborn approached. "What is it?" he muttered.

"Mistress Josselyn bids me deliver a message to her uncle."

Rand frowned. Osborn should know better than to interrupt this way. But his captain's eyes were steady and Rand's tension eased. "Go ahead then; deliver it."

"Well, man? What does she say?" The Welsh translator interpreted Clyde's anxious words.

Osborn faced Clyde respectfully. "She bids me tell you that she will stay willingly as hostage if it will keep peace. She does not wish for anyone to die," he added.

A deep satisfaction settled over Rand. She was a smart lass, and loyal to her people. He watched Clyde as Osborn's words were repeated in Welsh. The old man's brow furrowed and he stared past Rand to the place where Josselyn must stand. Rand resisted the urge to turn and look at her too, but instead concentrated on the Welsh leader. And when Clyde again met his gaze, he knew he'd won this skirmish.

The older man studied him a long moment before speaking. The translator said, "I need some assurances. She needs a chaperone. It is not seemly that she stay alone in a camp with only men."

It was Rand's turn to frown. A chaperone? He hadn't anticipated that. Then again, if he truly meant to wed her to Jasper, a chaperone made sense. Brutally he beat back his own selfish desire for her. Politics came first and if he did not concede this one point Clyde would have no reason to trust him. And in the meantime he could send for Jasper and decide whether this plan of his would work.

"A chaperone is a worthy idea, but I doubt any Welshwoman will want to spend all her time among us, and I am not willing to allow any of your people the freedom to come and go in my camp. I propose a compromise. I will allow Newlin an occasional visit."

Clyde frowned. "That is not the same as having a woman at her side."

"It will have to do. I trust the bard, as I gather you and Josselyn do also. It is either him or no one."

Clyde stared at him, working his jaw back and forth. "Very well. For now." He paused, then added, "Naught can come of this."

"I want naught, save peace," Rand answered.

"Eventually you must release her to us."

"When my walls are tall enough to ensure the peace, then I will return her safely to you."

Their eyes met and held. Clyde ap Llewelyn might be beyond his prime, but he was not afraid. Nevertheless, it was clear the man did not relish the idea of war. But there was still the question of Owain ap Madoc. "Tell me of this man you have betrothed her to."

Clyde shrugged. "You will find him more difficult to deal with than I."

"Has he no care for her safety, then? Ah, but this is a political match." Rand answered his own question. "If he cannot have her to wife, you cannot have his forces to combine with your own."

Clyde's eyes glittered. "You have taken something Owain has laid claim to. He will not allow the slight to go unanswered."

"Then it falls to you to restrain him." *If you can,* Rand silently added. A part of him wanted to see this man who would wed Josselyn, to test his own strength against him and lay him low while Josselyn watched. He wanted to vanquish the man she'd pledged herself to, and see her glory in his victory. He wanted her to open her arms gladly to him afterward—

No! He gritted his teeth against the perverse image that had so swiftly taken root in his head. He had no intention of fighting Owain ap Madoc for a woman. For land, yes. But not for a woman.

He scowled at Clyde. "Well, old man? I offer you peace but I am fully prepared to wrest it from you at the point of my sword, if I must."

The wiry translator glared his hatred, but Clyde was more restrained in his response. "I will send Newlin to visit her. But we are not done with these talks, Englishman. Your people have come before, and you have not lasted. This time will be no different."

Oh, but it would, Rand vowed as the man strode away, head high and shoulders square. He'd come here to establish a permanent stronghold for this rebellious part of the English realm. He might not intend to stay forever, but Jasper and his heirs would.

He looked over and spied Josselyn. She was watching her uncle's departure, but as if she sensed the touch of Rand's gaze, she turned toward him. At once he felt the rise of an urgent desire. She looked like a wild creature of the night with her face pink from the cold and her hair coming loose at her temples. Alan kept a firm grip on her arm, but she seemed oblivious to the man.

She stared at Rand and more than anything he wondered what she thought. Despite the practical voice that warned him away from her, he crossed to where she stood.

"You may go," he told Alan, who promptly released her arm. But the smirking puppy did not go away, he simply stepped back a few paces and, like Osborn, continued to observe Rand and Josselyn.

Rand fixed them both with a lethal glare. "Good night."

With a wink and a sly look the pair melted into the darkness of the predawn. Only then did he turn to Josselyn.

She stood, staring now at the place where her uncle had been, staring in the direction of her home village, he realized. She looked both brave and vulnerable, like the willows along the river that bent before the winds, yet always survived to stand tall another day.

He resisted the urge to touch her. "Your message was timely. It eased a difficult moment and I thank you."

"I did not do it for you."

"I did not think you had." *Stubborn wench. Look at me!*

Slowly her head turned. "How long will it take to build your wall?"

"You mean, how long must you suffer in our midst? I remind you, Josselyn, that you are the one who first sought my company. 'Tis you who sought employment in my camp. If our presence did not offend you then, I see no reason why it should do so now."

Her eyes glittered with emotion. "I came then to learn what I could of the enemy that had invaded our lands under the guise of peace. Do not make more of it than there is."

"Ah, but there is more," he replied, galled by her easy dismissal of those first days of their acquaintance. "You have laughed with me, or have you forgotten? You have kissed me." He lowered his voice to a husky whisper. "You have trembled in my arms."

Her answer was to start stiffly for her new lodgings, but he caught her by the arm. "Do you deny it?" he persisted. "You have trembled with passion in my embrace. I can make you do so again."

"Then you are even more vile than I thought. Would you force me? Would you force me, then turn around and wed me to your own brother?"

He released her so fast she nearly fell. She had heard. How he wanted to deny those intentions, but he could not. So he said, "It is but one possibility. I have not yet made a final decision."

"*You* have not made a final decision. *You?* What of *my* final decision? I am as likely to agree to marry him as I am to marry a dog. Besides, I vow he will not be pleased to marry the shrew that he will fast discover me to be."

Rand felt a brief twinge of ill-placed humor. How he would enjoy seeing his younger brother rebuffed by an angry Josselyn. It would do the troublesome whelp a world

of good. But no matter how she tried to rebuff the lad, in
the end, if Rand deemed it politically expedient, she would
wed with Jasper. And he could find no humor in that at all.

"I'll be certain to warn him," he muttered.

"I will not be wed to him," she vowed. "I will not."
Then she turned and fled.

Rand did not stop her but instead followed. She was fast
but he knew he could overtake her should she try to escape.
But she did not try to flee the camp, and in the end, she
burst through the door of his own sturdy quarters. Before
she could turn and close the door against him, however, he
shoved his way in.

She was winded, as was he, and in the weak light of the
guttering candle she was more beautiful than ever. She
roused his blood like no other woman did, whether she
smiled on him, raged at him, or rejected him completely.

Could he truly see her wed to his own brother?

At that moment Rand did not think so.

"Get out," she ordered.

"These are my quarters."

"Then I will gladly leave them to you."

"I want you to stay."

A man in charge of his own fate—and hers—would not
have termed it so. Rand knew that at once. He should order
her to stay. Command her to stay. Force her to stay. Instead
he requested that she stay. A clear sign of his weakness for
her, he feared. Yet when confusion flickered in her vivid
eyes, he knew he'd somehow turned a key in the gate she'd
erected between them.

He closed the door behind him and the click of the latch
settling into place seemed to lock out everyone else. Her
uncle. His brother. Even the king and all the reasons that
had brought Rand to Wales.

"What are you doing?" she asked in a decidedly less
strident tone.

"Tomorrow Newlin may come to see to you. Tonight,
however, we are alone."

"I . . . We . . . we should not be alone. My uncle will be furious."

"Yes. No doubt he will. But will *you* be furious? That is what I must determine, Josselyn."

"This makes no sense!" She backed around the table. "You make no sense. First you make love to me, then you reject me for being an innocent. Then you take me hostage and say I must wed your brother, and yet here you are trying to . . . to . . ."

She trailed off, but Rand finished for her. "And here I am, trying again to make love to you."

"I am still a virgin. That stopped you once before. Mayhap the reminder will stop you again."

"No." He unfastened his sword belt and laid the weapon aside.

"I do not want this. You will have to force me."

"No. I won't." He shrugged out of his hauberk and tossed it onto a trunk.

"It will be rape, for I will never agree. You would rape me after promising my uncle I will be safe? You would rape the very woman you say you will give to your brother?"

He heard panic in her voice and saw fear in her flashing eyes. Fear and hatred. While he was confident he could eventually overcome her fear, her hatred was another thing entirely.

Though it pained him sorely, Rand knew he must change his tactics. Irritated, he flung himself into a chair, raised one booted foot, and plopped it on the table. "I will concede the point. For now. Nonetheless, I am loath to abandon these comfortable lodgings when they are so recently completed."

"Then I will abandon them."

"Ah, but this is the sturdiest building we have, and therefore the best prison for my hostage." He spread his arms to encompass the whole room. "It appears we will have to share it."

"No."

"We need not share the bed—unless you desire it." *As I desire it.*

She shook her head vehemently. "I do not trust you."

"Nor do I trust you. But we will manage despite that. Here, come remove my boots so that I may enjoy what little is left of this night. To sleep," he added when her eyes narrowed.

"Surely you jest! I have no intention whatsoever of serving you. You are my enemy and I refuse to offer you any sort of comfort. Nor will I—"

She jerked when his fist slammed down on the table, rattling the candle stand and a pewter dish. "Be grateful I am giving you a choice!" he exclaimed, frustrated by her obstinacy. "You are a prisoner here, not a guest, and you will work for your keep. Serve me in my bed, or serve me everywhere else. You choose. But do so quickly, else I will make the choice for you. I believe we both know what my choice will be."

It was no choice at all. He knew it; she knew it. He watched the play of emotions across her lovely face. The struggle between feelings and logic. That she hated him in that moment, he did not doubt. That she could control that emotion with logic, however, interested him even more. How often had he fought that same battle in his dealings with the king and his most powerful barons? To repress his true feelings, to tame them with logic and practicality, had brought him many rewards. A woman possessed of similar talents, however, was a novelty to him.

What a pity she was not English. With her courage and shrewdness, she would make a perfect wife for an ambitious lord.

But she was not English.

He clenched his teeth and repressed his own emotions beneath the iron hand of logic. "Decide. I grow weary of this cat and mouse game we play."

Fury sparked in her eyes. But she held it back, albeit

with considerable effort. He waggled his foot back and forth, and her eyes darted from his face to his leather boot and back again. "What sort of service do you mean—tending to your quarters and your possessions?"

"And my person," he added, enjoying the way her eyes darkened at his words.

"Perhaps you could be more specific." Her voice was laced with acid.

"Why certainly. You would help me dress. And undress." He waggled his foot once more. "You can start by removing my boots."

Ah, but victory was sweet, he thought when, after an endless hesitation, she started forward. He should have been disappointed. After all, he needed her in his bed more than he needed her to clean and scrub for him. But she would be dressing him—and undressing him—and that was a step in the right direction.

She muttered a curse when she reached the table. He wasn't sure of the meaning of the Welsh phrase, but he was certain it did not flatter him.

"I will also want to continue our lessons in the *Cymraeg* tongue," he said as she reached for his mud-encrusted boot.

"You trust me to teach you the correct meaning of words? How do you know I won't tell you wrong?"

"Perhaps you will tell me wrong. But as time goes by your anger will abate, Josselyn, and with it your need to oppose me. Now come. Enough of this contest of wills. Help me undress and we will sleep. The dawn comes soon enough, and our labors with it."

Josselyn knew he was right. She knew that it would not benefit her to oppose him any further. He'd given her an alternative to his bed, and for now she must content herself with that. After all, she'd resigned herself to a marriage with Owain. In truth, serving Randulf Fitz Hugh was not nearly so loathsome a task as lying with the cruel Owain.

For a moment she allowed herself to wonder. What would lying with Rand be like?

Not loathsome, she admitted, then immediately condemned herself for so traitorous a response. She would serve him as he ordered, but she would *not* succumb to his masculine wiles. And if he thought to seduce her by their proximity, he had much to learn of Welsh pride. She would listen and learn and somehow try to escape. She would not end up naked in his bed with his hard warrior's body sliding over hers—

"Gwrtaith," she cursed again. Then she reached for the boot and began to pull.

The boots proved to be easy; the stockings far less so. For his stockings were warm, and once removed, they revealed portions of his person she'd not previously laid eyes upon. Large pale feet. Strong ankles and muscular calves sprinkled with dark hair.

He was not as dirty as most men. Her nose wrinkled. Nor did he stink. Those were intimate details about him, however, that she did not wish to know.

"Now my chainse," he said, leaning forward and extending his arms.

Josselyn flinched and scrambled to her feet. He did not grab at her though. Rather, it was his laced cuffs he wanted her to untie.

He grinned at her discomfiture. "I know my English clothing is unlike the garb of your people, but surely these simple lacings are not beyond your ken."

She could get through this, she told herself. She could. Without speaking, she made swift work of the laces, then rudely tugged the loose garment over his shoulder and head. "I will wash this in the morning," she muttered, refusing to look at his naked chest. Unfortunately, the linen shirt, even warmer than his socks, unsettled her as much as did the man.

"What of my braies? The crossbandings are knotted."

"You are well able to manage them on your own." She backed away from him, flinging the chainse into a corner.

"I am well able to manage all my clothing needs on my

own. That is not in question. Since you will not attend my other needs, you must attend these. Remove my braies.''

Rand waited, watching her, aroused by her presence, annoyed by the predicament she put him in. He wanted her, yet to take her when she would be of more use wed to Jasper was unwise indeed. But that didn't prevent him from wanting her all the same. This game they played was frustrating, and yet he could not make himself stop.

Josselyn was no less frustrated herself. He was a man like any other, and yet unlike any other. Bower was as tall; Owain as brawny. Dulas had bluer eyes and Dryw a more charming manner. Added to that they were all Welsh, whereas he was a hated Englishman. Yet it still remained that he was the one who stirred her senses. None of those others made her skin tingle or her breathing cease. None of them. She hated him, and yet he moved her in ways she did not comprehend.

Still, that did not mean he could defeat her.

She lifted her chin to a defiant angle. ''Very well.'' Gritting her teeth—staring anywhere but at his naked chest and arms—she crossed to him. He stood as she knelt to fumble with the crossbanding knotted just below his knees. Beneath her fingers he was warm. Her entire body heated from the warmth he radiated.

Somehow she freed one knot, then concentrated on the other. It loosened, but before she could back away she felt his hand in her hair.

''Josselyn . . .''

She foolishly looked up, up the impressive length of him, past his thighs and loins, and broad muscled chest, to meet his overheated gaze. His palm cupped her cheek and for an endless moment she was caught in the trap he'd set, caught by his tantalizing allure, by the forbidden nature of it. She knew he was aroused. The bulge in his braies was not an excess of linen.

Unfortunately, she was aroused too. At least that must be what these foreign feelings were. Her heart raced; she barely remembered to breathe; and every portion of her, from toes to belly to cheeks, was on fire.

"Josselyn," he repeated, and were it not for the English cadence of his pronunciation, she would have been lost. But he spoke as an Englishman and that one fact drew her back to reality.

With a cry of dismay she scrambled backward. "I am done. Are you satisfied? Now let me be. Let me be!"

She did not dare look at him again—she was that weak— and she prayed fervently that he was satisfied with the torture he'd already inflicted upon her. Only when she had barricaded herself in the corner, with a rug wrapped around her and her cloak over all, did she allow herself a sidelong peek at him.

He had turned away from her, though the sight of his naked back was no less disturbing than his naked front. Still, it signified that he would trouble her no more this night. She heard his harsh breathing. She watched him strip off the loose braies.

She should have looked away, but she could not. Beneath his small cloth his arousal appeared even more pronounced.

"You see what you do to me."

Her eyes jerked up to meet his. But there was no amusement in his face this time. Only honesty, and that affected her more than anything else might have. He stroked himself once and groaned, and it set her already simmering senses aflame.

Then he blew out the candle and she heard the creak of the ropes as he climbed onto his bed.

What you do to me. She heard his words echo in the dark. She did that to him. Did that mean he knew what he did to her? She stifled her own groan and shifted miserably in her corner.

"If you change your mind, there is room up here for you," he said into the lively silence.

"I won't," she swore in a hoarse voice.

"You might."

She would not bandy words with him, she told herself. Besides, she feared the truth too much to tempt the fates by lying. For the truth was, a wicked, wanton part of her wanted to accept his invitation. To add to her fears, she realized that with enough time and provocation she might very well give in to that temptation.

Sweet Mary, but she needed to escape before that happened.

Twelve

Owain ap Madoc rode into the village like a marauder. Dogs tucked their tails and ran. Women snatched up their children and hid in their houses. The men, taken by surprise, raced for their weapons.

Had Owain meant them harm, Clyde realized, he could have slaughtered people at will and set the village aflame before a substantial opposition could have been raised.

Clyde clenched his fingers around the stout oak staff he carried and waited for Madoc's rebellious son to approach him. The late dawn had brought with it a cold rain. It was that which had muffled the horses' hooves of the dozen riders. Otherwise the watch would have sounded an earlier warning. Besides, Clyde reasoned, they had no cause to expect an attack from anyone. The English enemy held Josselyn precisely to prevent the advent of war. And the village had no reason to expect attack from fellow countrymen, not when they all faced a much greater enemy.

So why did his heart hammer as if battle were imminent?

Because Owain ap Madoc was unpredictable and cruel. The man seemed possessed of a need periodically to let blood. If he had no real enemies to fight, he was wont to fashion one from imagined slights and insults. Not for the first time Clyde wondered if marrying Josselyn to Owain would prove to be of any real use.

Dewey ran up, gasping for breath, his round face red from exertion. "He wants to attack. To retrieve Josselyn from the Englishman by force."

Of course he did, Clyde thought. In a pitched battle Clyde could be easily killed; whether by an English weapon or Welsh one would not matter to Owain. A few other key losses and all of Carreg Du would then be vulnerable to Owain's greed. It was not enough that he marry Josselyn and thereby make his claim. He needed to leave his mark on Clyde's people, to make his imprint. To leave no one in any doubt about who was the most powerful lord in this northernmost part of Wales.

Clyde grimaced. He should never have convinced Josselyn to wed the brute!

"You have lost my bride!" Owain accused Clyde as he pulled his wild-eyed steed to a plunging halt just short of trampling Clyde. Clyde met Owain's scowl with a scowl of his own.

"She is not lost but stolen, as I informed your father."

Owain's eyes flashed with dangerous fire. "And what plan do you make to get her back?"

Clyde met the younger man's challenging stare. "I do not intend to attack the English camp until I am certain he will not make good on his threat to harm her."

"In other words, you plan to do nothing but sit here and wring your hands. Like a woman," he added with a sneer. Then he spat on the ground in front of Clyde's feet.

Dewey's hand flew to his sword grip, but Clyde stayed him with a quick hold of his wrist. He stared unflinchingly at Owain. "Finesse will carry us further than brute strength, for the English possess more brute strength than do we."

"So you say. I'll trust my own judgment—"

"On my lands you will trust *my* judgment!"

As if a signal had sounded, an ugly silence fell. The two men glared at one another, the one young and fiery, the other older, calmer, but equally adamant. As the silence stretched out, the men of Carreg Du gathered round their leader, some mounted now, as were their tenuous allies.

There was no predicting Owain's reaction, Clyde knew. But he would not allow the headstrong man to bully him, or to jeopardize Josselyn's safety. On impulse Clyde stepped forward and caught Owain's mount's lead. "Dismount and take refreshment with us. I will relate my conversation with Randulf Fitz Hugh."

"You would have us talk while that bastard ravishes my bride!"

"He is a man of his word, I think, and of some level of honor. Rape is not a part of his plan." Clyde tightened his hold, keeping the horse's head low. "Dismount, Owain. Share in our hospitality as we work to free my niece—and our lands—of this new oppression."

After a long breathless silence, Owain relented. But even when he did as Clyde asked, even when he and his lieutenant, Glyn, entered Clyde's home with a grudging show of civility, Clyde felt the weight of a dark despair. Was he to free Josselyn of one oppressor only to deliver her to another? "Where is your esteemed father?" he asked as he waited for Nessie to serve them her best wine.

Owain grunted. "He awaits my message. Should we require more men, he will come."

They would require no further men, Clyde swore to himself. His judgment might have been lacking in the past. His caution might have been too great. But he was not so foolhardy as to welcome an even larger contingent of men under Owain's control into his village.

He'd been a fool to think linking his family to Owain's would ease tensions between them. If anything, it had emboldened the ruthless fellow. No, this matter of Josselyn's freedom was up to him to negotiate. But how he would deal with two enemies vying for his niece was a matter with no easy answers. Perhaps, he feared, no answers at all.

*   *   *

After the long day of physical exertion, Rand should have slept like a dead man. Instead he tossed restlessly in his bed, unable, despite his profound weariness, to find any relief in sleep.

It was due to Josselyn, of course. Though she had kept as still as a frightened mouse, huddled down in her rug, Rand had been unable to ignore her presence. He'd lain there, half waking, half sleeping, remembering tales from his youth and confusing her with the women in them. Paris and Menelaus had fought battles over Helen of Troy. Would he be forced to battle for Josselyn of Wales? The ancient King Arthur had been devastated by a woman. Would he suffer the same fate?

Now, though dawn barely nicked the horizon, he threw back the plain wool blanket and rose from his torturous bed. "Up, woman." He faced the huddled lump in the corner. "Your duties begin when I rise, and I am risen."

"Ci ffiaidd."

He heard the muttered invective and took a perverse pleasure at her obvious ill humor. If he had to suffer for her presence, then by damn, so must she suffer for his. "Up," he repeated. "Fetch me water and help me with my morning ablutions."

With another curse she shoved the rug down and glared bleary-eyed out into the dim room. *"Myfi casau ti.* That means I despise you," she translated. Unfortunately, her voice, made husky by her slumber, imparted a different sort of message entirely. She was rosy from sleep. He could see that even in the shadowy light. Her hair was loose and tangled, and her clothing rumpled and askew. Altogether a delectable eyeful, were it not for the baleful expression on her face.

"I have needs of my own," she muttered. "Needs I must attend before I can tend any of yours. In private," she added when he did not immediately respond.

"Of course," he answered when her words belatedly registered. He pointed in the direction of the chamber pot, then turned for the door. "Be quick about it. There is water in the ewer."

She did not thank him. He did not expect her to. His disappointment, however, was not for her lack of appreciation but rather that he wanted to hear her voice again, that low thrum of feminine warmth, that breathy, arousing murmur, even if it was only to curse him anew. Something in her voice aroused him and though he should not want her to exercise any more power over him than she already wielded, a part of him could not resist. He wanted her husky words breathed in his ear. He wanted her, warm and tousled from sleep, lying in his bed beside him. Wrapped in his arms.

The foolish desires of a lunatic, he told himself as he opened the door, stepped outside, and slammed it closed behind him. Then he breathed deep of the bracingly cold air and willed sanity back into his head. Letting a woman dominate his thoughts was a colossal mistake. Letting one who was his avowed enemy do so could be deadly.

Around him the camp stretched and yawned, slowly coming awake. The morning shift had already relieved the night guards and the castle workers were rising now to begin their labors. Nothing had changed, he reassured himself. And now, thanks to yesterday's daring raid, nothing would. He'd purchased additional security when he'd captured Clyde's niece. He'd secured time enough to finish the first tier of the wall. Though the Welsh were bound to bluster and threaten him, so long as he kept her safe, he was certain they would not attack the camp directly.

Then Rand spied Osborn headed his way, scowling, and his self-satisfaction began to wane.

"Who's to cook?" Osborn demanded without preamble, before he'd even reached Rand's side. "The women did not come and the fire in the kitchen is gone out."

Like a disgruntled shadow, Sir Lovell trailed him, a worried expression on his face. "Gladys is not here. You don't think anything unfortunate has befallen her?"

"She's not comin'," Osborn snapped at the other man. "They're not any of them comin' because that damnable Welshman won't allow it."

The frown on Sir Lovell's face deepened. "How can you be certain?"

"I'm certain. Am I the only man here not besotted by one of these Welsh females?"

"They're not coming as much by my order as Clyde's," Rand said. "I told him I would allow no one but Newlin in the camp while Josselyn is my hostage. We'll have to cook for ourselves. We've done it before; we can do it again."

Both men stared at him as if he'd just sentenced them to torture. "What of *her*?" Osborn asked, jerking his thumb toward Rand's quarters. "Why can't she cook for us?"

"I've given her other duties."

At that Osborn smirked. "I don't see why that should interfere with her cookin' for us."

Sir Lovell's mouth turned down in concern. "What duties have you given her?"

"Nighttime duties," Osborn answered before Rand could.

"I did not lay a hand on her," Rand swore. *Though I wish I had.*

"And you'd better not," Sir Lovell stated with a boldness usually reserved only for matters related to construction. "She is being held hostage and is to be returned unharmed to her people. You said as much to her uncle."

"And I meant it," Rand bit out. He glared at the two men. When Osborn was hungry he was like a tenacious bear. He wanted a woman in the kitchen and Rand knew he would badger him until his stomach was filled and content. As for Sir Lovell, he had a moral streak that would not abide seeing a woman harmed in any way. Not that Rand meant to harm Josselyn. But he doubted the master builder would ever understand that.

Perhaps it was for the best, he told himself as he met

their expectant stares. If Josselyn was busy all day she would be less likely to try to escape.

But then he would not have her exclusively to himself.

He chewed on that undeniable fact a moment. Before he could respond to Osborn's suggestion, however, the door shoved open and slammed into his back.

"Ow! Move, you big oaf!"

Josselyn emerged, her hair barely tamed, her face still damp with wash water. She was no longer rosy from sleep; her voice had lost its smoky timbre. But even pale, angry, and shrill, she brought every one of Rand's senses alive.

"I refuse to be discussed as if I am not here," she stated, planting a fist on each hip.

"Can you cook?" Osborn demanded to know.

"I have a moderate talent for cooking, more so than I have for washing and mending," she added, shooting Rand a cool look.

"Then come along," Osborn said, grabbing her by the wrist and starting for the kitchen.

"Hold on!" Rand caught her other hand and for a moment she was caught between them, like a tasty morsel claimed by two birds of prey. He didn't want to share her, at least not just yet. Unfortunately, she knew it, if the glitter in her eyes was any indication. She might be his hostage but that would not prevent her from fomenting any trouble she could. And nothing affected the men under his command so universally as did the issue of food—more particularly, the desire for good food and great quantities of it.

Though he wanted to throttle her, he knew it would do no good. She meant to fight him, to thwart him, in any way she could. In her position he would no doubt do the same. But the mark of a good leader was not to overreact, to know when to retreat and when to advance. This was clearly a time to retreat.

"I give her leave to prepare the meals. But first she and I have a few issues to clarify between us."

He released her wrist. At once she jerked her other arm

free of Osborn's hold. She looked at Rand. "What issues? Do you need me to comb your hair for you?" she asked, stretching out the words in an overly innocent tone. Amusement glinted in her turbulent blue eyes—amusement at his expense. It was time to remind her who was in charge here.

He turned to his men. "She will be along directly. Osborn, inform your men that the morning meal has been delayed but it is coming. Sir Lovell, tell your workers the same." When they didn't move right away, his brow lowered. "Go!"

Josselyn tried to slip away with them, but his boot, planted squarely on the trailing edge of her cloak, halted her in her tracks. "Not you. Not yet."

Osborn grinned. He'd achieved his aim, so he strode off in the direction of his guards milling about near the empty kitchen. Sir Lovell was less certain of Rand's intentions toward Josselyn, but after another dark look from Rand, he quit their company.

Finally Rand was alone with her. Except that they were not actually alone. In the open camp they were visible to anyone who wished to observe them—and it seemed on this morning that everyone wanted to do just that. Rand's only consolation, though meager, was that the others were all beyond hearing.

He kept his voice low and calm. "Do not congratulate yourself too quickly on your success, Josselyn. This skirmish you have won is only that. A skirmish. And in truth, not even that. You had but to ask me and I would have granted you access to the kitchen."

Her smug expression faded, and he suspected why. She'd never wanted access to the kitchen, nor to the hot labors that cooking for so many men entailed. She'd wanted only to counter him, and so she had. She'd not anticipated the benefits that would accrue to him. He would take great pleasure in reminding her.

"Gruel will be sufficient for breakfast. Keep it hot and make plenty of it. I'll send an extra man to help you and

Odo with the midday meal. I suspect you will want to cook fish while they are so plentiful.''

"You trust me not to poison you?'' She glared at him.

Had her garb been finer and her hair more intricately coiffed, her haughty expression would have marked her a queen, or at least a woman of rare breeding. Certainly as noble as any woman at the royal court. But the plain wool cloak and the loosened curls blowing against her cheek reminded him that she was Welsh. Her value was not slight, but the royal court was not where she belonged either.

Though it pained him to admit it, he'd been right to consider her for Jasper. It was the only solution that made any sense. But that understanding weighed heavily on his mind.

He answered her in a somber voice. "You will not poison us for the same reason your uncle will not attack me. The consequences would be too dear.''

"Should I choose to poison you there will be no consequences save the one you will suffer.''

"You cannot poison us all,'' he snapped. "But I warn you, Josselyn. Should even one of my men sicken at your hand, it is your people who will pay. Your village that will suffer.''

Their angry gazes clashed and held. Would she truly try such a foolhardy scheme? Rand was not about to take that chance. "You will taste your preparations in my presence before anyone else eats.''

She shrugged, but she could not entirely hide her annoyance with him. "Whatever you wish. My lord,'' she added, sneering at what should have been a term of respect. She turned to go, but again he held her back. She jerked her eyes back up to his, clearly prepared to snap at him. But they were closer now, their faces but inches apart, and as the moment stretched out, the tension between them grew.

"One thing more, Josselyn. When the meal is done, return you to my quarters. I will want a bath. And my hair needs cutting.''

Her arm was slender and warm in his hand. Her eyes wide and blue. He could hear her breathing, and her scent of soap and warm skin filled all his senses. She said, "If you seek by such activities to make yourself more acceptable to women, you do but waste your time and mine."

"My thanks," he answered, deliberately misinterpreting her insult. "But I believe there is always room for improvement."

"*Twpsyn,*" she muttered. "That means half-wit," she added with acid sweetness. "May I go now?"

Rand released her, though it was not what he wanted to do. Had they been anywhere else, he would have kissed that tart mouth to silence. He would have responded to the challenge she presented and let the battle between them exhaust itself where he knew it should—where it would if the circumstances were only different: in his bed.

But there were other considerations he could not escape. There was much more at stake than this ungovernable need he had to take her to his bed. He'd come unwillingly to Wales but he meant to make the best of it. He meant to leave a powerful castle and a powerful legacy behind him here, and in the process increase his king's indebtedness to him. Josselyn was not a part of that plan, save as a lure to his brother. He must remember that.

Still, he couldn't help thinking that he should have taken her in that little clearing while he had the chance. He'd been a fool to stop just because she was an untried maiden. She'd been willing. That should have been enough. Now . . . Now he feared he'd always hunger for the woman who would wed his brother.

He watched her march stiff-backed to the kitchen. The men moved apart to let her through. Not a coarse call was made to her; not a crude offer or an insulting suggestion. They might be starved for the warm company of women, but they were even more starved for satisfying victuals.

Only when she finally disappeared into the kitchen did he let out a harsh exhalation and turn away. "*Twpsyn.*" He repeated the insult she'd cast at him. He was most assuredly a half-wit when it came to Josselyn ap Carreg Du. She robbed him of half his wits and all his sense.

But not anymore, he told himself. This was all for the best, keeping her busy in the kitchen. Were she languishing at this moment in his quarters, on his bed, he'd never get a minute's work done.

Still, as he strode down the hill to the lowest part of the new wall, deliberately avoiding breakfast, he could not escape the image that lingered in his head. Josselyn bathing him. Josselyn bending over him. Josselyn trimming his hair, her fingers threading through the—

"Twpsyn." He broke off, cursing himself again. *"Twpsyn."*

Who was the half-wit? Josselyn asked herself several hours later. She'd prepared a simple gruel for the morning meal, then immediately begun a hearty fish stew. Odo had learned enough from Gladys to take charge of the bread baking and now, with the meal complete and the washing up left to one of the workers who'd sprained his ankle and could not work on the wall, she was finished with her tasks.

Yet still she lingered in the kitchen. She was hot and tired, and in sore need of a good washing herself. But she did not want to return to Randulf Fitz Hugh's quarters. What if he was there?

She filled a dipper with fresh water and took a long cooling drink. Then she poured the rest on a strip of clean cloth and bathed her face and neck as best she could. Her hair was a knotted mess, loosely braided then rebraided in an effort to keep it out of her way as she'd worked. She had no *couvrechef,* nor even an apron. She'd had to make do with a torn length of fustian to protect her skirt, and had rolled up her sleeves.

The work had been hard, hot and—ultimately—for the best. She'd had precious little time to worry about Rand, though she'd noticed when he did not approach the kitchens, either for breakfast or the midday meal. So much for his threat to have her taste the meal under his watchful eye.

But why had he stayed away?

She gave herself a mental shake. Why should she care? It wasn't as if she worried he might starve to death. One of his men had probably carried food to him.

She didn't care at all why he stayed away, she told herself as she wrung out the cloth, then draped it over a line that ran across one corner of the kitchen. She needed to think and one thing she knew was that when he was around her mind turned to mush. She turned into the half-wit she'd accused him of being. So even though she dearly wished to get out of the overheated kitchen, she was unwilling to signal her captor that her labors were complete. She settled herself in the one window and stared out at the sky. She needed to calm herself and collect her scattered wits. She needed to think and plan.

She needed to escape.

She propped her chin on her hand. Escape would be difficult. Even though she was not locked in a prison, the fact that she was the lone female in the camp made her more noticeable than ever. Every one of the Englishmen knew her situation. Every one of them would make note of her comings and goings.

That did not mean she ought not try to escape, should the opportunity present itself. It only meant that she must consider other means of securing her freedom—especially if Rand was determined in his plan to marry her to this brother of his.

The very thought infuriated her. The gall of the man! How could he threaten seduction one moment, then in the next plan to give her to his brother? The wretch! No doubt he and this brother were two of a kind. Big oafs so sure of their appeal that they thought no woman could resist them.

Then her anger gave way to panic. God help her if the brother possessed anywhere near the appeal Rand did.

She sat there quietly, trembling with terrible self-knowledge. If Rand pressed her too hard she feared she would give in to him. And then what would become of her? Was she truly to live out her life as wife to Rand's brother?

Panic strengthened her resolve. She had to escape! But how? And how long until this Jasper arrived at Rosecliffe?

All at once she sat up straighter. Her breath caught in her chest as a sudden thought burst fully formed into her head. If she could not escape, perhaps her arrogant captor could be convinced to let her go.

He'd taken her hostage. Why couldn't her uncle play that same game? Why couldn't he lie in wait for Jasper Fitz Hugh?

Surely Rand would release her in trade for his precious younger brother.

Thirteen

Jasper Fitz Hugh frowned down at the parchment in his hand. He'd had more wine than he needed last night, as well as more women than he could rightly handle. His head ached, his body was stiff, and he worried, only half-jokingly, that his manhood might one day fall off from overuse. And now, with the sun only half-risen, he was awakened with a message that made no sense at all.

He lifted his eyes from the swimming ink letters, grimacing at the pain generated by that cautious movement, and stared at the weary messenger. "Why this change of heart? Why does my brother bid me come to Wales without delay when before he ordered me to stay in London?"

The other man shrugged. "I cannot say, milord. But I've made the journey by horseback in record time on his orders. We're to leave this very day." The man shifted from one foot to the other when Jasper squinted incredulously at him. "Them's his words, not mine, milord. I'd just as soon rest a day or two," he added under his breath.

"He expects me to leave today?"

The man nodded, then took a wary step back when Jasper lurched to his feet. As if he had the ability to do anything beyond stand there, swaying, Jasper thought. "Send my squire in," he muttered. "And wait outside."

Only when the door was closed and Lawrence stood waiting did Jasper speak. "We leave tomorrow for Wales. Send up a bath—and a wench to keep me from drowning in it. Then take yon fellow to the kitchen. Feed him. Ply him with wine—the best." He rubbed his face and fought down a wave of nausea brought on by the thought of actually sitting on a horse while wine still sloshed through his veins. "Do whatever is necessary to find out what's afoot in my brother's household. Find out what has changed in the short time he's been gone. And hand me that pot—"

Lawrence was gone before the first retch. As Jasper emptied his stomach into the chamber pot he wondered why the man bothered to remain in his employ.

Still, that mystery was of no moment. More important was the truth behind Rand's change of heart. Whatever Lawrence learned, however, it would not stop Jasper from going to Wales. And with any luck, by the time he arrived he would have sobered up and his head would have ceased pounding.

There would be far less drinking in his brother's household, but for once Jasper would not be sorry. There would also be no women, he realized, and that thought drew him up.

He rinsed his mouth with stale wine and spat it out, then wiped his mouth with the back of his sleeve. There would be no Englishwomen, but there would be women. And though they might not speak his language, he'd learned a bit of theirs already. Besides, there was one language all tongues spoke.

Welshwomen, he mused. He was tired of English wenches, anyway, whether they were lowborn or of the noblest breeding. A lusty Welshwoman sounded better and better.

He looked around and cautiously stretched, tilting his head from one side to the other.

"Lawrence, where's my bath?" he bellowed, only wincing a little at the pain that shot through his head. After all, what was a little pain to a knight of the realm? He'd be as good as ever come the afternoon. Rand would not be disappointed that he'd sent for his younger brother, Jasper vowed. He would prove his worth to Rand this time. He grinned to himself and scratched his belly. He'd prove his worth.

It was one thing to plot against Rand. It was another thing entirely for Josselyn to put her plan into action. After an afternoon weighing one idea against another, one possibility versus the next, she was certain of only one thing: she would have to place herself directly in harm's way if she was to learn anything helpful to her escape. She would have to accost Rand instead of avoiding him. And she would *have* to keep her wits about her.

"He's an Englishman, and I hate all Englishmen," she reminded herself over and over, chanting the words like a prayer. "He's an Englishman and I hate him." When she spied him with Sir Lovell near a section of wall that still remained only a ditch—a section that was nearer the forest than any other section—she decided to put her plan into action.

"Wait," Odo called out to her when she slipped out the door and angled away from the kitchen. But Josselyn paid him no mind. She didn't head straight for Rand, however. It would be interesting to see how swiftly he noticed her.

Swift indeed. She had not progressed beyond the nearby half-constructed alehouse before a burly soldier pulling a cart loaded with scaffold poles called out, "Here, miss. You're to stay in the kitchen or in Sir Rand's quarters—"

She ignored him as she had Odo, and strode across the stony ground as if she owned it—which, in truth, she did.

"Wait!" the man cried.

From the corner of her eye she saw Rand look up. She was not near enough to the woods to win a foot race with him, and anyway, a gang of workers laying rubble between the slowly rising wall faces labored squarely in her path.

No, she would not attempt an escape today. But he needn't know that.

She increased her pace, still watching Rand. Only when his determined strides turned into a run did she veer in his direction. She marched purposefully toward him while he slowed to a stop.

"Where do you think you're going?" He blocked her path and crossed his arms across his chest. The perfect image of male arrogance, she decided. She met his stormy glare with a placid expression. "Why, I was looking for you. What else could possibly lure me from my labors in your kitchen?"

He grinned at the sarcasm that crept into her tone. "You chose to work there."

"So I did. What other choice was I given? To sit and stew in my solitary prison, darning your stockings?"

"It needn't be solitary. You have only to beg my presence and I will gladly join you there."

"Beg your presence?" She bit back any further retort, for she knew it pleased him to see her riled. She crossed her arms, mimicking his stance. "If I am to be forced to play the role of hostage while you build these ugly walls, the least you can do is provide me the minimal comforts."

"My quarters are not comfortable?"

"Your quarters are furnished to meet a man's needs, not a woman's."

Again he grinned. "If you wish to sleep in my bed, you have only to ask."

How she wanted to slap that smug expression from his face. "What I want is a change of clothing, my own combs, and the other small possessions that make a woman's life more comfortable."

"I see." His dark gaze moved over her, head to toe and back again, a slow, assessing survey that raised goose-flesh on her arms and shoulders. "You are lovely as you are, Josselyn. If you were any more so . . ."

He let his husky words trail away and for an endless

moment Josselyn could not breathe. Why must he say such things to her? Why did she react so foolishly?

She tilted her face away from him and reminded herself that he was her enemy whom she hated. She could goad him just as he now goaded her. "Your opinion of my appearance is irrelevant, I'm afraid. 'Tis your brother I needs must impress. Not you."

She glared up at him and after a long silence he exhaled harshly. "Yes. My brother." He paused before he spoke again. "Tell me what you need. I will send a messenger to your uncle."

A messenger. That would do her no good. Josselyn stared at the woods that lay between Rosecliffe and Carreg Du. The wind carried the scent of the rousing spring, of the forest and its creatures. She'd long taken that particular mixture of scents for granted. But not anymore. "Shall I write down a list?"

He let out a snort of laughter. "And write some other message I cannot translate? I think not. Just relate to me what you want and I'll see the message delivered."

Inwardly she groaned. What good would that do her? Then, as she stared longingly at her beloved wildwood, Josselyn spied a movement. She glanced at Rand but he was watching her. She feigned a sigh and looked toward the woodland again. One of her uncle's men? Someone come to rescue her?

On impulse she moved nearer the wall, a hip-high barrier at this point. Hip-high, but wider than she was tall. "Let me think," she murmured, delaying as much as she could. She stopped at the wall, conscious that he was less than an arm's length to her left. She searched the forest. "I'll need a clean chemise." Where was that man she'd seen? "Fresh stockings." Had she imagined the movement?

Then something swayed in the low branches of a holly tree and to her relief—and then horror—she spied Rhonwen!

"Fresh stockings," she repeated, glancing away and then

back to the holly. What was Rhonwen doing here? Why hadn't Gladys kept her closer to the village? But then Rhonwen seemed ever to oppose her mother's wishes.

"Anything else?"

Josselyn gasped at the reminder of her captor's presence, then peered warily at him. He watched her with a curious expression. What would he do if he discovered the child?

The answer came to her, simple and surprising. He would not hurt Rhonwen. Josselyn could not explain why she was so convinced of that, but she knew it was so. Her fear for the girl vanished, replaced by cunning. "It seems we have a visitor." She gestured toward the child's hiding place.

At once his focus shifted to the woods. Like the warrior he was, his every muscle tightened in anticipation, in preparation for a fight if necessary. He did not move or so much as twitch. Yet Josselyn sensed his tension as if it were a tangible thing.

"Get back to my quarters."

She smirked. "Could it be my countrymen come in force to rescue me?"

At once he yanked her behind him and drew the short sword that hung at his side. The sound of steel slithering against the steel-and-hide sheath killed what little humor she was taking of the situation. She grabbed his sword hand and held on. "It's only Rhonwen. The little girl. You know the one."

At that moment a stone came sailing across the clearing. It fell short and rattled on the wall, but it was followed by another.

"Let her go, you pig!" the shrill voice screamed in Welsh. *"You vilest of vile creatures! Let her go!"*

His tension vanished. She felt his grip loosen on the hilt of his sword and his fingers flex. Only then did she realize she still held on to his hand. She released it as if he burned her.

Rand slid the sword back in its sheath and, after a searching look at her, turned his attention back to Rhonwen. "Begone, brat!'' he yelled at the invisible child. He brandished his fist. ''Get you home where you belong.''

''She doesn't understand a word you're saying.''

''Then you tell her,'' he grunted. ''Tell her to keep well away from here else I'll make her my prisoner too.''

''You wouldn't.'' Josselyn shook her head. ''That's an idle threat and we both know it.''

She hadn't realized she was smiling until he gave her a half-grin. ''You know me that well?''

She averted her eyes from his gleaming ones. *He is my enemy and I hate him,* she reminded herself. She must take advantage of this situation and not become distracted by him no matter how attractive he was when he smiled upon her. She cleared her throat. ''She's worried about me. If she sees I've not been harmed, she'll be appeased. I'll try to reassure her.'' She turned toward the forest. ''Rhonwen, *is that you?*''

''Run, Josselyn, run! If he pursues you I'll hit him in the head with a rock.''

''What is that about a rock?'' Rand asked from just behind her.

''She says she's going to hit you in the head with a rock.''

''Humph. Tell her to go home. That you're not being mistreated.''

''Listen to me, Rhonwen. Listen carefully. I've not been harmed but you must carry a very important message to my uncle.''

''Why don't you run away?'' the child called back. The tree branch shook and one foot appeared, then another. With a graceful leap the child landed on the ground. *''Hurry. You can run faster than he can.''*

''What did she say?'' Rand asked.

''I'm having a hard time convincing her that I won't be harmed. After all, you just drew your sword and you won't let me leave. What else is a child to believe but the worst? This might take a minute or two.''

"Then get on with it. I don't have time to deal with children."

Josselyn suppressed a grin of triumph. *"Listen closely, Rhonwen. They want me to wed an Englishman. This one's brother. Tell my uncle to watch for his arrival. To capture him and then purchase my freedom in exchange for his."*

"Marry an Englishman?" Even from this distance Josselyn could see the horror on the girl's face.

"If my uncle can capture the man first, I won't have to marry him at all. But you must explain that to him. Can you manage it?"

There was a short pause and Josselyn prayed Rhonwen would realize how important this was. Then the child thrust her hair out of her face and spat on the ground.

"I hate these English. They killed my father. But I won't let them kill you."

"You'll tell my uncle?"

"I'll tell him."

"Well?" Rand asked. "She seems calmer."

"I told her not to worry."

"Tell her what you need. The clothes and the combs. Maybe she'll rest easier if she can be useful to you in some way."

At that odd remark Josselyn looked over at him. He was staring at the little girl across the way. "All right," she said, still puzzled. *"Rhonwen, something else you can do for me. Tell my aunt to send me a few things. My combs. Some clothing. I may be here for a while. At least I want him to think I will."*

"I'll tell her," the child replied. *"Don't you worry, Josselyn. We shall set you free. And we'll stab all these English and send them back to their king, bleeding all over his ship."* Then with a wave and a flash of skirts she was gone.

"What was that last? I heard something about English and ships."

" 'Tis said her father was murdered by the English. She'd like to return the favor."

"Bloodthirsty little wench, isn't she?"

"She has good reason. But that is neither here nor there," Josselyn said, conscious now that he'd turned all his attention on her. "She will tell my aunt what I need, and you will not need to send a messenger."

"How convenient for me. Or perhaps you?" One of his brows arched in that infuriatingly superior manner he had. "Pray tell me, Josselyn, what were you about when I intercepted you?"

"I was looking for you," she replied with a shrug. "Why do you ask? Do you fear I might attempt to escape?"

"I'm sure you'd attempt it did you harbor any hope of success."

"Yea, I would indeed."

They stood a little apart, the wall and forest to one side, the English encampment on the other. The sun broke through the patchy clouds and glinted in his midnight hair. Josselyn swallowed hard. "Well, I'll be going back to the kitchen."

He caught her by the arm. "But you haven't said why you were looking for me."

She shivered at his touch, so impersonal and yet somehow not impersonal at all. Was she hot or cold? She did not know. She forced herself to answer him. "Though I see now it was a foolish endeavor, I had hoped to convince you to set me free. To abandon this foolish plan to keep me as a hostage to peace."

"I see. And you had no notion that one of your kinsmen hid within hailing distance."

She bristled. "How could I have known that? And what good would it do anyway?" She pulled away from him and he let her go. "Will you release me?"

He shook his head "Nò." His eyes slid over her as if he measured her value, but whether for himself or his brother, she did not know. "No, I will keep you until there is no longer a reason to do so."

"Ci ffiaidd!" Furious—unsettled—she whirled and stalked away. She could hear his steps close behind her.

"Fetch me some victuals from the kitchen," he called out to her back. "And tell Odo to heat water for my bath. Then come you back to my quarters. Your labors are not yet done this day."

Josselyn kicked a stone out of her path, and only just resisted snatching up another and flinging it at him. Curse his soul for tormenting her so! Well, two could play at this game. She'd discovered certain weapons she could use against him. At least three. And she meant to make the most of them. Or perhaps they were better termed weaknesses.

First among them was that he possessed a core of honor. A core of decency. He might be her enemy, but she'd recognized that much about him in the short time she'd spent in his company. Her second weapon was his plan to wed her to this Jasper. This brother. She did not believe he would harm her and then turn around and make her his sister-in-law. Some men might, but not him.

The third cudgel she wielded over him, however, was one that could easily hurt her as him. He desired her. If she could just control her own response to him, she could torment him with that desire, while using his honor and his brother as a shield to protect herself. She could torture him unmercifully—*if* she was very careful.

And in so doing, he might grow careless and she might escape. *If* she could resist him.

She reached the kitchen out of breath, but whether from the brisk walk or from her heightened emotions, she could not say. She glanced back. He had halted to speak to Alan, but he looked up and met her gaze.

She looked away, her heart pounding anew.

This would not do, this reaction to his every glance. She gritted her teeth and clenched her fists. She would feed him. She would bathe him. And she would remain unaffected by him. It was the only chance she had to return to her people.

And to Owain?

No, she decided once and for all. She would not marry Owain. She could not. She and her uncle would have to find another way to marshal aid and drive the English out. She could not do it through a marriage to Owain.

It's all due to Randulf Fitz Hugh. Because you desire him, you cannot stomach the idea of sharing Owain's bed. But that dismal truth could not change the other, greater truth. *He is my enemy and I hate him.* She hung on to that reminder as she girded herself for the bath to come.

Furious with her contradictory emotions, she shoved open the kitchen door. "Heat water," she ordered the startled Odo. "And lots of it. Then carry it to your master's quarters."

"He wants another bath?"

"He doesn't know what he wants," she muttered, though more to herself than to the manservant.

Odo grinned. "I'd say he knows very well what he wants, miss, and you're it."

"Do your work and save your wit for someone who appreciates it!" she snapped at the grinning Englishman. But her cheeks burned scarlet.

Everyone knew what Rand wanted and everyone believed he'd get it. It would come as no surprise to her if they laid wagers on it. They wagered on everything else.

But they had much to learn about Welsh pride, and so did Randulf Fitz Hugh.

She just prayed that she would be the one to teach him.

Fourteen

Odo came with the valuable tin tub, then, in short order, with two double-loaded buckets of steaming water. Josselyn made no move to help him with his tasks. She was too consumed with the fears that beset her.

Would Rand remove all his clothing in front of her? Would he require that she bathe his entire body, or only those portions not submerged in the oval tub? She'd never seen a tub of that sort before. Her only bathing had been done in the ice-cold river. Any other washing was done with a cloth and a bucket and a sliver of the prized soap she helped her aunt make. She'd never taken a tub bath of the sort he intended, so she did not know what would be expected of her.

One thing she knew, however, was that he could manage very well without her help if he wanted to. The whole point, unfortunately, was that he did not want to. He wanted her help. Or something else.

She swallowed her terror as best she could, and when Odo gave her a grin and a wink, she scowled. "Go on about your work. And if someone from Carreg Du arrives with a bundle for me, bring it directly here. Do you understand?" she added when he continued to gawk at her.

"You needn't fuss at me, miss. 'Tis milord Rand wot has you in such a dither, not me. More's the pity," he continued in a voice he did not even try to mute.

"Begone from here, wretch!"

Yet once he was gone she wished him back. Anyone's company, even a foolish English servant's, was preferable to being alone with her fears. She stared about the room. Dusk was creeping in, turning the room shadowy, and its corners vague.

She needed more light to stave off any hint of seduction. Not that she didn't mean to torment him with his desire for her, for she full well intended to do so. It was the only real power she held over him. It was her own perverse desire for him that she needed to keep at bay. Though freedom beckoned as a reward for her daring, she knew her plan was fraught with danger. So she lit a twig in the banked fire, then lit the one lamp and four candles she found.

Much better, she decided as the golden light chased the shadows away. She should build up the fire as well, but why make the room more comfortable for him? The colder it was, the briefer would his bath be. With any luck his overheated cock would freeze and fall off.

She laughed at the thought, then paused. How much easier a place the world would be if certain men could be castrated that way. A magical bath, off it fell, and suddenly their power was gone. She had no doubt whatsoever that the loss of virility would render the most ruthless of men helpless. Should Owain have his manhood removed, perhaps then all his meanness would disappear.

Were she forced to wed him, Josselyn pondered, she might be forced to test that theory.

But Owain was not her problem now. Randulf Fitz Hugh was. And as if responding to her thoughts of him, his step sounded from beyond the door. Josselyn had just enough time to sit upon a three-legged stool near the hearth before he strode eagerly into the room.

"What a cozy scene greets me this evening." He grinned at her. "A steamy bath, a platter of food, and a beautiful wench to serve me." He pulled off his gloves and hung his sword belt on a peg. "I'll bathe first, then eat. Come, help me disrobe, Josselyn. Set the food nearer the fire to keep warm—" He broke off. "Why is there no fire?"

"Did you want a fire? I don't recall you asking for a fire."

He pulled his cowl over his head, tossed it aside, and stared boldly at her. "If you did not stoke the fire in the hearth, then perhaps it was because you plan to stoke another sort of fire in me. The embers already burn," he added, caressing her with his eyes.

He is my enemy and I hate him, Josselyn reminded herself. She gave him a disdainful look. "Is your brother equally possessed of such limited interests as are you? Does he look at every woman and see only a receptacle for his lust?"

He sobered at her words, but only a little. "If he has earned the reputation given him, then I'm afraid he is precisely as you describe. But you must know, fair Josselyn, that I see you as far more than that."

"Oh, yes. I am also a political pawn that you can use to get your way."

"I was thinking more that you were a convenient serving wench, well able to scrub away the sweat and dirt of my labors."

"A serving wench—"

"Let me finish. I see you also as a talented translator and a capable teacher."

He said the last with such sincerity that Josselyn felt somewhat appeased. But it did not last, for with a grin he threw himself into his chair and held out one booted foot. "At the moment, however, 'tis neither the translator nor the teacher I need, but the serving wench. So come, wench. Remove your master's garments so he may soak in yon water before it cools."

Somehow she buried her fury. Somehow she suppressed her urge to use his own sword to separate the source of his male power from his arrogant male body. She'd gone down this road with him once before and she knew she could not win. So she undressed him swiftly. Boots and stockings. Tunic and chainse. Braies and lacings.

"You can manage the rest," she muttered, turning away on the pretext of searching out a length of toweling. She did not intend to remove his small cloth.

"So I can. However, I'd prefer you do it," he said in a husky voice.

She swallowed hard. *Ignore how he makes you feel. Remember instead your need to escape him.* She made herself face him, but kept her eyes fixed upon his face. "I am unused to Norman ways. Does a wife do this task for her husband? Will I be forced to perform this ritual for your brother?"

His brow lowered at her reminder of the brother he meant her for and she felt a grim satisfaction. She pressed on. "Am I to practice this bathing ritual on you in order that I will be more proficient for your brother?" She smiled and waited, well aware of the muscle that jumped in his jaw.

"I have never had a wife. I don't know what little tasks they perform for their husbands. I suspect that each couple is somewhat different." Then still facing her, he began to remove the small cloth himself.

Somehow she kept her eyes on his face. This was his way of challenging her and she refused to let him win. But it was difficult beyond the telling, because she wanted to see. She wanted to see the whole of the man, to study him, and determine just what it was that drew her so unwisely to him.

But she knew better than to give in to that temptation. So she stared fixedly at his face, counting backward, first in Welsh, then in Norman French, then in English, until he let out an indecipherable oath and stepped into the tub.

Only then did she breathe. Only then did she blink and unclench her stiff fingers. Her palms hurt from the crescent marks her nails had left, but that was all right. That was fine. She'd resisted him when she'd feared she could not.

Now it was time to learn if he could resist her.

"Well? How does a Norman wife bathe her husband?" she asked, moving deliberately in front of him. Head high. Breasts thrust forward. Hips languidly swaying.

Another muffled oath. This one in the coarser English tongue. "First, she builds a damned fire in the damned hearth!"

"Very well." She gave him a sweet, sarcastic smile and turned to that task. Though she concentrated on the kindling and small branches, building a strong, careful fire with three larger logs tented above the small, licking flame, she was acutely aware of his presence.

He did not reach for the cloth or soap. He did not shift in the tub or splash the water. He only sat there. Were it not for the rhythmic sound of his breathing, she might have thought herself alone. But she was well aware that she was not. When the fire was well taken and she had no further reason to crouch there with her back to him, she finally stood and turned. He was watching her, as she'd known he would be.

"Perhaps I should not wed you to my brother."

Her heart leapt at that dark, unexpected remark and pounded a fierce new tattoo. Why she should care what he planned for her was something she didn't want to examine too closely. So she picked up the soap and tossed it unceremoniously into the water between his projecting knees. "Plan whatever you want. The fact remains that in the end you and your brother—and your masons and diggers and soldiers too—will all be gone from here while we Welsh remain. And then I will wed whom I will."

"Owain ap Madoc?"

She snatched up the bathing cloth and flung it behind the soap. "Owain is almost as repulsive as are you."

"You find me repulsive? I hadn't noticed."

"You are English. That's enough to make you repulsive to any true daughter of *Cymru*."

He relaxed back in the water, stretching his arms along

the rolled edge. "So you say. Perhaps I should warn you that I've heard tales that Jasper tempted not one but two nuns to his bed."

Josselyn stared in astonishment. Two nuns? Surely not! She closed her gaping mouth with a snap. "You're lying."

" 'Tis what the gossips say of him. When he arrives you can ask him the truth of that tale. He was meant for the Church himself, but he was not well suited to the life." He paused, watching her. "If nuns cannot resist him, I wonder how a wench of your passionate nature will fare."

He dunked down in the water, submerging his head. When he rose sputtering and wiping his eyes, Josselyn had not moved. A fallen churchman who tempted nuns? Whether Rand's tale was the truth or only a portion of it, she knew more than ever that she must renew her efforts to escape. Rand affected her more than any man ever had. This brother . . . She did not want ever to meet this brother he boasted of. But she must not let him know that.

With a nonchalance completely feigned, she approached the tub. "If he is as appealing to women as you say, mayhap I will not be so unhappy with him as I imagined. When is he to arrive?"

"Soon."

Soon. She needed more information than that if her uncle was to intercept the man and capture him. Unfortunately, Rand's face revealed nothing of his feelings, which raised her anger from a simmer to a seething boil. He would not get the best of her. She pushed up her sleeves, then without flinching away from his relentless gaze, she reached down into the water.

Thank goodness her fingers found the washcloth before they found anything else. "Shall we get on with it?" she snapped. "Tell me, how will my Norman husband wish me to proceed?"

"In the same manner a Welsh one would. First, he would advise you to find the soap."

"If you will hand it to me, I will begin."

"You're the one who threw it in the water."

He was going to make her find it and he didn't think she would. Josselyn could see the gleam in his eyes. But she refused to let any English lord get the best of her. Especially this one. With a brazenness that surprised even herself, she plunged her arm back into the water. This time, however, she did not worry about avoiding his naked legs. With deliberate calculation she let her knuckles graze the slippery slope of his thigh.

"Where is it?" she wondered out loud as she felt around the floor of the tub. Her arm bumped one of his bent legs, then the other. She heard his sharp intake of breath; it mirrored her own. She was playing a dangerous game, she knew, yet a perversely exhilarating one. Her arm was submerged over the elbow and her shoulders were tilted toward him. Her head was very near his. If she raised her face to look at him . . .

She found the soap between his feet and started to straighten up. But his legs came together to catch her arm, and when she looked up, her triumph faded to alarm. She'd been caught in a trap of her own making. His far hand clamped down on hers, forcing her fist that still clutched the soap down into the jointure of his thighs.

"You see what you do to me?" His voice was husky with desire as he rubbed her fist against the hard length of his fully aroused manhood. "You see?"

Josselyn could make no answer. She'd meant to taunt him, to torture him using his brother as protection against his inappropriate desire for her. But she'd sorely underestimated her own desire and her meager ability to resist it.

His other hand came around her neck, tangling in her hair, and the soap slipped out from her fingers.

"You see what you have wrought with your teasing?" he murmured as he drew her face inexorably to his own. Then his lips closed over hers and any thoughts of teasing him—of escape or his brother or anything else—fled her mind. When their lips met, all the old possibilities melted away. Only one possible future lay before her now, one new possibility, urgent and consuming. She must kiss him and be kissed by him, and follow this dizzying spiral of emotions wherever it led.

Their mouths met and slanted, seeking a closer fit, a more perfect union. He tugged at her lower lip, teasing her until her lips parted and he gained full entrance.

At the same time he released her trapped hand and circled her shoulders to draw her nearer. Her hand found his thigh, hard and coarse with hair. She slid her palm up, trying instinctively to brace herself from falling fully onto him, and found the smooth flesh of his hip, then the ridged muscles of his belly and chest.

His tongue invaded her mouth at the same time his wet hand curved over her breasts.

"Wait—"

"No more waiting." With one tug he pulled her off balance so that she sprawled over him. She was suddenly wet, overheated, and utterly confused by the war of foreign emotions raging inside her. What was she doing?

But Rand obviously knew what he was doing and what he wanted her to do. For he deepened the kiss, using his tongue to excite all her senses. Did he know how the rhythmic stroking of her inner lips lit a fire in her belly? Did he know how his palm circling her breasts sent sparks of lightning shooting through her? Did he know how swiftly he'd converted her opposition to enthusiasm?

For despite all logic, she tried now to do the same to him, to excite him with her tongue and tease his flat male nipples with her fingertips. He would not rob her of all control. She could master this game. She could master him.

But when he slid one hand down her back to bunch up her skirts, then moved beneath the voluminous fabric to find the bare skin of her hip and thigh, she knew she had no control at all. He possessed it all. She was a novice in the hands of a master, a simple instrument played to perfection by one who knew how.

"Let's be rid of all this wool." He straightened up so that the water lapped over the side. Now her skirts were wet too. She was kneeling in a warm puddle that cooled quickly on the stone floor. "Where are the ties?" he asked as he felt for the side laces of her simple gown.

"Wait. You can't . . . What are you doing?"

He drew her down for a kiss and did not relent until her full weight melted against him. How did he woo her so easily?

"I'm teaching you how a man likes to be bathed. Any man," he added as he slipped the neckline of both her gown and her smock off one of her shoulders, then blessed her newly bared flesh with a trail of searing kisses.

"This . . . This isn't bathing," she gasped, then kissed him when he turned his face back up to hers.

"It's a prelude to bathing." In a moment he had her laces untied. With another tug he had her bodice off both shoulders and then pulled farther down so that her breasts were suddenly revealed. Only then did he pause.

Josselyn still knelt upon the floor. Her arms were trapped now against her side by the opened neckline. Rand sat upright in the tub, his eyes feasting upon her newly exposed flesh. No man had ever seen her thus. She'd certainly not intended to let him do so. Yet as his eyes ran over her, Josselyn quivered with excitement. Her nipples pebbled, dark and rosy, standing out pertly from her pale skin.

He reached out with one finger, tracing a circle around first one, then the other. A small sigh escaped her lips. He thumbed over one taut peak and her entire body jerked in response. This time she groaned.

"Shall I kiss you there, Josselyn?" He lifted his gaze to her face. "Is that what you want?"

"Yes."

That could not be her response to such an outrageous question. Surely not. But it was, and when he drew her nearer, then licked first one, then the other of her straining nipples, Josselyn knew it was she. How else could she possibly answer?

"I'm going to bathe you with kisses," he murmured as his mouth trailed across her fevered flesh. "I'm going to lick every portion of you," he whispered between nibbles so intense they were almost painful. Almost. "I'm going to eat you up. Consume you. Make you mine . . ."

Make you mine.

"What . . . what of your brother?"

He cupped her breasts, one in each hand, and looked up at her. His expression was one of fierce possession, of burning desire. "Forget about my brother."

He thumbed her nipples with excruciating precision. She nearly fainted from the overwhelming pleasure of it. But she knew she must not succumb. Not yet.

"Then I shall not be forced to wed him?"

He moved as if to kiss her nipples again, but she managed to catch his head between her hands. "I have to know what you plan for me. Will you make me wed this Jasper?"

He shook his head. "No."

She gasped with relief. She hadn't known how desperately she'd wanted to hear him say that he would not foist her upon his brother. "Then what *will* you do with me?"

His eyes had become clearer, though desire still ruled him. "I should think it clear, even to a virgin, what I plan to do with you."

It was clear indeed, especially when he stood, and stepped from the tub, dripping wet, fully aroused. He pulled her flat against him. "I plan to make love to you. Here. Now."

He gave a hard tug on her abused gown and she heard a small rip as a seam gave. He pulled again and it fell to her hips, though her hands were tangled still in the sleeves. She tried to free them but he wouldn't let her. With her naked breasts pressed to his damp chest, their faces were but inches apart. When he tried to kiss her again, however, she tilted her head away.

"Am I to remain your hostage?"

He grinned. "Yes, but I promise to make you a very willing one."

"So I need not wed this brother when he arrives." It had suddenly become more important to her than ever that he was being honest about that.

"No." He sought her lips again, but still she eluded him.

"How long must I remain your hostage?"

She felt his sigh. The wet curls on his chest teased her nipples and sent new quivers through her. "Nothing will change by our joining, Josselyn. You remain my hostage so long as I need to ensure peace between our people."

Not an unexpected answer. Still, it was not the one she sought. "So you will take me to your bed—for who knows how long—then return me, ruined, to my family?"

In the long tense silence she heard his answer and her heart sank. She'd had no reason to hope for more from him, but it seemed she foolishly had.

She began to struggle away from him but he caught her chin in his hand and forced her to face him. "Did you expect me to offer marriage to you?"

"I would never marry the likes of you!" she spat.

"If I thought you could be—" He broke off and something changed. His eyes became opaque. His expression shuttered. "It appears neither of us wishes to wed the other. But it is equally apparent what we do want from one another." For emphasis he thrust his hips against hers, then held her there with a hard hand over her backside. "You want to know the secrets of womanhood and I want to teach them to you." He splayed his hand and rubbed it in a slow circle over her derriere until she squirmed at his fiery touch.

"I don't want it." She shoved against his chest but he only laughed.

"You lie. Shall I show you?" So saying, he bent her back over his arm and took one of her breasts in his hand. She struggled to right herself, but to no avail. He was too strong. Then he began that small, scintillating motion, just his thumbs grazing back and forth over her sensitized nipples, and she could feel her opposition melting away.

"You are forcing me. This is . . . This is rape." She murmured the word even as her eyes fell closed and she began to pant.

" 'Tis anything but," he retorted, and she knew it was true. Oh, what a pitiful creature she was!

Somehow he walked them to his bed. Somehow he tugged her gown past the swell of her hips. Somehow she found herself lying on her back with his magnificent warrior's body weighing hers down onto the mattress. The bed ropes, so newly strung, stretched and creaked.

His lips had taken over the task of his thumbs, and his stubbled chin scraped her skin. But the pain was a part of the pleasure, just as the wrong of what they did was entwined so thoroughly with the right of it. Like the devil had tempted Eve. The demon serpent was so beautiful, the apple it offered was so sweet. But it was wrong just the same, and like Eve, she knew the cost of tasting of the fruit would be high.

"You must not. Rand—"

He heard her and he raised his head. Their eyes met. He lay sprawled half on the bed, half off, his hips between her knees, his chest pressed against her belly. She was completely exposed to him: naked, open. The very picture of wanton desire. Against his wide muscled shoulders her hands looked small and ineffectual. She was no match for him, not his raw strength, nor his raw appeal. But he was a man of some honor, or at least she believed so. She had to try to stop them both before they went too far.

Before she could collect her scattered wits, however, he spoke. "You want this as much as I do." So saying, he slid his body lower against hers, trailing hot kisses and small bites down her stomach to her navel and farther still.

She caught his dark hair in her hands, staying his progress before she entirely forgot her intent. " 'Tis wrong. I . . . I wish to save myself for my husband."

He looked up at her. In his eyes there burned desire, hot and hungry. Yet he was not so far gone as to be oblivious to her words. "You wish to remain a virgin?"

She hesitated. Of course she did.

Of course she did!

She had to force herself to nod.

His jaw clenched; his breathing came fast and harsh. Finally he nodded. "So be it."

Flooded with relief, overcome with disappointment, Josselyn scrambled back on the bed, pushing with her heels and elbows. She needed to cover her nakedness, to escape the overwhelming aura of sex and desire that vibrated in this room. But his hands caught her hips and without warning he pressed the side of his face against her lower belly. "I will leave you a virgin, Josselyn, if that is what you truly want."

"It is." She whispered the lie.

Then the breath caught in her throat, for he began to kiss the dark curls that guarded her feminine core. She began to tremble when his tongue parted those curls and found her most vulnerable spot. And when he began a rhythmic stroking, hot, wet—impossible to fight—her very heart seemed to stop.

His hands sought her breasts. His thumbs moved in concert with his tongue and lips. He urged her on and though a voice in her head—the voice of reason, and caution and rational choice—told her to fight him, to escape him any way she could, she hadn't the will to do so.

She arched into his sinful caresses. She opened her legs and her arms to him. Her entire being. And when she could bear no more, she erupted beneath him, giving him everything he wanted and more. Her free will. Her woman's body.

Her Welsh heart.

Fifteen

How long Josselyn lay there, she could not say. She was roused from her sated state only when Rand loomed above her, damp with perspiration, rigid with his own unfulfilled desires. Without thinking, she stroked her fingers up the powerful contours of his arm, marveling at the restraint in those hard, bunched muscles, the heat seething beneath his smooth, unmarked skin.

"That's only the half of it, my sweet. There's more pleasure still to be had. Better. Far sweeter."

She looked up at him, too drained to speak, too befuddled by the sensations he'd wrought in her to think or argue. Taking her silence for consent, he drew her legs up and she felt the prod of his manhood. She was frightened, and yet enticed. Somehow she knew he did not lie. She knew it would be incredible.

She wanted him inside her.

He began to push, and she felt the moist pressure, the stretching. It hurt a little, but it felt good as well.

She stared at him. In the golden glow of the candles he was a gilded being. A god of old come down to earth. Certainly he was more than any mere man, for he'd cast a spell on her that she was unable to break.

As he came farther into her, her lethargy fled. With short rocking movements, in and then out, he roused her anew.

Just like before, and yet it was somehow different. The pleasure was centered lower, it was more basic. The other had been sex in all its physical delights. But this was more. This was mating.

The very thought brought tears to her eyes and they spilled over before she could prevent them. He frowned at the sight, then gently kissed them away. "It will not hurt for long. Just a moment to breach your maidenhead."

He caught her mouth in another stinging kiss, long and hard and unbelievably sweet. Then, when she gave herself up to the kiss, arching up to him, his hips thrust forward again. She gasped as something gave way and he rested wholly inside her. He let out a groan, half relief, half frustration, it seemed—and someone pounded on the door.

"Rand! Are you asleep? Rouse yourself, man! One of the boats is on fire!"

Josselyn and Rand both froze as reality, cruel and unflinching, invaded the room. He lay over her, pinning her to his bed with the hard proof of his masculine prowess. Sweat beaded on his brow, passion burned like coals in his eyes. But reality would not relent. The fist thumped its harsh interruption.

"Come on, man! I know you're in there. 'Tis the Welsh. They've set fire to one of the boats on the beach!"

With a particularly foul English oath, Rand rolled off her. "Damn you, Osborn! Damn your pitiless soul!" He shoved up from the bed and yanked on his braies.

Josselyn remained where she lay, dazed. And yet she suddenly saw everything with startling clarity. Dear God, what on earth had she been thinking? Lying with her enemy, sharing his passions. Welcoming his seed. He needed no one to dress or undress him. He needed no one to assist his bath. Every step of the way, every word, every caress, had been calculated to seduce her. To lure her in and demolish her resistance. To gain him that ultimate power that every man sought to wield over a woman. And she'd provided him with precious little opposition.

While her countrymen plotted her escape, she'd opened her arms—and legs—to her enemy. But not anymore. She would not be seduced by him ever again.

She stared wildly around. Had she a dagger she would have severed the source of all his male arrogance, all his male power over her. She would sever it from him and feed it to the pigs!

"Stay here," he ordered as he jerked on his boot. He glanced only briefly at her, and if his expression was at all regretful, it was only that he was as yet unrelieved of his disgusting male seed. She meant to ensure he remained unrelieved.

She glared at him. "If you think—"

She broke off when Osborn burst into the room. "God's knuckles, Rand."

"Dammit, man!"

"Uffern dan!" Josselyn yanked the sheet over her—not that it could disguise what had just happened. *"Cer!* Begone from here!"

To his credit Osborn did not stare but instead averted his eyes. But he did not leave. "Alan is hurt. 'Tis bad."

"Did he see anything?"

Osborn glanced at Josselyn then away. He did not answer.

"Bloody hell." Rand tugged on the other boot then snatched up his chainse and started for the door. "I'll be back," he said, giving her a brief parting glance. He gestured for Osborn to leave before him. Only then did his grim expression ease. "Stay right where you are, Josselyn. We will finish this ere the night is through."

Slowly she shook her head. "We are finished already."

His eyes glittered in the faltering light. Cold outside air rushed over her but his gaze was as hot as ever. "You and I are far from finished. If you wish to rage at someone, I suggest you rage at your countrymen. 'Tis they who have interrupted our lovemaking."

Then with the sharp crack of the solid door against the

oak frame, he was gone, leaving her no one to rage at save herself.

Heads would roll, Rand swore as he strode through the chill night. They had but three boats, two small tubs and a larger flat barge. They were for fishing and ferrying supplies from the seagoing vessels that would call periodically at the partially sheltered cove beneath Rosecliffe. But now the barge was gone, if the orange glow down the cliff path was any indication.

Damnation!

"Who was on the watch?"

"Geoffrey. If Alan hadn't come upon the marauders when he did, it would have been worse."

They picked their way down the path that hugged the cliff face. On the narrow strip of beach the blackened frame of the barge showed like the bones of a great sea beast come awkwardly to its final rest. A cluster of men doused the remaining flames with buckets of seawater, but it was clear the damage was grave. As for Alan and Geoffrey . . .

With the harsh orange light of the fire gone and only the smoky flickerings of the stubborn embers remaining; the two soldiers lay like gray lumps upon the shore, one hunched over, holding his head, the other prone and not moving at all.

The figure so deathly still was Alan.

"He saved me skin," young Geoffrey moaned, unconcerned by the tears coursing down his dirty cheeks. "He took the blade meant for me." He sniffled and wiped the back of his hand across his eyes. "He won't die, will he? Will he, milord?"

Alan's face was so pale and the bloody stain on his tunic so large that Rand feared the worst. A man bent over Alan, stanching the bloody flow with a wad of cloth. "How fares he?" Rand asked.

"Bad, milord. But he yet lives. And he's a strong lad," the man added hopefully.

The stench of smoke mingled with blood was not unfamiliar to Rand. It was the smell of battle and his nostrils flared in recognition and rage. Someone must pay for this. Someone *would* pay.

"Make a litter," he ordered one of the guards. "Take him to the kitchen." Then he turned to the shaken Geoffrey. "Tell me everything. What was said. What you heard. I want every detail, starting with how many there were."

"I . . . I only saw three, but there may have been more. I was . . . I was sitting there," he stammered, pointing to a grassy hummock where a torn fustian blanket lay in a heap. "I wasn't asleep, milord. I swear it."

"Where did they come from, land or sea?"

"I didn't see any boat."

"We've searched the area," Osborn put in. "The only access by land is down the path and we know they didn't come that way."

Rand was silent a moment. "Three men or more come in by sea, yet not on a boat. Were they wet?"

Geoffrey blinked and slowly nodded. "Aye. The one as held me was wet. D'ye think they swam here?"

Rand did not reply but asked another question, one he knew the answer to already. "What did they say? Did you hear any names?"

Geoffrey grimaced. "They was Welsh. I couldn't understand a blessed word they said."

"Not even a name?"

"Wait a minute! Maybe that's what he was sayin'. The one that cut Alan. He wiped the bloody blade clean over his chest, then he laughed and said owin' at mad dog. He said it twice. Owin' at mad dog."

"Owain ap Madoc," Osborn mused out loud. He met Rand's steady gaze and nodded once. Then he hurried back up the narrow trail.

Rand turned away and stared blindly out into the black night hanging over the sea. So it was begun. He did not often pray, but in the dark, with the sea lapping peacefully—deceptively—at the thin gravel shore, he prayed. *God, save Alan. He is a good soldier and a good man, and he's too young to die.*

He didn't pray for help finding Owain ap Madoc, however. When it came to revenge, Rand needed no one's help—least of all God's.

Two hours later there was every hope that Alan would survive. The cut in his side, though bloody, had sliced through muscle only. No entrails spilled through the fleshy wound. Alan had roused briefly and despite his pain had confirmed Geoffrey's story. Three men and Owain himself at the fore. The man already wanted his bride back, Rand mused. Would he want her now that she'd been ruined?

He frowned, then quaffed the bitter dregs of the red wine in his cup. He'd heard the Welsh did not value a woman's purity so highly as did Englishmen. Under their law, Welshwomen could not be forced to wed, though likewise, they could not marry against their father's wishes. Some English lords allowed their daughters a similar freedom, though they were not required to do so. But it was on the issue of a bride's virginity that the Welsh and English parted ways. An unmarried Welshwoman could even take a lover if she so desired, without it reflecting poorly on her eventual husband.

He gritted his teeth and worked his jaw back and forth. Josselyn had done no more than that. Taken a lover. Owain would not be shamed before his people by that fact.

But Rand wanted him shamed. He wanted him dead.

And he wanted to finish what he'd started this night with Owain's woman. With Josselyn.

He slammed the cup down and shoved to his feet. It was the darkest hour of the night, with neither moon nor stars to break the cavernous blackness. The watch had been doubled. Alan slept. It was time for him to visit his lonely hostage.

To his surprise two men stood guard, one at the door, the other at the window.

"She tried to escape, milord," the shorter man said. He took a step away from Rand. "We had to tie her up."

"You what?" Rand's anger flared like a pitch torch. No one had the right to touch Josselyn save him.

"She was like a wild woman!" the man cried as Rand advanced on him. "She nearly scratched my eyes out. See?" He pointed to a jagged scratch on his upper cheek.

"And she tried to set fire to your bed!" the other man said while keeping his distance. "She tried to burn your quarters right down to the ground. But we put out the fire before it could rightly catch."

Rand drew up. Fire? That conniving little bitch! She would be well matched with that bastard Owain. "Go find your own beds. I'll see to her the rest of this night."

The two men exchanged glances, relief being their first reaction, followed swiftly by a leering understanding. But Rand didn't care what they thought. He slammed into the room in a cold rage. He could not mete out punishment against Owain. Not tonight. But he could damn well mete it out against Josselyn. And he would.

She was tied to the bed, slumped against one of the posts. Her arms had been lashed behind her, her hair tumbled over her face, and the neckline of her gown was torn, exposing her chest and the upper swell of her left breast. Despite his fury toward her and her countrymen, a sick knot twisted in Rand's gut.

They hadn't taken advantage of her, had they? They hadn't fondled that creamy flesh or feasted their eyes on her rose-tinged nipples?

God help them both if they had!

"Josselyn?" Even to his own ears he sounded far too concerned for her welfare. She was his enemy, a willful warrior bitch who would do anything to drive him out. He'd best think with his brains, not with his cock.

She lifted her head slowly, then tossed her hair out of

her face with an arrogant jerk, and glared her hatred at him.
A smudge of soot marred her fair skin, but otherwise she
appeared unharmed.

He could not say the same for his bed.

The sheets were charred and a hole in the close-woven
mattress cover let burned straw protrude. Wet, burnt straw.
The room stank of smoke but at least there was no blood.
Rand expelled a long breath as weariness stole over him.
What more madness could this night hold for him? He
braced himself against any show of weakness and met her
scowl with one of his own.

"You have sealed your fate. Any freedoms I might have
been disposed toward granting you are no more."

"Freedom to labor on your behalf? Ha! 'Tis just another
sort of servitude."

She had straightened and stood now as haughty as anyone could while tied to a bedpost. Her hair fell to her waist,
hiding her partially exposed breast. She had lost one of her
shoes in her struggles with his men. But for all that, she
looked like a queen. No wonder Owain wanted her.

But he would not get her—

Rand stopped in the act of laying aside his sword. Owain
wanted her back and no doubt he would try again to free
her. Only this time Rand would set a trap and take the
Welsh rebel captive. Once Owain was locked in a dun-
geon—or else sent back to London for Henry's justice—
the Welsh rebellion would falter.

Then he would have to decide what to do with Josselyn.

But he need not make that decision tonight.

He put his sword down. "The labors I have given you
are not so hard. Especially those you performed in here. In
fact, they have every potential to be rather enjoyable. I
thought we agreed on that earlier."

"We agreed on nothing!" But the hot color that stained
her cheeks made her words a lie.

He advanced on her. "Perhaps 'tis only that you need
another demonstration to remind you."

"I don't. Stay away from me you . . . you coward."

He stood before her, close enough to touch any portion of her soft, strong body. But he didn't. She smelled of smoke and fear. And of sex. He sat on the bed and she twisted as best she could to face him. It brought her jutting breasts nearer to his face, and he felt the rise of desire.

"Did you burn this bed as a symbolic gesture? Or mayhap it was a tribute? We had built a considerable fire of another sort in it before I was so abruptly called away."

Her chin trembled. Or did he imagine it? It was clear, however, that she did not want to be reminded of the passion that had ignited them both in this bed. He vowed not to let her forget.

"Strange, isn't it, that water—a bath—was what led to our own fiery union." He reached a hand up and, though she flinched away, he rubbed his knuckle across her sooty cheek. "You bathed me very well, Josselyn. Truth be told, I cannot recall a more memorable bath. Now 'tis my turn to do as much for you."

Josselyn watched Rand with increasing alarm. What was he up to? She'd had too much time to rage and worry in the long hour since she'd failed in her bid to escape. The two English thugs who'd barred her way, then doused the fire before it could fairly catch, had been crude and threatening when they'd tied her to Rand's bed. The shorter one had become hard at the sight of her struggling against the leather bindings. He would have raped her, she was certain, had not the other man warned him away. Fear of Rand's reaction had been the only threat that had kept the man's erection in his braies.

Now, however, Rand was here, with no one to prevent him doing what he would with her. And though she feared what he might do, she feared just as much her own response to the man.

When he wet a cloth from the chilly bathwater and rubbed soap into a thin lather, her fear trebled. But she would rather die than reveal that to him, so she bit the inside of her lower lip and glared her hatred at him. Though she knew it was hopeless she twisted her face away when he tried to wash the soot from her cheek.

"Don't touch me."

" 'Tis only a bath, Josselyn. You will sleep better when you are clean."

"I'll sleep better when I am free from the likes of you!"

He caught her chin and forced her to face him. "That may be a very long time."

"And then again, it may come much sooner than you think."

He wiped her cheek, gently. Firmly. His hand was warm, the cloth was cold. She shivered in dismay.

"Owain will try again, no doubt."

So it was Owain who'd fired the boats. She'd wondered.

"But he will not succeed," Rand continued. "He must want you very badly. I wonder, though, if he will want you as much when he learns we have lain together."

She could not turn away from him, but she did avert her eyes. Otherwise he would have seen the truth: that she would never lie with Owain as she'd lain with him. She knew now that such a thing would be impossible.

She forced her words, however, to mislead him. "Owain will not care. Once he and my uncle drive you English from our shores, he will rejoice in the greater victory and not care about the small losses along the way."

He moved the cloth to her lips. "English mothers wash their children's mouth with soap when they catch them in a lie." But it was not the cloth that smoothed over her lower lip. It was his thumb, and her eyes jerked up to his.

He was so near, his chest but inches away, his feet arrayed on either side of her own. He surrounded her. He overwhelmed her. In an instant he had pushed her hair behind her shoulders, then wrapped one hand in her tresses and gripped the post behind her head, so that she could not turn her face away from him.

Did he mean to take her here, up against the bedpost,

like some prize of war? She'd heard the men's tales of battle. She knew what happened to any woman captured by an enemy army. In truth, all men were the same. English ones. Welsh ones. And yet she'd somehow imagined this man different.

Past the lump that formed in her throat, she forced herself to speak. "If you mean to rape me, have done with it now."

"I don't mean to rape you."

She felt his breath against her cheek. She saw the lantern light reflect in his eyes, gold glimmering up from those midnight-dark depths. Despite his words, his intent was clear.

"It *will* be rape," she said, though the husky tremble in her voice belied the words.

"No."

He was close enough to kiss her, but he didn't. Thank God, she told herself. Thank God. For if he kissed her he would feel how she strained toward him. He would feel the traitorous arch of her body, the betraying desire on her lips.

Instead of kissing her, he moved the cloth down her neck and, with a perverse thoroughness, began to bathe her skin. The hollow of her throat. The line of her shoulder. The swell of her breasts. The bathwater had long ago cooled and her skin prickled with the cold. But inside she burned.

Would he remove her gown? Surely not.

"Don't," she warned breathlessly.

He raised his head and met her tortured gaze. "I won't. Not until you ask me to."

"I'll never ask that."

His answer was a smile of such blinding male beauty, of such wicked worldliness, that Josselyn felt faint. He meant to seduce her and he probably could.

"This . . . this is not fair. At the least release my bindings."

"I will. Eventually." He knelt then and began to bathe her feet, her ankles, then slowly moved up her legs. Relentlessly he moved the soapy cloth upward, bunching her skirt ever higher, revealing the flesh he bathed.

By the time he reached her inner thighs she was trembling so violently that were it not for the leather cords, she would have collapsed. His head was bent to his task and she was desperate for him to go on, to touch her there, where she ached for him. But he looked up instead, his eyes burning with the force of his own desire.

"Shall I continue?" he asked, hoarse and low. His left palm slowly slid up and down her thigh, the thumb so near the apex of her thighs, yet never quite making it there. "Tell me, Josselyn. Tell me what you want."

The breath caught in her throat. He knew her answer, for every part of her proclaimed it: trembling legs, flushed skin, fevered eyes. But he wanted the words.

It was the only thing she still possessed that she could withhold from him.

"I want you, Josselyn. I want to taste every sweet morsel of you, beginning here." He pressed a kiss against her belly, against the rumpled wool that yet covered her there. "You liked it before when I did that to you. You'll like it even more this time. I promise."

She bit her lip, anything to deny him the admission he sought. But a whimper slipped past, a sound of helpless assent, and with a groan of his own, he buried his face against her.

"Damn you!" he swore, digging his hands into her derriere and pressing her into him. "Damn you!"

He stood abruptly, unfastening his braies with one hand while he pulled her gown up to her waist. Then he pressed fully against her, letting her feel the full strength of his warrior's body, the full desire of his male arousal. And even as he loosened the leather thongs that held her in place, he lifted one of her legs and entered her.

"Rand," she gasped, but he swallowed her words, her very breath, with a fierce kiss. The last of her good reason was abandoned. The last remnant of logic burned to cinders in their fiery embrace. She circled his neck with one arm and rose into the kiss, and reveled in his possession of her. Her other hand remained behind the post, held there by Rand's fierce grip as he finished what they'd begun hours earlier. He pushed past all her defenses, taking her hard against the unyielding bed frame.

But it was not rape. He had been right in that and Josselyn rejoiced for it. They came together willingly, violently. Inevitably.

And when he drove her past her ability to bear any more, when she erupted around him and dissolved into him, she felt his answering culmination. She felt the hot burst of his strength into her.

Only then did he release her hand. Only then did she slump into him, holding on to his shoulders so that she did not melt quietly away into the floor.

He held on to the post, keeping them upright a little longer. She felt the unyielding oak behind her and suspected she would be bruised. But as her senses returned and she felt his hard body up against hers and realized her one leg curved still around his hips, she knew that the bruises to her body were of no moment. What would happen next, she did not know. But the bruises he could inflict on her heart would stay with her far longer than any bruises of the flesh.

They might very well kill her.

Sixteen

He did not allow her to speak, but put out all the lamps and took her to his bed. Despite her exhaustion, Josselyn did not believe she could possibly sleep beside him. But she did—until he awakened her and they made love again. When she tried to protest, he silenced her in ways she'd never imagined, with kisses and touches in places she'd never known could be so erotic. He was bold and voracious and she was too consumed by the fire he built in her to object.

Somewhere along the way they abandoned their clothes, just as she'd abandoned her modesty and her virginity. But she couldn't think about that now, not when he had tucked her against his chest and curved his magnificent body around hers, as if he meant to protect her even as he slept.

To protect her—or to prevent her from escaping him? Some remnant of suspicion rose to make her wonder. Josselyn tried to reason out which, for she knew it was an important distinction. But her exhaustion was too great and her body too replete. Reason had been numbed by sexual satiation. Her last clear thought before she succumbed once more to sleep was to wonder if her reason would ever fully return.

A hard fist on the door dragged her back to awareness. Hadn't she been awakened thus before?

But that knock had been urgent. This one was less so. And it had been dark, not the hard light of morning. She burrowed into the bed, hiding her face against a warm chest—

A warm chest! She leapt back as if scalded.

"Good morning." Rand's head rested on the same pillow she'd just abandoned.

She backed off the bed then, realizing she was naked, tried to pull the sheet over her. But Rand caught her wrist and with one easy tug brought her sprawling across him. "You don't have to leave," he said, positioning her, despite her struggles, over him. She felt the morning heat of his masculine body and felt the hard arousal of him too.

The fist pounded the door once more. "God's bones, Rand. Can't you come up for air long enough to hear that we've company?"

Rand's playfulness disappeared. "Company? Who is it, man? More of the Welsh?"

"It appears to be Simon Lamonthe," Osborn answered. "If the pennant they fly tells the truth of it."

More Englishmen. That chased away the last cobwebs of Josselyn's interrupted slumber. Her body ached from Rand's invasion of it. His repeated invasion of it, she recalled with hot shame. But she had no time for remorse. More Englishmen. Had he sent for them? Did he plan to retaliate against Owain?

Did he plan to attack Carreg Du?

She tried to push off him but he held her with hands of steel. "Is he here yet?"

"Almost."

"Send for wine and whatever Odo can muster in the kitchen. I'll greet them here."

After a moment Osborn cleared his throat. "What of your . . . hostage?"

"Send for two guards—not the two who guarded her yesterday." Rand's eyes bored into Josselyn's though he spoke to his captain. "She'll be ready to accompany them in a few minutes."

The captain of the guards grunted but he did depart. That left Josselyn lying naked over her enemy—her enemy who had become her lover. A sheet separated them, but it was a useless barrier. She felt every muscle, every bone, every hollow of his well-honed body, as he now knew the contours and textures of her own. But she knew nothing of his thoughts, and his carefully shuttered gaze ensured she would not.

"You will go with the guards and stay strictly out of Lamonthe's view."

"Why must he not see me?" she responded, her voice tart. Her emotions were too overwrought for her to be logical. "Welshwomen have always been the spoils of war for you English."

A muscle jumped in his jaw and his eyes narrowed at her sarcastic tone. "Put whatever name you will on this night, Josselyn. But it will remain a night of pleasure in my memory—and yours, if you are honest. As for Lamonthe, he will see you and he will want you. He is one who *does* see Welshwomen as spoils for the taking." He paused, his gaze as hard as his words. "Do you want him to take you?"

What she wanted was the privacy of a good cry. How could he act so unaffected by what had occurred between them? "Would you let him?"

Inside dust motes floated in the single beam of sunlight streaming through the crack in the shuttered window. From outside the muted sounds of a camp coming awake drifted in to them. But where they were and why they were in this terrible situation did not matter. Would he give her to another English lord if the man demanded it? After what had happened between them . . .

"I've told you before. The women of Wales are safe under my rule. I do not condone rape."

She pulled away, not fully satisfied by his words, and

this time he let her go. She turned away, searching frantically for her cast-off clothing. Smock, kirtle. She found only one stocking. Then covering her terrible dishevelment with her voluminous cloak, she shoved her bare feet into her shoes and crossed the room. He blocked her way with a hand splayed flat on the door.

"Wait for the guards to come. They'll protect you."

"I don't need protecting. I need my freedom." She faced the door, acutely conscious of him just behind her. Was he dressed? Sweet Mother, but she hoped so, for if she turned they would be face-to-face, mere inches apart.

If she turned. She did not dare do so.

His voice was a low rumble. "I cannot set you free. Not yet."

"Why not?" What answer did she want from him—that he couldn't bear to be without her? How pitiful a creature she'd become after only one night with him. She needed him to need her. Only he didn't. Not in the way that was most important.

"Never mind," she said, before he could respond. "I know when. Once the walls are higher than a man's head you will release me. How long will that take?" she added, unable to hide the bitterness in her voice.

"A few months. Before winter arrives."

"And am I to warm your bed during that time?" An awful thought occurred to her and she swallowed hard. "Or do you plot still to wed me to your brother when he arrives?"

His hand on the door before her curled into a fist. So he didn't like her to remind him of his brother and his threat to wed her to him. That knowledge goaded her recklessly on. "Does your brother arrive with this Lamonthe? Shall I meet this paragon fellow today, perhaps? Or tonight?"

He jerked her around so fast she nearly fell. He shoved her back against the door, pinning her there with his hands. He was dressed, she noticed. And he was furious.

"Beware that sharp tongue of yours does not bring you to grief, Josselyn. 'Tis enough for you to know that I will make that decision. You are better served by keeping me content rather than riling my temper.''

She left it at that. His anger boded well for her—she hoped. He did not want to share her, not with this new English lord, nor with his brother. But what he did want of her, beyond the immediate, she could not fathom. She tried to content herself that he had her closely guarded for the rest of the morning in the kitchen.

She washed her limbs and her bruised body as well as she could. Then as boredom overtook her, she decided to help with baking the bread. But she refused to dwell on what had happened between her and Rand last night—or on what might occur during the coming one. She must learn instead why this new group of Englishmen had arrived and what repercussions would follow last night's raid by her countrymen. She must remember that she was Welsh and that Rand was English. She must remember that they were enemies and very likely would be forever.

''How many extra loaves are required for the visitors?'' she asked as she divided a batch of dough and began to knead. Slap the dough down, push and fold, push and fold, then slap it down again.

Odo did not look up from his tasks. His good humor was lacking in this, the second day of his elevation to cook. He much preferred helping Gladys to managing on his own.

''Ten men, five loaves,'' he grunted. ''And nearly as many gallons of ale, I'd warrant.''

Josselyn divided the dough into three loaves, shaped them up, and crisscrossed their tops with the edge of a spoon. Odo had been ordered to keep her well away from any knives. ''You'd think this Simon Lamonthe would wait until accommodations were better before he came calling,'' she remarked, hoping to draw some information from Odo regarding the visitors.

'' 'Tis just as well. They're less likely to linger.'' Then he shot her a sharp look. '' 'Course, if you Welsh are plannin' to burn us out, I ought not to complain about ten stout Englishmen come to our aid.''

Josselyn glared at him and dropped the second batch of dough onto the floury table. ''These are Welsh lands, not English.''

''King Henry says Wales is a part o' Britain. Always has been. We're one bloomin' island, or hadn't you heard?''

''If my reasoning was as faulty as yours, I'd say that gives Wales the right to claim English lands as our own. After all, we're one bloomin' island,'' she sarcastically echoed him.

He scowled then pointed at the unfinished loaves before her. ''Finish your work. If you don't work, you don't eat.''

''I don't have to do this.'' She met his angry look with a superior smile, and folded her arms across her chest.

''If you want to eat, you do.''

''No. I don't.''

He looked so exasperated that for a moment Josselyn felt sorry for him. He was hot and tired and sorely overworked. But she was not the cause of his situation, she reminded herself. Rand was. And though Odo wanted to vent his ill humor upon her, she refused to let him do so. She sat herself down on a three-legged stool and began to remove the fragments of dough that clung to her fingers, watching all the while as Odo's frustration grew.

''Have it your way, then,'' he sneered. ''Do nothing. But I'll wager you're not so surly when Lord Randulf makes you earn your keep on your back.''

He ducked when she threw an empty crock at him, then circled the table when she snatched up the wooden pele and came after him. ''Guard. Guard!'' he cried, warding off her swings with the long bakery tool.

Josselyn spun around when the door burst open. ''Stay away from me, you vile pig! Stay back or I'll burst your crown wide open.''

''Here, missy. Don't be startin' any more trouble,'' the

grizzle-faced guard warned. "I don't want to draw my sword 'gainst a woman."

What she thought she might accomplish with the wooden bread paddle against a seasoned warrior, Josselyn could not say. But emotions had taken over where good reason ought to reign, and she was not about to back down.

"Remove yourself from that doorway, and you'll have no reason to draw your weapon."

"Now, miss. You know I canna do that. Himself would have me head."

"She's gone full crazy," Odo swore, sidling up to the soldier. "First she won't cook. Then she threatens me."

"Keep a decent tongue in your head and I'd have no reason to threaten you."

The guard glanced at Odo. "I hope you haven't done nothin' foolish, lad. She's Lord Randulf's woman, or ain't you heard?"

"Oh!" It was simply too much. Did the whole world know what had happened last night? Had Rand regaled all his men with the details of his conquest, like the details of a battle, told and retold and embellished each time?

With a swing borne of utter frustration, Josselyn struck out at Odo. He barely escaped a whizzing slice at his head. But in the process of avoiding the pele, he lurched into the guard and they toppled in a tangle of arms and legs and flailing sword.

Josselyn saw her chance and took it. Out the door and across the yard she sprinted—and directly into the path of trouble. For three mud-splattered soldiers approached the kitchen, and before she could veer out of their path, one of them caught her by the arm and spun her into the grasp of another of his comrades.

"Here, an' wot's this?"

"Looks like a bedwarmer to me," the third man said. "D'ye think Fitz Hugh welcomes all his visitors with one of these?"

"A Welsh bedwarmer, from the looks of 'er," the first

man said, grabbing the paddle from her before she could make use of it against any of them. "Here, I've a treat for you, sweetheart. How'd you like a taste of good English meat?"

Josselyn was too angry to be afraid, too frustrated that they'd stymied her escape to be cautious. "If it's meat you want, the kitchen is there." She indicated the building with a jerk of her head. "Now, release me. Ere you anger Lord Fitz Hugh," she added by way of threat. Unfortunately, her dubious threat was lost in their great guffaws of laughter.

"Meat from the kitchen!"

"Mutton or beef?"

They laughed and leered, yet Josselyn could make no sense of it. Were they all mad? She saw no humor in her words.

Then one of them grabbed his crotch and suddenly she understood. Her disgust was instantaneous and overwhelming. So was her retaliation. While they roared with laughter, the one who held her let his grip loosen a little. In a moment she snatched his dagger from the sheath he wore at his hip. She sliced through his sword belt with a swift downward movement, then pointed the blade up between his legs, holding it steady against his thigh. "Would you like to see a Welshwoman carve good English meat?" she asked in a deadly quiet tone.

His eyes bulged, jerking from her face down to where she held the blade against his manhood. "Get 'er off me!"

"Touch me and he loses what he values most," she swore. "And do not make the mistake of thinking I do not know how to use this blade. All I want is safe passage to the forest. Now."

For a moment she thought they would agree, for they hesitated and did not respond. But then someone new entered the fray.

"You cannot escape me so easily as this, Josselyn."

Rand! Josselyn fought back an overwhelming urge to look at him, for she sensed that to break eye contact with her hostage would be her downfall. God's bones, would this nightmare never cease? She pressed the blade higher, until the man began to blubber with fear. "Release me or he dies," she vowed.

"Kill him, then," Rand replied from much nearer, behind her and to the left. "He's not one of my men so I'll not mourn his loss. Besides, he's not likely to die from losing so useless an appendage."

"Here, milord. That ain't—"

"Silence!" Josselyn ordered the terrified man. "If I cut him, you can be sure he will bleed to death from the wound. Now back away, all of you. And you too," she told her captive, pricking his manhood with the point of her blade.

He was quick to comply and they made three steps together, like dancers locked in an obscene sort of embrace. Three steps away from the kitchen, down the incline toward the forest and freedom. Three steps, with the first drops of blood seeping onto her hand.

"Ow! Ow! She's cuttin' me somethin' fierce!"

" 'Tis only good English meat," Josselyn sneered. Then as abruptly as it began, her escape ended. An arm shoved her aside. The Englishman screamed, and she landed hard on the ground, pinned there by none other than Randulf Fitz Hugh.

It was hard to remember that only hours before he'd pinned her in a sexual embrace. For he was no gentle captor now, no considerate lover bringing her to pleasure before he found his own release. He was an enemy knight, sworn to defeat her and her people.

And she'd just shamed him before his own countrymen.

"Bloody hell," he swore, for her ears only. "That was a stupid move."

She swung her fist but caught him only a glancing blow on his thick English skull. Before she could rally, he yanked her upright, twisting one of her arms behind her back. It hurt her shoulder, but not as much as it hurt her pride to be held so helplessly amidst her enemies. How dare these English asses laugh at her!

"I believe your orders were to keep her safe," Rand bit out. His voice was as cutting as cold steel, and Josselyn saw the guard who stood just beyond the English soldiers swallow hard, then nervously bob his head.

"Yes, milord."

"You blasted fool!" The Englishman Josselyn had cut swore at Rand's guard. "You let a slip of a girl get past you—"

"She got the best of you as well."

That was said by yet another stranger. He was well dressed and well ornamented, with a huge gold buckle on his cloak, and an ornate girdle. Simon Lamonthe, Josselyn deduced at once. And she'd just threatened one of his men. He was of only average height and build, and no match physically for his men, but she feared him just the same. There was power in his manner, a cruel power she instinctively recognized. His eyes, a pale silvery color, moved over her with an avidity far more frightening than his men's.

Without realizing it, she leaned back against Rand. His hand curved over her shoulder and though she resented the possessive gesture and everything it implied, she did not fight him. Not while this other man stripped her naked with his eyes.

"I'll deal with you later," Rand muttered to her. He gestured for his humiliated guard. "Take her back to the kitchen."

But the silver-eyed Lamonthe intercepted him. "I can think of far better uses for her than as a kitchen drudge. I've found Welshwomen to be a spirited lot. Most certainly this one is no tame kitten."

His eyes lowered to her breasts and Josselyn trembled with outrage and disgust. And fear. God help any woman who fell into that man's power! Surely Rand would protect her from him.

Rand's fingers tightened around her shoulder in what she

took to be a reassuring gesture. His words, however, were not so comforting. "When I tire of her, I'll send her to you. For now, however, I'm not inclined to share her."

Lamonthe smiled, though without any trace of warmth. His men laughed coarsely—at least two of them did. The man she'd cut only glared at her as he crudely rubbed his crotch. A threat, she knew, and once again she leaned into Rand.

But he thrust her toward his guard, and with a warning slap on her derriere, he released her.

Josselyn was wise enough not to react to that last patronizing gesture, but oh, how she wanted to snatch the long pele from Odo and crown Rand with it. Instead she followed Odo, trying without success to jerk her arm from the guard's unforgiving grasp.

"Stupid bitch!" the guard snapped once they were in the kitchen.

" 'Tis you who appeared stupid," she countered, jerking free of him at last.

"You made Lord Randulf look the fool," Odo hissed. "D'ye think he'll forget that?"

Josselyn glared at him. "Why should he care what that other man thinks?"

"Simon Lamonthe, Lord of Bailwynn, is not a man to trifle with, nor one to appear weak and foolish before."

"He's a powerful lord," the guard added. "He's got the king's ear and 'tis said he rules the hills south of here like a king himself."

"So?" Josselyn turned away from them, but though she appeared unimpressed, it was pure affectation. For she recognized the name Simon Lamonthe now. His cruelty to the Welsh was legend. The fortress he'd built to the south, almost to Radnor Forest, was said to be impregnable. And now he was here. But for what purpose?

"There's work to be done," Odo pointed out. But Josselyn ignored him. She'd cooked her last meal for Englishmen. She'd kneaded her last bowl of dough for their consumption. What could Rand do to her that he hadn't already done?

He could give you to Simon Lamonthe.

Her heart began to race. He could. But he wouldn't.

But what if that man requested the use of her body? Could Rand deny the demands of the powerful Lamonthe if he forced the issue? Would he even try?

She sat in the farthest corner of the kitchen, stiff and unrelenting, while Odo and his haphazard assistant prepared an unappetizing fish stew. The loaves came from the oven, small, hard, and only half-risen. But they were not burned. Indeed, in the confusion of the hasty preparations, the loaves were barely cooked.

A just God would see them all choked on the sticky mess, Josselyn decided. It was very likely a sin of grave proportion to instruct God in the handling of His affairs. Still, she did not believe a just God would begrudge her this tiny irreverence.

As time grew shorter, Odo cast her many an angry look. But his beseeching ones had not moved her, and neither would his irritated ones. Josselyn had far more serious matters to consider than the rising of dough and how hot the oven was.

In the span of one day her life had been turned upside down. Worst of all, however, she did not know what to do about it. Even should she escape, she would be caught in another trap. For the pattern of her life pointed in one direction, but it was a direction in which she did not wish to go: marriage to Owain. Complicating things further still, Owain's efforts on her behalf could not be ignored.

And yet were her wishes of no moment?

More importantly, what *were* her wishes?

The low rumble of thunder rattled the sky and rain began abruptly to fall. Outside men swore while inside she tried to rejoice. They could not work in the rain, could they? They could not raise their cursed wall.

She stood, stretching her stiff limbs, trying not to recall

the activities that had made her so sore. "I need a moment's privacy," she told the guard.

The man scowled at her. "I've learnt my lesson. You'll not be trickin' Horace again."

"This is no trick but a plain fact of life." She planted her fists on her hips. "I'm surprised you don't have a similar need by now."

He shifted from one foot to the other, then glanced uncertainly at Odo. "What d'ye think?"

Odo was sweating, with flour dusting his arms and a big greasy stain on his apron. He sent Josselyn a desperate look. "Can we come to an agreement?"

Her first instinct was to say no. The English could starve for all she cared. But reason had cooled her anger somewhat. She gave him a curt nod. "We can."

His eyes widened. "You'll take over the baking?"

"Wot's this got to do with anything?" Horace demanded.

When she nodded at Odo, he turned to the guard. "I can't have people pissin' in me pots. Take her outside somewhere. But watch her closely and bring her back immediately. And keep her away from any of Lamonthe's men."

She had only a few minutes, but Josselyn made the most of them. Simon Lamonthe's men clustered near Rand's quarters. No doubt the two lords plotted inside. The rain fell but lightly now, a drizzle that did not slow labor on the walls after all. The building meant to eventually house the soldiers, but which now was to serve the masons and laborers as well, was nearly head high. By day's end it would be ready to receive the roof timbers.

The work was progressing much swifter than she could believe. Had Rhonwen delivered the message to Clyde about Rand's brother? Would they intercept him? And would Owain try another ploy to free her?

As she trudged back to the kitchen she asked, "How fares Alan?"

"Don't tell me you're feelin' guilty for the poor lad's miseries."

"It's a simple enough question. Will you answer it?"

"He lives," the man grunted. He yanked open the kitchen door and gestured her in. "That's all I know."

Josselyn was silent as she approached the baking table. Alan was little more than a boy. It pained her that he had been so grievously wounded in Owain's attack. But many more Englishmen would suffer, she reminded herself, and Welshmen as well, before this struggle was ended. She could not fret over these English warriors who'd invaded her lands.

She stirred the embers in the oven and added more oak to even out the heat. Warriors fought, they were wounded, and often they died. It was the way of the world, just as women married to benefit their families.

The difference was, it was your enemy whom you expected to hurt you, not your ally. In her case, however, she was certain Owain would hurt her more than Rand ever would, even considering his curt behavior today.

Rand, however, was not one of the choices given to her. His brother was.

As she worked, shaping the loaves, using the pele once more to ferry hot loaves out of the oven and freshly risen ones in, she tried not to think of this Jasper Fitz Hugh, nor of Owain. Nor, especially, of Rand. Instead she thought of her conversation with Newlin not so long ago—and yet it seemed an age: winter's end was nigh. The end of her old life. The beginning of a new season for her, and mayhap her people too.

The rain outside washed the winter away and brought the new softness of spring. The walls rose as did the reborn fields and forests.

Would the wild roses of the cliffs one day clamber up the stone walls the English built? And if they did, who would be there to pluck the fragrant blooms, English women or Welsh?

She was heartily afraid to learn the answer to that.

Seventeen

The meal was only a little better than palatable. Half the bread was a waste of flour, even coarse barley flour, and the poor quality of the other half would not encourage the visitors to stay.

But that was for the best, Josselyn decided later, as the sun retreated behind a heavy layer of clouds. It was clear to her that Simon Lamonthe and his men were not welcome at Rosecliffe. They should have been, for they were English, and Josselyn would have expected Rand's welcome to be sincere. But instead it was strained; she sensed that even though she'd not seen either of the men since her futile attempt at escape. There was a caution among Rand's men and a watchfulness among Lamonthe's that spoke of suspicion rather than mutual support.

How interesting. She'd always supposed the English to be a united front of mighty lords, determined to make Welsh lands their own. Were it not for the rough terrain of the northern Welsh lands, her country's fragmented families, who were suspicious and always warring among themselves, would have no chance against the full force of English might. But the English were not so united as they seemed, despite their king and his claim to the contrary.

Why did Rand mistrust this man? she wondered. And why had Lamonthe come to Rosecliffe?

The answer was obvious: to spy. He'd come as she'd initially come, to see what Rand planned. To consider how he might be thwarted.

Did that mean Lamonthe might be an ally for the Welsh?

Her fingers stilled in their restless combing of her tangled hair. Lamonthe was not a man to be anyone's ally for long. She knew that instinctively.

She watched through the window as outside a bonfire flared to life, silhouetting several clusters of men in its orange glow. Ale flowed freely now that it was too dark to work. The masons and carpenters and diggers drank and talked, growing more and more boisterous. But no soldiers drank, she saw. At least not to excess. Neither Rand's men nor Lamonthe's.

Her curiosity piqued, she crept quietly from her corner. Odo had deserted the kitchen as soon as the supper had been offered up. Horace still watched over her, but for the past hour he'd been fighting to keep his eyes open. As she watched, his head nodded forward and he began to snore.

Did she dare creep outside? And if she did, should she try to escape or, rather, try to determine the source of the tension between Rand and Simon Lamonthe?

In the end the choice was not hers to make. For as she opened the door, it creaked. Horace awoke with a start, and she was caught. Though she did not run, his fury was unabated.

"I merely needed fresh air," Josselyn protested as she tried to evade him.

"Save your lies for Lord Randulf. As for meself, I'll not be made a fool of twice."

"You were born a fool," she muttered. "Keep your hands off me!"

But he caught her and rudely bound her wrists behind her despite her struggles. Then he looped the rope through one of the pot hooks embedded in the new fire box, leaving her to fume and heap curses upon him in Welsh, English, and French. She remained in that ignoble position when

Rand strode in and her fury turned at once from the guard to the man who gave him his hateful orders.

"You will rue the day you treated me thus!"

"Simon Lamonthe seeks an audience with you."

Her angry invective died in her throat. Hot rage turned to cold fear, and her heart began to thud.

He glanced at Horace. "Go." He waited until the muttering Horace shut the door before continuing. "He wants a woman for tonight and you are the only woman here."

Josselyn could not believe what he was saying to her. He could not mean to simply give her to this man! And yet when he crossed to her and began to loosen her bindings, it seemed he meant to do precisely that.

"I will not go!" She tried to twist away from him, unwilling to be untied if it meant being handed over to Simon Lamonthe. "I won't do it. I'll fight him—"

"He'd like that, Josselyn. He would relish your every struggle, then take you just the same."

Tears sprang unbidden to her eyes. Bad enough the fate that awaited her. But how could he so easily hand her over to that man? She shook her head, paralyzed by unaccustomed fear.

Only then did his implacable expression alter. His eyes searched her face, as if he sought to delve into the deepest corners of her mind. "I told him you are my woman," he finally said. "But he believes he can woo you to his bed with coin."

Josselyn shuddered. "There is not enough coin in the entire British realm."

Rand cocked his head. "You enjoyed our bed sport. Why would you avoid it with him?"

Suddenly she sensed a trap. She tried to compose herself, to weigh her words. To decipher his. "I am no whore to leap from one man's bed to another's—nor to accept coin for the use of my body."

"Then what of last night?"

Josselyn turned away from him. She had no answer for

that, at least none she could share with him. " 'Tis not last night which concerns me now, but tonight. Will you turn me over to him?"

She felt rather than heard him move up behind her. She waited for his touch, hating herself for wanting it. Hating him for making her feel this traitorous longing.

"I will turn you over to no one."

She trembled at the husky possessiveness in his voice. "Not even to your brother?"

He did not answer and though she knew it should not matter, for his brother would be captured by her uncle and Owain long before he arrived at Rosecliffe, she nonetheless needed to know. "Will you wed me to him?"

"If I must."

She shifted farther away from him, though her wrists were still tethered to the pot hook. "Who's to say you must, save for yourself?"

"I want peace here, Josselyn, between your people and mine. If your union to Jasper is the only way to achieve that end, then I have no other choice."

She glared at him. "So. You will not make a whore of me with Lamonthe, but you would do so with your brother."

A muscle jumped in his jaw. "No more so than your uncle would. Come," he added. "You'll sleep in my quarters."

"I will not lie with you again."

His eyes narrowed. "We shall see."

"I'd rather lie with Lamonthe!" she swore.

His jaw clenched again in irritation. "We both know that is a lie. But do not force my temper, woman, else I may decide the pleasure you afford not worth the aggravation." Then unmindful of her wishes, he turned her around, unknotted her bindings, and gave her a curt shove toward the door.

She rubbed her wrists as they headed across the loose sort of enclosure created by the kitchen, his quarters, and the new wood shed. Daily the Englishmen progressed in their frenzied building program. Already the cluster of buildings at Rosecliffe felt more like a village than merely an encampment. Once the walls were raised the English would be nearly impossible to rout.

As if to confirm her dark thoughts, Rand's hand moved to the small of her back, a reminder that she was his hostage. A reminder also of the perverse power his simple touch had over her. She moved faster to avoid that distressing touch. "Where is Lamonthe?"

"He has a pavilion."

"So you do not take me to him."

"I told him you were mine and not available no matter the price."

They reached his quarters and halted outside the door. She looked up at him accusingly. "You had no intention of giving me to him. You said that only to frighten me."

He paused before responding. The glow from the distant bonfire limned his face with the faintest gold, but it cast no light on his expression. "You came here to spy on us. You agreed to teach me Welsh only to give yourself the opportunity to learn my plans. You deceived me about who you were and conspired against me. I would be a fool not to wonder why you took me to your bed—"

"You can hardly call it that! *You* seduced *me*!"

"Perhaps. Nevertheless, I wondered if you would try the same ploy with Lamonthe."

"The same ploy? 'Twas no ploy. Oh!" Enraged that he could think so little of her, Josselyn backed away from him. "I will not share a chamber with you again. Most certainly I will never share your bed!"

"Even if I seduce you?"

Like a caress, the sensual promise in his low-pitched voice washed warm and revealing over her. Her skin prickled and she wrapped her arms across her stomach. "I am not so foolish as to fall into that trap again."

"Indeed. I'd wager that you are more susceptible than ever."

A coarse laugh and the tramp of approaching steps saved her from responding to that provocative remark. When the shadow of three men loomed near, Rand shoved her protectively behind him.

"So, Fitz Hugh. Have you reconsidered my offer?" Simon Lamonthe asked. Josselyn would have recognized that cold, amused voice anywhere. "Or mayhap you have not relayed it to the wench. Three gold coins," he said to Josselyn. "Three gold coins and a night you will never forget."

"Her wishes are immaterial, Lamonthe. She is my hostage. You will have to wait until I release her before you solicit for her pleasures."

Josselyn could have kissed Rand for that. She wanted to throw her arms around him and kiss his broad back and thank him for protecting her from Lamonthe's revolting offer. By rights she should be angry at Rand's reminder that she was nothing more than a hostage to him, and the implication that her favors could be bought. But at that moment she did not care about such details. He kept her safe from Lamonthe and for now that was all that mattered.

"So be it," the other man said, after a long tense silence. "I'll be waiting when he sets you free," he said to Josselyn, jiggling his purse. But the clink of coin on coin sounded ugly in her ears. Ugly and threatening.

"And Fitz Hugh," he added before he left. "Beware you do not fall into the same trap that has ruined so many an Englishman. She is a warm body, no more. A hot quim to serve your needs. Do not be fool enough to engage your heart else you will find that she has cut it out and served it up to her bloodthirsty brethren." Then laughing, he turned and strolled off into the darkness, his hulking soldiers laughing along with him.

Without speaking, Rand opened the door and thrust Josselyn inside. The bolt came down, an abrupt scraping of wood on metal. Then they were alone. Even more than before, Josselyn was grateful to have escaped the repugnant Simon Lamonthe. But his reference to her as no more than a convenient object for sex left her feeling dirty and defiled. She knew it was no less than Rand already thought of her, yet hearing the ugly truth out loud depressed her anew.

"I will not share your bed," she muttered as she watched him divest himself of his weapons and tunic.

"As you wish. I am too weary to argue the matter."

That surprised her, but she knew better than to trust him. "I do not speak lightly. If you intend me for your brother, I cannot lie with you again."

As she watched for his response he pulled his boots off, then with one smooth movement tugged his chainse over his head and flung it aside. He was barefoot and bare-chested and when he looked over at her, unsmiling, she swallowed hard. What a sight he made in the meager light of one candle. What a powerful, virile sight. Her mouth went dry; her pulse went wild.

"It has been a long day, Josselyn, following on the heels of a night when I slept but little. I plan to sleep now though, as, I trust, will you."

He meant what he said. A modicum of relief washed over her. Then he added, "But you *will* share my bed."

"What?"

"It's that or be bound to my chair. I cannot risk you making another bid for freedom."

"Then I prefer the chair. I'd rather be tied in a chair all night than share a bed with you."

"So you say. But I will not sleep well if I know you are uncomfortable. My bed is soft and big enough for two."

"No."

"Yes." He started toward her, stalking her. "You need not fear my intentions, for I plan only to bind you to me." He held up a length of chain. "That way you cannot hope to escape without rousing me."

Josselyn shook her head. No matter what he said, she

knew where this was leading. "What if I promise not to escape?"

"I am to believe that? Tell me, I have promised not to touch you in a provocative manner. Do *you* believe *me*?"

Her heart sank. She was trapped.

She waited as he crossed the room to her. Her back pressed against the rough stone wall. Her palms grew damp. The chain swung from his hand. Pretty. Ominous. It was curious in design, with a narrow cuff at one end. He clicked it closed over her left wrist, then using a small lock, fastened the other end of the chain around his wrist. She twisted the cuff but could find no lock. When she looked up at him in frustration, he gave her a half-smile.

"An Eastern curiosity, but exceedingly useful. Now come. I weary of this constant battle between us."

She had no choice, but that did not make it any easier to comply with his demand. She followed him reluctantly to the bed.

"Do you need help removing your gown?"

Josselyn scowled. "I have no intention of shedding any of my garments."

He shrugged as if he did not care. Then still holding her gaze, he released the ties on his braies, unwound the crossbands, and stepped out of the loose garment.

She averted her face. She could not, however, hide the rush of hot color to her cheeks. She feared that would be visible even in pitch darkness. "Is your brother as crude in his manner as are you?" she muttered. The phantom Jasper was her only defense against Rand. But did she invoke Jasper's name to warn Rand away or to warn herself? She feared to examine her motives too closely.

"I am not privy to the particulars of his behavior with women. But leave off these delaying tactics, Josselyn. I wish only to sleep."

He tugged on the chain that bound her to him and she took a step closer. But still she kept her eyes fixed on the

wall somewhere above his head. "How . . . how old is he?"
she stammered.

The bed ropes creaked beneath his weight and her cheeks
burned hotter. That sound would forever remind her of . . .
of what she should put completely out of her head.

"He is ten years my junior. Son to my father's second
wife. Lie down, Josselyn." He tugged and she sat down
abruptly on the bed.

"Have you a wife?" she blurted out.

"No." After a moment he added, "Nor am I seeking
one."

The insult implied in his answer restored her to anger.
"Yet you would seek one for your brother."

"I want peace between the English and Welsh. I want
him wed to a Welshwoman. You are the obvious choice.
Enough of this." He caught her around the waist and pulled
her down on the mattress beside him. "Enough of this,"
he repeated, yawning against her hair. " 'Tis time to
sleep."

Perhaps for him, Josselyn thought as she lay there on her
back, stiff and unmoving. His arm lay heavy across her
waist, a warning for her not to escape. His breathing grew
slow and even, a warm, rhythmic wave rustling her hair,
tickling her ear. His bent knee pressed against her thigh.

It might be time to sleep, but their intimate proximity
precluded it.

Yet somehow, at some point, she did sleep. Somewhere
between wondering if she could break the chain and trying
to squeeze her hand through the cuff, she fell into the
heavy, dreamless sleep of the truly exhausted. She awoke
only when someone shook her.

Rand.

Her eyes blinked, he smoothed the hair back from her
face, and it began again. The terrible tension. The impossible attraction.

He leaned over her, backlit by the unshuttered window.
Silent. Strong. For that moment, between the dreams of

night and the reality of day, he was only a man, neither Welsh nor English. He had not come to conquer or rule, but simply to offer her pleasure.

She stared up at him through the haze of morning light, through the haze of feelings unaffected by reason or responsibility.

Then he shifted and his leg slid along her thigh. Her bare thigh. With a start she realized that during the night her gown had edged up so that it bunched now around her waist, leaving the rest of her naked.

As naked as was he.

His hand moved down while his eyes held steady. "Did you sleep well?" His long fingers found the smooth skin of her hip. His palm did as well.

"Yes."

"And are you refreshed? Renewed?" His voice was husky with sleep . . . and with desire. It awakened an answering desire in her.

"You promised only sleep," she whispered.

"Do you want to go back to sleep?"

What she wanted she could not speak out loud, neither in his language nor hers. "Please, Rand."

He shifted her near him so that her hip nestled against his groin. He was hard and ready for her, and suddenly she could hardly breathe. Once more he toyed with her hair. "When you say my name, Josselyn . . . Say it again."

"Rand," she repeated, like one mesmerized.

He groaned and closed his eyes as if in pain.

She did that to him, she realized. She made him desire her just as she desired him. It was a heady thing to wield that sort of power over a man like him. Yet what could she do with that power save ultimately destroy herself?

She would enjoy it for a moment more. That was all, she told herself. She lifted her hand to his face to cup his lean cheek, to thread her fingers in his dark hair. But the chain caught beneath her elbow and prevented her. Her hand stopped halfway to its goal. The silver cuff winked morning light at her, reminding her of the grim reality that lay between them.

He saw it too, and when their eyes met she thought she spied regret on his face. Certainly she saw frustration.

"There are those women who enjoy the limitations of bindings," he murmured. "You did yesterday."

So she had, and it shamed her to admit as much. But this was worse than physical bindings, whether they be rope or silver chain. For he meant to bind her with the love of his body, then give her to another. To his brother.

"No," she said, closing her eyes.

"You say no. But I hear yes." This time he slid fully over her, pressing her into the mattress, thrilling her body with the hard weight and heat of his own. He kissed her closed eyes. "Say yes, Josselyn. We shall both of us be glad for it."

She made herself look at him. She made herself struggle against the powerful tide sucking her along with him. "Tell me you will not wed me to your brother."

He started to say it. She was certain of it. He opened his mouth and began to form the words. But then he stopped.

He caught her face between his hands and gazed earnestly into her eyes. "We both have our duty. Your loyalty is to your people and you will do whatever is necessary to preserve their well-being, just as I do the same for mine."

"Lying with you and then your brother cannot help my people," she countered.

He hesitated. He had no good answer to that. "Marrying you to Jasper will keep a reasonable sort of peace between your people and mine, long enough to prove that we can prosper together, Welsh and English, side by side."

"You are wrong in that. I can understand why you wish to believe it. Still . . . still, that does not pertain to this . . . To us . . ."

"To us," he repeated. He was close enough and there was enough light for Josselyn to see the stubbled growth on his cheeks, each individual dark hair. She saw also the hairless scar on his cheek and the hungry glitter in his clear gray eyes. "This desire that lies between us," he continued, "need have nothing to do with anyone else, Josselyn. We desire one another. There is no impediment to—"

"There is every impediment! Even were your brother not a part of it, I am your hostage. You are my enemy."

He swore under his breath. "I could force you."

"Don't."

His eyes burned into hers. "I can seduce you."

"I know," she admitted in a whisper.

A vein throbbed in his neck, pumping the blood that made him warm, that made him so alive. That made him the man who moved her so violently. Had he pressed her—had he bent down and kissed her then—she would have caved in to his demands, to the demands of her own pent-up desires.

But he didn't do that and she knew she ought to be glad. He pulled away. His hands fell away from her face, and with a curse and then a groan, he rolled off her.

They lay side by side, tethered by the chain he'd placed on their wrists, but as far apart as duty and politics could place them. Josselyn wanted to weep, though it was the unlikeliest of reactions. He was her enemy and he did not mean to force her. That was cause for joy, or at the least, relief. Certainly not for sorrow.

She made herself speak. "Will you remove this cuff?"

He removed it then dressed himself in silence and left without further word. Josselyn remained in the bed until he was gone. It was a new day. Pray God it would be easier than the previous one.

She rose, sluggish, her body clumsy, not yet fully roused from the heavy sleep she'd sunk into. An ewer of water refreshed her. The barred door depressed her.

She should never have agreed to teach her language to Rand. She should never have ventured into his camp at all. She would not be in this agonizing predicament if she had only resigned herself to marrying Owain.

A shudder ripped through her. Marry Owain? Never. It took only the touch of Rand's hand—or lips or any portion of his body—for her to know she could never share such intimacies with Owain.

"Why must he be English?" She muttered the unhappy question out loud. But even that was not the biggest impediment, she realized. The fact remained that while he would have his brother marry her, he would not do so himself. Whether English or Welsh, if he did not wish to marry her, there was no one who could force him to do so.

That meant this Jasper would become her husband unless her uncle succeeded in their desperate plan. But when would that happen?

She spent the day waiting. One of Odo's kitchen helpers delivered her a tasteless meal of undercooked bread and scorched eel. The new guard at the door gave her a small bundle—her personal items at last. Someone had quite obviously searched them, not that Josselyn was surprised. It was just one more ignominy, a minor one in the face of all the others she'd suffered—and was yet to suffer.

But news of Rand's brother Jasper did not arrive that day. Nor the next. And when it did come, it came through the unlikeliest source, and before the actual event had even occurred.

Eighteen

The guard Horace ushered Newlin in, giving the twisted bard a suspicious look and a wide berth. Josselyn could have kissed them both, she was that overjoyed to see one of her own people. She was also fairly bursting with questions. Two days alone had left her desperate for company. She should have guessed that Newlin was the only Welshman Rand would allow in his camp. For his part, Newlin appeared equally pleased to see her.

"You are well treated?" he asked, circling her, scrutinizing her with his one good eye.

"As well as can be expected. The food is awful," she added in English, aiming those words at the departing guard.

" 'Tis your own fault," the man muttered before slamming the door on his way out.

"My fault. *My* fault!" Josselyn turned to Newlin, throwing her hands up in the air. "What manner of men are these English that they expect their prisoners to labor on their behalf, preparing them delectable meals so that their workers are satisfied and can proceed more swiftly than ever to obliterate us from our own lands? They are madmen, every one of them, most especially the one who leads them." She paused in her tirade. "And they are driving *me* mad," she finished in a less strident tone.

" 'Tis the separation from your family that tortures you so," Newlin stated.

"Indeed it does."

"And the confinement to this single room, the inability to feel the wind and climb the hills."

"Oh, yes. I miss that terribly."

"No doubt the absence of the Englishman makes it worse."

"It does. *Not*. It does *not*," she corrected as soon as she realized her mistake. But it was impossible to lie to Newlin. He fixed his unblinking gaze on her, his odd, unfocused stare, and with a sigh Josselyn gave up. She turned away from him and began to pace. "I do not understand any of this."

"You do not speak of politics but of your own feelings."

Resigned, she nodded. "I cannot understand even a portion of them, and I don't believe I ever will. But it is not for you to interpret my perverse emotions," she continued. "That is not the purpose of your visit. Tell me about everyone. Does Nesta worry overmuch? Did Rhonwen deliver my message? Does my uncle think it a worthy plan?"

"Yes to all of your questions," Newlin responded as he wandered the room, examining Rand's belongings. He ran a finger over the inkwell and three quill pens. He smoothed his hand along a roll of parchment, then across the locked trunk where Rand kept his personal possessions. "He is avoiding you, I think."

"Uncle Clyde?"

Newlin looked up at her and smiled. "Randulf Fitz Hugh."

Josselyn frowned. "And well he ought to."

"His brother comes."

"He has been sighted?" Josselyn's heart began to pound. Would her plan work?

Newlin tilted his head and stared somewhere beyond her. "They take him now, south of Bryn Mound, near the ford below Raven Hill."

"Now? This very minute?" Josselyn stared at the bard and the skin on her arms prickled. He could not be right. How would he know? And yet she could hardly doubt him. How he knew such things she could never say. No one could. It was enough that he did, and that he'd come to tell her.

"What will happen next? What will my uncle do first?"

Newlin's face reflected no satisfaction as he studied her. "Owain will torture him, I think."

"Owain? But this is not his concern."

"You are his betrothed. When you first disappeared, your uncle suspected Owain of capturing you. There are yet hard feelings between them for his mistake. But Owain has not been deterred by the insult. He has roused many of the younger village men on your behalf. Where your uncle would be cautious, he is bold."

Dismay crept over Josselyn, robbing her of hope. "It was he who fired the English boats and nearly killed Alan."

"It was."

"And it is he who has captured Jasper Fitz Hugh."

Newlin stared at her, not blinking. "So it would seem."

Josselyn sat down, sick with dread for anyone who fell into Owain's power, even this Jasper, whose capture would lead to her escape. But this was war, she reminded herself. People were bound to be hurt. People were likely to be killed.

Still, this was the first time she'd caused such pain, and even though her involvement was indirect, she felt no less guilty. She swallowed hard. "Does Rand know?" Then she realized how foolish her question was. The ford near Raven Hill lay more than three hours' hard ride to the south. "Will you tell him?" she amended.

"I did not see him in the camp."

Josselyn sighed. Rand had stayed away these past two days. Two long, drawn-out days. "They will tell you where he is if you ask."

"When he hears the news, he may well take out his anger on you."

Josselyn suspected as much, but hearing her fear expressed by the wise bard sent a shiver of apprehension up her spine. After a long moment she said, "Surely my uncle will not allow Owain to torture him."

"No doubt he will try to prevent it."

"Will he succeed?"

Newlin's answer was a noncommittal shrug.

Agitated, Josselyn pushed to her feet. "This should never have happened. I sent that message to my uncle. Why has he let Owain take over this way? He should have known Owain would ruin everything! Don't you see, Newlin? If Owain hurts Jasper—if he kills him—Rand will never let me go. And he'll never forgive any of us. He is a man of honor, notwithstanding that he is our enemy. He will avenge his brother's death. I know he will, Newlin. You have to stop Owain before this goes too far."

" 'Tis out of my hands, child. Better for you to think on your own situation."

"Does Owain even plan to offer Jasper in trade for me?"

Newlin took a long time to answer. "The day will come, and not far off, when you will be free to marry into Owain's family."

Josselyn's nostrils flared and she shook her head vehemently. "I could never marry a man so bloodthirsty as Owain ap Madoc, a man so cruel as to torture his captives."

"Then marry another."

Newlin's words lingered long after he was gone. Marry another. And yet to shun the Lloyds now would be to ensure their undying enmity—unless she married another from among their number. That gave her pause. Madoc ap Lloyd had no other sons, but he had nephews and brothers and cousins. Surely one of them was yet unwed or perhaps widowed.

Like Madoc himself.

Josselyn ceased the restless pacing she'd begun on Newlin's departure. Marry Madoc, Owain's father. Would he agree? Did he even desire another wife? And then, could she agree to lie with a man old enough to be her sire?

The answer was horrifyingly simple. She could resign herself more easily to the aging Madoc than to the cruel Owain.

She sagged back against the wall and covered her face with her hands, then slid slowly down until she sat huddled on the floor, sick with the choices left to her. She was but chattel in the war games played by the men who surrounded her. Her body was a prize to them. Uncle, enemy, betrothed—they were all the same in their view of her and, indeed, of all women. Her body was a prize while her feelings were of no consequence at all.

She was too sick with dread to cry. Too crushed by despair to weep. Her plan to infiltrate Rand's camp and somehow save herself from Owain seemed now but the dreams of a foolish girl. She could never defeat any of these men. No woman could.

Rand found her thus when he ventured into his quarters a short while later. He'd allowed Newlin's visit and he'd wondered what they'd conversed about. Though he'd made a solemn vow two days previously to avoid being alone with her again, the bard was not an hour gone before Rand reneged on that vow. To see her so subdued, so beaten down, alarmed him.

When the door shut behind him she looked up, then rose slowly—painfully, it seemed—to her feet.

"What ails you?" he demanded to know. "Josselyn?"

She refused to look at him. "I long for my freedom," she answered, wrapping her arms around herself. "Is that so surprising?"

It was not. Yet he knew there was more that she was not saying. "What news has Newlin brought that leaves you in such a state?"

She turned to face him and her eyes were bleak. Something had happened, and while logically he knew that what-

ever news depressed her would more than likely have the
opposite effect on him, he nonetheless felt an inkling of
alarm. Without planning to, he took hold of her shoulders.
''What has happened?''

She pulled away from him—recoiled, it seemed. Though
he did not want to, he let her go. She crossed the room,
hugging her arms around herself again, avoiding his searching gaze. It must be grim news, indeed, for her to react this
way. But what? His men had engaged no one in battle.

Unless it was conflict between the Welsh, conflict between her uncle and her betrothed, neither of whom apparently trusted the other.

He studied her, noting her pale color, her agitated movements, and sorrowful demeanor. From nowhere the unlikeliest emotion rose in his chest. He wanted to comfort her.
If someone she cared for had been wounded or killed, he
wanted to comfort her.

Unless that person was Owain. If it was Owain she
mourned, he wanted to wipe the man's memory completely
from her brain.

He clenched his fists and forced himself to stay where
he was, to allow her to reveal the problem to him at her
own pace.

She rubbed her arms, then drew a fortifying breath. He
saw her gather her courage and turn to face him. But he
was so taken with the totality of her womanly beauty, the
beauty of her face and form, the beauty of her rare strength
and fortitude, that the words she said did not initially reg-
ister.

''Your brother has been captured.''

Their eyes met and held until he blinked. ''What?''

''Your brother . . . Jasper. He has been captured.''

Reality felt like an interloper in the cozy room he'd given
over to her. Reality was too ugly to exist here, between
them when they were alone. But her slender body, so tense,
and her compelling face, so pale, lent strength to the inter-

loper, and in the space of a heartbeat reality slammed like an unblunted lance into his gut.

He did not want to believe her, but he knew instinctively it was true. A cold calm settled over him. An icy fury. "Who has captured him? Your uncle?"

She bit her lower lip. "Owain."

"Where is he?"

"At Raven Hill. Three hours from here."

He planted his fists on his hips, never taking his eyes from her. "I assume he plans to trade Jasper for you. Why did Newlin not relay the terms to me directly?"

She looked away. He fancied he saw her tremble. Why was she so afraid? Then his heart stopped in his chest. "He's not dead, is he?"

Her startled face turned back to him. "No. At least . . . at least I don't think so."

"Damn you, tell me what you know!"

He thought she'd shrink back beneath his fury, but instead she stiffened and met his accusing glare. "It has just happened. I cannot explain how Newlin knows such things, but he does."

"It has just happened three hours' ride from here and he already knows of it?" Rand shook his head. He would not believe such foolishness. How would they even know Jasper was en route?

The answer stood just before him: from Josselyn.

The facts spun through his head in dizzying sequence. His drunken revelation to Osborn and Alan within her hearing. She'd told Newlin—

No. Newlin had already departed that night. Then suddenly he knew. "It was the little girl in the woods. You sent word through her."

She didn't have to admit it, but to her credit she did. "I cannot be your passive prisoner. I cannot stand idly by while you take our lands, while you carelessly pair me with your brother. I told Rhonwen and she told my uncle—"

"And he sent Owain to hunt Jasper down."

"I don't know the particulars of what happened beyond my own part in it," she said.

Rand wanted to rage at her. He had no reason to expect any loyalty from her, and yet perversely enough, he did. He felt betrayed. But he'd as lief grovel at her feet as admit it. How she would gloat to know the true depths of her triumph over him.

And yet there was a strange lack of satisfaction in her bearing. "Why do you not rejoice in this victory of your betrothed over my brother?"

She looked away.

Something was not right, he realized. Something about her reaction made no sense. "Don't you want to be traded for Jasper? Don't you want to leave here and return to your beloved Owain?"

Her little involuntary shudder at the mention of Owain's name revealed much to Rand, all of it welcome. "You do not have to marry him, Josselyn. Not if you do not wish it."

She drew herself up. "Do you refer to Owain, or to Jasper?"

He hesitated only a moment. "Owain."

"What of your brother?" she persisted.

He expelled a slow breath. "I will not force you to marry him."

She considered that. "You would support my wish to select my own husband?"

"I cannot allow you to wed anyone who will join your family in opposing me. Surely you can understand that."

"So I would remain unwed, for you will deny me any man of Wales, and I will not marry any of your Englishmen."

That suited him perfectly. But there was still the matter of Jasper. "What else did Newlin tell you?"

"You avoid my question."

"Tell me first of my brother."

Her eyes flickered away from his, then back. "Newlin fears for Jasper's safety in Owain's care."

Rand forced himself not to react, at least not outwardly. But inside he howled with rage. Impotent rage. "Is Owain so careless of the hostage I hold? Does he not consider that I will behave in a like manner?" He advanced on her, his arms rigid at his side. His fists were clenched so hard they shook. "Does he truly believe that because you are a woman I will take the torture of my brother without reacting?"

He stopped but inches from her. She was small and slender before him, no match for his angry strength, defenseless against any punishment he chose to mete out.

And he did want to punish her. He wanted to punish her for making him behave like a fool. She'd deceived him about her identity, then entranced him with her innocent passion. He'd been so overcome with desire for her that he'd revealed information she should never have been privy to, information which could cost any number of lives.

And first among those was his brother's.

Still, she'd done no more than any loyal soldier would do. She'd ascertained her enemy's most vulnerable spot, then attacked him there. And he had let her. His brains had been in his braies—a condition he'd oft accused Jasper of.

He glared down at her, hating her for the way she'd played him for a fool. Even now, with his younger brother's life hanging in the balance, he was making stupid promises to her. By God, he ought to shackle her to the vilest man he could find!

Josselyn saw the fury Rand struggled to rein in. *See how it feels to worry for your kin? My aunt and uncle have felt that same fear for me, and all on account of you.* But though she knew she should enjoy his frustration and his fear for his brother, she simply could not.

"I am hopeful my uncle will prevent Owain from harming him."

He gave her a contemptuous look. "We speak of a man

who makes you shudder. I saw you," he added before she could deny it. "Tell me the truth, Josselyn. Will he kill Jasper?"

"I . . . I don't think so," she stammered. Then honesty compelled her to add, "But only because he would be blamed for any resultant punishment that might befall me."

A muscle ticked in Rand's jaw. "Will he torture him?"

Another shudder ripped through her. "I believe he might."

In the silence that followed, her feelings of dread increased tenfold. For a look came over his face. A light glittered from deep in his eyes. Gone was the seductive captor, the charming captor. Even the frustrating captor she'd raged against. In his place appeared an iron-willed lord, an English knight with vengeance on his mind and murder in his heart. She'd never seen him in battle, but she knew he must be formidable. The English king would not otherwise have sent him here.

Once more she rued the day she'd so foolishly thought to spy in his camp, to cook and clean and teach him Welsh and thereby come to know her enemy better. She knew him too well now, far better than she'd ever intended. Well enough to empathize with his pain. Well enough to desire him above all men.

But any connection they might have had, no matter how unwise, had been severed this day. Owain had captured Jasper and she'd helped him. Now Rand would want his revenge.

As she watched he turned and began to gather specific items. A short leather hauberk. His heavy riding gloves. His sword.

At the door he paused and she thought he would speak to her. But his stare was so hard, so cold and assessing, that she was glad he did not. The door closed with a dull thud. The bar fell into place and he was gone.

Owain held Jasper. Rand held her. In the hours to come Josselyn feared there would be hell to pay.

*   *   *

"A finger will suffice."

There was no mistaking the man's meaning. Jasper lay on his side where he'd been dropped. How long had he been insensible? His head throbbed like Scottish war drums. His shoulders were wrenched back to an unnatural degree, and his hands were numb from the tight cords that bound them. He didn't know where he was or who held him, but from what he could make out of the difficult Welsh tongue, it seemed they meant to cut off one of his fingers.

He didn't know whether to be grateful or curse the day he'd decided to learn Welsh. He'd done it to impress Rand. His older brother thought him a failure in everything and he'd wanted to show him he was wrong. But instead he lay in a muddy corner of some mean hovel, using his newfound skill to translate his own fate.

"A hand will prove we should not be taken lightly!" said another.

A hand! One of *his* hands?

Sweat popped out on his head and, without being aware he did so, he began to twist his hands back and forth. A sharp poke in the ribs drew a grunt from him and a child's voice announced, "He's awake. The Englishman is awake."

"Get that girl out of here," ordered the man who wanted Jasper's hand cut off.

"Begone from here, Rhonwen. Dewey. Take her home." That was the man who'd opted for the finger only.

"What if you need a translator?" the man addressed as Dewey asked.

" 'Tis Randulf Fitz Hugh we'll be communicating with, not his brother."

Jasper had known this concerned Rand, but how? What intrigue had his older brother gotten him involved in? There was a commotion at the door then the child cried out, "If you hurt his brother, then he'll hurt Josselyn!"

Jasper winced at the pain her shrill voice started up in his head. Who in the name of hell was Josselyn?

Outside, with the door slammed rudely in her face, Rhonwen could not hold back her tears. She'd been so frightened. Ever since Josselyn had been taken hostage by that wretched Englishman, she'd lived in utter terror of losing her. Then today they'd dragged the Englishman's brother into Carreg Du, and she'd been so relieved, for they had the means to make a trade for Josselyn. But now, instead of saving her, they argued about which portion of the man's body to cut off and send as proof of their threat. Were they so stupid that they could not see what would happen to Josselyn if they hurt this man too badly?

"Rhonwen, child. Where have you been?"

Rhonwen whirled at the sound of her mother's voice. Though her mother had not been drunk in weeks, Rhonwen still did not trust her. With Josselyn gone, Gladys might still slip back into her old, careless habits.

Rhonwen scowled and shifted aside when her mother reached out to her. "I wish Papa was here. He'd know how to help Josselyn."

As always, the reference to Tomas stopped Gladys in her tracks. She swallowed hard and twisted her apron in her hands. "Perhaps he could. But he's not here and you're just a little girl, too young to interfere with such goings-on."

"But Josselyn told me that we must be the smart ones. Women may not be as big or strong as men, but we have our own strength and cunning—"

"Dear, she did not mean in matters of this sort."

"You're just afraid! And you're just as stupid as they are!" Then throwing the vilest curse she could think of at her mother, she barged past her and ran full tilt toward the wildwood and its blessed solitude, where she could cry and rage, then cry again for the woman she'd come to love better than anyone.

But even the dense forest offered her no peace, for someone already lurked there, perched in the ancient yew she claimed for her own. She sensed his presence before she spied him, but when she squinted up through the tangled branches, he did not try to hide himself.

How dare he be here!

"Get out of my tree!" she demanded, focusing all her impotent rage on the dirty-faced child. "Get out and take your puny self away from here."

He stared down at her, not in the least intimidated. "And who's to make me?"

That cheeky response pushed Rhonwen past all endurance. With a cry of utter fury, she scrambled up the tree. She would push him down from his perch. She would toss him out of her tree and chase him away and he would never dare invade her territory again!

But he proved to be just as tenacious as she, and just as quick. From branch to branch they maneuvered, she in pursuit, he always managing to evade her. He was smaller than her, and younger, but he was not afraid.

"What's a'matter? Too slow to catch me?"

"Who'd want to catch a thing that smells so bad as you?" she sneered. "I just want to kick you down from my tree before I faint from the stench."

She pulled herself onto a higher branch. He retreated to the other side of the main trunk.

" 'Tis you who stinks," he taunted.

She pinched her nose. "You reek, boy. Haven't you ever heard of washin' yourself now and again? What kind of mother lets her child go about so shabby?"

"Me ma is dead, so just you shut your trap!"

"Well, my pa is dead. What of it? You still smell worse than a pigsty."

They glared at one another, both breathless from their exertions. "What are you doing here anyway?" Rhonwen asked. "You're not from Carreg Du."

"I'm Rhys ap Owain. I'm with the soldiers of Afon Bryn. Who are you?"

Rhonwen stared at him, answering, "Ap Owain? *He's* your pa? That man that's going to get Josselyn hurt?"

The boy spat at the ground, then wiped his mouth with his grimy sleeve. "I hope she dies."

Rhonwen gasped in horror. How dare he speak such atrocities?

With a cry of rage she leapt at him. Her hand caught his leg but not enough to unbalance him. He started to laugh at her, but when she grabbed onto his branch, pulling it down with her weight, she caught him unprepared.

For one precarious moment he teetered, grabbing wildly for another branch. But that branch was rotten and snapped beneath his hands. While Rhonwen watched, swaying madly from the tree limb that had held him, the boy crashed down through the branches. He hit the ground hard, then lay still.

Rhonwen stared down at him, terrified. She'd achieved exactly what she'd wanted, except that she hadn't meant to kill him.

Was he dead?

Somehow, despite her violent trembling, she managed to shimmy down. But she hesitated approaching him. Death was contagious. Like deadly fevers, bad luck leapt from one body to the next. The fact that she was the one who'd killed him only made it worse.

But what if he wasn't dead?

She blinked back frightened tears and saw the shallow rise and fall of his chest. He was alive!

As quickly as that her guilt fled. He was alive but his father was going to be the cause of Josselyn's death—or at least great harm. Maybe if she took this boy hostage, his father would have to listen to her.

The boy coughed then groaned, and she made up her mind. She must be daring; she must be brave. She could not let Owain cut off that man's hand, no matter how much she hated the English. That was not the best way to save

Josselyn. So she would use the boy to bargain with the father.

But first she would have to tie up the boy.

She bent over him and began to remove the dirty cord knotted around his grimy oversized tunic. Her nose wrinkled. He smelled even worse up close.

"You're my prisoner," she told him when he groaned again, then blinked and looked up at her, still dazed. She knotted the cord around his ankles, then removed her own girdle to bind his hands. "You're my prisoner and the first thing I'm going to do is give you a bath."

Nineteen

It was very late before the Welsh contacted Rand. Three men came up the hill from the darkened valley carrying torches. They stopped at the *domen* and waited for Rand to approach.

Dusk had settled over the land hours ago. The north wind blew in erratic gusts, and a storm threatened. The English encampment was usually asleep by this time. But Rand had been gripped by an unholy rage all day and his black mood had infected the rest of his followers. Every soldier was primed for battle. Every weapon was honed to its sharpest edge. No one knew what had caused these sudden preparations, but no one had the nerve to question Rand about it, save Osborn.

It was indicative of how far Osborn had come that he did not doubt the bard's message to Josselyn regarding Jasper. But they could do nothing until they were contacted by Madoc—or Owain.

Now, as Rand and two of his men strode down the hill, the wind at their backs, he hoped for the best, but feared the worst.

He recognized Clyde and his translator, but it was the other man who accompanied them that drew his attention. The man was young and fit, of moderate height and burly build. But he had a cruel twist to his mouth and an arrogant glint in his eyes. Owain ap Madoc. He could be no other.

"We would offer you a trade." Clyde spoke first through his translator, Dewey.

"How do I know you actually hold my brother?" Rand demanded to know.

Clyde's brows lifted in surprise. Owain's lowered in anger. "How have you heard of this?"

"Suffice it to say I have. But what assurance do I have that this is not an elaborate bluff?"

Without warning, Owain tossed a small bundle at him. Rand caught it with one hand. "He is your height, but slighter," Dewey translated Owain's words. "His hair is not so dark as yours. Open the sack," he added, while Owain grinned.

Rand held the cloth bundle at arm's length. An unreasoning fear gripped him and he fought the urge to throw the bundle down, anything to avoid looking inside it.

But it was not Owain he feared. If anything, he relished meeting the man in combat. The day would come when they would battle to the finish. He would have to kill Owain; there was no other way. Now as they glared at one another they formed a silent pact of death.

But he still must open the cloth bundle.

His hands were steady. His face betrayed no emotion. But the sight that met his eyes brought bile rising in his throat.

It was only a finger. It could have belonged to anyone. But it wore a ring he recognized. One that bore the Aslin family crest. It was his younger brother's finger and it had been hacked off because Rand had miscalculated. He'd underestimated his enemy, and not merely Owain.

He raised an impassive face to Owain. "You will pay for this with your life."

The other man laughed. Then his expression turned ugly. "If you have soiled my bride, I will hack you apart, piece by piece. Fingers. Hands. Feet. I'll keep you alive as I tear you apart."

"Atal!" Clyde cried. He stepped between the two younger men. "Stop this. My niece is what I want. Returned safely to me."

"Not until I see Jasper."

"Agreed."

"Where is he?"

"In a safe place. We can return here with him soon enough."

"Bring him here at dawn."

"Why wait so long?" Dewey translated Owain's question.

"I want to see him approach from afar, on foot. When he walks up the hill, I will send Josselyn down. God help you both if he is unable to manage without assistance."

"He will manage it," Clyde said, forestalling Owain with a sharp gesture. "At dawn."

Josselyn sat before the hearth. Her arms wrapped around her bent legs, her forehead nestled on her knees. She was fully dressed.

The night was not so cold. The fire glowed and the fireplace radiated heat. But still she shivered.

She hadn't seen Rand since his silent departure. He'd barred the door and shuttered the window, and shortly afterward, a guard she did not know had been posted. She questioned the man twice, but with no response at all. So she'd resigned herself to wait, and all the time she worried.

She did not worry, however, whether the swap of hostages would occur. Rand would not risk his brother's life by refusing to release her. Though it must gall him to negotiate with the same people he'd come here to rule, he would have to do so. Jasper's life would otherwise be forfeit.

What Josselyn worried about was her own murky future. If Owain had been the one to capture Jasper, he was sure to take credit for her release. He would be hailed a hero and he would undoubtedly expect their marriage to take place at once. She shuddered even to imagine herself wed to him.

But what if she revealed her intimacy with Rand? Would Owain still wish to marry her if he knew she'd lain with another?

She was not sure.

Her people were less obsessed with the purity of brides than the English and French were said to be. But Owain was not like other Welsh men. He was cruel and selfish, and she knew instinctively that he would punish her for her loss of innocence—especially to an Englishman. He would punish her and continue to punish her all the days of her life.

She fought back a wave of panic. She could not marry Owain. She would have to face his rage and perhaps her uncle's. But she would never consent to become Owain's bride.

She considered the few options left her, and once again her thoughts turned to Madoc ap Lloyd. Owain's father was the only man who could hold Owain in check and also guarantee aid to her uncle.

She paused. Aid to her uncle. Aid to beat back the English. Aid to maintain Welsh freedom from English rule. Once the battle with the English was won, however, the Welsh families would no doubt return to their old habits of fighting among themselves.

Oh, but it was all so hopeless. Was there no way to an enduring peace in her troubled land?

Josselyn lifted her head and stared blankly at the fire, and for the first time allowed herself to consider another scenario. What if the English stayed? What if Rand built his castle and ruled these lands? He'd vowed to protect one and all from oppression, to build a walled town where English and Welsh could live side by side, secure that he would keep the peace. Did he mean it? Could he ensure it?

Would that offer a better life for all who resided in the valley drained by the River Gyffin?

She was prevented from pursuing that disturbing line of thought when, with a crash, the bar was thrown down, the door flung open, and Rand burst in. He was breathing hard. Fury emanated from him in waves.

He closed the door with a chilling thud, then held up a bundle of rags. ''I have met the man who claims you.''

''Owain?'' She stood up warily. ''Has he brought your brother with him?''

''No.''

There was something ominous in that solitary word. Something dangerous. Yet that danger was less frightening than not knowing what was going on. ''Doesn't Owain have Jasper?''

He tossed the cloth bundle to her and she caught it. When he only stared at her, his expression bitter, his eyes cold, Josselyn's heart turned leaden. Was there something within this small package that answered her question?

Suddenly she knew. She raised stricken eyes to his and thrust the rags back at him. His expression turned even more forbidding. ''Open it.''

She shook her head. Some portion of his brother rested in the cloth she held. Some proof that Owain held him. Jasper had been a stranger to her before this, an anonymous Englishman whom she hated without even knowing. Now he was one of Owain's victims and her heart ached for him. Then guilt rushed over her and she bowed her head. If not for her . . .

Her trembling fingers fumbled with the cloth. There was blood, and she gagged to know she'd caused this pain. Was it his ear? His nose?

She remembered her brief fantasy about removing certain men's private parts and thereby sapping them of their masculine strength. Please God, not that!

She gasped when she saw the finger. Relieved. Horrified. The fingernail had turned blue. The flesh was unnaturally pale. A ring still circled it, and she could not look away. Just hours ago blood had pumped through that finger. It had been warm; it had moved. It had gripped a knife, touched a woman, scratched an itch. But not anymore.

Consumed with remorse, she dragged her eyes up to Rand. "I'm sorry—"

"Shut up!"

Josselyn flinched but did not back away when he snatched the finger in its nest of dirty cloth and placed it on the table. When he turned back to her, however, she shivered with fear.

"I have you until dawn," he said. "And I intend to make you pay for the pain you have caused him."

He did not even bother to undress. His dagger lay at his side; he left it on. He did not care about her clothes either, for with a deft move, he caught her by the arms, shoved her backward onto the bed, and jerked her skirt up to her waist.

Josselyn was too stunned to react, too numb to struggle. If he were anyone else she would have fought back. She would have kicked and clawed and screamed her hatred at him. But she did not hate him.

He hated her though. That was plain as he forced her legs apart with his knees, then fumbled with the closure of his braies. He hated her and he meant to rape her, to destroy whatever rare scraps of good there might have existed in the tortured relationship they'd forged.

She did not have the will to stop him.

But neither could she watch. She turned her face to the side and struggled to breathe—and struggled not to cry.

She was destined to fail. For when he pushed her skirt higher, baring her legs and hips and belly to his furious gaze, she began to tremble. And when his hands, hard and unfeeling, gripped her waist and dragged her closer to him, the first tear leaked out.

She heard his harsh breathing. His wool-clad legs abraded the inside of her widespread thighs.

He has been here before, she told herself. *This is no more than what I've done willingly with him.*

But that logic failed her. This was nothing like the time before. She was not willing and he did this now in anger, not desire. He wanted to punish her and she understood that. But still she could not bear it.

Another tear leaked out, hot and telling, then another and another until she could not make them stop. She wept silently as he positioned her for his unfeeling possession. She could not believe he would do this to her. Didn't he know how she felt about him? Didn't he know how easily she could have loved him?

Her weeping turned to sobs, hard choking sobs that she'd not wanted him to hear.

But Rand heard them, and though he fought to blot them out, he could not. She was sobbing. This woman who'd been brave and loyal to her people was finally broken. And he'd been the one to do it.

He should have gloated. He should have taken her then, proven to her who the victor was in this struggle between them. But he couldn't. The very idea sickened him. Even if he had wanted to finish what he'd so crudely begun, his body would not cooperate. There was no pleasure in possessing her this way. No joy. Only disgust that he had come so near to doing it.

He drew back, appalled at his behavior, then turned away. God in heaven, when had he become so depraved?

He stumbled toward the door. He had to get out of this room, out of her presence. But at the door he stopped, unable to leave. She wept still. When he peered warily at her he saw she'd curled onto her side. Her legs were still bare, her derriere also. She was pale and vulnerable and heartbroken, and all on account of him.

But what of Jasper? his angry side reminded him. What of his brother tortured by the man she was to wed? Did Jasper count for nothing? Was his finger of no value?

Then why not sever one of her fingers? Why try to rape her? He knew that torturing her as Jasper had been tortured would do no good. So why had he thought raping her would? Thank God he'd come to his senses.

But he could not leave her like this.

He turned to face her again, as unsure as a chastised child, as terrified as an untried warrior. He took a step nearer her then stopped. "You needn't fear me," he muttered gruffly. "I will not harm you."

Instead of easing her tears, however, his words seemed perversely to increase them. She curled up tighter, covering her head, as her entire body shook with the violence of her weeping.

"Josselyn. Don't—" He broke off. He didn't know what to say to her, how to make her stop. That he wanted to comfort her made him angry. She was his enemy and he should not care how miserable she felt. But he did care and he didn't know what to do about it.

With a muttered curse directed at his own perverse nature, he crossed to the bed, flung her skirt down to cover her legs, then backed away. But still he could not leave.

After a while, to his enormous relief, her sobs began to ease. She shuddered a few times, then wiped her face on the bed linens and finally pushed up and cautiously glanced around. When she spied him, she averted her eyes.

That fearful gesture wrenched something in Rand's gut. Fear had never been the emotion he wanted to evoke in her. But fear was all she'd ever know now. That and loathing.

He cleared his throat. "You need fear me no longer, Josselyn. My fit of fury is spent. I regret that I vented it upon you."

She peered sidelong at him again. Her eyes were red and swollen. Her dark lashes clumped together in wet spikes. With her garments in disarray and her hair loosened from its neat coiffure, she looked buffeted and misused. His need to comfort her increased tenfold.

It was his turn to look away. "The exchange will be made. You for Jasper."

After a long moment she replied. "Then your brother lives?"

"He does."

"I see." Another pause. "When is this exchange to occur?"

He turned back to her and met her damp gaze. "At dawn."

"At dawn." Moving stiffly, as if she were an old woman, she pushed herself to the edge of the bed. She smoothed her skirt as best she could, then folded her hands in her lap. "I . . . I am sorry for what Jasper has suffered at Owain's hands."

Rand's fists tightened. He didn't want an apology from her. She'd not been the one to cut Jasper's finger off. "I should not have summoned him here." That left much unsaid between them. But in her eyes Rand saw her understanding of the rest. He should not have threatened to marry her to Jasper.

He should have wed her himself.

He reared back at that unwelcome thought. That would never have worked, for he did not plan to remain long in Wales, and she would be sorely out of place in England. It was only his physical desire for her that made him think such foolishness. He'd always wanted her. He wanted her now.

"You need only wait until dawn," he said, trying to suppress his inappropriate longing for her.

"I see." She took a long breath, as if she gathered her strength, and her breasts strained against the bodice of her gown.

Blood rushed at once to his loins and he muttered another curse. That was done between them. She was lost to him now, as much by Owain's doing as by his own. He would find some other woman to vent his lust upon. An Englishwoman, this time, with no complications between them.

Then she stood and moved slowly toward him, the last thing Rand expected. Her expression was impossible to read, hesitant and yet determined. Sad but somehow relieved.

"So we have until dawn?" she asked when she stopped before him.

She was so near. Too near. Her face tilted up to his.

"We have until dawn," she repeated, her voice a hoarse whisper in the silent room. "And after that I must wed a man I do not want. I must lie down with a man I do not desire." She hesitated, then he watched as she gathered her courage and spoke again. "But I desire you. I desire you, Randulf Fitz Hugh."

He searched her face, unable to believe what she was implying. He shook his head. "You don't understand, Josselyn. It's not necessary for you to do this. In a matter of hours you will be free."

She smiled sadly. "No, 'tis you who do not understand." She placed a hand on his chest, her palm flat, her fingers splayed.

He should have questioned her last words. What did he not understand? But her touch, though light, was powerful. It was overwhelming. The desire he fought to hide leapt fully formed to life. He covered her hand with his, knowing he would regret this, but knowing as well that he could no more resist her entreaty than he could choose to cease breathing.

This time they removed all their clothes. Or rather, she removed his and then her own.

This time no fist pounded interruption on the door.

This time he guided her to mount him, and afterward, while they were both still breathless and damp with their exertion, he rolled her onto her back and made love to her again.

There were few words. There were no promises. It was good-bye they said to one another, for with dawn's arrival, they would become enemies once more.

But for the waning hours of this night, they were lovers,

and urgency demanded they wring every moment of pleasure they could from it.

Inevitably, however, the dark began to recede.

Josselyn was the first to acknowledge it. She lay with her back to him, snuggled in the curve of his body. Both their heads rested on his bent arm. His other arm was draped over her; his hand enveloped hers, their fingers twined. She lifted her head, bumping his chin. " 'Tis time, Rand."

She thought he was asleep, for he did not respond. But when she tried to slip her hand from his, his fingers tightened. For a moment, one foolish, hopeful moment, she thought he would not let her go. But then he slid his hand from hers, and she knew he had no more choice than she. His brother's life hung in the balance.

She rose, grateful for the shadowy dark that hid her naked flesh, as well as the naked emotions she could not quell. She did not want to leave him. It was irrational, of course, but no less true. He was a man with considerable capacity for good—certainly more so than Owain. But he and she were caught between their countries and there was no escaping that fact.

So she donned her smock and kirtle, pulled on hose and found her shoes. She gathered her few belongings, then sat and began to finger-comb her hair.

Rand had lit a lantern and she heard his movements as he too dressed. The room was cool and yet the heat and scent of their joining overwhelmed her senses. That was how it was meant to be between a man and a woman. Would she ever again know such a night?

Her lower lip trembled but she pressed her lips together until her weakness passed. The answer to that question was no, she would never again know such a night. She should be grateful to have had even one such night, she told herself. Many women were denied even that, married to men they did not love.

Love? A lump rose in her throat. Was that what she felt

for Rand? Was this intense longing, which was as much emotional as physical, love? She feared it was. But did he feel the same toward her?

She did not know, and anyway, love could not change their present circumstances.

She resumed her efforts on her hopelessly tangled hair, but her fingers stilled when Rand crossed to her. She looked up at him, meeting his eyes for the first time. He was dressed as a warrior in his studded leather hauberk, with short sword and dagger at his side. He lacked only his chain mail to complete the picture. But he held a comb out to her, and his expression, though somber, was not fierce.

"Thank you," she murmured. Their eyes held an endless, shattering moment.

"Don't marry Owain."

Josselyn's heart began to race. Her chest hurt from its terrible pounding. "What are you saying, that I should stay?"

He shook his head. "You cannot. I must protect my brother. You have to go. But . . ." He took a harsh breath. "Owain will treat you badly. It's in his nature."

Josselyn broke the hold of his eyes. "I know his nature."

"Then don't agree to wed him."

Suddenly she was angry. "Why? Why, Rand? So his family and mine will not unite against you?"

"No!" He threw the comb in her lap. "Damn you, it's your well-being I'm thinking of, not mine! Your people cannot hold out against English might. These lands are claimed for Henry and England, and they will remain English lands for a thousand years and more. No matter who you wed, nothing will change that." Then his temper eased. "I don't want to see you hurt, Josselyn. That's all."

How final that sounded. That's all. She'd wondered if he loved her. Now she had her answer. There would be no offer from him, she realized. No request that she wed him as assurance of peace between the English and Welsh. What had he said once before—that he would not long remain in

Wales? Once the castle at Rosecliffe was built he would be gone. She'd known that all along, so why had she allowed herself so stupidly to hope?

She turned blind eyes away from him and began automatically to comb her hair. The knots were stubborn, but she yanked through them, oblivious to the pain. Time to go. Time to bid him good-bye.

Part Two

To Mercy, Pity, Peace, and Love,
All pray in their distress

—William Blake

Twenty

Dawn was a nebulous thing. The clouds hung low and leaden. Sorrowful, Josselyn thought. She and Rand did not speak on the grim walk to the wall. Down the stony hill the land lay in shadow. If her kinsmen were there, she could not make them out.

They stopped at a place where the wall was but knee high. He stepped up onto the rubble packed solid between the flat courses of facing stones, and offered her his hand in assistance. But Josselyn could manage without his assistance. She would have to manage the remainder of her life without him; she could certainly manage this wall.

And yet it was this very wall and all it stood for that kept them apart; it was the wall between England and Wales, the wall between his ambitions and hers. The wall Owain had raised a hundred feet high when he'd sent Jasper's finger to Rand.

She looked over at Rand. The least she could do was reassure him that she would not agree to marry Owain. But as she turned, Osborn called from just beyond him. "There he is. See?" He pointed and they all strained to make out the two figures that emerged, ghostlike, from the forest edge.

The two walked through the mist, floating, it seemed, on a cloud that enveloped their feet and legs. One of them

walked stiffly, like an old man. As he came up the hill and
the mist fell away, they could see he cradled one arm, and
that his hand was bandaged. Jasper, she realized, with
Owain triumphant beside him.

Bile rose in Josselyn's throat and she fought the urge to
retch at the sight of Owain and his vicious handiwork. Had
Rand not caught her by the arm and started the two of them
forward, she could not have made herself approach him.

They jumped from the wall then marched down the damp
hill. The grasses swept their legs with a soft sigh, the coarse
gravel crunched beneath their boots. But other than that
there was only silence. Even the small creatures of the earth
cowed in Owain's murderous presence, she fancied. Or perhaps it was Rand's fury they shrank from.

She glanced sidelong at him. His narrowed gaze focused
on the approaching men. She could feel his tension, his
readiness to do battle with Owain.

On impulse she stopped. She would not give Owain the
chance to hurt Rand too.

When she stopped, Owain did also. "Send Josselyn forward," he called from fifty paces away. Josselyn translated
for Rand, then she started forward, anything to forestall
combat between them. But Rand caught her arm. "Don't
marry him, Josselyn, unless you desire soon to become a
widow."

She lifted her face to his. Fear for him and for herself—
indeed for all the peoples of these hills who must suffer the
wars to come—made her voice bitter. "That would solve
all our problems, wouldn't it? I wed Owain to please my
uncle and Owain. You kill Owain to please me and you.
Everyone receives some portion of their desires. But then
what? For all that unhappiness, nothing would have
changed. Nothing ever will." *Because you will not choose
the most obvious path to peace.* But she would not say that
out loud. She could not. So she turned and fled and he let
her go. Tears welled in her eyes, blinding her. But she knew

where she was going. Down the hill. Away from Rosecliffe, never to return.

She paused in her headlong descent only when Rand's brother started forward. They stopped midway and studied one another. One of his eyes had swollen shut. His lip too was swollen and split on one side, crusted with blood. He cradled his mutilated hand against his chest.

"I'm sorry," she whispered, horrified by the abuse he'd suffered, filled with guilt.

He stared suspiciously at her with his one good eye. "I'll recover. Mostly. But surely those tears are not for me. Has Rand used you so poorly?"

Her chin trembled. She shook her head. "No. I have not fared so poorly at your brother's hands as you have at his." She indicated Owain with a gesture.

"Josselyn!" Owain called. "Come. Now!"

She saw Jasper's jaw clench with hatred, but to her he gave only a painful smile. "Farewell Josselyn ap Carreg Du."

"Good-bye, Jasper Fitz Hugh." *Man that I might have wed.* Though their exchange had been brief, she knew he would have made a far better mate than Owain.

What if she turned right now and fled with Jasper to Rosecliffe? What if she wed him, as Rand wished her to do? Wouldn't that be better for everyone, even her?

But how could she? How could she live in Rand's household and yet be his brother's woman? She could not.

She started away. Every step was an effort. Every step nearer Owain was a step farther from Rand. As she neared her brutish countryman, she could not look at him, he repulsed her so utterly.

If he noticed, he did not care. He caught her arm in a crushing hold, then drawing his sword, he hustled her back toward the woods, toward safety, and toward a future too bleak for Josselyn to contemplate.

*   *   *

The village of Carreg Du was in an uproar. The influx of men from Afon Bryn had the two streets crowded and muddy, and thick with the droppings of their many horses. Every villager housed a soldier in their cottage. Talk was loud, tension ran high, and weapons were everywhere in evidence. The women kept to their kitchens, their children close beside them. Only the men moved about, and Josselyn sensed they were as uneasy with Owain's presence as they were with the Englishmen's.

They all watched as she trudged into the village, flanked by Owain and her uncle, and trailed by two very separate sets of guards. She'd slept but little, and her physical union with Rand had taxed muscles that were unfamiliar to her, yet neither of those was the source of her exhaustion. Her emotions were overwrought, stretched to the breaking point. When she spied her Aunt Nesta smiling a tremulous welcome, Josselyn could be strong no more. With a sob she rushed into her aunt's embrace, buried her face in her warm, comforting shoulder, and wept like a little child.

"I'll kill the bastard," Owain growled.

How her uncle responded Josselyn did not hear, for Nessie hustled her into the kitchen and shut the door against the intrusion of men. There was no privacy in the kitchen either, for Gladys and Rhonwen tended Cordula and Davit there. Still, it was the domain of women, and Josselyn took some comfort in that.

Gladys hugged the two younger children to her and stared silently at Josselyn. Like Nesta, she obviously had some idea of the treatment Josselyn had suffered in Rand's care. Rhonwen, however, was a child. She saw no obvious injuries and so rejoiced.

"We have defeated them and got you back! You were right. We women *are* smarter. We can outwit all of those stupid men!"

"Rhonwen!" Gladys rebuked her.

Rhonwen turned and sent an impatient glare at her mother, and when she did, Josselyn gasped. The child sported a bruised face almost as ugly as Jasper's. "What happened to her?"

The two women were silent but Rhonwen gave her a triumphant grin. "I outwitted them all, Owain and that awful Englishman. And also that ragged brat, Rhys," she gloated.

"Rhys? Owain's boy?" Josselyn remembered an angry little boy heaving curses and stones at her. "He did that to you?"

" 'Twas Owain did it," Gladys bit out. "Not the boy, but the father."

"But why?" Josselyn asked. Concern for Rhonwen had banished her own miseries. "Why would he strike a child so viciously?"

" 'Cause I made his stinking son my captive."

Josselyn's disbelieving eyes darted from the boastful little girl to the silent women. When they both nodded, she looked back at Rhonwen. "Why?" was all she could say. "Why?"

Rhonwen crossed to stand in front of her. "To save you. Owain wanted to cut off that Jasper's hand and send it to his brother. Not just his finger. But I was afraid of what the English lord would do to you, so when I found Rhys, I made him my hostage."

"Your uncle agreed with Rhonwen and so Owain was forced to back down," Nesta said.

"Owain did not like being bested by a child," Gladys added.

Josselyn cupped the unmarked side of Rhonwen's face and stared down into the child's guileless eyes. Nine-year-old Rhonwen had held Owain's son hostage to ensure Josselyn's safety? Could such an outlandish tale be true? But clearly it was. If Nesta and Gladys had not confirmed it, the purple bruise on Rhonwen's face did.

God, but she hated that man!

"Is it very painful?" she asked, past the lump in her throat.

Rhonwen shrugged. "Not very." Then she grinned. "It was worth it to see you set free. And also to see *him* so furious."

Josselyn could only imagine how livid Owain had been. He'd hit Rhonwen. Had he vented his anger on his son as well? "Where is Rhys now?"

"That ragamuffin?" She sniffed in disdain. "He's pro'bly rooting in the refuse heap. He stinks, that one does."

Josselyn's brow creased in a faint frown. She hoped he was all right. "I know he is a troublesome lad, but remember, he's had no mother to tend him and we all know what sort of father he has. At least you have a mother who loves you, Rhonwen."

The child met her steady stare, and though Josselyn could see resistance in Rhonwen's eyes, she knew it would not last. When the child averted her eyes, then peered warily at her mother, Josselyn gathered her up in a tight hug. "Your mother loves you," she whispered into the child's tangled hair. "You know she does. And you love her too. We women must remain united if we are ever to achieve our goals."

Rhonwen looked up at her. "What are our goals?"

Josselyn hesitated. What indeed? "Peace, I suppose. Peace and a good harvest. Husbands who honor us, and healthy children."

The two other women murmured their agreement, and after a minute they turned to the task of preparing the midday meal. But as Josselyn worked alongside them, her own words echoed in her ears. Admirable goals she'd outlined for them. But in truth, women had no power to achieve any of them at all. Peace was dependent on men. A good harvest relied on the weather. A husband could not be forced to treat his wife well, and the health of a child rested in God's hands.

Her shoulders slumped as defeat weighed heavily on her.

Fine goals indeed. But she'd not live long enough to achieve even one of them. No woman ever would.

Jasper's face was pale, save for the enormous purple bruise that sealed his eye. He'd been bathed and fed, and his mutilated hand had been freshly bandaged. Now he sprawled back in Rand's chair with his eyes closed.

Rand studied his younger brother, the brother he hardly knew. The boy had been barely out of swaddling clothes when Rand had been fostered out. After that he'd seen him but rarely. Rand had then gone into the king's service. Jasper had been sent to the abbey in Walsingham, and three years further had passed with no contact between them at all.

Then suddenly Jasper had left the abbey and become squire to their father's good friend, followed soon thereafter by his knighting. Rand had suspected he was not truly prepared for a life of warfare. Now he was here at Rosecliffe, his face battered, his finger crudely severed—his boyhood come to a rude end. And for what purpose? Rand had not wanted him here. For a brief moment, however, marrying him to a Welsh heiress had seemed a convenient solution to the political situation here.

Except that Rand had deflowered the would-be bride, while her betrothed tortured Jasper.

God's bones, but he should never have sent for the boy! He shoved up from the stool he perched upon, toppling it back with a crash. Jasper jerked upright, startled from his exhausted doze.

Rand cursed. "I'll have that bastard's head on a pike."

Jasper grimaced and shifted into a more comfortable position. He clearly knew of whom Rand spoke. "What of *her* head? 'Tis the woman, this Josselyn ap Carreg Du, who didst betray you more so than Owain ap Madoc." A knowing grin lifted the unmarked side of his face. "Or was bedding her so sweet as to put you in a forgiving frame of mind?"

Osborn sat across the table and his brows rose. But he did not laugh at Jasper's crude jest. It was a measure of how well he knew Rand's moods—and how little Jasper did, Rand decided. He fixed his brother with a fierce look. "Her marriage to Owain will solidify Welsh opposition to us. It will make our task here all the harder. More blood will be lost than the paltry amount you have spilled."

"Then why did you trade her for me?" Jasper snapped. "You've had no use for me in the past."

"And I have no use for you now," Rand growled. "But you're my brother."

"Half brother."

Better than John, who is my full brother, Rand thought, though he could not bring himself to say it out loud. "Half or no, you are of my blood," he responded grudgingly. "I would not leave you to languish in Owain's murderous clutches."

Rand poured himself a mug of ale, aware his brother watched him closely. It was pointless to hide the truth from Jasper, so when the question came, he was prepared to answer.

"Why did you send for me to come here, when previously you bade me stay in London?"

"I planned to wed you to Josselyn, and in that way ensure the peace here."

Jasper digested that in silence. " 'Twas a logical plan," he finally said. "Though I would not have agreed to it."

Rand sent him an irritated look. "You would have if I promised you control of Rosecliffe upon its completion." He watched his brother weigh that momentous pronouncement.

The younger man shrugged. "Mayhap I would have married her at that. She was not unpleasant to look upon. And Welshwomen are said to be a lusty lot, though I've not had one yet myself. How was she?" He grinned at Rand.

Rand held his temper in but barely. Jasper wanted to rile him but he would not succeed. Besides, Rand did not wish to discuss that devious wench with this whelp. " 'Tis a moot point. She is lost to us and will no doubt wed some Welshman."

"You say that as if you think she will not wed Owain. God pity her if she does," the boy added more bitterly. "He wanted to sever my entire hand, you know."

"Clyde stopped him?"

Jasper stared at his bandaged right hand. "He did not know I am left-handed, so meant to cut off what he thought was my sword hand. Clyde argued against it, saying the small finger was adequate proof of their intent. But Owain would have none of it. It was a child, a little girl, who swayed the man."

"A little girl? His daughter?"

"No, a child of Carreg Du." He shook his head and grimaced. "She was a bloodthirsty little wench. She swore she would be content to see me hacked to pieces and sent to you in two willow baskets strapped to a donkey's back. But only if Josselyn were safe. She feared you would retaliate in kind against Josselyn if my hand were cut off so she insisted on only the little finger."

Rand could not believe such a tale. "Owain listens to a child? He accepts the commands of a tiny maid?" Then he shook his head. "How would you know what was said, anyway? They are Welsh."

"I have not been idle these last months," he answered hotly. "When I learned you would come to Wales, I made it my business to learn the tongue. After learning Latin, it was no difficulty at all. As for the girl, she held her own hostage."

It was Osborn's turn to express his doubt. "A child holding a hostage?" He smirked. "That blow you took has addled your brains, boy."

Jasper leaned forward, intent. "She held Owain's son hostage somewhere in the woods. There was a terrible row over it. Owain struck the child down, then Clyde struck him down. I thought they'd kill one another and me as well.

But in the end I was returned with my hand still attached, and all on account of this girl child.''

Rand stood, crossed to the hearth, then stared into the spitting embers. He remembered a brave little girl, first in the woods that day he met Josselyn, later in the trees beyond the wall, throwing rocks at him in a vain attempt to gain Josselyn's freedom. Could she be the same one Jasper spoke of? No doubt it was. She'd been brave then, but she was even braver now to incur Owain's wrath, brave and loyal and foolish in the extreme. Owain was not a man to forgive anyone who bested him, least of all a girl. She'd made him a laughingstock and he would not soon forget it.

Would he vent his rage upon Josselyn as well?

Rand suppressed a shudder, afraid for her and for the girl. He should not feel that way. After all, they were his enemies. He should rejoice at the dissension among the Welsh, for it only did him good.

He turned away from the fire, banishing any concern he felt for either of them. Josselyn had made her loyalties plain. She'd wanted to escape the English camp, and so she had. Now she would have to live with the consequences, as would they all.

Twenty-one

The first day of Josselyn's return, the people of Carreg Du rejoiced.

The second day they cowered beneath Owain's rage.

The third they watched silently as marriage united their village to that of Afon Bryn.

It would not be an easy union, every last villager knew that, and the celebrations were subdued. For her part, Josselyn vowed to be a good wife and loyal to her new husband.

Madoc ap Lloyd was the only one who appeared well pleased with the situation. Owain did not even attend the wedding. But his soldiers did, for they were Madoc's soldiers first, and with his assertion of authority—and Owain's humiliation at the hands of a child—they had all been reminded who still ruled the Lloyd holdings.

Let Owain rage that his father had wedded the woman he'd thought to make his wife. Madoc reveled as one who'd rediscovered his youth. He laughed. He ate. He toasted his beautiful young wife.

He drank too much and fell asleep in his marriage bed, and did not even attempt to consummate the union.

Josselyn lay beside him, listening to his snores, desperately preparing herself to do her duty. What he'd not done last night he was certain to do upon waking, and if not then, then tonight once they returned to Afon Bryn.

She was his wife now and she should be glad, for he would make a far better husband than would Owain. Still, her skin crawled at the thought of lying naked beneath him. She sickened at the idea of his tongue inside her mouth, his mouth feasting on her flesh, his manhood thrusting inside her.

With a strangled cry she rolled from the bed and huddled in the farthest corner of the room. Though she knew she should not, she thought of Rand. She would not feel this revulsion were he her husband.

But that was no comfort. Rand was the one that should repulse her. He was her enemy, and she should be revolted by her easy acquiescence to him. But the truth was, she wanted him. She wanted him in her bed, just as he resided already in her heart. It was not that Madoc was old. It was that she was besotted with Rand. Even Rand's brother, young and virile, had not appealed to her. He was not Rand. No other man could be.

But Rand does not want to marry you, she reminded herself. He might have solved his woes by doing so, but he'd chosen not to.

She was a fool to mourn his loss when he clearly did not mourn hers.

Did he know she'd not wed Owain?

Rand learned Josselyn had not wed Owain when Newlin appeared, seated on top of the *domen* one misty morning a week later. The bard had been absent, as had all the Welsh people. They'd stayed close to their village, venturing out only into the forests and hills away from Rosecliffe. Rand knew because he'd posted a discreet watch on Carreg Du.

His men had strict orders not to accost anyone, save in defense of their own lives. But they were to report every movement, and what little they'd seen had depressed him mightily—and angered him as well.

A large party had left Carreg Du, a woman amongst

them. They'd traveled under a heavy drizzle, so little else could be noted. She'd ridden beside a man, both of them mounted on the finest horseflesh, and he'd known at once that the deed was done. She was wed. With that single act the Welsh had united against him and he had lost Josselyn.

He'd told himself it was the former he'd most wanted to prevent. Now, mired in his darkest and most private thoughts, the truth would not be denied. He could fight the Welsh, united or not, and eventually he would make them see the value of one powerful lord to keep peace in these lands. But he could find no remedy for Josselyn's absence from his life.

Even when Newlin revealed the identity of Josselyn's new husband, Rand was little consoled. "At least he cannot be so cruel as his son," he muttered. Then he fixed Newlin with a hard gaze. "Am I wrong in this?"

Newlin sat staring at a finch that scolded some unseen intruder in its domain. After a while he blinked and turned to face Rand. "Owain is his father's son. Madoc was a hard man in his youth. Hard on his first wife, who bore him but the one son. Hard on his second, who died giving him a daughter. Hard with an anger he took out on anyone so unwise as to cross him. But he is old now. He covets his fire and his comforts. And if his new wife does not bear him another child . . ." Newlin shrugged his shriveled shoulder. "I do not think he will care, so long as she sees to his other needs."

They talked of other matters after that. Of the wet weather, and the quarrying of native stone, and the strengthening signs of spring. But in the back of Rand's mind lurked an image of Josselyn lying beside an old man. An older Owain. Rage rose in his throat to choke him, and he fought the urge to throttle someone. Anyone. He cut the bard off in mid-sentence.

"If she thinks she has outwitted me—If any of them think that due to their union I will abandon my plans to

raise a castle for my king on this site—they are wrong.
They cannot fight me and think to win.''

Newlin's odd face creased in a frown. "Is there no other
way?''

Rand did not answer. Perhaps there had been another
way once. If instead of sending for Jasper, he'd seriously
considered marrying Josselyn himself . . . But he'd refused
to consider it. His political ambitions had come first, and
she didn't fit into them. He'd refused to consider it then,
and it was too late now for him to indulge in regrets.

Summer came with green meadows and new lambs. Fledgling birds took to the skies, and everywhere were the signs
of burgeoning life.

Josselyn felt them too. Her breasts grew heavier. Her
monthly courses ceased. Her waist thickened even as her
appetite paled. But she hid the truth, if not from herself, at
least from all the others. She carried the beginnings of a
child deep inside her. Only it was not her husband's child,
and therein lay her terrible dread.

Madoc had tried. The first night they'd returned to Afon
Bryn. The second also. He'd stripped her naked and rubbed
his hands over her, pinching her nipples, though not too
painfully. Josselyn had lain still and fought any sign of
revulsion. She'd agreed to this. She would not renege on
her vows.

But his manhood had remained flaccid.

He'd forced her to touch him, to rouse him. And so she
had, but again without success. In the end he'd drunk himself into a stupor and so the pattern had been set.

Now, however, she carried a child. Rand's child.

Madoc was not an unkind husband, though he treated her
more as a daughter than a wife. Still, he made twice-weekly
visits to her bedchamber and she went along with the cha-
rade.

For her part, Josselyn was acutely attuned to his needs.
She learned his habits, his favorite foods and drinks. She

carved him the best joints of meat, kept his clothes in perfect repair, cleaned his weapons as he requested, trimmed his hair, and bathed him once a week. She prepared a concoction of mint and wormwood and juniper berries to aid his digestion, and a poultice of hyssop for the itch that plagued his feet. He slapped her bottom when he was pleased with her. Otherwise he did not much concern himself with her. There was, after all, a battle to be fought against the English.

This particular morning was wash day, not a day she particularly looked forward to. She and Meriel gathered the soiled clothing and household linens in a basket and carried it between them to the village well in the square just beyond the front door. From across the village women came to scrub and talk and pass the time away from their husbands and fathers. The younger children and babies accompanied them and Josselyn found herself staring at the babies with uncommon interest.

Meriel gave her a sly look. "Mayhap there will soon be one of them in your arms, eh?"

Josselyn concentrated on sorting the laundry. "I suppose it is every woman's desire to bear children."

"So it is," Meriel replied, but in such an odd tone that Josselyn looked up. The other woman's lips were set in a thin line and she looked angry. Then Josselyn remembered that Meriel's marriage had produced no children. Though the woman was nervous and sly, she was the only female companionship Josselyn had. The last thing she wanted was to alienate her.

"I'm sorry if my words were thoughtless, Meriel. It must be a hard thing to want a child and not have one."

Meriel's brow lowered further. She jerked a bed sheet so hard Josselyn heard a small rip. "When a woman has no children after ten years with one husband, no other man will have her. They all believe it's the woman who is at fault." Then she looked up and stared straight into Josselyn's eyes. "Sometimes it's the men who can't do their part, if you know what I mean."

Josselyn could do no more than nod. Her heart beat like a drum. Did Meriel know about Madoc? Is that what she was implying? For if she did, she would know also that the child Josselyn bore could not be his.

And she would guess whose it was. Would she then run to Madoc and tell him her suspicions?

There was no help for it. Josselyn had to tell him first.

She waited for him that afternoon. He'd ridden out early with a small party of men, armed as if for battle. In the past two months there had been much debate on how to drive the English out. But beyond several raids and the theft of one cow, it amounted to little more than talk.

It was because Owain had departed the village, Josselyn suspected. He was the fire and daring of this village. Madoc was too old. Owain and the three men closest to him had departed Carreg Du the day her marriage to Madoc had been announced and had not been seen since.

Josselyn had been much relieved by his absence. Owain's son, Rhys, had also disappeared. Madoc had expressed no concern for either his son or grandson, nor had Meriel. But one evening when he was well into his cups, Josselyn caught him fingering a wooden sword, a neatly carved miniature of a warrior's weapon. A child's toy, she realized. Rhys's?

When he'd seen her watching, he'd thrust the thing aside. But Josselyn had rescued it from the rushes and placed it in a cupboard for safekeeping. As she sat now, waiting for Madoc on a bench in the sunshine, she bent to her sewing, worrying about her husband's reaction to her news. Would he beat her? Would he kill the child?

The breath caught in her throat as panic assailed her. He wouldn't be that cruel. He couldn't. She pressed a hand to her stomach, cradling the new life in her. Her child. Rand's child.

Two women passed by and she bent again to her stitching.

"Anxious to see your husband?" Meriel came up and sat beside her, wiping her hands on her apron. Her fingers were knobby from work, the skin red and cracked.

"I can make an ointment for your hands with dog grass."

Meriel snorted. "These are not times for foraging in the open places where that grows. Madoc would not like it."

"Perhaps I can convince him to accompany me," Josselyn answered, more tartly than she ought. There was something in the other woman's tone, some sly undercurrent that Josselyn neither liked nor understood.

"Hah! He's no lovestruck lad to be trailing after you. 'Tis not his nature, and well should I know it. He and I were born but two weeks apart. Cousins but raised like brother and sister—" She broke off and stood. "He may have wed you, but he'll not play the fool for you."

Josselyn shook her head. "I want no fool for a husband."

Meriel shot her a look of intense dislike, an emotion more honest than any other Josselyn had detected. But their conversation ended in the thunder of hooves, for up from the valley rode Madoc. Josselyn stood to watch and saw with swift dismay that her husband led a larger party than before.

Owain rode at his side.

The news spread like wildfire. Owain had returned—cruel, powerful Owain who would one day lead them and whose goodwill was sought by one and all. Owain had returned with his three men, his snarling child, and a very pretty, very frightened wife.

Madoc watched closely as Owain greeted Josselyn. "My good stepmother." He took the hand she extended and kissed it, displaying no anger either in his hold, his voice, or his expression. His restraint, however, only frightened her more. "You are grandmother to my son now. Rhys."

He shoved the boy toward her, clamping his fingers over the boy's shoulder.

The child was not so adept as his father at hiding his emotions. He glared at Josselyn. "Tell that girl I'll slice her to ribbons when next I see her!"

Owain cuffed him, then laughed when the boy cursed and slithered away. "Bested by a girl. My other sons will not be so puny." With that he drew the silent woman forward. "I present to you my wife, Agatha."

The gathered throng began to murmur their surprise. Madoc was obviously well pleased with Owain's unexpected marriage, for he beamed with pleasure. He knew his son's vengeful nature. Had he experienced second thoughts about having taken Josselyn away from him?

Not that he had actually taken her away. Josselyn had resolved not to marry Owain under any circumstances. But that would not have deterred Owain's fury with his father and they all three knew it.

Perhaps, however, this pretty wife had softened his anger. Diverted it. Madoc clearly hoped so. "Welcome, Agatha. You are wife to my son and now you are daughter to me. Josselyn, come greet Agatha who will be as your sister. As your daughter," he amended. "Come," he entreated everyone. "We shall celebrate, for my son is returned to us and with him a new wife."

The night proved grueling. While the men celebrated, the women labored to prepare the food, deliver the drinks, and keep the peace—to the limits that they could. More than one fight broke out among the drunkards, fights that were either egged on by shouts of derision and encouragement, or else doused by the well-aimed toss of a bucket of cold water.

Josselyn endured it. Agatha as well. Perhaps she would find an ally in this poor, frightened child, Josselyn speculated, for Meriel eyed this newest interloper in her household with ill-disguised contempt. When Owain summoned the girl, however, she scurried immediately to do his bidding.

During the course of the evening Josselyn had been lulled into thinking herself safe from Owain's cruelty. He'd not looked once at her, but had turned all his charm upon his father and the other old men of the village. Now, however, when he stood up and drew his wife full length against him, making no bones about his intentions, he stared straight at Josselyn.

"My pardon, for neglecting you, my sweet bride. My juicy morsel." He licked his lips once, slowly, still staring at Josselyn. Then he abruptly tossed Agatha over his shoulder, and giving her a sharp smack on her bottom, carried her up the stairs, much to the delight of the revelers he left behind.

"Swive her good!"

"Plant a strong lad within her!"

"Teach her who her husband is!"

Josselyn's stomach roiled at their crudity. Abruptly setting down the ewer she carried, she bolted for the door. No one noticed as she lost her meal in a dark corner of the kitchen garden. No one followed her, concerned, carrying a damp cloth and ale to rinse out her mouth.

No one else heard the coarse grunting that came from the window above her head, nor the barely stifled sobs as Owain took his wife with no care for any pleasure but his own.

Josselyn clapped her hands over her ears when she recognized the hideous sounds, and she staggered away, fighting tears. That could have been her. Thank God she'd been strong enough to prevent it.

But did Agatha suffer even more due to Owain's fury at *her*?

Josselyn ran, dodging drunks and roving dogs, and even a couple that copulated in the shadow of the alehouse. But she could not outrun her fears or her guilt. Only when she was beyond the village did she stop. She collapsed against a tree while tears streamed unheeded down her cheeks.

Oh, God, she could not endure life here. She did not want to bring her child up in this horrible place with these horrible people.

Then something sounded, as of a foot turning upon a small stone, and she scrambled up in alarm.

"So. 'Tis brokenhearted you are," a boy's voice mocked.

Rhys. She didn't know whether to feel relief or dread.

The boy went on. "You heard him givin' it to her and you can't bear it, can you? Well, best you get used to it, 'cause he does it all day long. He plans to get her with child afore his da can get one in you," he added smugly.

Josselyn's heart ached even more for Agatha, for the harm she'd inadvertently done the unsuspecting girl. But she steeled herself to deal with Owain's unpleasant child.

"Why should that matter to Owain? He's Madoc's heir, as you are his."

Rhys snorted. "You don't know nothin' 'bout men, 'specially my da."

"Nor does he know a thing about women," she snapped.

"What's to know? They cook. They sew. They spread their legs," he sneered.

He was working hard to hurt her with his cruel disdain, and he was succeeding. But Josselyn would not be bested by this boy. What he said reflected on his limited knowledge, for he had only his father to guide him, the most wretched example of manhood she knew. But she was here now, as was Agatha. Though it pained Josselyn to think what the poor girl must endure, she vowed to befriend her—and also to befriend this vicious pup of Owain's.

She drew a steadying breath. "It seems your father would keep you as ignorant as is he. Were your mother alive still, she would no doubt have seen to your complete education. 'Tis a pity for a boy to grow up knowing less than those he will one day rule."

She turned and walked away, not certain she'd made an

impact on him. But as she drew nearer the noisy house that had become her hated home, she heard his thin cry through the darkness.

"Stupid bitch! You don't know nothin' 'bout nothin'. And you're not my ma! Nobody will ever be my ma!"

"Twice you've said that," Josselyn whispered to herself. "You must be sore in need of mothering to deny it so vehemently." Then girding herself once more for what she must endure, she opened the door and went inside.

Madoc was too drunk to talk to that night, and the next morning too disgruntled. But Josselyn could not put off this matter of her pregnancy. If he hit her, so be it. If he sent her back to her uncle . . . Sweet Mary, how she prayed he would! She would accept any punishment her husband meted out, so long as he did not harm the innocent babe she bore.

She followed him when he made his daily trek to the village latrine. When he emerged she met him with a mug of hot ale and bade him walk with her. "Just to the edge of the meadow," she pleaded, forcing herself to smile.

"A child," he repeated when she confessed the truth to him. His gray brows drew together and he stared at her stomach as if searching for the truth. Then his mouth turned down in a scowl. "Is it Owain's?"

Josselyn stepped back, horrified by the very implication. "No! No. How could you think such a thing?"

"You and he were alone that time and—"

"No!" She swallowed hard, for nausea rose like a beast in her throat at the thought of Owain doing to her what he did to Agatha. "Your son disgusts me," she blurted out, not caring how her words might anger him. "He always has. That's why I refused him and sought a union with you instead."

Madoc's jaw worked back and forth. Then his eyes narrowed. "Does the father know you bear him a child?"

Josselyn shook her head. "No."

"Do you know who the father is?"

She held her breath. How was she to answer? Then he
grinned, a sly stretch of his lips over his long yellow teeth.
"Aye, you know. And so do I." Then his grin vanished.
"But no one else is to know. I will claim the child—and
protect it," he added. "So long as you present it as mine.
Mine. Do you understand?"

Josselyn nodded. She was too stunned to do anything
else. She'd imagined all sorts of reactions, but never that
he would want to claim the child as his. Relief made her
knees weak until he caught her by the arm. He pressed his
palm against her belly, squeezing his fingers just enough
for her to feel the strength in them. He might be old, but
he was not weak. "Come, wife. Let us go and announce
the good news."

They started back to the village. He walked with a
jaunty, confident stride. She stumbled trying to keep up. In
the shadow of the hall, however, he paused then pressed
her flat against the door frame. He nuzzled her ear. A man
passing by chuckled. Two lads tittered then ran off to
spread the tale.

But Madoc had something other than love sport on his
mind. Though he pitched his voice low, Josselyn heard the
threat in it. "I caution you, wife, to have a care for this
child you bear me. I know you are skilled in foreign
tongues, but I will not have a child of mine speak other
than the language of its *father*." He emphasized the word.
"No Norman French. No coarse English. This babe speaks
Welsh only—or it speaks not at all."

Josselyn swallowed hard. Her heart ached in her chest,
as if a crushing weight bore down on it. As if it would
break. But she knew her duty.

"Yes, husband. I will do as you say."

"Always."

"Always," she replied.

Twenty-two

The people of Afon Bryn celebrated again that night, though Madoc did not drink so carelessly as before. Instead he sipped from his goblet and watched his son, and kept his wife close beside him the entire evening.

Josselyn did not understand his reaction. Why would he claim another man's child as his own? To save face? But as the evening wore on, she began to understand. Madoc was not ready to cede his role as their leader. He was not blind to his son's power and the way their people reacted to it. To father a child at his age increased Madoc's stature with his men. To do so before Owain could get *his* new wife with child was sweeter still.

So Madoc drank but lightly at every toast hoisted, and petted Josselyn as if she were the love of his heart. He also watched his son and gloated.

Josselyn was relieved by Madoc's unexpected response to her news, but she was not much reassured. Owain's hatred was no light matter. He hated his father; he hated her; and now he would hate her child. She shuddered and would have slipped away to the meager privacy of her bedchamber, but Madoc trapped her hand upon the table.

"Stay," he ordered.

She bowed her head. "I am sore tired, husband."

"You are never to be alone," he told her, even as he

smiled and acknowledged another toast to his manly prowess. "Never," he continued. "Do you understand?"

Josselyn wanted to cry. Was she not to know a moment's privacy? "No, I don't understand."

In answer he stood up. "Let us raise our cups this time to my son, Owain. May he be as fruitful with his wife as I am with mine."

Everyone drank, but for one long moment Owain's pale eyes burned into Josselyn's, malevolent with fury. Mad with frustration and revenge. It was only a moment. Then he laughed and drank and made a coarse remark about planting his seed in his wife three times, in three different places.

The men all roared with laughter.

"Mayhap that is the reason for the delay," Madoc jested.

Josselyn didn't understand their ribald humor, but she did understand Madoc's warning now. She was never to be alone because he did not trust Owain. Did he truly think Owain would go so far as to hurt his father's wife?

Foolish woman, she immediately chastised herself. Owain would not hesitate to hurt either her or her child. She shivered with fear. He probably wouldn't mind ridding himself of his father either.

"Do you understand?" Madoc repeated when he sat down again.

She nodded. "I do."

"If you hope to bear a healthy child, you will heed my words on this. For there will be no other children for you." His hand closed over her wrist. "I will not have it."

This time she raised her eyes to meet his. "I am mindful of my duties as a wife," she stated. "I am no faithless creature to ignore the vows of fidelity I made to you, husband."

"Good." Then he caught her chin in his hand and gave her a hearty kiss. Their audience roared once more with approval. Though Josselyn was disgusted by the slobbering display, she knew better than to show it. So she played the role she'd been given. She ducked her head against his chest as if from shyness and endured the crude innuendos and drunken advice.

She understood very well what was expected of her in exchange for her child's legitimacy. She understood that she was caught in the vicious struggle between father and son, and that her innocent and defenseless babe would be trapped in that same terrible struggle.

She understood also that Madoc was not likely to win that struggle. Time was on Owain's side. And when Owain finally won . . . When that happened she must be prepared. To do what, she did not know. But she would think of something.

Her hand moved to her stomach. She had no other choice.

Rand watched Jasper in the tilting yard. The boy handled a sword with considerable skill. He improved daily on the jousting runs, and even in hand-to-hand combat he acquitted himself well, considering he'd spent five soft years in the care of priests, monks, and other novitiates.

He and Alan were well matched now that they'd recovered from the wounds Owain had inflicted upon them. They practiced together, drank together, and brawled together. Rand frowned and scratched his chin.

"The lad's come a long way," Osborn said from atop an empty ale keg.

Rand grunted. "He can fight."

"And that displeases you? What more do you want of him?"

"He has the skills of a man, but not the heart. Surely you can see that."

"He is but eight and ten."

"He takes nothing seriously. He but plays at this practice."

"Then make him work at it."

Rand glared at his friend. "That would not be wise."

Osborn refused to look away. "Why?"

Rage rose, hot and boiling in Rand's veins. The whole long and tedious summer it had been thus. His rage seethed.

He'd held it in most of the time, but he'd not been able to vanquish it. Twice it had exploded. Twice he'd shed other men's blood. To take up the sword against his brother, the only available source of his rage, would surely lead to disaster.

"I fear I would kill him."

Osborn shook his head. "He is better than you think."

"That would only make matters worse."

"Matters cannot get any worse!" Osborn exploded. "You have been in a rage ever since he arrived. You say it is anger at Owain. But it is anger at Jasper. Why? Because you had to trade Josselyn away to save him? Jesu, man, she was only a woman. Get another!"

"He should not have been taken by Owain. If he'd been alert—if he took his duties seriously—he would have defeated Owain and arrived here unscathed!"

The two men faced one another, posture tense, fists knotted. Across the yard Jasper and Alan fought on, unaware. Metal clanged on metal. Grunts and friendly taunts filled the air. Finally Osborn blew out a harsh breath. "If you will not relieve your anger in the practice yard, then you must release it somewhere else." He planted his fists on his hips. "You need a woman. We all do. What say you I buy some wenches in Chester? The men will freely give their time to build a stew house to shelter them."

A stew. Rand had thought to build a chapel, but the truth was he and his men needed a stew house more. The irony of it was painful. God's bones, but nothing was turning out as he'd planned.

Peace? A fool's dream.

Passion? A fleeting moment.

Contentment? He feared he'd never know it now.

He gritted his teeth and fought back despair. Peace could be maintained, if only by might. Passion could be purchased in a stew house. As for contentment . . . He stared across the yard. Jasper and Alan leaned on their swords now, sweaty and laughing, much as he and Osborn had done when they were young. Mayhap Osborn was right. Mayhap Jasper could be trained to hold Rosecliffe Castle while Rand returned to London.

Mayhap contentment was something he'd yet find.

He nodded his head, mindful that Osborn awaited his response. "Go to Chester, then. Find women for us. But not the marrying kind. I want no men fighting for the right to wed them. Bring hardened whores only, without any artifice," he added, remembering a soft woman who'd deceived him.

"See to it," he muttered, turning away from his friend and back to the work that must consume him until he could safely leave it to Jasper. Rosecliffe Castle, the bane of his existence. The reason for it. The walls could not rise fast enough to suit him, but they *were* rising.

The imprint of Sir Lovell's plan was now clear on the rocky site. The smooth inner face of the wall had risen to chest height, though the outer face was not everywhere so tall. In between, rubble piled up daily as the quarry works produced cartloads of the dark stones. The long days of summer had increased their output considerably, as had the incentives Rand offered his men. Once the walls were head high and winter demanded they cover the uncapped walls with straw, the workers would be free to construct their own dwellings in the land he'd set aside for the town. The promise of homes for those who had wives and children, and a boat to deliver them come spring, had turned Rosecliffe into a beehive of activity. Sir Lovell spent his days grumbling, but he was well pleased with the progress.

To a lesser degree, so was Rand. But his problems were larger than Sir Lovell's. Materials; food stuffs; safety; defense. One way and another, the Welsh were a constant threat to every aspect of Rosecliffe's survival. No massive attack had yet been mounted against the rising castle. Indeed, Rand sometimes wondered if that would ever occur. Instead the devious Welsh mounted lesser, insidious attacks. Two quarry workers felled by archers. Another fire set, but not boat or building this time. No, they'd been craftier, and during a hot, dry spell more than half of the hay field, meant to provide fodder for the animals during the worst of the winter, had been ruined.

Now the hunting in the surrounding forest had become poor. Alan had found traces of other hunters there and the conclusion was obvious. The Welsh had concentrated all their hunting in the forests nearest Rosecliffe in an effort to deplete the woodlands of their game. But if they thought to starve the English out that way, they would not succeed. Although the very sight of fish had begun to sicken him, Rand knew the sea would keep them alive, even should every other source of food disappear.

Still, he meant to eat more than fish and oysters. He ordered the hunters to venture farther afield, but in larger parties, and with at least one fast horse so the alarm could be carried back should an attack occur.

He sighed and gazed beyond the castle walls, sweeping the wildly beautiful countryside with his eyes. Then he focused on the *domen*, symbol of everything Welsh, and he felt the profoundest urge to wreck it, to tear it down and use the stones as rubble within Rosecliffe's walls.

" 'Twould change naught.''

Rand was not startled by Newlin's words. How the little man with his awkward gait approached so silently—how he managed to read a man's thoughts—Rand did not ponder. Suffice it that the bard could do so. Once more Rand sighed and his shoulders sagged. "You have no cause for concern. 'Twas only a passing thought.'' He paused then added, "A mad thought proffered by a madman.''

They stood in silence a long while. Around them circled sounds of construction. The creak of heavy cart wheels. The solid thud of rock fitted to rock. The constant click of the masons' tools as they shaped the rocks. Half a year only had they been here, and yet the change was profound.

"There's more to this land you have adopted as your own than merely this outcropping, wild and beautiful though it be." Newlin's one good eye focused on Rand. "There are villages and mountains. Wild places and towns. Fairs and marketplaces."

Marketplaces. Rand scratched his chin thoughtfully. He needed to scrape his cheeks before his beard grew as long as a Scotsman's. He did not understand the odd-looking bard, but he did trust him. "Is there a market or fair nearby where supplies might be purchased with English coin?"

Rand, Osborn, and ten handpicked warriors rode to Llangarn, heavily armed but with peaceful intentions. The Saint Ebbe's Day Market was a tradition, sponsored by the abbot of Llangarn in tribute to their patron saint. That it coincided with the harvest and allowed the monks to purchase their winter needs without sending carts out to collect it was of no consequence. For many in the wild hills of northern Wales, the Saint Ebbe's market was the only time in the cycle of seasons when they deviated from the routine of their lives: labor six days, worship one. Labor six days, worship one. But Saint Ebbe's day was different.

Fully twenty score people crowded the flat meadow alongside the river, where the fair was held. The High Road bisected the site, with coarse goods displayed on the riverside, and finer goods against the abbey walls.

Rand surveyed the scene as they made their way down the road. He noted the fierce scowls of the Welshmen, as well as the worried frowns of their women and wondering stares of their young. The Welsh were not likely to initiate a fight with so many women and children in their midst, not so long as they were not provoked. He had no intention of provoking them.

A hum of apprehension rippled through the crowd, a warning passed from mouth to ear and on, dousing all other conversation. The market grounds grew unnaturally still, though the bear baiting continued without pause. Rand could hear the dogs' excited yipping and the bear's painful bellow. Then a trio of brown-clad monks hurried forward to greet the newcomers, clearly anxious to maintain calm, and the taut muscles in Rand's shoulders eased. He was right to have come. Everything would be fine.

The monks stayed close to the Englishmen as they progressed through the stalls. Rand had come to purchase Welsh goods, and so he did. Two barrels of salt, a keg of honey, and three willow fish baskets. Also a team of oxen, four dozen hens, two cocks, and a pair of pups newly weaned from their dam. The two carts he'd brought grew heavy with his purchases, and as he bought, the angry stares directed at him eased. Somewhat.

The sounds of the market returned. The entertainments resumed. A family of acrobats drew a throng, including several of his own men. A fire-eater mesmerized a fearful crowd. The three religious eventually drifted away from the Englishmen, reassured that no conflict would erupt and ruin the most profitable day of their year.

" 'Tis not so unlike an English market," Osborn remarked as he eyed a platter of meat pies, steaming their fragrance into the early autumn air. Then the warrior in him took control once more. "It grows late, however. Unless we plan to camp next the abbey walls, we should begin our return to Rosecliffe. What say you, Rand?"

But Rand was not listening. A small party had arrived on horseback. Seven men. Two women. And one of them was Josselyn.

His hand tightened on the reins and his well-trained mount obediently backed up, nearly upsetting a plank table stacked high with bolts of kersey, twill, fustian, and lawn.

"Hey!" cried the cloth merchant.

"My pardon." Rand muttered. *"Esgusodych fi,"* he added, hoping he had the words right. Without thinking, he urged the horse forward. He'd known he might encounter Madoc or Clyde. Or Owain. That's why he'd left Jasper at

Rosecliffe. If there was a battle and he was killed, Jasper would finish Rosecliffe. But he'd not allowed himself to imagine Josselyn here.

Not that it mattered.

His jaw set in stern lines. So she'd come to market with her husband. Suddenly furious with her, he jerked his horse around. He'd not yet offered his good wishes to the happy couple.

"Come," he ordered Osborn. Then he rode straight toward the woman he still dreamed about, and her husband who was old enough to be her sire.

Josselyn saw Rand before her husband did. She'd had no reason to look up, but she had, and the sight of him threw her into utter turmoil. It was as if she had sensed his presence, and in the scant seconds before Madoc spied him too, her eyes swept greedily over him. She took in his manly profile, his easy control of his mighty destrier. As he neared, she saw also the gauntness of his face, the new lines that bracketed his mouth. He was brown from the sun and weary from his labors. She'd heard that the walls of Rosecliffe grew steadily taller, that his men worked every minute of daylight and often by torchlight, and that he worked harder and longer than them all.

She'd heard also that he'd brought in women to service his men—and no doubt himself. Not that it mattered to her. And yet a spark of righteous anger burned in her chest. Had he no shame?

Judging from the hard expression on his face, he did not.

In a belligerent gesture Madoc urged his horse in front of hers, as did her uncle. Then Rand and Osborn drew up.

Like a contagion a new silence grew, rippling out in waves until even the shouts of the wrestlers faded to naught, and only the squawking of the crated hens pierced the unnatural quiet.

Nesta's horse sidled up to Josselyn's and the older woman reached a hand to her. She meant to comfort her, but no one could do that. Josselyn stared at Rand, hungry for every detail of his appearance. She'd thought herself successful in putting him out of her mind, but knew now that she'd failed. To see him was to want him. Only he had never wanted her as much.

Already he turned away from her to face Madoc.

"Congratulations on your marriage," Rand said in creditable Welsh.

Madoc stared coldly at him. "Have we met?"

Clyde leaned forward. "This is the Englishman, Fitz Hugh. Fitz Hugh, this is Madoc ap Lloyd, husband to my niece."

Josselyn pressed her lips together and kept a painful silence. Madoc would countenance no interference from her. This was men's business, not women's. But it felt very like her business. Her life had been made forfeit to the posturings of these three men who sat their horses before her now.

Madoc shifted to a more comfortable position. His saddle creaked. His mouth quirked in a smug smile. "I accept your congratulations. But you may not know that further congratulations are also due me."

Josselyn sucked in a hard breath. No! He could not mean to say anything about that. He could not be that foolish!

As if he heard her thoughts Madoc glanced at her, and the warning in his eyes was clear. Nesta's hand tightened as if to caution Josselyn against angering her husband. She was right of course. Nothing Josselyn said or did would alter Madoc's plans. Though it felt as if she were agreeing to have her heart ripped, whole and still beating, from her chest, Josselyn did as she must. She averted her gaze, a good wife, obedient to her husband's command, and listened as Madoc gloated.

"My wife bears me a son."

There was no response from Rand, and when Josselyn could bear it no longer, she looked up. "My wife bears me a son," Madoc repeated. Then, "Stupid Englishman. He does not understand."

But he did. Rand stared blankly at Madoc. He understood

the man's words. Josselyn was with child. What he did not understand was the crushing sense of loss that struck him. Josselyn bore this old man's child?

Or was it *his*?

He looked sharply at Josselyn, at her slender figure astride the dappled mare. How could she be with child? She showed no evidence of her condition, unless she had just learned of it. It had been four months since he'd been with her. Were it his child, she would be further along.

He raised his eyes from her waist to her strictly controlled expression, and his sense of loss soured to bitterness. He jerked his gaze back to Madoc. "Let us hope your heirs and mine will be at peace with one another," he said in Welsh. Then he nodded, turned his horse, and rode away.

Josselyn watched him go. She made no sound or move that might betray anything of her feelings. But inside, where no one could see, she wept. He knew it could be his and yet did not care.

Madoc chortled with glee, well pleased with his revelation, for neither Clyde nor Nesta had known of it either. Everyone was pleased, it seemed, for Nesta reached over and hugged her, and Clyde shook Madoc's hand.

Josselyn smiled. She answered Nesta's concerned questions and nodded at her words of advice. But inside she wept. She approved her husband's purchases and made suggestions for the quantities of spices and cloth and household items to be purchased. But behind the placid expression affixed to her face she wept.

Only when she lay down alone in her bed that night did she loosen the tight bands that held her emotions at bay, that kept her walking and talking and performing as she must.

But even then she did not release the tears that threatened to choke her, to drown her in their sorrowing depths. She lay dry-eyed in her bed and wondered how she would endure the coming months, let alone the years that would follow, empty and leaden in their wake.

*   *   *

Josselyn's child was born in the midst of a howling storm,
a tiny girl with dark eyes and no hair. She'd gone the full
nine months, yet still she was too small. Josselyn had at-
tended other births and she knew it was not a good sign.
But the baby was perfectly formed, a beautiful infant with
a pure soul. Josselyn had loved her on sight.

The whole winter prior to the birth Josselyn had been
listless and ill. Owain's presence had not helped, nor had
the signs of rough usage that showed in Agatha's countenance. Meriel's furtive watchfulness made it worse, as did
Madoc's constant boasting about the child she bore him.
At times he seemed almost to believe it was his, for his
twice-weekly visits to her bed had become a trial. For the
most part it was only for show. But three times he'd tried
to mount her, and three times he'd been unable.

The last time her relief must have been obvious, for he'd
cuffed her and sent her tumbling from the bed. The bruise
had colored her cheek for over a week. But he'd not tried
again.

He'd seemed almost relieved when the child was born a
girl. The truth of her parentage was not so important as if
she'd been a boy child. Since the birth he'd appeared to
have lost all interest in both Josselyn and the child, whom
she'd named Isolde.

Agatha had conceived sometime during the fall, but
she'd lost the child before she'd even been certain of her
pregnancy. She'd not told Owain, but he'd somehow
learned of it and berated her soundly.

No doubt Meriel had told him. The older woman seemed
to become more secretive and watchful every day. She'd
acted eager for Josselyn's company when Owain had been
expected to wed her. But Josselyn's marriage to Madoc was
an altogether different matter. Meriel rebuffed every attempt to befriend her, and though it was frustrating, Josselyn tried to understand. Meriel had run Madoc's
household alone for many years. Now she'd been usurped

first by Josselyn, then by Agatha. Once when he was drunk
Madoc had referred to her as his ugly old cousin, and Josselyn had seen the stricken look on her face. But she'd
scowled at Josselyn, warning her away, and Josselyn had
been too steeped in her own unhappiness to try to pierce
the shell Meriel held around herself.

But at least Josselyn had Isolde. How she prayed that the
frail baby would survive. So many did not. She stared down
at the tiny girl, wrapped warmly and tucked into a cradle
next to the fire. Did she breathe?

"Isolde?" She touched the child's cheek fearfully, then
sighed when the baby's mouth began reflexively to suckle.
At once Josselyn's breasts tingled with the need to nurse
her. But Isolde needed to sleep. The child would awaken
when she was hungry. In the meantime Josselyn needed to
fetch fresh water to her room.

It was midday. In the main hall Madoc snored in his
chair. Owain and Agatha were nowhere to be seen. Meriel
sat in the only window repairing Madoc's torn hose. By
rights Josselyn should be the one to tend her husband's
garments. But she knew better than to challenge Meriel
about it. Nor did she truly want to. Madoc was a self-
centered bully, only a little less cruel than Owain. If Meriel
wished to wait hand and foot upon him, so be it.

The two women did not speak while Josselyn filled a
bucket, and as she trudged up the stairs with it, Josselyn
felt guilty. She should try harder with Meriel. She was an
old woman with no daughter to care for her.

Josselyn set the bucket on the floor outside the door, and
rubbed her aching back. When had she become so weak?
Then she heard a noise in her chamber and her weariness
fled. Who was in there? She burst in and surprised Rhys
bending low over Isolde's cradle.

"What are you doing!"

The boy sprang back, his dirty face looking guilty, his
posture defensive. His gaze swung toward the door, but she
barred the way.

"What are you doing in here? What are you up to?"

He scowled, a miniature version of his unpleasant sire. "I was lookin' at her. That's all."

Fighting down her panic and the unreasoning fear that Owain might have sent Rhys to harm Isolde, Josselyn moved purposefully to the crib. "She's asleep. Now is not a good time to visit her." She touched the infant's cheek and once more she suckled in her sleep. No harm had been done. Had any been intended?

She looked up at Rhys. He'd sidled nearer the door, but he hadn't left. His nearly black eyes darted from her to Isolde then back to her. "She's awful small."

"She'll grow."

"Meriel says she's more like to die."

"Meriel is wrong. She's wrong," she repeated. She reached for Isolde. Asleep or not, she needed to hold her close, to protect her from the ill will in this awful place.

The boy watched as she settled Isolde in her arms. "Girls can't inherit nothin'."

"She's no threat to your inheritance, nor to your father's. You have no reason to fear her."

"Fear a baby? Not me," he boasted. But still he did not leave.

Josselyn studied him. He was tall for his age though thin. But he was always filthy. On impulse she said, "If you wash up, I'll let you hold her."

He bristled. "I don't want to hold her."

Josselyn shrugged. She looked down at Isolde's sweet face and smiled. "I love holding her. She's so helpless and so good. She makes me want to be good too, to be better than I usually am."

When she glanced over at him, he had an odd expression on his face. Such a lonely child, she realized. Lonely and ignored, and in the long months she'd been here, she'd ignored him too. She smiled at him. "It's natural to be curious about her. After all, she'll be like a little sister to you."

"She's not my sister, and you're not my ma."

"No, I'm not. But once she can walk, 'tis you she'll be trailing after. Come closer, Rhys. Come see how little her fingers are. How tiny her fingernails." She smiled encouragingly at him. "Come on. She'd like to meet you."

He lingered a long while in her chamber, until Madoc's raised voice reminded him where he was. But before that happened he'd washed his hands and face, held Isolde while she slept, then held her again after she'd nursed. He actually grinned when Isolde let out a startlingly loud belch.

"Rude little bit, isn't she?" He laughed, and it was the first time he'd truly sounded like a child.

Josselyn laughed with him. "We'll teach her manners in due time."

But now he was gone, and though Josselyn crawled into bed with Isolde beside her, she could not sleep. It was easy to forget that Rhys was but eight. He was Owain's son, as unpleasant and aggressive as his father. But he was also a child, alone in a harsh world. She should try to befriend him. She should try to civilize him.

If nothing else, she might succeed in making him Isolde's ally and protector during the years to come.

Twenty-three

The winter was harsh, but it left in a rush. The ice melted. The rooks and becks tumbled to the sea. Spring erupted in all its green glory, and the creatures of the northern hills bred with wild abandon. But as the hills heated their way toward summer, so did the bitterness between the Welsh and English heat and rush headlong toward confrontation.

It began in April when the sheep were first released to their spring pasture. Owain stormed into the hall, threw off his fur cape, and glared at his father, rage mottling his features. "You would not heed my warning. Now see what your damned caution has wrought!"

Suspicion clouded Madoc's brow; alarm colored the faces of the three village elders who conferred with him. "What now?" Madoc grunted.

Josselyn skimmed fat from a broth of bones and withered vegetables. Agatha sat stitching near the fire. But at the sound of angry male voices they sidled uneasily toward the stairs. Owain angry was a fearful thing. Madoc raging against him was equally dangerous to anyone in reach. Only Meriel leaned forward, keen to know what had roused her cousins to such a pitch.

"A shepherd is murdered, fifteen ewes stolen, and a ram butchered!"

Madoc lurched to his feet. "Who has dared to steal my sheep?"

" 'Tis your wife's sheep they have dared to steal. 'Tis Carreg Du that is attacked. And the guilty party cannot be in doubt. The black-hearted English have begun their campaign to bring us to our knees. They will starve the people of Carreg Du, then they will turn for us." His nostrils flared in disdain for the four old men. " 'Tis clear enough you are content to sit and let them do it." He beat his chest with one fist. "But I will not!"

In the ringing silence that followed, all eyes turned to Madoc. Owain had thrown down a challenge. It could not be interpreted any other way. Josselyn saw Madoc's fists tighten. But the man's voice was remarkably calm. "What does Clyde say to this? Does he send for our help?"

With a roar Owain whipped out his dagger. Everyone fell back, including the women. With one swift lunge he plunged the wicked blade down into the table between him and his father. It barely vibrated, he stuck it so deep. He glared at his father. "Clyde will do nothing. He is a coward. But I will retaliate. With you or without you, I will no longer wait."

Josselyn watched the confrontation with mounting alarm. If Madoc did not act, Owain would soon wrest power from him. But more alarming even than that was the fact that one of the shepherds of Carreg Du was dead—and by Randulf Fitz Hugh's order.

"Who was killed?"

Agatha caught her arm in warning, but Josselyn would not be put off. "Who was it? Do you know his name?"

Owain turned his head to see her, and in his eyes Josselyn could swear she saw triumph. "A lad nearly of an age to become a warrior. Strong and smart." He paused. "He had no chance. His head was severed from his shoulders with one vicious swing of a long sword."

Bile rose in Josselyn's throat. She had to press her lips together to stop their trembling. "What was his name?"

He held her eyes for a long moment, delaying. Deliberately tormenting her. "Gower. I'm told his name was Gower. Do you know him?"

Josselyn's knees went weak. Gower. Only son of the widow Holwen. Her heart ached for the old woman, and she felt the profoundest need to clutch Isolde to her. But she held herself stiffly, unwilling to give Owain the satisfaction of seeing her pain. She nodded. "I knew him."

"Then you will understand my decision to wreak vengeance on those who would strike down a green lad and in so cold a manner."

As much as Josselyn mistrusted Owain, in that moment she agreed with him. Why Gower? He was a simple lad and good to his mother. Who would see to Holwen in her final years?

That day had marked the beginning of the bloody spring. The men of Afon Bryn and Carreg Du prepared for war, and through the planting months of April and May, it was the women and boys who tended the fields. The attack on Gower gave birth to a murderous retaliation. Though Josselyn was far removed from Carreg Du, word of the troubles there reached her daily. Another English boat burned and this time the two watchmen were killed. A skirmish between the Welsh and an English hunting party. Three Englishmen killed, two Welshmen.

Under Rand's leadership, the English response was equally ferocious. He drove the Welsh from every part of the land between Rosecliffe and Carreg Du. But Clyde still held the village, though most of the women and children had fled to Afon Bryn.

Her Aunt Nesta stayed, however, and Josselyn worried for her daily. Gladys also stayed, but though she kept young Davit with her, she sent Rhonwen and Cordula away. Josselyn did not see as much of her people as she would like, however. They stayed in outlying cottages spread around Afon Bryn, while she resided in the main hall.

July arrived, scented with the smoke of war and the

stench of death. Agatha was with child again, though no one spoke of it for fear of cursing the babe. Owain was usually gone, fighting the English, and in his absence, Agatha seemed more relaxed. Her timidity eased. Rhys also appeared more regularly at his grandfather's abode. He ate constantly, anything placed in front of him. Josselyn was pleased to see his narrow face begin to fill out.

Isolde grew as well. She was still small, but she had become plump and healthy. She smiled and gurgled and sang to them. At least that's how it sounded to Josselyn, who had fallen hopelessly in love with her daughter. Isolde was perfection itself. She was pink and soft, and when her hair came in fair, it was more like Madoc's than Rand's.

Rand.

Josselyn tried not to think of him, but the day did not pass without her wasting endless hours trying to make sense of the man. He was ambitious and ruthless. He'd seduced her then vowed to give her to his brother. He was awful— and English—and he'd killed Gower. All this she knew.

And yet she also knew that Rand had not been the first one to attack. Owain had. Rand had not allowed any woman to be raped, whereas Owain . . . well, she would not put it past Owain. He was cruel with his own wife; what would he be with the wives of his enemies? Rand had seduced her. But only because she'd been so willing. Even on his threat to marry her to Jasper he'd wavered. In truth, she did not think he'd known what to do with her.

How would he react if he knew he had a daughter?

"Look how strong she is."

Rhys's voice drew Josselyn from her reverie. He sat cross-legged beside Isolde's cradle, grinning as the baby gripped his fingers. "I believe she can pull herself all the way up. Can I try?" he added, glancing at Josselyn.

"No, dear. I don't think she's quite ready for that."

But Rhys did not agree. "She's got the same blood as me, strong blood come from her father, my grandfather. She can do it."

"No, Rhys. She's too young."

But the boy was stubborn. Before she could stop him, he pulled Isolde upright. The baby blinked and laughed, as if entertained by what she'd done. Then abruptly she let go, and with a thud, her head hit the side of the cradle.

Josselyn scooped her up before the first wail was out. Rhys leapt back as if he feared punishment, and lurked just out of reach.

"She shouldna let go," he muttered while Josselyn consoled the sobbing babe. "It wasn't my fault." He didn't notice Meriel's approach, so her sharp cuff to his head caught him unawares.

"Ow!" He ducked out of her way, holding his hand over his ear. "Stupid old bitch!"

"Hurts, doesn't it? If you're to be a true man you must know more than how to mete out pain," Meriel cried. "You must know also how to take it."

She struck out at him again, but he danced just out of her reach.

"Stupid old bitch. Everyone knows women don't get to hit men. Didn't my grandfather teach you anything?"

"He never hit me!" Meriel screeched.

"Then why did you moan and scream?" the boy taunted. "I hear how Agatha moans with my Da. I heard you too, with my grandfather, before he married her." He pointed at Josselyn.

Though Josselyn rocked the still sobbing Isolde, she glared at the two, the old woman and the young boy. "Stop this arguing. Stop it now!"

But Rhys had been a wild creature for too long to have been tamed by a bath and a few kind words. "You're not my Ma! You can't tell me what to do!" Then he fixed her with a smug, knowing look, so like Owain's it made her shiver. "Why don't you scream when your husband comes to *your* bed?"

How she would have answered that disgusting question she was never to know, for at that very moment Agatha lumbered into the hall, holding her increasing belly with her hands. "There's a messenger from Owain." She stared resentfully at Josselyn. "But he won't speak to anyone but you."

It was bad news. They all knew it, and only Isolde's lingering sobs broke the quick, oppressive silence. Meriel did not wait for Josselyn, but hurried to the door. Josselyn followed more slowly.

Outside Owain's man, Conan, drank from a jug. When he saw her, he wiped his face on his sleeve. "Madoc is grievous ill. Owain bids you come."

"Grievous ill? What is wrong with him?" Meriel cried.

The man ignored Meriel and stared boldly at Josselyn. "He suffered a seizure of the chest. He's callin' for his wife."

As if she sensed her mother's unease, Isolde began once more to fret. Josselyn hugged her closer and tried to think. "I cannot leave my baby."

"Then bring her."

Josselyn did not want to go. Duty demanded she do as she was told, but some unreasoning fear made it impossible. "She's too young to travel."

" 'Tis but two hours."

"By horseback. I'll need a cart."

The man shrugged. "He bids you come."

"I'll go in her stead," Meriel interjected. "I'll go with you to heal him. I've healed all his aches and pains these many years. I should—"

"You're not his wife," the man sneered. " 'Tis her duty, not yours."

"Where is he?" Josselyn asked.

"In your uncle's house."

Her uncle's house. That changed everything. "I'll prepare for the journey at once." To be in Carreg Du, with Uncle Clyde and Aunt Nesta, sounded like heaven, even under these circumstances.

They left within the hour and arrived at dusk. By then

Josselyn felt heartily ashamed of herself. Madoc's well-being had not concerned her nearly so much as her own. Though their marriage was based on mutual convenience, that did not lessen her duty to him. He gave Isolde a name; she gave him the appearance of manly vigor. She had no right to complain.

But now he was struck down, and for his sake as well as her own, she must nurse him back to health.

Nesta greeted her with open arms. "Ah, but she is a tiny thing!" she exclaimed, taking the wide-eyed child immediately into her arms.

Josselyn smiled down at Isolde. "Tiny and sweet, like a fairy child."

"Do not say such things," Nesta whispered. "There are those superstitious souls who would think ill of her if they heard you call her such a thing."

Josselyn stroked Isolde's cheek, then sighed. Some things in her beloved country would never change, superstition and strife being primary among them. "I must see to my husband. Will you mind Isolde?"

"Of course." Nesta settled Isolde in her arms. "He is in the chamber that was yours." She stared at Josselyn. "It does not look good."

Madoc would have to die for it to look any worse, and Josselyn feared that condition was imminent. He lay on the bed that had once been hers, bathed, draped in clean linens, and still as a corpse. His body had no marks on it—at least no new ones. The old scars, the battle marks of his youth, but no outward sign of this new affliction.

"He grabbed his chest and fell," the woman who sat with him told Josselyn. "Since then he opens his eyes and tries to speak, but he cannot. 'Tis like the devil has hold of his tongue," she finished in hushed tones.

Josselyn ignored that last remark. "Did this happen during a battle?"

The woman hesitated. Her gaze slid away from Josselyn, then crept back. "They had gone to set fire to the English fields." Her voice lowered further. " 'Tis said the only true battles he fought were with his son. With that Owain." Her lips turned down in distaste.

There was no surprise in that. Nor was there any surprise when during the night Madoc's heartbeat, already erratic and weak, ceased altogether.

Josselyn had dozed on and off while she sat with him, and when she nursed Isolde around midnight, she spoke softly to Madoc. But when she checked on him he was still. His skin was cold. His soul had fled.

And she was a widow, who had hardly been a wife.

She moved Isolde to the main hall, and though she dreaded it, she searched out Owain. He'd returned to the village late and she'd not seen him. But Nesta told her that he'd taken over the priest's house as his own. Josselyn carried a lantern across the stony road and told the guard to summon Owain. Instead, the man pushed her rudely inside, called out to Owain, then slammed the door, shutting her in with him.

To her shame, she panicked. She yanked frantically at the door, to no avail.

"Well. If it isn't my dear stepmother. And in the middle of the night."

Josselyn whirled around. Owain stood in loosened chainse and braies. In the background something moved—a woman, Josselyn saw when a face peeped from beneath the bedcovers. Her panic turned to disgust at his infidelity. "Your father is dead. I thought you would want to know."

He grinned, then with one hand slowly beat his chest, in an awful mockery of grief. "He is gone. My beloved sire."

Though there was no reason to think it, Josselyn wondered momentarily whether he'd somehow caused his father's death.

"But I forget," he continued. "You have lost a husband. Come, Josselyn." He extended a hand to her. "Let us comfort one another."

"No. Just tell your man to let me out of here. Your

companion awaits you," she said, in case he'd forgotten
their audience.

He grinned again. "As you wish. But Josselyn," he said
more lowly. "The time will come when we will . . . talk.
About you. About your child."

She stared at him, instantly on guard. "There is nothing
to talk about."

He gazed at her boldly and she knew he was the same
malevolent wretch he'd always been. But he was infinitely
more dangerous now than before. "I know the truth," he
murmured, coming nearer. "I always have."

She backed up until she collided with the door. "You
know nothing."

"I know enough. That child is your weakness. Her well-
being means everything to you."

For a moment only, Josselyn felt relief. He hadn't meant
the truth about who Isolde's father was. Then a far worse
emotion gripped her; an icy fear and an icy rage. He was
threatening Isolde.

She faced him, filled with a hatred so swift, so violent,
it terrified her. Yet somehow her voice came out cool and
controlled. Mocking even. "Yes, you've found me out. I
love my child. Now, open the door."

He raised a fist and she flinched. Then he laughed and
banged on the door beside her head. But before she could
leave he added, "If you get lonely in your empty marriage
bed, just let me know."

She fled without responding. Why had he threatened
Isolde? Did he know Madoc was not Isolde's father? And
if he did, what was the worst that could happen?

Isolde would be named a bastard. An English bastard.
She paused, breathless outside her uncle's door, and tried
to calm herself. A bastard English child would be hated by
her Welsh countrymen, especially now.

Still, that was not the worst of it. Owain had implied he
would hurt Isolde if Josselyn did not respond to his demands. She shuddered to think what those demands would

be, yet the alternative was so much worse. She did not doubt him capable of hurting a child. She'd seen Rhonwen's bruises, and Rhys's. He enjoyed bullying people; he always had. So long as he was anywhere near Isolde, the baby would not be safe.

Somehow she must protect her. She left the baby with Nesta as she prepared Madoc for burial. Two men carried his lifeless form into the hall where she bathed him, dressed him, and wrapped him in clean cloths, then stood candles at his head and feet. Only then did she seek out Isolde and take her to her breast. It was as much to console herself as the fretful babe, for Josselyn was afraid. With Madoc gone there was no one to control Owain.

That proved true first thing in the morning. The village priest came to pray over Madoc. Clyde and his people, and Owain and his soldiers, gathered around the body in the open square. In the weak morning light, Josselyn could better see the changes one year had wrought at Carreg Du, and she was appalled. It was more a warriors' outpost than a village. Few women; fewer children. And Owain's men nearly as numerous as her uncle's.

Apprehension shivered up her spine. She'd expected to feel safer in Carreg Du, but she did not. Not anymore. Unexpectedly, Newlin moved up beside her. Though he did not touch her, she felt a certain reassurance.

"... killed by our enemies as surely as if an English blade had run him through," the priest said. While the men of Afon Bryn all murmured their agreement, the priest looked over at Owain. Josselyn saw Owain's faint smile and the priest's sigh, as if from relief.

Had Owain told him what to say? But why should he?

Still, Josselyn could not rid herself of the idea that Owain had some part in his father's death. She worried over what it meant. That smile. That sigh. Not until she heard her own name did she realize that Owain spoke.

"... his wife, Josselyn, and I will take his body to Afon

Bryn to be buried with all the honor due him. We depart in an hour.''

"Be careful, child," Newlin murmured. "That one is not to be trusted."

Josselyn swallowed hard. "I don't want to go back there." She hadn't meant her voice to carry, but Owain heard her and strode up.

"You must go. 'Tis your duty as his wife. And as mother to his child," he added, showing his teeth in a smug smile. An evil smile.

"Bower and Dewey will accompany you," her uncle announced, taking her arm. He stared at Owain until the man shrugged his acquiescence.

They all knew Owain was evil, she realized. But everyone was afraid of him and what he might do to the people of Carreg Du should they oppose him. In trying to drive out the enemy English, they'd allowed another enemy—a far worse one, it seemed—into their midst.

By the time they reached Afon Bryn, Josselyn was beyond exhaustion. She'd spent two days traveling now, and in between, a night with precious little sleep. Meriel and Agatha greeted the travelers with a hearty meal.

Meriel wept as she served the hungry men. Josselyn tried to comfort her, but the older woman would have none of it. She'd loved Madoc, Josselyn realized. Not merely as a cousin, but also as a man. That's what Rhys had overheard in the past, Madoc taking Meriel. But he had not wed her. Instead he'd married Josselyn and thereby bested his son, albeit temporarily. No wonder Meriel had been so hostile toward her.

As for Rhys, she caught a glimpse of the boy only once. As always, his father's presence drove him to the edges of village life. He skulked around the periphery like a cur dog, drawn to the man, yet terrified of him.

The displaced people of Carreg Du gathered round her as Madoc was buried. But they could not protect her when night fell and Owain ruled in the house that had been his father's.

She went to bed with Isolde in the cradle beside her bed and Bower and Dewey asleep outside her door. But she awoke abruptly in the darkest hour of the night, her heart hammering with fear. She was not alone.

"Perhaps I'll wed her to my son."

Josselyn jerked upright. In the dark the malevolence in Owain's voice threatened to smother her with fear. Was it him or was it the devil come to earth to torment her? Then he moved and she saw the outline of Isolde in his arms, and she knew that Owain *was* the devil himself.

She leapt from the bed. "Give her to me."

"Shh. You'll wake her. I intend her no harm, Josselyn— if you do as you're told."

Cold dread seeped into her veins, an invasive fear that froze her in her place. "What does that mean?"

He chuckled, an ugly, amused sound. "What I could not have within the bounds of marriage to you, I would now have outside those bounds."

Fear made her want to flee. But he held her child and she would die before she abandoned Isolde. She moved toward him. "Give her to me."

"She is a pretty babe. Much like her mother. She and Rhys will make a good match."

He did not stop her when she took Isolde from him, nor when she backed away. Though she knew what he implied by proposing such a match, Josselyn needed to know for certain. So she said, "Isolde is your half-sister. Though younger than him, she is Rhys's aunt. He cannot marry her."

"She's an English bastard."

The words echoed in the darkened room.

"You cannot prove that."

"But Meriel can."

Meriel. So it was as Josselyn had feared. Meriel knew that Madoc had been unable to consummate their marriage.

She squeezed Isolde to her. The sweet baby scent of her provided a small comfort in the face of Owain's over-powering evil. Her voice trembled. "If you do anything to hurt her—"

"I'm not interested in your brat. 'Tis you I want. You can buy her safety easily enough. Though you are no virgin, I won't hold that against you. Now put her down."

Terror overwhelmed her. Fury energized her. "I'll scream and Bower and Dewey will come."

He laughed and her fear trebled. "They are not likely to hear a thing."

She gasped. "Have you killed them?"

"Don't worry. They are only drunk."

"No." She shook her head. "Neither of them would be so incautious."

Again he laughed. "It seems their ale was rather strong. In any event, we will not be interrupted. Now put her down."

She was trapped. With no other choice, Josselyn turned and laid Isolde in her cradle. The baby blinked and opened her eyes. "I'm sorry, sweetling," she whispered. Then as she straightened, she pinched her daughter's thigh.

Isolde's response was immediate. Her shrill cry rose in protest and at once Josselyn snatched her up again. She turned on Owain. "This is not the time or place for your perversions," she hissed.

But Owain was not one so easily thwarted. He wrenched Isolde from Josselyn's arms and tossed her carelessly onto the bed. The baby shrieked with renewed terror, but when Josselyn tried to get to her Owain caught her and flung her against the wall. Her head cracked painfully against the plaster, and before she could evade him, he pressed his full weight against her, trapping her as he caught her arms in a vicious hold.

"I'll have you, Josselyn. Whenever and wherever I de-sire. If you would keep your bastard alive, I suggest you cooperate." His free hand pinched one of her breasts, then moved to shove crudely between her legs. Only her thin smock blocked his entrance.

"It can be easy or it can be hard. You choose." Then he bit her neck until she cried out in pain. "I prefer it hard," he hissed in her ear.

He let her go and she nearly collapsed. Isolde's shrill screams assaulted her ears. From the hall she heard one voice, then another. As she scrambled across the room to Isolde, the door opened then closed, and he was gone.

But he was not gone, not really. Josselyn held Isolde and rocked back and forth, back and forth, as the terror of her predicament sank in. She had to escape Owain else he would kill her. There was no pretending otherwise. But it was not for herself that she feared. Not anymore. She cared because of Isolde. Her baby must be safe. That was all that mattered anymore.

Twenty-four

Rand rode slowly across the blackened field. No bird called out. No bee or cricket or butterfly flitted across the barren landscape that just yesterday had been golden with wheat. Only the charred remains of a slat-sided cart and the furrows blackened with the ash of wheat stalks gave evidence of what had been there before.

Six months' hard effort, gone. Wheat enough to provide most of their needs for the coming winter, gone.

His nostrils flared at the acrid smell stirred up by his restless destrier's hooves. There was no wind, only the heavy press of clouds in the humid afternoon. The river would run black when next it rained.

His fist tightened around the reins. When he caught Owain ap Madoc it would run red.

As if to underscore his dark thoughts, thunder rolled low and ominous across the open field. Farther down the valley, under the protection of a heavily armed band of knights, a gang of workers cleared the low-hanging branches of the trees that edged the field. Since Saint John's Eve, three laborers had been picked off by Welsh archers. One had died. The other two, plus over a dozen others, refused to work the fields any longer. They'd rather tote backbreaking loads of stone up from the quarry than risk the deadly arrows of the enemy Welsh.

He looked back at Rosecliffe. In spite of the constant harrying of the Welsh, the walls rose steadily upward. Until the loss of the wheat crop, he'd planned to keep the full complement of workers at Rosecliffe this winter. The temporary shelters along the inside of the wall were adequate, and between the stable and the nearly completed great hall, there would be enough space to keep the workers busy during the long hours of the winter. Rough stone could be trimmed for flooring. Oak beams could be measured, planed, and carved. The armorer could make hinges and bars.

But now there was no wheat for bread, no food to provide for so many. He'd have to send most of them back to England until spring.

"God's bones!" he swore. At this rate he'd be trapped in Wales till his dotage. Already he'd suspended construction on the town outside the castle walls. No one would bring their families to live in such a hostile and dangerous place. Without workers he could not raise food. Without food he could not import workers. He was caught in a vise of Owain's making.

"The south field is not entirely ruined," Osborn reported when he galloped up. "A quarter of the field, say one and a half arpents, was saved."

"The field farthest from the castle, and hardest to defend."

Osborn shrugged. "Fish and cheese. 'Twill be a lean winter. And here I'd nearly regained the girth I lost last winter on such a diet," he joked.

But Rand could not make light of this newest setback. Up to now he'd only reacted to Welsh harrassment. But that policy had obviously not worked. He must become more aggressive. " 'Tis time I made an example of these Welsh marauders," he muttered.

"So we wage war now, not peace?"

Rand turned his horse and the two men headed back to Rosecliffe. "These people do not respond to peace. I see now that they war among themselves due to their nature. They have a need to fight with someone. Well, I will give them a fiercer enemy than they've yet faced.''

Osborn tugged on his beard. ''Does this mean we will take the village?''

Rand leaned forward and his horse responded with ever-increasing strides. ''We will take Carreg Du. I will confront Owain, and he and I will settle this matter once and for all.''

''What of Madoc and Clyde?''

''They are old. They will choose peace over war once Owain is gone. With no strong leader to take his place, the Welsh opposition will fade. I will take Carreg Du,'' he repeated. ''I will take Afon Bryn as well, if I must.''

And I will take Josselyn too if she is so unwise as to place herself in my path.

There was no mistaking the signs. The English warriors practiced, dawn to dusk. The armorer's fire never died down. Even when Newlin sat on the *domen*, soaking in the solemnity of the night and the wisdom of the stars, he could hear the dull clang of hammer against heated rod.

He shifted his bulk on the level slab, unable to find the mental quiet he sought. He sniffed the air, alert. Alarmed.

War was imminent. The skirmishes of the past year would be nothing compared to the bloodletting the English would unleash upon the land. Newlin was impressed that the English lord had restrained himself this long. His younger knights, most especially his brother, had chafed under the restraint. Now they would make up for their frustrations of the past year.

Newlin did not like war, no matter who fought or how they justified it. He respected men of honor, and women. And children too, he amended, thinking of spirited young Rhonwen. But he did not interfere in the lives of those around him.

Usually.

He focused his left eye on the bright star near the western horizon. The people attributed great powers to him. But were he even half so powerful as they feared, he would long ago have made his eyes focus together. Shutting down the mental blinders on one or the other of his eyes was ever a distraction and a strain.

He focused on the star again.

He should not interfere, but he had a particular fondness for Josselyn, and he knew he would like her child, were it to survive Owain's threats.

His mind quieted. He visualized the child. Over the summer she had thrived. He'd seen her on the feast of Saint Swithun, all pink cheeks and fair hair coming in. But she would be dark-haired someday. Like her mother.

Like her father.

He thought of Rand. He did not know he had a daughter. Did Josselyn mean ever to tell him?

Then he frowned. Josselyn was afraid for her child. His focus shifted. Left eye. Right eye. He closed both eyes to make it stop. It was not for him to interfere. And he would not. But how he longed to steer another child's mind. Josselyn was a woman now, with a woman's concerns. Rhonwen was still afraid of him. But Isolde . . .

He smiled into the night and his focus returned. The brilliant star flickered in response. He would not interfere. He would not take sides. But even ancient bards needed to eat through the cold, bitter months of winter. He would do what was necessary to ensure he had an adequate supply of food.

He heard a step. No one ventured beyond the walls of Rosecliffe Castle after dark, at least not alone. But this night walker was alone and unafraid. "Welcome, Randulf Fitz Hugh."

"I hoped to find you here, Newlin. I come to give you warning—you and all the Welsh who reside along the River Gyffin. My patience is spent."

" 'Tis not your intention to drive me from this place."

"No—"

"Nor to drive out those who have peopled these wild places since the time of the three goddesses," Newlin continued.

"I wish only to drive out those who refuse to live in peace."

The moon limned the Englishman's face and Newlin was reassured by what he saw. He focused even more intently on him. "Madoc is dead."

Madoc is dead. Rand heard the bard's stunning words. Madoc was dead. Josselyn was now a widow. Her child was orphaned.

Then he shook his head. He didn't want to think about that. The real news was that Owain now led the Welsh in this valley. What happened to Josselyn didn't matter.

But Newlin had a different view. "You once wished to wed her to your brother. Perhaps that is again the way to the peace you say you desire."

Rand gave a bitter laugh. "There can be no peace when only one party desires it. If anything, Madoc's death will rouse Owain to even more murderous acts."

"That does not address my suggestion."

Rand did not want to address Newlin's suggestion, and he suspected the strange little man knew it. How much else did he know of the tortured emotions Josselyn roused in him? "I'll worry over issues of peace when I have resolved the issues of war," he stated.

The bard was quiet. A lone night bird called. An owl preparing for the hunt. "I've come down here to warn you," Rand continued, "so that you may be prepared. It will be bloody, and it will not end until I face Owain."

"I will not leave these lands," Newlin answered simply. "Nor will most of these people."

"Nor will I."

"You now intend to stay?"

Rand frowned. "I don't intend to be driven out. When I leave it will be because I am no longer needed here."

"Needed here," the bard echoed.

The man was trying to provoke him. Rand crossed his arms. "I came at the king's behest to build a fortress mighty enough to ensure peace for all who live here, English or Welsh. When that task is done, I return to London."

"But your brother will remain."

And need a wife.

The unsaid words hung in the air.

Rand gritted his teeth. "He will need a wife and I will encourage him to wed a Welshwoman. If he decides upon Josselyn, so be it. Meanwhile, I would know how Madoc died."

The bard shrugged his one good shoulder. " 'Tis said he had a seizure of the chest. His heart, I am told. Though there are those who say he grasped himself lower. His stomach."

"His stomach?" Rand went very still. "Poison?"

Newlin looked away. "Who can say? He was an old man."

"Who would want to poison him?" When the bard did not answer the question, Rand did. "A son who would rule in his father's stead. Or perhaps a young wife who tired of an old husband."

"Is that what you believe?"

Rand looked away. What demon prompted him to say such a thing? "No, I do not. But is Owain such a coward as to poison his sire?"

"Is there a lack of such cowardice in your English courts?"

Rand snorted. "There are cowards in every land. In every village."

"As there are the misguided and the misinformed. But we veer away from the purpose of your visit. You intend to rout the opposition to your English presence in our land. Is there anything else?"

Rand suppressed a sigh. There was nothing more that he

was willing to express out loud. But he wondered about many things, more now than when he'd first come down the hill to see the bard. And chief among them was whether Josselyn mourned her husband. Whether she would be compelled to wed Owain. Whether she wanted to.

"Owain has a wife."

Rand blinked, startled as always by Newlin's uncanny ability to read his thoughts. "He may have a wife," he muttered. "But she will soon be a widow. Then she and Josselyn can comfort one another. Take care," he added, "that you are not caught in the war between Rosecliffe and Carreg Du. I bid you good evening."

Rand left, almost sorry he'd come in search of Newlin. He'd hoped to find some reassurance regarding the offensive he meant to launch against the Welsh. Instead, as he made his way up the track that led through the unbuilt town, he felt more confused than ever. Josselyn no longer belonged to Madoc. She was free.

Perhaps now, after suffering the touch of an old man, she would be more willing to become mistress to a younger, more virile one.

The day would come when he would face her again. Then he would have the answer to that question. At the moment, however, he did not know whether he longed to hear her answer, or dreaded it.

The English attacked Carreg Du just before dawn on a day that threatened rain, a day that wisdom said boded ill for large destriers on slippery ground. But it did not rain and once Rand's best men captured the several watchmen that circled the armed village, his mounted knights and foot soldiers advanced on the village.

Osborn took the left flank. Jasper led the right, while Rand commanded the central thrust into the heart of Carreg Du.

The alehouse was put to fire, and the wind-borne smoke panicked the few women and children remaining there. The

Welsh fought gamely, but the English slew all who opposed them. Those who threw down their weapons, however, were spared.

It had been three years since Rand had led men in battle. He remembered the fear and the anticipation, the fury that would grip him. But he'd forgotten how fast his blood lust could rise. How violently.

He confronted one brawny Welshman and dispatched him with a quick thrust and a bone-crunching twist of his blade. Another beside him hesitated, then engaged Rand in battle. His demise mirrored his compatriot's. A third man started forward then, when confronted by Rand's wicked long sword dripping blood, threw down his weapon. *"Trugaredd,"* he cried.

Rand was hard-pressed to honor the man's plea for mercy, for his blood was up and all around him the din of battle—the cries and grunts and stench—urged him on. But murder was not his goal. He seized the man's sword and shield, and gave him into Alan's keeping. Then he charged back into the fray.

The battle raged the length and breadth of Carreg Du. Before the sun reached its zenith, however, the English held the town, though at a grave cost. Nine men killed; eleven wounded. But the Welsh had lost fourteen, plus twenty-two wounded and sixty-three more captured. All in all, a decisive victory for Rand.

Josselyn heard news of the battle from Nesta, who had been sent on to Afon Bryn with the few who'd escaped Carreg Du. The entire village was in an uproar, vowing to free their captured comrades, vowing death to all the English. Even Rhys and Rhonwen found unity on the issue of their hatred of all things English.

But while Afon Bryn took in the wounded, gathered supplies for those who still fought, and cursed the English, Josselyn worried. She worked alongside Nesta, but her thoughts were in Carreg Du.

Had Rand been hurt?

She should be hoping he'd been felled by a mortal blow, but she could not. Instead she prayed for his safety, and that someday he might know he had a daughter. When Isolde awoke, demanding with her tiny strident cries to be fed, Josselyn went gratefully to her. She secreted both of them in her chamber, and as she nursed her daughter, she worried for Rand.

Late, just before dusk, Owain rode furiously into Afon Bryn. He slammed into the main hall, cursing, screaming for food and ale. Meriel and Agatha scurried to serve him. Everyone else disappeared. Within the hour, however, Meriel burst without knocking into Josselyn's chamber.

"He'll see you now. Best you don't keep him waiting," she added with a cackle that sounded ominous.

"Why does he wish to see me?"

"I'm sure he can answer that better than I. Go on, girl. Oh, and he says you're to bring her." She indicated Isolde, asleep now in her cradle.

Bring Isolde to Owain? Josselyn's heart began to pound. She edged nearer her precious child. "She's asleep. I'll not wake her."

Meriel smiled, showing her long brown teeth. "All right then. Why don't I stay here to mind her while you go to Owain alone?"

Josselyn had never before feared Meriel would harm Isolde. Now she did. With no choice left her, she scooped up the babe, and telling herself it was better to know what Owain was plotting than to remain ignorant, she steeled herself and descended to the hall. But she was afraid as she'd never in her life been afraid. Owain was dangerous and unpredictable, and for the moment she could not escape him. But as soon as she could manage, she vowed to flee this place.

"I'll keep you safe," she whispered against Isolde's downy hair. "I'll keep you safe, even if that means delivering you to your father."

Owain's angry voice carried up the narrow stairwell.

"Are you deaf? Did you not hear me say step lively?" She heard a sharp slap and a muffled cry. Then Agatha rushed past the stairs, tears streaming down her face, mingling with the blood from her split lip. Josselyn froze, panicked anew. Maybe she should have left Isolde with Meriel.

"Go on." From behind the older woman shoved her into the lighted hall. " 'Tis your turn."

Owain spied her at once. "Come here," he ordered, fastening his eyes on her. Agatha hurried past with a fresh mug of ale, but he spared her none of his attention.

Something terrible was going to happen, Josselyn realized. Something terrible. Only when everyone else left the hall and Josselyn found the courage to draw nearer did he speak again.

"I have a task for you."

A trap, more like. But Josselyn kept her fears to herself. She hugged Isolde tighter. "What sort of task?"

He grinned, the awful grin of a murderous wolf, not above devouring his own kind. "Go to Fitz Hugh. I have no doubt he will receive you. Draw him out so I can kill him."

Josselyn fought to still her trembling. Help Owain kill Rand? She shook her head. She could never do that. "He will not see me."

"You lie! He will see you!" His voice lowered and his leering eyes roamed over her. "He will want to fuck the woman who rejected him."

Josselyn swallowed hard at his crudity. "No. He won't—"

"He will. You rejected me and I want to fuck you—and the day will come when I will. Why should he feel any differently? He'll want to fuck you if only to punish you. Meanwhile, you will be the bait to draw him out."

Josselyn tried to think. She tried to conquer her panic with reason. She could never turn on Rand that way. But it would be madness to reveal that to Owain.

Then again, perhaps this was her chance to escape his foul clutches.

He must have sensed the turn of her thoughts, for as he quaffed the contents of his mug, he once more grinned. He wiped his mouth on his sleeve—a sleeve stained with someone else's blood. "Just to ensure your loyalty, Josselyn, while you are bait to him, I will keep that babe of yours as bait for you."

"No!" Josselyn gasped. She backed away in horror.

Owain lurched out of his chair. "Yes," he countered, hissing the word like a serpent. "Flush him out and she will live. Fail me . . ." He began to stalk her. "Fail me," he repeated in a voice filled with venom, "and she will die in his place."

Josselyn came up hard against the rough stone wall. Owain stood less than an arm's length from her. He reached out and pinched Isolde's cheek hard enough to awaken her. As her fretful cries filled the room, he leaned forward.

"I can snuff her life out with a snap of my fingers. Smother her. Break her neck. It would be no more to me than killing fowl in the yard. But I'd prefer to kill her sire. Will you help me do that, Josselyn?"

It was so mildly asked, so casually worded, that Josselyn fought the obscene urge to laugh. This could not be happening.

But it was, and when she hesitated, he reached out again for Isolde.

"I'll do it!" Josselyn cried, trying to shelter Isolde from him. "I'll do it."

He laughed, and his hand caught her chin instead of Isolde's cheek. "What a good mother you are. If you succeed, I'll return your child to you unharmed. If you do not . . ." He shrugged. "But I have faith in you, Josselyn, and when Fitz Hugh is dead, you will have your reward."

The next hour was a nightmare. Owain's threats toward her were of no moment. But Isolde . . .

She watched as Meriel took her child away, and though she sat calmly, inside, where no one could hear, she screamed her agony. She did not trust Owain. She did not trust Meriel. If she could just get word to Nesta or Gladys—to anyone from Carreg Du. But Owain was too crafty to allow her to see anyone who might aid her.

He rode with her alone to the forest edge, giving her instructions. She was to seek refuge with Rand, to pretend she wished to help him defeat Owain. She was to pretend to lead him to Owain's secret hideout in Wyndham Wood, where he could then surprise and capture the rebels. But in actuality Owain would be lying in wait to slaughter the English. It was simple and comparatively easy—and her reward would be great, he reminded her.

For her part, Josselyn listened and nodded, and tried not to shatter into a thousand pieces.

He pointed out the direction she must take. He gave her no shawl against the evening chill, and only a half-lame packhorse to ride. "He's more likely to believe you escaped me if you are hungry and tired." He laughed.

"Don't hurt her," Josselyn pleaded. "I'll do as you say, but you must abide by your promise. Don't hurt her."

Dusk painted the land in violet shades, the color of bruises. It showed Owain's face in all its evil. "Don't give me a reason to hurt her," he answered, smiling coldly.

Had she a weapon, she would have murdered him right there. She would have gouged out his eyes, ripped out his bowels, and carved out his heart.

But she had no weapons, no power at all against his evil strength. So she kicked her pitiful mount forward, urging him blindly into the woods, heading north. She would find Rand. She would make up some reason, some excuse, to draw him out so that Owain could capture him.

She would not hesitate. She would not consider what was right or wrong. She would do what she must to save her child, even if doing so would kill the man she loved—and a part of herself as well.

Part Three

A little door she opened straight,
  All in the middle of the gate;
The gate that was ironed within and without
Where an army in battle array had marched out.

—Coleridge

Twenty-five

Josselyn found Alan first. Or rather, he found her at her lowest moment, when her poor horse had gone lame, the suffocating darkness had disoriented her, and she feared never to find her way to Carreg Du. He found her and brought her to Jasper. The English patrolled the southern arc of the valley below Carreg Du, an ominous presence in the dark, dripping night. They were tired from the long day and night, and yet still jubilant over their victory. They'd captured three Welshmen hiding in the forest. Josselyn made four. Only she'd come forth willingly.

"I must speak to your brother," she told Jasper. She'd told Alan the same thing but he'd insisted on bringing her to his immediate superior.

"So. We meet again." Jasper dismounted and stood before her. He was Rand's height, but not so thickly muscled. He was younger than she'd realized, from the one time she'd seen him. Younger and more handsome, with bold features and a sensuous mouth. But there was the callowness of youth about him. The arrogance not yet warranted.

He would make some woman a most difficult husband.

But that was not her concern. Her business was far more urgent than that. "I must speak with Rand."

"Rand, is it? Not Sir Randulf or Lord Fitz Hugh, but Rand." He grinned. "And what is it you have for him?

Information to sell?'' His eyes ran over her. ''I'm as like
to buy what you're offering as he is.''

She glared at him. She had no time for this; Owain held
Isolde hostage. ''I assure you, he will not appreciate any
delay in learning what I have to say,'' she bluffed. She
turned to Alan. ''I would not come here, were it not sore
pressing. You know that is true, Alan. So tell him.''

Alan clearly did not like having to side with her, but
after a moment he grimaced. ''He will want to see her. But
you'll find him a far different man from the one you be-
witched last year,'' he added to her. ''Your tricks will no
longer work on him, nor on any of us.''

''Speak for yourself,'' Jasper interrupted. ''I'm willing
to be a victim of her bewitching tricks. What do you say?''
he added, tugging the *couvrechef* down from her head.

Josselyn swatted his hand aside. ''Find yourself a nun—
or two,'' she snapped. ''Just tell me where Rand is. I'll
search him out myself.''

In the end they took her to Rand, her half-dead mount
stumbling along between their finer animals.

When they reached Carreg Du, it looked the same, and yet
somehow it was different. It had changed from the home of
her childhood to an armed camp under Owain's leadership.
Now it was an occupied town, controlled by the English.
Physically the village remained as it had always been—save
that the alehouse had burned. She spied a few Welsh faces,
those captured in the fighting. But with the English presence
everywhere, it felt like a foreign place. Would it ever again
be simply the home of free Welsh people?

She approached her uncle's house—Rand's base of command. Just outside the door she hesitated. What was she to
say to him? How was she to begin? Would he trust her
enough to follow her into the trap Owain prepared for him?

Could she really lure him to his certain death?

She stared at the door, one she'd passed through a hundred times before. A thousand. But this time was different.
This time she entered with murder in her heart. If she led

Rand to Owain, she would be participating in a murder.

And yet there was Isolde to consider. Pain pounded like a drum inside her head. What to do? What to do?

But Josselyn knew what she must do, and with a prayer for Isolde that was, she feared, a curse upon Rand's head, she pushed into the house.

To her surprise the place was empty, save for the man who sat in the lord's chair before the cold hearth. Rand, alone with his thoughts.

When he looked up he did not appear surprised to see her. Yet she, who thought herself prepared to meet him again, felt a profound shock. He was here. Rand. Isolde's father. Her only lover. The man she'd thought she'd fallen in love with.

In the past year she'd doubted that emotion. But with one glance, one moment only of his dark eyes meeting hers, she knew the fearful truth. She loved him, now as much as before. How much harder did that make her awful task?

But the impassive expression on his battle-hardened face reminded her of another bitter truth. He hadn't loved her then; he certainly did not love her now.

She swallowed the disappointment that caught her unawares. It wasn't his love she'd come for. It was her child's safety. She must go forward with this mad plan to lure him into Owain's clutches no matter how she felt. There was no other way.

He didn't rise. After an awkward moment, she advanced into the room. "I have come—" Her voice cracked and she took a breath to compose herself. "I have come to beg your aid."

Slowly, deliberately, he steepled his hands beneath his chin. "To beg my aid? What sort of aid would a staunch Welsh rebel want from her enemy? Unless, of course, you come here to lull me into complacency. To distract me from my purpose." He pursed his lips. "I wondered what you would do with your husband gone. In truth, I did not expect you to come to me. But you are here, so begin. Distract me, for I am sore in need of distraction."

Josselyn shook her head. " 'Tis not what you think. I care nothing of this war you and Owain wage—"

"You care nothing? You cared before. You cared so much you wed yourself to an old man to ensure there would be a war."

The truth was a bitter thing to hear. And yet there was so much more to it than that. "You don't understand," she began.

"Nor do I care to. 'Tis sufficient that I maintain peace in the lands drained by the River Gyffin. As for aiding you . . . " He ran his eyes over her, a crude assessment that made her shrink away. "I have only one form of aid to give you. If you would have it, take off your clothes. Otherwise, begone from here."

She hadn't meant to cry, but she could not hold back the tears that stung her eyes. "You may think what you want of me. You may use me in that way, if you wish. But I beg you, Rand, hear me out. I have come here to help you."

"Help me?" He laughed, a cold, contemptuous sound in the empty hall. "How can you help me? Your husband is dead. Your village is lost. You have no power to help me, save to serve Owain up. Will you do that?"

She stared straight into his eyes, eyes so like Isolde's that it hurt. But it was that likeness that gave her the strength to tell the lie Owain had given her. "Yes. I can serve him up to you."

Those gray eyes of his narrowed with suspicion, and between them the silence grew deafening. He did not believe her, but he had his doubts. She sensed the mental debate that raged in him.

"Why should I believe you?"

"Because . . . Because I have no reason to lie."

"You have every reason to lie."

"No. No, you have it wrong. Owain is a madman." That much, at least was true. She advanced farther into the room.

"He leads my people to their doom. Wasn't the slaughter here proof of that?"

"Madoc is dead and Owain has assumed leadership of the Welsh. Meanwhile, your uncle is no match for him and your village is now in my control." He crossed his arms and studied her. "You are caught between him and me—as you always were. But whereas you once thought Owain the lesser of two evils, it would seem you now cast me in that role. Is that a fair assessment of your present predicament?"

Emotion caught in Josselyn's throat. There was truth in his words, and yet there remained so much unsaid. That she'd loved him but he'd have given her to his brother. That they had made a child together. But all of that was in the past. The present was her concern now. That, and Isolde's future. "Yes," she finally said. "I see now that life under English rule is better than life under Owain."

She thought she'd convinced him, for he was silent a long time. Then he rose and approached her, his eyes suspicious once more.

"How do you propose to help me?"

The lie came easily to her tongue, yet the taste of it was bitter. "I can lead you to the place in the forest where he plots his retaliation. You and your men can surprise him there."

"I see." His fingers flexed, tightened, then flexed again. "So you would lead us to the place where we can slaughter your people. Do I have the right of it?"

Put that way, it sounded hideous. But was that any less awful than what she planned for him? Swallowing her doubts as best she could, she nodded.

"I see." He turned and slowly walked away. Josselyn sagged under the weight of her guilt. But she did it for Isolde, she told herself. For Isolde.

Suddenly he turned, shaking his head, pinning her with his sharp eyes. "You lie. You might betray Owain, but betray your people? No. That does not ring true. Owain has put you up to this, hasn't he?"

"No! No, he knows nothing of this—"

"Then where is your child?"

"What?"

He'd come closer, and now he circled her, like a great stalking beast. "Where is your child?" he repeated from behind her. "Who keeps her while you are here?" he asked as he came around to face her again.

The blood began to roar in her ears. "My aunt," she lied.

"So, your aunt knows you have come here. Who else knows?"

"No one. No one," she stammered. "I sneaked away—"

"Not even Owain?"

Her heart thundered to a halt. "Owain? No. No, he does not know—"

"I think he does. I think he has your child and holds her hostage to ensure you follow his orders. You would not otherwise leave her."

She wanted to tell him the truth. Oh, how she wanted to tell him! Only fear—utter terror—for their daughter stopped her. He must believe her tale. He must! Isolde's life depended on it. But though she struggled to find the words that would make him believe her, she could find none.

His eyes bored into hers, seeking her lie. Seeking the truth.

"She is with Nesta," she repeated, as panic overwhelmed her.

He let loose a contemptuous laugh. "Owain is no fool. He cannot best me in a head-to-head fight. But to catch me by surprise, to trap me, would sway the odds in his favor." When she would have turned away from him he caught her chin in his iron grip. "The truth, Josselyn. Tell me the truth."

She wanted to, but to do so was to condemn Isolde, her sweet and innocent babe. "No. You have it all wrong. Owain did not send me."

He thrust her away from him in disgust. "Begone from here. The very sight of you sickens me. Crawl back to Owain with this message. He has lost his lands to me. I will wrest them from him and I will ensure that no spawn of his will ever inherit them. My children will rule these lands for the good of all. Mine, not his. Take that message to him, Josselyn ap Carreg Du. Take it and go.''

Josselyn stood there trembling, unable to go. Unable to stay. She had failed. She had failed, but Isolde would be the one to pay. Tears burned her eyes, then spilled over. She stared at Rand. He was so filled with hatred for her and her people. But she could not accept defeat. She would not. She reached out a hand to him. ''Please, Rand, you must listen to me.''

He made a sound of disgust. ''You lie with your lips. You lie with your tears. You've lied to me since first we met.''

Josselyn flinched at his hard accusation. She had lied to him. But she could lie no longer, she realized. Lies had failed her. She had only the truth to help her now.

With the heels of her hands she brushed her tears away. ''You're right. You're right,'' she conceded, choking on a sob. ''I did lie. Owain did send me to you.''

She'd thought he would gloat, but if anything, his expression grew more shuttered. He crossed his arms and waited. She took another breath and went on. ''But I only did so because he holds my child hostage. He knows she is my weakness.'' She paused. ''He knows also that she is your child.''

Silence echoed, a dark and sudden cavern around them.

Rand's eyes narrowed. After a moment he shook his head. ''More lies. I know she is not mine.''

''But she is. I swear it!''

A muscle began to twitch in his jaw. ''It gains you naught to lie to me, woman. You forget, I saw you at the Saint Ebbe Market. You showed no signs of the babe. I know, because I looked.''

Tears again stung her eyes, but she refused to cry. ''She was a small babe and very nearly died. Even now she is tiny. But she is yours, Rand.''

He gave a hollow laugh. ''What do you think to gain by presenting me with this pitiful tale?''

"Owain has her!" Josselyn cried. "If I do not succeed in the mission he set for me, he will kill her!"

He shook his head, dismissing that possibility. " 'Tis only a threat. He will not harm his own sister."

"But she is not his sister, and Owain knows it. He knows it," she finished in a horrified whisper.

But Rand remained unaffected. He poured a goblet of wine and downed the contents in one long pull. Then he speared her with his hard eyes. "How would Owain know that? Or did the father share his wife with the son? Mayhap this child is Owain's spawn," he bitterly added.

The very thought made her shudder. "Be cruel to me if you must. But do not seal your own child's fate because you despise me, Rand. Madoc could not—He had lost the ability to perform his . . . his husbandly duties. Owain learned of it and drew the obvious conclusion as to her parentage. He has no hesitation about using Isolde to control me. She is your daughter. I swear it on my life!"

Something in his eyes flickered, and Josselyn clutched at the hope that she'd swayed him. But his next words crushed those hopes.

"She is not mine. No. I cannot help you, save to do as I already plan: to crush Owain. Until then, if you would protect your child from his rage, you'd be better served to do for him as I suspect you were prepared to do for me. Promise him the delights of your body. Lure him to complacency in your bed. Protect your child by placing yourself in his power. 'Tis what he's wanted from you all along," he taunted.

Josselyn fell back a step, then another, as if beneath pummeling blows. He did not care. He would not intercede. Why had she ever believed he would? When she found the strength to speak, she could only mutter over and over, "She is yours, Rand. Yours . . ."

But he refused to hear. He turned away from her and refilled his goblet from the ewer. His hand did not shake. He was so calm, so completely unaffected by her words.

He did not believe her and nothing she could say would change that.

Defeated, she turned and made her way blindly to the door. Her movements were stiff and off balance, as if the ground had tilted beneath her feet. She'd known he hated her. And yet, still, some part of her had been convinced he would believe her. That he would want to know his child. Some part of her had expected him to rush to Isolde's aid. She saw now that she'd been utterly, disastrously wrong.

She left the house and walked unsteadily across the village yard. Several of his men followed her with their eyes. But they did not prevent her leaving on foot through the well-guarded gate. The sun would soon be up. She could see the dark outline of the trees and the gray shadow of the eastern mountains. A lone cock crowed his dominion over all within hearing.

But Josselyn had no eyes to see her beloved lands, nor ears to hear the pulse of its life. Isolde was the true center of her life, not these lands. Isolde, so tiny and yet so alive. So vulnerable.

Josselyn steeled herself to face this newest dilemma. Somehow she must find a way to appease Owain. He would be furious with her, but she must not let him vent that rage upon Isolde. She would offer him her body. Once. Twice. A thousand times. She would do anything to save her child, for Isolde's father refused to do so.

Rand caught up with Josselyn below Carreg Du, in the place where the damp meadow gave way to forest. First light sparked the tips of the beech and wych elms, but she moved still in the shadows, a darkly clad figure, slender and small. Vulnerable.

Did she lie to him?

He'd debated that question since the moment she'd left. Did she lie?

He reined in his mount and watched her struggle up the hill toward the protection of the forest. She'd been sent to

lure him and his men to certain doom. She'd admitted as
much. Now, like a fool, he followed her, while any number
of her countrymen could be waiting. Maybe this was all a
part of the trap Owain planned.

He scanned the edge of the forest with a practiced eye.
His men held these woods. There were no Welshmen lurk-
ing in the lands around Rosecliffe and Carreg Du. But even
if there were, he had to speak to her.

Why did she lie to him? What purpose did she have to
claim this girl child was his?

The answer was obvious. Josselyn feared Owain and
wanted Rand to rid her of his threat. But he intended to do that
anyway, as she must already know. It was not for her sake,
though, but for his own and that of all who would prefer peace
to war. She would be safe from Owain soon enough, as would
her child, so there was no reason for her to lie to him so ur-
gently. Did that mean she was telling the truth?

It was that niggling possibility that had driven him to
follow her.

He urged his horse forward, his eyes fixed upon Josselyn.
He saw her stiffen when she realized she'd been followed.
Throwing a fearful glance backward, she lifted her skirts
and hastened her weary strides. But he came on steadily.
She could not outpace him. Then she looked back and
halted. She knew it was he.

He reined his mount to a standstill and stared down at
Josselyn's upturned face. Lines of exhaustion marked her
face; her red eyes gave proof of her tears. She was beautiful
in spite of it all, however, her mouth voluptuous, her body
ripe. He did not want to see that beauty, nor respond to it,
and yet it was not her feminine appeal that drew him and
refused to let him look away. It was the desperate hope-
fulness in her eyes. She was afraid to hope he had changed
his mind, and yet she could not help but do so.

She loved her child. There could be no doubt of that.
But was it his child?

He expelled a long breath. Did it really matter? "I will rescue your child from Owain."

A near silent sound, a small sucking intake of breath, a half-sob—whatever it was, she made no other response, at least none that involved words. But she placed her hand on his foot in the stirrup nearest her. It was a small enough gesture, but it carried with it a mighty impact. Gratitude. Trust.

It moved him profoundly.

He was reminded of the oath of fealty he'd sworn to King Henry, kneeling before his liege, holding out his palm so that the king could place his foot upon it. Now, in the shelter of a wych elm she seemed to swear him silent fealty.

It was not what he wanted of her.

It should be though. It should be *all* he wanted of her: her loyalty as a citizen of the lands he would rule. The loyalty of even a few Welsh was a step in the right direction.

But from Josselyn he wanted more.

With a silent oath he repressed that idiotic notion and turned the horse away from her, then dismounted. "Where is Owain?"

She pressed her lips tightly together. "At Afon Bryn."

"And the child?"

"There as well. Or at least she was. He could have taken her anywhere," she added, staring at him with huge, frightened eyes.

He steeled himself against the need to offer her comfort. "Go to Owain. Tell him you have convinced me. Elaborate in any way you must. Where did he plan to ambush me?"

She straightened, as if renewed strength flowed into her veins. A stray beam of early sunlight glanced off her hair, brilliant against the ebony thickness. It was of no moment, and yet his eyes noted it.

"There is a narrow place along the river, before it reaches the lower meadows. In a place call Wyndham Wood, the forest encroaches on one side. On the other the hill is steep and the footing precarious."

"So he will wait in the woods?"

"I do not know all his plans. Only that I must send you along that route."

He looked past her, into the wildwood. "When?"

"As soon as possible."

"Tomorrow then." He glared at her, willing any soft feeling for her out of his heart. "You know many will die. Many of your people."

She bowed her head. "I know."

He exhaled a long breath. Was he a fool to believe her when she'd lied to him so many times before? He would find out tomorrow. "Go. Go back to Owain."

She looked up at him and stepped closer. Too close. "Rand," she began.

"Don't," he bit out. "Don't make more of it than it is."

But she did not listen. "She is your child. You will see—"

"No. For all I know, she is Madoc's child or Owain's—or anyone else's but mine. It doesn't matter whose she is. It doesn't matter to me whom you lay down with."

Only it did. The very thought of anyone else touching her turned his blood cold. Even now, more than a year later, he had not learned how to control this insane possessiveness she fired in him.

He did not want to feel it, but the truth was, he still wanted her. Not just her body. He knew he could have that. She was that grateful to him. But he wanted more than gratitude from her, more than just the use of her body. More than her vow of fealty. He did not want to put a name on what he wanted of her, but that did not banish it. Though she'd spurned him and chosen her people over him, though she'd betrayed him and very nearly brought about Jasper's death, the truth of his longing did not waver.

He wanted her to love him.

"Go back to Owain," he muttered, denying the feelings that clawed for release in his chest.

She nodded, then averted her face. But before she could back away, he grabbed her arms. She looked up, as startled as he by his impulsive gesture. But before he could see acquiescence in her eyes and know it sprang from gratitude, he crushed her to him and took her mouth in a savage kiss. That she didn't fight him—that she accepted the onslaught and rose into it—only pushed him recklessly on. He wanted her to respond to him instinctively, with no time to think or consider or weigh all the practical reasons why she must submit. He wanted to taste true passion and feel total capitulation, and know she did not pretend.

And he did.

He was rough with her, very nearly brutal. But she welcomed him at every turn. He took her there, against the ancient elm, crudely. Swiftly. When they were done he rested heavily against her, gasping for breath—and for sanity. He'd accomplished nothing, nor assuaged any of his doubts. All he'd done was reveal his weakness for her.

For all he knew, one of her people could even now have an arrow aimed at his back.

He thrust himself away from her and glanced swiftly around, then adjusted his garments. In truth, however, he was stalling. When he finally looked over at her, he knew he'd handled things badly.

"Are you all right?" His voice was gruff.

She gave a small nod.

He cleared his throat. "Tell Owain I assemble my men. Tell him I will strike at his camp tomorrow at dawn. I will do my part to dispatch Owain. It falls to you to see to your child's welfare."

Again she nodded. "I will do whatever is necessary. She is so innocent." Her voice dropped to a lower pitch. "She's the only true innocent among us."

For no reason, jealousy stabbed daggers into his heart. She loved this child, no matter who had sired it. She hadn't loved her husband, nor did she love him. But she loved her child. "What do you call her?"

"Isolde. I have named your daughter Isolde."

" 'Tis pointless to call her mine," he muttered. "The proof of her parentage will ever be in doubt."

"If you believe that, then why have you agreed to help us?"

"Because I desire you," he answered, denying all the other reasons that demanded he come to her aid. And to Isolde's.

She recoiled at his bluntness, but she did not turn away. She lifted her chin and stared at him, her face pale but composed. "I will make myself available to you as long as you desire me, if you will save my daughter."

He did not respond to that. He could not. He'd been cruel in what he'd said to her. Now, in her honesty, she was being even more cruel to him. He wanted her, yes. But not in payment for services rendered.

But in his pride he had made certain he could have her in no other way. She would come to him out of gratitude, a gratitude rooted in fear for her child. That was little better than her coming to him in fear, much as she would have to do with Owain.

He took no comfort in the fact that she feared Owain more than she feared him. She would respond to each of them in the same manner, if that was the only way she could protect her child.

His stomach knotted and he fought down the bitter gall that burned his throat. Snatching up the reins, he flung himself onto his horse. She stood beside the wych elm, disheveled from their lovemaking, fearful and yet hopeful.

"Thank you," she whispered, so grateful he had to close his eyes against it.

"Don't thank me," he muttered. "Don't ever thank me again." Then, unable to bear either her nearness or her distance from him, he urged his horse down the hill, away from the forest, to the safety of Rosecliffe's mighty walls.

He had to plan for tomorrow's confrontation. He had to clear his mind of her and focus on the matter at hand.

He had to hide from the fear that Isolde might be his daughter—and that she might not.

Twenty-six

Josselyn hurried, but her beloved wildwood seemed to conspire against her. The bracken caught her skirts, the steep hills pulled her back, and time and again the rocky path tripped her up. She followed the same path, paralleling the river, keeping to the trees wherever she could. But she was so tired she could hardly force one foot before the other. Fear drove her on, however.

She needed to get back to Isolde. She needed to hold her child and deliver her message to Owain.

Yet fear was accompanied now by something else. She would not call it reassurance. Until Isolde was well beyond Owain's evil grasp she could not be reassured. Nor could she call it comfort, for Rand's promise of help had a dark underbelly. He did not believe Isolde was his. And though he was willing to bed Josselyn, it was clear he had no interest in having her to wife.

She stumbled over an exposed root and fell, scraping the heel of one hand. For a moment only she allowed herself to lie heavily upon the damp ground, savoring the stinging pain as her due. If nothing else, it focused her on the task at hand. She must find the energy to keep going. She must put Rand out of her mind, for she had no control over him or his actions. She trusted him to honor his word though. That would have to be enough.

She pushed on beneath the sullen dawn, into the gray threat of another day. As she drew nearer the scattered village rain began to pelt her, as if warding her away. But nothing would keep her from her child.

A guard hidden within the yellowing leaves of a drooping sycamore was the first to hail her. "Show your face!"

She raised her head and lowered her *couvrechef*. With a grunt he gestured her on. But as she angled down the hill, following a deer path through the undergrowth, she was met by Owain. She drew up, repulsed anew by the sight of this man who would kill a child if he thought he could gain from the deed. She might live the rest of her life with the guilt of other Welsh lives that would be forfeit by her doing, but she would feel no guilt for Owain.

She faced him, not hiding her hatred from him. "I have done as you asked. Where is my child?"

His lips curled in a smug smile. His glittering eyes moved over her. "So you have succeeded in the task I set you. That is good, very good." He grinned. "You must have fucked him very well to win him over so swiftly."

Josselyn wrapped her arms around herself. Just that easily did he turn the intimacies she'd shared with Rand into an ugly thing. God, how she hated him! "Where is Isolde?" she repeated.

He gestured vaguely. "She is safe. But tell me more, sweet Josselyn." He caught her by the arm. "When will he strike at my hidden camp?"

"Tomorrow at dawn."

"At dawn. How unimaginative." Then he laughed. "By dawn, I fear, your English lover and his men will be long dead."

Josselyn had stiffened at his touch. Now she tried to pull away, alarmed by his words. "What do you mean, they will be long dead?"

"Just what I said." He jerked her up against him. "Did you truly think I would trust a woman with the truth, especially a woman who has already betrayed her people by

spreading her legs for her enemy? I see his marks on you.''
He rubbed his stubbled cheek against the tender places
Rand's rough kisses had left on her cheek and neck.

Josselyn twisted and fought him, but he was too strong.
'' 'Tis my turn, bitch. I'll have you now, and for once it
will be good Welsh juice that fills your belly.''

He yanked her skirt up. She heard it rip. Behind her his
men laughed and her blood turned to ice. Though she'd
vowed to do whatever she must to survive, she could not
bear to be raped here in the open while his men watched
and jeered—and waited their own chance to rape her too.

"No. No!" With a strength born of pure hatred she
rammed her knee into his groin.

He screamed and fell backward, and she did not pause
to think. She ran for Afon Bryn, for the last place her
daughter had been, to the dubious safety of her aunt and
uncle and their men. Pray God they were there.

Pray God Isolde was still there!

Her side ached from her effort as she skidded down the
track into a small knot of women. Agatha and Nesta,
Gladys and all the others, gathered round the well. Amidst
their startled looks, she fell into her aunt's arms.

"Josselyn! I was so worried—"

"Where is Isolde? Where is she!"

"Asleep in the hall. But—"

In a moment Josselyn was in the hall. Isolde was there,
peacefully asleep. But Josselyn snatched her up anyway and
held her close. She would never let her go again. Never.
He would have to kill her first.

"She's been well looked after," Nesta said from the
doorway. "Meriel has seen to that."

Josselyn looked over at her aunt. Nesta didn't realize
how pervasive the evil was in this place.

Behind her aunt stood Meriel, a smug grin on her narrow
face.

She would do anything to help Owain defeat Rand, Josselyn realized, including sacrificing an English bastard, and

a girl baby at that. Should Owain triumph, everyone would be completely at his mercy. There would be no one to stop him from doing anything he wanted.

She must get word to Rand, Josselyn realized. She must. But she would not leave Isolde this time. She could not risk it.

"I am weary," she said. "I've done as Owain asked. Now I must sleep." Before she could escape to the privacy of her chamber, however, she heard a commotion in the yard.

". . . the bitch! Where is she?" Owain burst into the hall, his face livid, his eyes mad for revenge. They landed on her. "I'm not done with you."

Her arms tightened around Isolde as he advanced into the hall. A crowd pushed in behind him. Women. Owain's men. But a few of her own kinsmen now too. Dewey. Taran.

"I have done all you demanded," she retorted, forcing her voice to be strong, to carry to all. "I have delivered your message to the English. You have no cause to punish me or my daughter any further."

His eyes glittered. "You have betrayed us. You took that man into your bed and betrayed your people. You told him I plan a trap." He glanced around, gauging the growing audience. Even Rhys and Rhonwen had been drawn in. "That child she holds is an English bastard, not a child of my father's at all. Tell them, Meriel."

The old woman stepped up. " 'Tis true. She bore the Englishman's seed ere she wed Madoc. 'Tis that which broke his heart and killed him."

"This is not about my child," Josselyn interjected. " 'Tis about Owain and the fact that I did not let him rape me."

All eyes swung to Owain. The charge of rape was a serious one.

But Owain only grinned. " 'Tis she who tempted me. Now she flies into a rage because I honor my marriage vows." His arm circled Agatha and his grin increased. "Ask Conan and Glyn. They were there."

"Enough of this." Clyde came belatedly into the crowded hall. He shouldered his way to Josselyn's side. The other men of Carreg Du moved to back them up. "We've more important matters to attend. A battle to plan—and to win. This spat avails us of naught."

But Owain was not willing to let it go. "She has raised a serious charge against me."

"And you have raised equally serious ones against her. I say it is enough to know the English come and we must be ready to meet them." He stared at Owain, his eyes unwavering.

In a fight Owain could beat him. In a battle, Owain's men outnumbered Clyde's and would defeat them. But there was no benefit in such confrontation and after long, tense seconds even Owain acknowledged it. With a contemptuous sneer he spat on the floor.

"She is a traitor to our people. Once the English are slain I'll not have her at Afon Bryn. Her or her bastard."

Nor would she willingly venture here ever again, Josselyn thought as the crowd began finally to drift away. She wanted only to return to Carreg Du, to raise Isolde and live in peace.

But that was not likely to happen. There would be no peace in this valley if Rand was slaughtered.

She caught her uncle's arm, staying his departure. "You must stop him."

"Stop whom? Owain?" He threw off her hand and glared at her. "So, 'tis true. You would forsake your own people for that Englishman."

Tears gathered in her eyes. "I forsake no one. I have betrayed no one—save for them who would trample on their own countrymen—"

"Is she his bastard?" He indicated the now restless babe.

"Her father is English—but I did not lie to Madoc or try to deceive him. He knew the truth before she was born.

Then yesterday I went to Rand on orders from Owain—he threatened Isolde if I did not! I told Rand the lie Owain gave me.'' She looked away from him. "But he did not believe me.''

With the back of her wrist she wiped her tears away then faced him once more. "To save Isolde from Owain's fury, I told Rand the truth. He is the only one willing to protect Isolde from Owain. He is the only man who can prevent the madness Owain will rain down upon us.'' She grabbed Clyde's wrist. "You know I am right. Owain will kill any of us who get in his way. We are not strong enough to prevent it.''

He didn't want to hear her. He didn't want to have to choose his lifelong enemy over his own countryman. She could see it in his face. His son had died fighting the English. So had his brother, her father.

But he also knew she was right about Owain.

He turned away, scrubbing his hands across his face. He was old and tired, she realized. Even in his youth he'd been a reluctant warrior.

She pressed on in a low, urgent voice. "Uncle Clyde, please. You know the kind of man Owain is. Do not allow him to slaughter the English. Once he holds all the power he will—''

"Enough!'' He lifted his graying head and stared at her with tortured eyes. "I know what Owain is. But still I cannot join with my enemy to fight my own people. I cannot, so do not ask it of me.''

His breath sounded harsh in the empty hall. "I cannot ally myself with the English,'' he muttered. "But . . . But I will not fight alongside Owain.'' He let loose a heavy sigh. "That is the best I can do.''

She nodded, blinking back tears. As concessions went, it was better than nothing. "I must tell Rand,'' she began.

He held up a hand. "I want nothing to do with your treason. In this you are on your own.'' Then he quit the room, an old man who could not control his world, nor adapt to the new one taking its place.

But Josselyn had no time to contemplate her uncle's misery. She had to get word to Rand.

That proved impossible.

Within the hour Owain marshaled his men to intercept Rand. Even Rhys was there, mounted on a pony, though Owain ignored his pleas to accompany the soldiers. When Clyde refused to join them, Owain made no pretense of his contempt.

"I have joined with you to honor my father's commitment. In his memory I will carry on, with you or without you. And when we are victorious, when the men of Afon Bryn defeat your enemy for you, do not think to join with us again. We will hold these hills. All of them." He beat his chest with one fist. "I am Owain ap Madoc! All will quake before me!"

His men roared their agreement. Then he pointed at Josselyn, and though outwardly she did not flinch, inside she quaked with renewed fear. "We take her and her bastard to ensure the safety of the women and children we leave here undefended."

Clyde frowned. "That is not necessary. We will keep them safe."

"How can we believe that when you have broken faith with us this day?" Owain sneered. "Besides, she has committed treason." Owain's hand moved to rest on the hilt of his sword. "She and her brat go with us."

Clyde tensed. As one his men bunched up behind him. Owain's followers did the same and Josselyn feared bloodshed was imminent. She could not bear the thought.

"I will go!" She stepped forward, thrusting Isolde into Nesta's arms. "I will go to satisfy Owain's doubts. But not my child. She stays here."

Clyde caught her by the arm. "Are you certain of this, Josselyn?"

No, she was not. But she could not let Owain slaughter

her uncle and his men, nor could she allow him to get hold of Isolde. "I am certain. But promise me you will keep her safe."

His promise was her only comfort in the hours to follow.

Owain's men viewed her with suspicion, but their very numbers protected her from Owain's revenge, as did the haste they made. By early afternoon half of Owain's force was secreted amid the woods that lined the narrow fissures along the River Gyffin. The other half hid in the rocks above the vale. The English must come one way or the other.

Nerves were taut. Josselyn prayed: for Isolde's safety first, then for Rand's. For herself she tried to be calm, to resign herself to whatever fate God planned for her. But oh, how she wished to present Isolde to Rand, to see pleasure in his eyes when he looked upon their child. She didn't know if he would feel such a pleasure, but she comforted herself with imagining it.

Clouds pushed in from the sea, dark and threatening. Lightning split the sky to the north. Thunder sounded, a delayed tremble from afar.

Then came a shout and a sharp cry, and everyone jumped.

"I can help. I can!" came a child's agitated voice.

By the saints, it was Rhys! He must have followed them.

Josselyn saw Owain rise, his face mottled with anger. He shot her a venomous look that he turned on his son when the boy was dragged into their presence. Rhys flailed like a wildcat, but Glyn held him by the nape of his neck. When the man shoved him to his knees, however, and Rhys spied his father, the boy's fury dissolved to fear. "I've come to help—"

"I told you to stay behind!"

"But I want to fight with you."

"Fight? Fight who?" Owain laughed as the child rose. "Go home, skinny pup. Go home and fight the other babies."

"But Papa—"

Owain's slap came out of nowhere. It knocked the child off his feet. "Begone, brat, and leave the battling to men."

Josselyn started for the boy. But he snarled at her and scrambled away. Only when he was gone did Owain laugh again. "He has guts, that one. He will make a great warrior one day."

"And he will hate you," Josselyn muttered.

Owain looked at her. "So he will, as I hated my father. 'Tis the way of the world. But no one will ever say I raised a coward."

Weeping in the woods, Rhys did not hear his father's perverse praise. A true warrior would not cry, but he could not stop. His cheek burned. His ear rang. He'd bitten the inside of his cheek and the awful taste of blood filled his mouth.

He wept anew, but he also cursed and vowed to prove his father wrong. Wiping his eyes, he turned his pony north. If he spotted the English before they arrived, his father would have to acknowledge Rhys's prowess as a warrior. He would see that Rhys was more important than this girl child Josselyn had borne, or the babe Agatha carried in her increasing belly.

He was the firstborn. No one else could claim that. He was rightful prince of these hills. He would let no other wife or offspring change that.

Twenty-seven

Rand and his men rode in bands of five. Slowly. Carefully. Rand suspected a trap. He'd pondered long and hard over Josselyn's visit. Had she been sincere? He wanted to believe so. She'd tried to betray him and failed. Only then had she confessed the truth.

But had it been the whole truth, or only as much as Owain had seen fit to reveal to her?

Rand planned to arrive at the Welsh camp long before dawn. But he knew Owain was too crafty to reveal his entire plan to Josselyn. It followed, then, that the Welsh ambush might come at any time and location along their route.

So he'd ordered outriders to sweep the hills along the way, and late in the afternoon his caution paid off. Jasper's party hauled in a Welsh boy, a dirty little wildcat who hurled curse upon curse at them, so fast neither Rand nor Jasper could interpret them all.

"What is it about these Welsh that their offspring are so vicious?" Jasper muttered, shoving the boy at Rand, then wiping his hands clean in a bunch of long, wet grass. "First that bloodthirsty little girl, now this brat."

Rand studied the child. "I know this boy. *Are you son to Owain ap Madoc?*" he asked in the boy's language.

The boy met his stare without flinching. *"I am, and my*

father will cut off both his hands for the way he has handled me," he said, referring to Jasper. Then he added, sneering, *"He plans to slice off your balls and feed them to his dogs."*

Rand grinned. "Beware, Jasper. This pup of Owain's threatens us." To the boy he added, in Welsh, *"I plan to capture your father and render him harmless. He will use his knife on no one ever again, least of all any of my people."*

"Yes he will!" the boy shouted. *"You'll see!"*

"So you believe, Rand said, goading the child. "Send him home. He cannot hurt us."

"Just you wait! Before you reach the next vale your blood will stain the earth red—" The child gasped and backed away. But it was too late for him to take back his words. Rand caught him by the nape of his neck.

"Hold him in a safe place," he told Jasper. "Send word down the line that the Welsh lie in wait just ahead."

But before he turned over the boy, he crouched down, holding him by both arms so that they were face-to-face. The boy obviously realized the gravity of his blunder, for no longer did he struggle to escape. Tears wobbled at the edges of his thick-lashed eyes.

"Where is Josselyn ap Carreg Du?" Rand gave him a little shake. *"Where is she—and where is her child?"*

The boy's chin trembled, but young as he was, he remained defiant. *"My father has her, and you'll never get her back. 'Cause you'll be dead!"*

Rand signaled Jasper to take the child. But that shrill voice echoed in his head. *My father has her. My father has her.*

Was Josselyn with Owain willingly or not?

And where was her child?

His child.

For the first time he feared as much for the unseen babe she claimed was his, as he did for Josselyn. But fear had no place in battle, he reminded himself. First he must defeat

Owain's forces. Then he would find Josselyn and Isolde.

The word was passed. They could engage the Welsh at any moment. They started forward, only half the men now, with two separate groups of reinforcements following close behind.

Then the signal came from the outriders: the shrill cry of a kittiwake. Once, and then again. *Immediately ahead* was the meaning it carried.

Through the trees Rand could make out a narrow clearing, a thin place in the deep forest. The heavy cloud cover lent a feeling of dusk to the afternoon light, a bruised purple. A chill.

Rand gestured to his men to brace themselves. Then he made a sign of the cross, fitted his small shield on his left arm, and urged his horse forward.

God save me this day, so that I may know my child, he prayed. *God save me that I might find Josselyn and profess my love to her. God save me that I might bring peace to this place someday, not bloodshed.*

Then a twig to his left snapped. The thunk of a bowstring. The whir of an arrow. He lurched to the side, jerking up his shield. Only God could have guided him so.

The arrow split his shield and grazed his shoulder, but buried itself harmlessly in a tree trunk beyond him. At once the sylvan glade turned to bedlam. The Welsh came screaming down upon them, swords slashing, battle-axes flying.

Horses shrieked and fell; men cursed; and the smell of blood swiftly drenched the woods in the awful stench of death. It was a stench Rand abhorred, and yet, as always, it worked on him like a black magic. His instincts took over, and he fought like an animal, not a man. He spun his horse and trampled two Welshmen in the process. One quick slice, a second merciless swing, and each of them fell, dead before they hit the ground.

Josselyn could see nothing of the battle that raged down

the hill from her. But she heard the screams of pain, the curses, and the grunts. The gasps for a final breath. Welsh or English, she could not tell. All men died the same, she realized. They lived for the same things—food, power, love. And they died the same way.

Why must they battle one another when they were so clearly alike? Why not join forces instead?

Horrified by the terrible battle, she struggled against the leather bindings that held her to the tree. But it was useless. Owain had wanted her near the battle, to watch her lover die, he'd said. Was Rand down there in the middle of the hellish fight? She knew he was.

Was he hurt, or even dying?

She prayed with all her heart that he was not.

She clawed at the ties until her fingers were raw, all the while assaulted by the shouts and cries of both men and beasts. Then a different sort of shout went up and she stilled. The crashing of another wave of warriors overpowered the sounds of battle.

Reinforcements. English reinforcements.

Then came a third wave of screaming attackers, from the opposite direction of the first, it sounded to her. More English soldiers.

A fresh fear shuddered through her. *Please do not slaughter them all, Rand. Show mercy to my people.*

Suddenly the battle seemed to surge in her direction. One man clambered up the hill, his head bloody, his weapons gone. Another came, carrying a comrade, slipping on a damp rock, then struggling up again. Owain's men were fleeing. They'd been routed.

But where was their leader? Where was Owain?

The answer was swift in coming. A horse burst up through the bracken and charged straight at her. Owain leapt off the sweaty animal and Josselyn instinctively shrank away from him, twisting desperately against the thongs that held her to the tree. Blood caked his hair; blood stained his leather hauberk. But it was not his blood, she realized, rather that of his enemies. Rand's?

He gripped his sword with one hand and his dagger with the other. Both dripped more blood still.

"You bitch!" he snarled. "You betrayed us."

"No. I didn't know enough of your plan to betray you," Josselyn swore. She tried to squeeze her hands free, but only rubbed her wrists raw.

"You knew enough to betray your own people." He was upon her now and she turned away, bracing for the blow.

I love you, Isolde. I love you, Rand.

But the blow never came. Instead he thrust his sword in the ground and caught her chin in a hurtful grasp. "You should have chosen me. You should have known I would soon succeed my father."

He was going to kill her. There was no other way he would allow this to end, she realized, and that knowledge provided her with a perverse sort of courage. She stared at him, for once unafraid. "You hastened his death, didn't you? Didn't you!"

For a moment he looked startled, then he laughed. "You should thank me for ridding you of him."

"How could you do that? How could you kill your own father? And Gower," she continued. "It wasn't the English that killed him, but you!"

His fingers cut into her jaw. "No one can ever prove that. Besides, I only did what I had to, to keep my people together."

"Killing an innocent boy? Killing your own father?" she spat, sickened by him.

"The boy's death roused the people to my side," he said, growing impatient now. "My father's death freed you so that I could have you."

"You already have a wife," she screamed at him, trying to twist away.

"And now I have you too." Though the sounds of his fleeing men surrounded them, he pressed his lips over hers.

It was a mockery of a kiss, for he wanted to hurt her with it, and he did. But though she could not escape him, she refused to give his tongue entrance.

He broke off with a guttural curse. "Cold bitch! You turn away from your own kind, yet embrace the godforsaken English. But I'll heat you up. I'll fuck you on top of your dead lover's body."

With a quick upward motion he cut through the leather thongs. She felt the sting of his blade where it nicked the base of her thumb. But that didn't matter. She was free of her bindings.

But she was not free of Owain. Manacling her wrist with his unrelenting grip, he dragged her away from the battle that was beginning to ease behind them. They reached his horse just as Conan limped up.

"Glyn is hurt. Bad," the man said. He sported a gash on his head as well as one to his thigh.

"Leave him!" Owain barked. He flung himself onto his horse, then dragged Josselyn, kicking and flailing, up before him. "Hurry. Fitz Hugh will be fast upon us. He wants his whore, but I have her. I have her and he'll have to come through me to get her back."

"He won't come," Josselyn swore, striking at his face. *Rand wouldn't come for her, would he?*

Owain shoved her down, then turned the horse, holding her too tight to allow escape. "He'll come, if only for pride. But I'll skewer him on his pride. And when I've had my fill of you, I'll do the same to you," he added in an obscene whisper. Then he kicked the animal and they were off, through the densest woods, into the rockiest terrain, into the rugged mountains that had ever been the last bastion of Welsh rebels.

Josselyn was nowhere to be found. Neither was Owain.

Rand paced the main hall at Afon Bryn. They'd taken the town with a minimum of opposition. He'd expected to confront Clyde and his men at the village, for they had not participated in the ambush. But they'd not been at Afon Bryn either. They'd not fought him at all this day. Had that been Josselyn's doing?

In Afon Bryn, few had remained beyond the old and infirm. Now as the prisoners were herded into town—the able carrying the wounded and carts ferrying the dead— more and more of the villagers ventured down from the thickly forested hills.

Rand had no interest in slaughter, and the sight of the wounded being tended must have convinced their wives and families. First one woman. Then a pair. Then a strag- gling line of frightened children. By sunset full half the village made their way down from the hills to see their men. But no sign of Josselyn or her child.

Outside a bonfire sent flames licking up to the sky, a sign to the craven Owain that his village had been taken. But Rand felt no triumph in his victory. What matter this mean village if Josselyn was gone? Had she lied to him again—or was she in mortal danger?

Or dead already?

"Christ's blood!"

He stormed out of the hall. He had to do something, else he would go mad. Outside his men caroused in the glow of the giant fire. Ale ran freely. Wine as well. The Welsh were subdued and confined. The English were victorious. His men wanted only women to complete the glories of this day.

Rand wanted a woman too—but not just any woman. So when a woman was led forward, timid and cowed, his lips curled in disgust.

"My orders were clear," he barked at his brother. "No woman is to be taken unwillingly, even by me."

"She asked for you in particular," Jasper replied in an injured tone. "When she learned I spoke her language, she asked for you. That doesn't sound unwilling to me. Her name is Agatha."

Rand looked at her, a small creature carrying an infant

in her arms. And if her thickened girth were any indication, she swelled anew with another babe.

"Deal with her," he snapped. "I have other matters to attend."

But when Jasper tried to oblige by steering the woman away, she began to cry. *"No, no. He must take the child. She is his. Take her. Take her!"*

His child! Rand spun around. "Is that Josselyn's child? *Josselyn's child?"* he repeated in Welsh.

The woman nodded and held the baby out. Rand swallowed hard. His eyes darted from her to the child and back again. *"Where is Josselyn?"*

A tear ran down the woman's pale cheek. *"Owain took her."*

"I'll kill the bastard!"

"No! Please. I beg you. I stole the babe away to bring her to you. Now you must spare my husband's life."

Again she held the child out to him, but Rand backed away. Was this really his child? How could he be sure?

The baby waved its arms. In the leaping light of the bonfire she was an indistinct creature. He raised his eyes once more to the woman who held her. Belatedly her other words registered. She was Owain's wife.

"Where has he taken her?"

"You must promise to spare him."

"Spare him! For all I know he has killed her!"

She shook her head and more tears spilled onto her cheeks. *"He would not kill her. He has always wanted her more than he wants me. But he is my husband, not hers! You must take her away from him so that he will be mine again. I brought you your child. I can help you find your woman. Spare me my husband. 'Tis not fair for her to have you both, while I have no one."*

In the end he promised.

He could not risk Josselyn's safety any longer. He did not share Agatha's confidence that Owain would not hurt

Josselyn. So he promised not to kill Owain. Then Agatha again held the child out to him.

Rand had not ever held a babe before, and panic swept through him, the likes of which he'd never before felt. He might crush her, or drop her, or somehow frighten her. But despite his fear, he took the child in his arms. A girl child. His child.

"Isolde," he murmured. She looked up at him, her eyes dark, her tiny face serious. Was she truly his?

God, he hoped so!

It was an illogical reaction but one he could not deny. He wanted this warm little thing to be his. His and Josse-lyn's.

He left Isolde safe in the hall with two guards and a maid to tend her. He rode now with three men into the ebony night, beneath grim spruce and somber oaks. Owls called into the darkness. Their frightened prey scurried along the forest floor.

He hunted Owain like the owls hunted the rodents of these hills. Unlike the mice and rabbits, however, Owain could become the hunter as easily as the hunted. And if he were cornered, there was no predicting what he might do to Josselyn.

They traveled through the night slowly, stopping often. Dawn found them in a chilly glade, just below the crest of a hill. They could smell smoke. It was faint but it was distinct. Someone was nearby.

Though Jasper objected, they left him with the horses. The other three crept to the top of the hill, keeping low in the gorse. The scent was stronger.

"If that's him, then he's a fool to have a fire," Osborn muttered. "Or else confident that no one has followed him."

"Or else setting yet another trap," Rand replied.

Over the hill they slowly crept. A horse blew out a breath and they froze. Then a man staggered out of a copse not a stone's throw from their position. Raising his hauberk, he relieved himself against a tree trunk. He was one of Owain's men, and Rand nodded to Osborn.

In a moment Osborn had him. Throat slit, body eased silently to the ground. No cry of alarm, save that of a bird that was startled away.

Rand made his way nearer the camp. Where was Josselyn?

"I count five horses," Osborn whispered. "Good odds for us."

Then a curse sounded, followed by a slap and a woman's cry, and all thought of caution fled. Josselyn needed him and Rand responded. He surged forward, drawing his sword as he ran, and burst into the campsite, screaming for blood.

Owain stood over Josselyn. Her gown was torn; her face bore the imprint of his hand. At Rand's bloodcurdling cry Owain spun around, grabbing for his own weapon.

Josselyn scrambled back from Owain at the first shout, unmindful of the stones that cut into her palms. Rand had come for her!

But as he rushed Owain and their swords hissed murder in the air, her elation turned to horror. Dear God, protect him, for Owain was a madman!

Where they found the strength to fight she did not know. Neither of them could have slept much, especially Rand. But they fought with single-minded intensity, parrying, feinting, each aiming with deadly intent to kill the other.

Owain fell slowly back and Josselyn rose to her knees.

Beyond them two other battles raged, and the air resounded with grunts and curses. Then someone screamed and went down.

Osborn lay crumpled in the trampled grass, his blood painted on Conan's blade. Without pause, Conan turned and lunged at Rand.

"Behind you!" Josselyn screamed.

By a hairsbreadth Rand missed being decapitated.

When he lurched aside, however, his boot skidded on the wet grasses and he went down. Conan was on him at once, stabbing with his lethal blade while Rand fought him off from his back.

Osborn was still down, and Alan fought his own battle. So when Owain rushed Rand for the kill, Josselyn did not pause to think. She launched herself at Owain, throwing him off stride, then clung to his back like an enraged cat.

"Bitch! Traitorous whore!" he screamed when she clawed at his eyes. But it bought Rand the time he needed. Somehow he shoved to his feet, parrying off Conan's renewed blows.

Meanwhile, Owain yanked Josselyn off his back. It felt like her arm came out of its socket. But instead of thrusting her aside, he jerked her up, holding her before him like a shield—and held the point of his dagger perilously close to her throat.

"Throw down your sword!" he yelled. "Throw it down or I'll gut her where she stands!"

Rand hesitated. His eyes locked with Josselyn's—just a fraction of a moment—before they fastened upon Owain. But there was a wealth of emotion in the connection they made. He'd come for her. He'd fought for her.

Did he love her?

She wanted to believe he did. But she did not want him to lay down his life for her.

Rand held his sword on Owain's henchman, but stared at Owain. "Just release her and you can go free. But harm a hair on her head and you're a dead man," he added in an astoundingly calm voice.

Owain laughed. Behind them Alan and the other Welshman still fought, but Owain's man was tiring and beginning to falter. "Call off your man," Owain ordered Rand. He pricked Josselyn's neck and she gasped. A trickle of blood started, hot and ominous, down her throat.

"Hold, Alan. Hold!" Rand shouted. Once more his eyes connected with hers. His chest heaved from his exertion and yet Josselyn again sensed that calm about him. Despite their hideous predicament, he would not lose his head. That knowledge was the only thing that kept her from falling apart.

She could be no less strong for him, she decided. So she forced a small smile, a private smile to her lips, that she prayed conveyed to him just how much she loved him.

"Throw down your weapons," Owain ordered. He was shaking with rage; she could feel it. "Throw down your weapons or she'll be the one to pay."

"No," Josselyn whispered. Once Rand's sword fell they were all as good as dead.

But Rand's attention was on Owain. "I'll put down my weapons when you let her go."

"Now!" Owain screamed, pricking her neck again.

Rand dropped his sword. So did Alan.

Owain began to laugh. "So. I have you both now. You and your whore. This will be even better than I imagined. Tie them up," he ordered his men. "Let him watch as I make good use of his whore. And if he objects, cut out his tongue. If he fights, take off his hands." He laughed again, then holding Josselyn by the throat, he forced her head back and licked the bloody trail on her neck. "I've waited a long time to have you," he hissed in her ear. "Make it worth my while, bitch, and I might yet allow you to live."

Josselyn's gaze had not veered from Rand, and somehow she knew what she must do. No words passed between them, but somehow she knew. Owain held her weight against him, so she simply let her legs buckle.

When she collapsed, Owain staggered backward, and his hold on her momentarily loosened. At the same time Rand lunged at Conan, and Alan tackled the other man. For a moment Josselyn thought she'd twisted free of Owain. But he grabbed at her hair and jerked her off her feet.

"I warned you. I warned you!" Owain screamed.

She saw the dagger flash. She braced herself for the blow. *Isolde. Rand . . .* That was all the prayer she had time to say.

Then a shriek rent the air and Owain collapsed on top of her.

They went down in a tangle of arms and legs, and his weight crushed all the air from her lungs. She was trapped beneath him. She could hardly breathe. But somehow she knew she wasn't dead, and she struggled to free herself.

Then she heard a new voice—an English voice—and the sounds of renewed combat. Owain slid a little aside, and she looked up to see Jasper holding a sword on Conan, and Alan holding the other Welshman at bay. Rand heaved the inert Owain aside. A dagger was buried to the hilt in his neck, and she shuddered, both horrified and relieved. Jasper had come just in time.

Then Rand pulled her up and enveloped her in his arms, and she clung to him as if she'd never let him go. He was so solid and warm, while she could not stop shaking.

"It's over. It's over. You're safe now," he murmured against her hair.

She raised her head and caught his face in her hands. "And *you* are safe," she whispered back. She stared up into his eyes, unable to hide any of her emotions from him. "I would have died if anything had happened to you."

Then reality, ugly and frightening, stole into her happiness. "I must find Isolde!"

"I have her in a safe place." He smoothed the hair back from her face.

"You do?" Her relief was so acute it hurt. "Thank God. Thank God!"

"Rand! Osborn is in a bad way!" Jasper called.

After that all their attention focused on Rand's fallen friend. Josselyn stanched his bleeding with a crude poultice of wild hyssop and the torn hem of her kirtle. Jasper and Alan made a litter for him, while Rand clasped his friend's hand.

"Hold on, Osborn. This is not your time. We've many a fight yet to share." He kept up a steady stream of reassurances and exhortations. Though Osborn did not respond, his breathing slowly eased and Josselyn was certain he heard.

Not until his wounds were bound and he was loaded onto the litter was she able to address Rand once more. "Where is Isolde?" she asked as he led her horse to her.

He stared down at her. "At Afon Bryn. I hold the town."

"I need to see her."

"We cannot travel very fast with Osborn."

"Yes." She took a steadying breath and searched his face. He'd come for her, despite all his doubts. It was time now for her to bare all her emotions to him. "I know we must go slowly. But you do not know, Rand, how I long to see my child resting finally in her father's embrace."

When he did not respond, she bit her lower lip and wrapped her arms nervously around her waist. "You must believe that she is yours," she continued earnestly. "I would not lie to you about that. I would not—"

"I believe you."

Her breath caught in her chest. "You do?"

Slowly he nodded. His eyes were the clearest gray, a dark color yet filled with light. "I do. But you must know that I will return her to you on one condition only."

"Whatever it is, I will agree—just so long as you do not send me away from you."

Their eyes locked. She held her breath and prayed. Then he let out a slow sigh. "I could never send you away from me," he said in a voice gone hoarse with emotion. "This past year . . . The past few days . . ." He shook his head. "I love you, Josselyn ap Carreg Du. I was a fool not to realize it long ago. I want you to marry me. I only hope that I have not been so big a fool as to lose you forever."

"You could never lose me," she confessed in a voice choked with emotion. "I love you too much for that."

She stepped nearer him, wanting to hold him and be held by him. But he held her back with a hand on each of her shoulders. "Don't say that out of gratitude," he demanded gruffly.

Above everything else he'd said, that was what brought tears to her eyes. He wanted her to love him for himself, because he loved her for herself. Thickheaded fool! Didn't he know she already did?

Her tears spilled over at the same time she started to laugh. "I love you, Rand. And I want nothing so much as to marry you—but not out of gratitude! If you believe nothing else, believe that."

Then she kissed him, sealing her vow and his, and he kissed her back.

They stood beside the horse and kissed one another in plain sight of everyone. It took coarse male laughter to break them apart.

"Is this the thanks I get?" Jasper jested. "I save the day and yet you end up with the beautiful damsel."

From the litter came Osborn's voice, weak but distinct. "You've still much to learn, lad. Your turn will come."

Rand smiled down into Josselyn's eyes, a smile filled with all the love in the world. "Your turn will come, Jasper. I only hope you can find a woman who will make you so complete as my Josselyn makes me."

Then he put Josselyn up on the horse and mounted behind her, and together they turned for home, for Isolde and for Rosecliffe.

Epilogue

Say, wilt thou go with me, sweet maid

—John Clare

Epilogue

Rosecliffe Castle, Wales
May A.D. 1137

Rand hoisted Isolde high onto his shoulders, and her squeals of utter delight only made his duty more odious. How he would miss this child of his heart!

How he would miss her mother.

He leaned from side to side, eliciting even more squeals from his precious daughter. She trusted him not to drop her, to always keep her safe. God willing, he would never fail that trust.

Across the bailey, in the newly constructed pleasaunce, he spied Josselyn. In the past two years she'd made Rosecliffe into a home. He'd raised the walls of a spacious and impregnable keep. But she'd warmed those walls of his with tapestries and painted frescoes. She'd scented the rooms he built with herbs, and furnished them with pillows and rugs. Most of all, though, she'd filled the sturdy walls of Rosecliffe with love. Love for him and love for their child.

He knew he must leave for the south, to confer with the other Marcher lords on this matter of Stephen's and Matilda's dual claims to the British crown. Ever since King

Henry's death, the country had been thrown into turmoil by their political machinations. Stephen demanded loyalty of the border lords, but Rand knew Matilda and her young son had the truer claim.

As much as he wished to stay apart from their conflict, he could not do so. Duty called and he must go.

Josselyn's determined cheerfulness in the face of their first separation only strengthened his love for her. She bore another child. She had not told him, but he knew it was so. But she didn't want him to worry, so she kept her secrets.

Sweet Jesu, but he loved the woman!

As if his emotions had reached out and touched her, she looked up and smiled. At once he started toward her, his boisterous baby rider secure on his back.

"Jasper sends word that the men are ready to leave," she said. Then her efficient manner broke and her eyes grew misty. She placed her hand on his chest. "You will be careful, won't you? I cannot like it that this meeting takes place in Simon LaMonthe's stronghold."

"I will be careful." He circled her with one arm while bracing Isolde with the other. Then he bent down to kiss her sweetly upturned mouth.

"What about me?" Isolde demanded. She patted his cheek and the top of her mother's head. "What about me?"

They broke apart, laughing. Then Rand slid their giggling daughter down so that she became the center of their embrace.

"How's that?" he asked Isolde in Welsh.

"Just perfect," she answered, circling each of their necks with one arm.

Yes, Rand thought. It was just perfect, this loving circle of a family they'd created. Unable to stop himself, he spread his palm gently over Josselyn's still flat stomach. When her eyes widened, he murmured, "I love you. All of you."

"Then hurry home to us," she whispered, leaning into him.

"Yes, hurry home, Papa."

Home. Rand took a deep breath. In his arms he held his family, and around them circled the safe walls of their home. Three years ago he'd wanted nothing but to do his duty here then return to London. Now leaving Rosecliffe even for a fortnight was tearing him apart. Politics called him, but family called him louder.

He hugged Isolde and Josselyn closer—and also the unnamed child that grew beneath her heart. "Never worry. I'll come home as fast I can. As fast as I can."

As Rand and his men departed the castle, a single file of knights with a double file of foot soldiers following, more than one pair of eyes marked their passage through the valley.

Rhonwen lurked in the shadows of a grove of hollies, watching. Brooding. Maybe with her English husband gone Josselyn might become more amenable to reason. 'Twas she, after all, who'd said that women could defeat men despite their greater strength. Women had but to be smarter. Craftier. Had she forgotten that? Had the English knight stolen that from her? Rhonwen pulled her shawl tighter against the damp chill. Perhaps now was the time to find out.

Rhys ap Owain watched from a place farther down the long hill. He perched high in a massive oak, sitting very still amid its clinging vines of mistletoe. The English left, both the lord and his nine-fingered brother. A just God would keep them away forever.

But God was not just. God had killed his mother and his grandmother, and He'd tricked Rhys into believing Josselyn cared about a lost little boy.

But he could manage without God's aid. Hadn't he taken care of himself and mad Meriel for these two years since his father had been murdered by Jasper Fitz Hugh? They might live in wretched poverty, but they did not starve. He'd seen to that. No one could match his skills at stalking the wild beasts and bringing them down.

His eyes focused on Jasper Fitz Hugh. Someday soon he

would stalk that one and make him pay for murdering his
father. If Owain ap Madoc still lived, these English would
be gone from Welsh lands. But Rhys meant to avenge his
father and save his people.

He spat at the faraway riders. He would kill Jasper Fitz
Hugh and his brother also. Then he would rip the red wolf
pennant down and live in the fortress they'd built. After
that no Englishmen would ever dare trespass on the lands
of Rhys ap Owain again.

Newlin watched the departure too, and memories of another day came to him.

Winter's end is nigh. Josselyn had said that once, before
the English had come. Before Owain had become drunk
with visions of his own power. Much had changed since
that blustery winter day.

" 'When stones shall grow and trees shall no', " he
chanted out loud. His good eye wandered toward Rosecliffe
Castle, toward the newly cleared lands below the town site,
and the walls that grew daily to newer, stronger heights.

Much had changed, yet much was still the same. Winter's end was nigh, yet for these hills the balm of spring
remained a long way off. Though Randulf Fitz Hugh was
a fair lord and kept the peace in this valley, there was yet
much discontent fermenting.

A vision of Rhonwen came to him, and the wild boy
Rhys. They were not alone in their hatred of the English.
Then he thought of Jasper and knew that hatred was not
one-sided.

But there was another generation to consider, those
children born of a Welsh and English union. Little Isolde and
the brother that followed her would lead the way to peace.

He smiled and turned back to the *domen.* Winter's end
was nigh, perhaps not right away, but soon.

Soon.

Please turn the page for an excerpt
from Jasper and Rhonwen's story,
the second book in
Rexanne Becnel's trilogy

Mistress of the Wildwood

coming soon from
St. Martin's Paperbacks

Jasper reached the river and dismounted, letting Helios browse freely while he took both ale jug and wineskin and clambered onto a boulder. The only good thing in the whole of his brother's considerable holdings was the quality of its ale and wine, he groused. He took a deep pull of the wine and settled onto the boulder.

Being left behind by Rand again was the final indignity, he told himself. The river rushed by, dark and cold. A perch broke the surface with a silvery flash. A crow's raucous cry echoed; another answered it. And all the while Jasper brooded and drank and subsided into morose daydreams, of adventure denied and daring suppressed.

When his brother returned, Jasper knew he must leave. He would attach himself to Stephen's army—or Matilda's. He didn't care which. He would fight battles and win rewards, and if he died, he didn't care about that either.

He drained the wineskin, then tossed it aside. What was a knight but a noble warrior? What was a man but a creature of blood and bone? He would fight with honor; he would win with honor; he would die with honor.

So he drank and he dreamed and the sun moved across the sky. It lit the opposite riverbank and cast him into shadow. He needed to relieve himself, but he could not move. He was too relaxed. Had the rock not been so hard, he could have slept.

He squinted at the diamond reflections on the river. If he kept his eyelids half-closed, one of the twisting willow trunks on the opposite bank very nearly resembled a woman. Slender and strong. Supple in the breeze.

Then the tree stepped nearer the water and into the sunlight, and Jasper blinked his eyes. The tree *was* a woman. *A woman.*

He pushed up onto his elbows and tried to focus. At his movement she looked up and spied him. He froze, praying she would not flee. A woman, and alone as far as he could tell.

His head began to pound from the effort of staring so hard. But he remained still, sprawled upon the boulder, no weapon in his hands. Perhaps that was what reassured her, for after a moment she advanced farther into the sunlight. Her hair was long and dark, as black as a raven's wing. It gleamed in the waning sunshine. And she was young. Her waist was narrow and her breasts high and firm. Jasper felt a portion of his own anatomy began to grow firmer, too.

She saw him and yet she did not shy away. One hundred paces and an ice-cold river full with snow melt protected her. It emboldened her, it seemed. As he watched, she put down the bundle she carried, then began to remove her dark green mantle.

Slowly Jasper sat up.

She stretched her arms high to let down her hair, then shook it out and began to finger-comb the thick, luscious length of it.

He was mesmerized. Was she real, or was she a lovely dream, some fanciful conjecture created of wine and ale and restlessness?

Then she removed her short boots, and tucked her skirt up, baring her pale ankles and legs. This time his heart stopped. She waded into the water. Did she mean to cross over to him?

He jumped to his feet—an unfortunate movement, for he'd consumed more spirits than he realized, and on an empty stomach. But he refused to succumb to his spinning head or to his traitorous stomach, for her breasts were such lovely thrusting things, and her legs were long and shapely. She wanted to wrap them around his hips. He was convinced of it.

God, but he must have her!

Across the river Rhonwen was shocked by her own daring. Baring her legs to a hated Englishman! But it had caught the scurvy knave's attention, for he stood now on

the flat rock that jutted into the river. He stood there swaying and she thought he would lose his balance and topple
over. What was wrong with the man? Though her feet were
turning numb from the ice-cold river, she squinted at him.
Was he drunk?

Suddenly she gasped. It was *him*! Brother of Sir Randulf.
Jasper Fitz Hugh, whom she'd first laid eyes on when she
was but a child and he a newly dubbed knight.

At the time he'd been the captive of Rhys's father,
Owain. Now, ten years later, Owain was dead by Jasper
Fitz Hugh's hand, and Rhys had become the scourge of the
English. Meanwhile, Jasper Fitz Hugh had no claim to
fame, save as English sot and despoiler of Welsh woman-
hood.

She'd seen him once or twice in the intervening years,
but only from afar, as now. But there were few as tall and
broad-shouldered as he. Even from this distance, she could
see the square jaw and straight nose that lent his face a
comeliness no man should possess. Especially an Englishman.

Yes, it was Jasper Fitz Hugh. Would he recall the wild
little girl who had saved his miserable hide?

She snorted. Not likely. Had she the opportunity to do it
all over again, would she save him a second time? Absolutely not!

Ten years ago she had saved him, but only so he could
be exchanged for her friend Josselyn, who'd been taken
hostage by Randulf Fitz Hugh. But Rhonwen's efforts had
all been for naught, for Josselyn had eventually wed her
captor. Jasper Fitz Hugh had recovered from his wounds
and stayed to become one more Englishman oppressing her
people.

Across the river, Fitz Hugh raised a hand to her in
drunken salute. Rhonwen frowned. The past was past. She
could do nothing to change it. But the present . . . The present demanded that she act. So she waved back at him, all
the while wondering what Rhys would do were he here.

The answer was uncomfortably clear. Rhys passionately believed that Wales should be purged of the English by whatever means necessary. Those who would not leave willingly must be killed.

The Fitz Hughs had long ago made it clear that they did not intend to leave.

So she steeled herself to do what she knew any true Welsh loyalist must do. Slowly she reached back for the small hunting bow she carried. Carefully she eased an arrow from the quiver that hung at her waist.

Then not allowing herself time for doubt, she swung the bow into place, notched the arrow, and let it fly . . .